Praise for
The Fallen

"[Bailey] stands on the brink of one of those remarkable careers, a writer who leaves his mark on a genre, a writer who makes a genuine difference."
—Fantastic Metropolis

"A great first novel . . . reminiscent of the work of horror legends like Stephen King with maybe a hint of H. P. Lovecraft. . . . I highly recommend *The Fallen* for fans of supernatural and psychological horror. . . . Stephen King says he's retiring—maybe he can lend his pen to Dale Bailey." —Scifi Dimensions

"Quietly draws you in one step at a time . . . a very thought-provoking story. *The Fallen* at times has a classic noir feel to it and I highly recommend giving this one a shot." —Horror World

HOUSE OF BONES

Dale Bailey

A SIGNET BOOK

SIGNET
Published by New American Library, a division of
Penguin Group (USA) Inc., 375 Hudson Street,
New York, New York 10014, U.S.A.
Penguin Books Ltd, 80 Strand,
London WC2R 0RL, England
Penguin Books Australia Ltd, 250 Camberwell Road,
Camberwell, Victoria 3124, Australia
Penguin Books Canada Ltd, 10 Alcorn Avenue,
Toronto, Ontario, Canada M4V 3B2
Penguin Books (N.Z.) Ltd, Cnr Rosedale and Airborne Roads,
Albany, Auckland 1310, New Zealand

Penguin Books Ltd, Registered Offices:
80 Strand, London WC2R 0RL, England

First published by Signet, an imprint of New American Library,
a division of Penguin Group (USA) Inc.

First Printing, December 2003
10 9 8 7 6 5 4 3 2 1

For Jean and Carson

Not a house in this country ain't packed to the rafters with some dead Negro's grief.

—Toni Morrison

The World Beyond the Fence

the Fence

WINTER 1986

1

The dead first spoke to Abel Williams when he was twelve years old, twenty-one years and half a continent away from Dreamland. As a boy, Abel could hardly have imagined the fate which awaited him. Few of them could have, that handful of strangers to whom Dreamland would one day have such cruel significance. Not Lara McGovern, only nine during that fatal winter when Abel first heard the voices of the dead, and not Fletcher Keel, a rangy blond man of thirty-three drifting slowly toward some awful catastrophe he could not yet begin to perceive. Certainly not Ramsey Lomax, already wealthy beyond his wildest dreams at the age of forty-six. None of them could have imagined what awaited them at Dreamland—*none* of them, Abel least of all. Yet it awaited them all the same, infinitely cold, infinitely patient, casting its shadow across their futures.

Dreamland.

So it was called on the street, though where the name came from no one could say for sure. Its official name, Harold P. Taylor Homes, had no poetry; it was a bureaucrat's name, and it honored the memory of a bureaucrat. But its designers had been poets all the same, soldiers in the service of a great society. The original specs approved by the Housing Authority called for eight shining spires of glass arrayed around a courtyard the size of a city block, for sidewalks radiating from a central fountain, for park benches and playgrounds, for towering avenues of shade trees.

But the bureaucrats had won.

There was no green there. Dreamland was a study in

dismal grays. It stood, brooding and implacable against a
lowering gray sky, eight pillars of soulless gray concrete,
drilled out at intervals with tall, narrow windows, like a
line of merciless gray eyes. The first floor of each building
was devoted to public space. Each of the remaining seventeen floors contained twenty-four apartments, ten along the
central corridor, seven on each wing—a total of four hundred eight units per building. Many of them thronged with
humanity, overflowing with sprawling multigenerational
clans of black women and their children.

Others were already empty. In some of the towers, on
some of the floors, more than half the windows had been
boarded over with sheets of flimsy plywood. Doors hung
from broken hinges on apartments empty but for the debris
of abandonment: a mattress too stained with semen and
blood to bother hauling away, an empty vial of crack on
the concrete floor, a shattered hypodermic. The poets who
designed the place were long gone. The bureaucrats were
leaving. Soon now, in a matter of years, the derelict corpse
of Dreamland would belong solely to those imprisoned inside its walls—by illiteracy, by drugs or drink, by the mere
genetic chance of skin color. For no human being would
live in such a place for long, and no one came there by
choice.

It had been that way for more than twenty years now.

It would be that way for at least another twenty yet, until
Abel Williams came at last—Abel Williams and the others,
who in that long cheerless winter of 1986 were wrestling
demons of their own, unmindful of Dreamland and the terrible role it would play in the futures that awaited them.

2

From the time he was a child, the watch hung in Abel's
mind like a talisman, so omnipresent in his imagination that
he sometimes wondered if it hadn't always been there, if it

hadn't begun gathering substance in the moment of his own conception, spinning itself into being in the formless dark of his mother's womb. In his first memory—if it *was* a memory, not some image summoned from the endless deeps of family mythology—it dangled before him, the hinged silver band glinting, the hairline fracture in the crystal touched with fire. His father's face hung beyond it, like the hemisphere of some enormous, tender moon. The night of the funeral, Abel had even dreamed of it: his father's smiling face, his own child's hand extended in longing, the watch itself turning and turning between them, always just out of reach.

That was the image that came to Abel as he slipped into his parents' bedroom. He stood quietly, listening to the clock tick atop his mother's bureau as he stared out the ice-sheathed windows. Mountains loomed dark on the horizon, like the curled fingers of a god. Gazing out at them, Abel was struck anew by the vulnerability of the town huddled in the cupped palm of the valley—the crumbling street below and the stooped identical houses, thrown up by Copperhead Coal four generations ago and now crumbling slowly into earth. Even the coal tipple towering among the ridges to the north looked fragile, a mocking reminder of how easy it would be for that fist to close, crushing them all.

Abel shivered.

A storm was coming. That's what his mother had told him over lunch, talking in the faintly querulous tones she'd adopted since the funeral. Now, staring up into a sky armored with clouds the color of roadside cinders, Abel thought she was probably right. That would be just their luck, everything they owned packed into the back of one of those gigantic yellow Mayflower moving vans, stranded for days by a late-February blizzard. They'd probably charge you extra for that, Mom had said. And it wasn't like she could afford it. It wasn't like she could afford *anything* since—

She hadn't finished the sentence. She just sat there for a minute or two, her lips twitching, while her soup cooled on the table. And then she abruptly burst into tears.

Remembering, Abel felt a twinge of dismay.

The move was all she talked about these days: how great

everything was going to be when they finally got to Pennsylvania, how happy Grandma was going to be to have them, how much Abel would like his new school.

The prospect didn't cheer Abel any.

But it was inescapable. The movers were due in two days, and the bedroom smelled of mothballs and unsettled dust, of closets disgorging the accumulated clutter of years. His father's clothes lay on the bed, neatly folded for Goodwill. Half-filled boxes loomed in the shadows. The whole house seemed suddenly haunted and strange, like a place seen in a dream, and not necessarily a pleasant one.

Abel laughed nervously.

He almost reached for the light switch. The truth was, though, he didn't quite dare turn on the light. Mom's lunchtime crying jag hadn't abated until she had dozed off on the sofa about an hour ago. But she was an uneasy sleeper at the best of times, and if she *did* wake up, the light shining down the stairs would be a dead giveaway.

He'd already had one taste of his mother's feelings on the issue of the watch, and he wasn't anxious for another. The day before the funeral, a solemn, dark-suited courier from the company had delivered a big, padded mailer containing his father's personal effects. When Abel had plucked the watch from the items Mom had spread atop the kitchen table—wallet, keys, a handful of change—she had snatched it back with a fury that had been both frightening and uncharacteristic. "I suppose you think it'll bring you luck as well," she'd snapped. "Right? Is that what you think? *Is it?*" She leaned toward him, brandishing the watch in one shaking hand, her face strained and ravaged—transformed, abruptly, terrifyingly, into an old woman's face. "Well, it won't, Abel! It didn't save him and it won't save you either, and I'm not losing anyone else, you understand me? I won't have it, *I won't have it*—"

Abel had fled as she dissolved into tears. When he returned twenty minutes later, the envelope and everything in it—watch, wallet, even the half-empty roll of Tums—had been cleared away.

He hadn't seen it since, despite half a dozen surreptitious searches.

Now, steeling himself, he slipped furtively across the

room. Kneeling by his mother's nightstand, he slid open the top drawer. This time luck was with him. The envelope lay just inside, wedged in atop a random clutter of odds and ends: a deck of cards, a pair of broken sunglasses, a couple of letters. He pulled it out and reached inside, his fingers skating across the smooth leather surface of the wallet to probe deeper—keys, change, even the Tums. Everything but the watch. His heart quickening, he emptied the envelope atop the bed and combed through it all again. Nothing. The watch was gone.

He swallowed and sat back on his haunches.

Okay, he thought. Fine. Be cool.

The watch had slipped out of the envelope, that's all. Turning back to the nightstand, he started through the junk inside the drawer. He pushed aside a tray of bicentennial quarters and an old paperback, his fingertips brushing a stiffened edge of paper. Curious, he withdrew a creased snapshot of his father coming off shift, just stepping down from the cage which carried him each morning into the graveyard depths of the planet. The face under the mining cap was gaunt and weary; the eyes looked like gray stones, stranded in a sea of glittering black dust. Abel slumped against the bed, still holding the photograph.

It was useless. The watch was gone.

Gone.

The word tolled inside his head like a bell. He stared down at the photograph, riven suddenly with grief, with a yearning so intense that it was an almost physical ache, like the hot throb of a twisted muscle in the small of his back.

"Dad," Abel whispered, "Oh, Dad—"

He peered down at the photo in the gloom, staring so intently into his father's weary, gray eyes that the room around him seemed to melt away—for the space of a single heartbeat he was there, *there*, inside the frozen tableau of the photograph as his father stepped out of the elevator, wearing battered work boots, coal-stained jeans, a denim shirt worn to the consistency of velvet.

"Dad?" Abel whispered.

As if in answer, a whirl of competing voices rose around him, like a radio tuned to a frequency where half a dozen stations bled together, an incoherent babble from which a single pair of syllables, hauntingly familiar—

—my name was it my name—

—floated up and died away in one long breath of air. A stir of echoes, that's all it was, like dry October leaves whipped to frenzy by a sudden gust of wind.

And then, whatever it was, it was over.

He was back in the bedroom, crouched on his haunches against the bed, his skin pimpled with gooseflesh, his breath frosting in the gloom—

—cold when had it gotten so cold—

—and his name *was* in the air. It was his mother's voice, rising up from the living room, plaintive and aggrieved, an old woman's voice.

"Abel?"

He crouched there an instant longer, trying to sort out what had happened, to summon it back, but whatever it had been, it was gone.

He stood, shoved the photo into his pocket, and scraped everything else back into the envelope. Jamming it unceremoniously into the drawer, he darted back toward the hall.

"Abel?"

"Coming, Mother," he said from the stairs.

3

They were talking about her again.

Lara watched from the viewing room as the stragglers eddied toward the foyer, where her parents stood. People had started flowing in at a quarter past seven or so; now, as the minute hand on her yellow Swatch inched toward nine, they had begun ebbing back toward the big double doors out front, which had been swung open to the chill air from the parking lot. It was like watching the tide go out, each receding wave of humanity swirling up against her waiting parents with another little burst of condolences, evanescent as wind-torn froth.

She could tell when they were talking about her. Dad, solemn in his dark suit, had a way of drawing himself up firmly and dipping his chin toward her mother, as though conceding that any matter involving the girls—

—*what girls it's just you now, Lars, it's just you*—

—fell naturally under her jurisdiction. For her part, Mom had a habit of stealing a swift look at Lara, as if assuring herself that her daughter was safely out of earshot before she began speaking. A stranger might have missed it altogether, but in the last couple of years, Lara had become well versed in reading the semaphore of her mother's inner life. She must have seen that veiled glance a thousand times—whenever the door of Lana's hospital room swung back to admit a doctor clutching a sheaf of test results or Father Preiss, cradling his Bible in his soft, perfumed hands.

The fact was, Lara had never quite adjusted to the adult solicitude occasioned by her sister's illness. There was something infuriating about it, something insulting, as though everyone secretly suspected her of being mildly retarded. They acted as though the funeral must have come as a surprise to her—as though she had somehow managed to miss the endless doctors' visits, the weary midnight drives to Duke, the whispered consultations in hospital corridors.

As though she had somehow managed not to notice that her sister was dying.

Tonight had been worse, though, because let's face it, when you could stretch out your arm and lay your hand atop a corpse, denial no longer remained a viable option—even for an adult suffering from the misconception that kids didn't become truly self-aware until they were twenty. So everyone who caught sight of Lara felt compelled to talk about it, to kneel before her and tell her in hushed tones that she had to be strong or ask her how she was doing or—and these were the worst, they practically made her livid with rage—say they supposed she would miss her sister, wouldn't she? "We'll *all* miss her," they invariably concluded.

And Lara *would* miss her—she would—but she was doing okay. She really *was*, cross her heart and hope to—

Lara swallowed.

She studied the half-sized casket, a gleaming lozenge of pink and ivory resting at waist level—higher actually, if

you were only nine—on some kind of platform draped in
billowing white. Someone had placed an enormous spray
of flowers—pink tea roses and gardenias, suffused with
sprigs of baby's breath—on the lower end, just where the
lid had been propped open. Lara could smell the gardenias
from here. She could taste their tickle at the back of her
throat.

She sniffed—she was okay, she *was*—and glanced into
the foyer.

Her parents were visiting with the O'Neils, the elderly
couple who lived three houses down. Mr. O'Neil stood by
with an air of long-suffering patience while Mrs. O'Neil
talked. Mrs. O'Neil was always talking (*she had diarrhea of
the mouth,* Lana used to say), and now she laid her hand
across Mom's forearm, patting it, and leaned forward to
speak in hushed, confidential tones. And then the whole
group—all four of them, even Mr. O'Neil—swiveled their
heads in her direction.

Something tightened inside Lara's breast. She gave them
a pinched smile. For God's sake, she wanted to scream, I'm
okay. And when they turned away, subsiding once again
into the rhythm of adult conversation, Lara found herself
drifting toward the casket, as if to prove it to herself. She
was okay.

She hesitated before she looked in, her fingers curled
lightly against the satiny white drapery. From this angle she
could see the dim interior of the little chapel where they
would hold the service in the morning. Pews cushioned in
red velvet receded into the shadows, where another door
opened into the neighboring viewing room. THE HEAVENLY
REST ROOM, the little brass plaque affixed to the wall had
called it. Lara had noticed the sign earlier, when she slipped
through the chapel to avoid having to talk with Mrs. Quillen, who had taught her to read way back in first grade.
Who had taught them *both* to read actually, which was the
principal reason Lara didn't think she could take talking to
her, because that was the year Lana had started getting
sick. Nobody had thought anything of it, either. Everybody
thought she had a cold, she was just a little tired—except
she kept getting more and more tired until finally Mom
had taken her to the doctor, and after that nothing had
ever been the same again.

So rather than having to think about all that, Lara had slid through the chapel, past a second sign propped atop a little podium (MARQUEZ FAMILY, it read), and into *The Heavenly Rest Room. Which is what*, Lana had inquired inside her head, *a toilet with a halo?* It was exactly the kind of thing she had always been saying, and normally it would have sent Lara off into gales of laughter. That evening in the decidedly unfunny *Heavenly Rest Room*, however, it had released a pent-up ocean of sorrow, a sorrow so deep and wide that Lara thought she might never fully plumb it, that it might keep sweeping over her forever, breaking in fresh waves every time she thought she had at last gotten her head above water, until finally she just gave up and let herself drift limply to the bottom, until finally she drowned.

On top of which, the room itself had turned out to be pretty much identical to the one Lana was lying in (THE CELESTIAL TRANQUILLITY ROOM, according to its little brass plaque). It even had its own casket, a full-size model in dark glossy wood. Lara had peeked over the edge at the very old man who lay inside. He didn't really look dead, just very, very sleepy.

Recalling this, Lara felt a little guilty. After all, she hadn't yet found the resolve to look into her sister's casket, had she?

Lara lifted her hand and let her fingers rest against the cool pink surface. Lana would have cracked wise about that too—would have despised the ridiculous pink lozenge her parents had chosen to bury her in, would have loathed the ridiculous pearl inlays with their embossed silhouettes of a little girl at play. For as long as Lara could remember, Lana had hated all things frilly and pink. She had refused to wear dresses and had turned up her nose in disdain the year twin baby dolls showed up under their Christmas tree.

You be the mommy, Lars, she'd said then. *You're the one who likes to take care of everybody.*

Which was true, Lara mused—except she hadn't done such a great job of taking care of Lana, had she? There wasn't any use in thinking about that, though. Besides, she was okay, she really *was* okay, she could lift herself up on her tiptoes and gaze right in at Lana, she could do it right

now, I mean how bad could it be, it was no problem at all
she was okay she was—

Lara took a deep breath.

Lana lay inside, swaddled in pink satin, her thin hands
clasped over her stomach, her eyes closed. The hair draped
artfully across the lacy pillow was exactly the same pale
blond as Lara's, but otherwise they looked nothing alike,
nothing at all. And that was freaky, because for most of
Lara's life, looking at her sister had been like looking in a
mirror. Everybody had mixed them up—their friends, their
doctors, even their teachers (Mrs. Quillen among them). It
had happened so often that Lara had sometimes wondered
if maybe their parents hadn't gotten them confused at some
crucial moment as well. How hard would it be? You wake
up bleary-eyed in the middle of the night, you feed the
babies, you burp them and change them, and maybe you
put them back in the wrong cribs—you're exhausted after
all, it could happen to anybody, and besides who's going
to know, except they go through the rest of their lives with
the wrong names, Lara is Lana and Lana Lara, both of
them playacting at lifetime roles without ever even knowing
it, and if that was the case then maybe she, Lara, was the
one who was supposed to be dead, maybe she was the one
who was supposed to be in the casket—

—but it wasn't a casket was it it was a coffin—

—yes a coffin and soon now they would be shutting the
lid and she would be all alone there, alone in the dark
waiting for the first spadeful of dirt to rattle—

Lara clutched the edge of the coffin.

The casket.

Their parents hadn't gotten them mixed up. It was a
crazy idea, that's all. Mom must have told them a thousand
times about the little ID bracelets they had worn. Lara had
seen them herself, pasted carefully inside the photo album
with their birth pictures and the wrinkled prints of their
tiny feet and a thousand other mementos of their
childhood.

Besides, they hadn't looked very much alike in nearly a
year now, had they? The change had been almost imper-
ceptible at first, but it had happened all the same. The
leukemia had slowly but surely turned Lana frail and wizened, like an old lady, so that looking at her was less like

looking into a mirror than looking through a window in time at the self she might become in seventy or eighty years. Lara had even gotten used to it after a while, that sense of her own discrete individuality, she had even—

—*yes,* Lana hissed inside her mind, *face it why don't you*—

—she had even grown to like it. And now something else came floating into her thoughts, a stark unpleasant memory dredged from the muddy lake bottom of her mind: waking up in the recovery room after they had taken her bone marrow and catching a glimpse of her own face in the mirror. She had been wan and tired-looking, pale from the anesthesia, and for a moment she thought she had seen Lana staring out from behind her own frazzled eyes—the *new* and not-so-improved Lana, the leukemia Lana. And in that moment, she had felt a fierce joy blossom like a terrible rose within her, joy and gratitude that it had taken Lana, not her, that Lana was going to be the one who withered away and died.

And now she had.

That's all. Lana had died. And Lara was okay. *I'm okay,* she told herself. It was something of a relief, actually, to look into the casket and see a stranger, someone so entirely *not* her, not even her sister, just a body, like one of those weird little space aliens you sometimes saw on television, all head, all eyes and face with a spindly set of arms and legs dangling below it.

Except Lana *wasn't* a stranger. Hadn't Lara herself given Lana the heart-shaped silver locket that even now lay pale and shiny against the pallid flesh of her breast? And if she reached down and opened that locket, wouldn't a photo of their twinned faces stare back at her? Wouldn't she see two sets of initials engraved on the inner side, hers and Lana's, and wouldn't they be the same initials? The answers were yes and yes and yes. Why?

Because Lana was her sister. Lana was her sister and now they would never again lie awake giggling into the small hours of the morning, never pass notes during class or watch television or play hopscotch on the front walk, never blow out the birthday candles on their cake together because Lana wasn't having any more birthdays, her birthdays were over, finished, kaput, done, Lana would never

do anything at all, ever again, except lie there and be
dead and—

—*you didn't take care of me, Lars, you wanted me to
die*—

"I'm sorry," she moaned, "I'm sorry, I'm so sorry," and
she leaned in over the casket to touch her sister's hand;
how cold it was, how cold and unyielding, the skin firm and
chill as she lifted the fingers to her face, saying, "I'm sorry,
Lana, I'm so sorry," and suddenly it was all too much for
her, Lana's flesh against her lips and the hum of voices
approaching from the foyer and the stench of the
gardenias—

—*like rot like things that were rotting*—

—so sweet and cloying that she thought she would be
sick, she could taste the bile flooding her mouth—

"Lara!"

Her mother's voice startled her, arcing through the rising
bank of hysteria like the beacon of a lighthouse, illuminating everything for a single glaring instant of flashbulb
lucidity—the casket on its pedestal and her parents moving
toward her in horrified unison, a dark-coated man from the
funeral home at their heels—before the fog closed in once
again. Words welled out of her, choked and panicky: "I'm
sorry, it should have been me, *it should have been me*—"

Lara turned back to the coffin, still clutching her sister's
hand. If she could touch her face, if she could only—

Lara felt her mother's hands on her shoulders. Her father's voice cut through her thoughts, sharp, admonishing—

"*Lara!*"

—but that was all so far away. If she could rest her face
against Lana's face, if she could only make her understand,
she hadn't wanted her to die, she *hadn't*, she was so tired
of watching her be sick, that's all, *she was so very tired of
feeling helpless, of*—

"Stop, Lara!"

"No!" she cried. "No, it should have been me, *it should
have been*—"

Her voice spiraled into incoherent sobs, alien and distant,
wholly apart from her, drowning out the strained, urgent
commands of her mother and father, the dark-suited
stranger. Hands clutched at her, pulling her back. Lara tore

at them, wrenched herself free, she needed to touch Lara, she needed to make her understand—

Lara never quite sorted out what happened next. Maybe her legs got tangled up with those of the surrounding adults, maybe her foot caught on the table—some kind of wheeled cart, actually, she saw—that lay under the enveloping white drapery. All she knew was that one minute she was crying in panic at her mother's hands, twisting to escape her father's embrace; and then, in the stark inert instant that followed, she found herself lurching with a kind of dread slow-motion inevitability toward the casket. She cried out, and reached for something, *anything*, to break her fall.

But it was too late.

Her hand slipped across smooth and marbled flesh—she felt the delicate silver chain around her sister's neck snap beneath her fingers—and then everything came down with a carpet-muffled crash: Lara, the three grappling adults, the ridiculous pink-and-white lozenge of the casket itself. Lara scrambled away, clutching the chain and its locket in one fist, her ankle giving with a white-hot twist of agony, and then she found herself staring into the glazed unseeing eyes of her twin, her twin who was no longer her twin at all, who had passed irretrievably beyond some border to a place where there were no twins anymore, where there was nothing, nothing at all, now and forever, but the cold stone weight of eternity. Weeping, Lara climbed to her knees and stared down at her sister's body, spilling from the pink-and-white casket like a broken Barbie doll, a painted plastic mockery of a human being. Makeup caked her pores. Her lips had parted slightly, exposing a shiny glimmer of wire and a thick yellow bead of adhesive.

She was dead.

Lara had failed her.

Lara's mother was weeping, a distant atonal hitching of breath, and her father was talking slowly, gently, in the sure steady voice you used to calm a frightened animal. Lara sensed the dark-suited man climbing unsteadily to his knees at the edge of her vision.

But none of that mattered. It might have been happening in another world. Nothing mattered. Nothing was real but the broken-Barbie-doll sprawl of Lana's body and the stark, icy fact of Lara's failure. And now, gazing down into the blind, staring emptiness of her sister's face, Lara found herself making a promise that she would never again fail anyone she loved, she would save them all, she *would*. She said it aloud, uttering the words in an incoherent rush, "I'm sorry I'll save them all I'll save them all for you I promise—"

"Lara, honey—"

Lara looked up into her mother's face, subsided back into the warmth of her embrace, the honeysuckle scent of her perfume.

"I promise," she whispered fiercely. *"I promise."*

4

The teacher hadn't wanted to notice the boy, hadn't wanted to pay him any special attention. On the first day she had greeted him as she had greeted all the children: warmly, with a smile designed to say, *You're welcome here. You will succeed here.*

It was her first job and she was lucky to have it; she knew that. Lots of girls she had graduated with would have killed for a place in such a school: affluent, sophisticated, as well-manicured as the community it served. And she was still young enough—idealistic enough—to believe that she could make a difference. She'd been trained in the best liberal tradition. She wasn't a racist, she knew that. Yet her eye was drawn to him all the same, and not alone because his was the sole dark face in the neat rows of small up-turned faces that greeted her every morning.

No.

It was that he was so strange, such a strange and silent child. He was intelligent, she had no doubt of that. His written work was flawless, a little frightening actually, it was so precocious. Still, more than half the year was gone,

and how often had she heard his voice? Twice? Three
times? How often had she seen him interact with the other
children? How often had she seen him do anything other
than sit in his desk and write, write, write, filling reams of
spiral notebooks with his cramped, careful hand?

He was obviously adopted: his parents were white and
pleasantly bland, perhaps a touch more prosperous than
those of his classmates, but otherwise indistinguishable.
And if they seemed blissfully unaware of his eccentricities,
she was partially to blame. The question of his parentage
made conferences a delicate matter. She never knew quite
how to finesse the issue—whether to openly acknowledge
it, skirt it altogether, or seek the safety of some yet-
undiscovered middle ground—so she had opted for cheerful
vagueness: *What a pleasant child, he's no trouble at all*, and
usher them out the door. Similar scruples had prevented
her from making inquiries among the staff. An excessive
interest would be unseemly.

She was new here, after all.

She sat now in a wash of late-winter California sun, polishing an apple idly against the hem of her blouse and
watching him across the rows of empty desks. It was
lunchtime, and the cries of children at play drifted up
through the half-open window, but neither of them noticed.
He was too intent on the lines he was inscribing in the
notebook atop his desk. She was too intent on watching
him.

He rocked as he worked, a steady soothing motion, like
the swing of a boat at anchor. He clutched his pencil so
tightly that tiny white crescents had appeared under the
neatly trimmed arcs of his nails.

The other children neither liked nor disliked him. They
simply went about their business as if they couldn't see him
at all—as if he radiated a subtle negative charge that sent
them skating off into new orbits whenever they got too
close. He had mastered the art of invisibility.

She took a bite of the apple, savoring the tart flavor, and
watched him some more. The room smelled pleasantly like
the classrooms of her youth: chalk dust and the faint, sweet
orange-peel odor of pencil shavings. The clock ticked steadily, drawing the hour slowly toward one, science, then social

studies, the lazy fag end of the day. In ten minutes the bell would ring, and the hall would fill with the shrieks of children, the clatter of feet against the stairs.

And still he wrote, his small dark face solemn and clenched, like a fist.

There was something . . . What? The word came to her out of the air: Obsessive. Yes. Something obsessive about it. Something disturbing, maybe even dangerous.

Later, the teacher would wonder why she did what she did next, and those were the words that would come back to her: obsessive, disturbing, dangerous. She would tell herself she did it out of concern, concern for his welfare, concern for the safety of the other children. The child needed professional help. She would be remiss in her duties—to him *and* his classmates—if she simply stood by any longer.

That was all rationalization, of course. The truth was, she did it out of curiosity.

She finished the apple, dropped the core with a bang into the empty metal wastebasket—

—he didn't react didn't even flinch—

—and stood, smoothing her skirt.

"Benjamin?" she said.

He didn't react to that either. He stared down at the notebook, his hand racing across the page.

The classroom seemed very quiet suddenly, the shrieks from the playground faraway. Her heels echoed in the stillness as she walked down the aisle and knelt at his side.

"Benjamin," she said quietly.

He reacted this time. He straightened abruptly, snapping the point off his pencil. It slipped from between his fingers and rolled to the floor at her feet. He turned to look at her, his brown eyes fathomless, opaque.

"What is it you're writing all the time?" she said, but he didn't answer. He simply returned her gaze, his dark face impassive, utterly devoid of emotion, and she said, "Can I take a look? Do you mind?"

He said nothing, but he didn't protest when she slid the notebook out from under his hands. He just stared at her, waiting.

"Everything's going to be okay," she said. "Everything's going to be fine."

Then she started to read.

5

There was an apple tree in the front yard which had leaned for so many years into the winter winds tearing down from the ridges that it never quite recovered come spring. It flowered late, and what little fruit it put forth was pinched and green, sour on the tongue. At midnight, Abel stood in his bedroom and stared out at the tree as the storm his mother had predicted hammered the house, hurling a fine grit of snow against his window. Beyond the faint condensation of his breath fogging the glass, it hunched arthritically, its stunted branches glistening in the yellow nimbus of the streetlight.

Shivering slightly, Abel turned away and slid beneath the threadbare covers of his single bed. As a child, he had often lain awake nights, gazing up into the darkness, chasing the shape of a future which would never quite come clear amid the tangle of shadowy branches printed on his ceiling. Even then he'd known he wanted nothing to do with his father's profession. Even then he'd sensed something false about his mother's daily demeanor: the veneer of cheerful normality with which she saw his father off to work in the morning and welcomed him home at the end of shift. Once or twice—when Dad was running late, or when he stopped for a beer at the Yellow Badger and forgot to call—Abel had caught a glimpse of the unplumbed depths of terror which lay just beneath that mundane surface. And so he'd sought the refuge of a future inconceivably far away from Copperhead, from West Virginia, from the dirty and often dangerous business of mining and the daily terror it induced. He didn't know what it would be exactly, that future, but he searched for it anyway, glimmering vaguely among the shadows on his bedroom ceiling: something different, something infinitely removed from the world he'd always known. Something glamorous.

Now, lying awake and listening to the storm rock the house, he watched a more ominous pattern take shape in the shadows overhead: the hunched form of a miner, his head twisting in terror as he heard the first premonitory rumbles in the vast density of stone overhead. The wind shifted, rattling the window in its frame, and in the play of branches on the ceiling Abel saw the shadow figure stumble, cowering as the terrific tonnage of rock collapsed upon it, a crushing, killing weight.

Abel winced, the knowledge of his father's death bearing down upon him like a black wind out of the mountains. Protected. All these years, his father had believed himself protected, and they had collaborated in propping up his fantasy—Abel and his mother both—imbuing the watch with powers it could not have possessed, as though, having saved his life once, it had conferred some kind of lifetime immunity upon him.

At two, Abel had been too young to remember the event itself, but he had heard the story so often that it had assumed the dimension of myth in his mind. He had merely to close his eyes, and he could see it, summoning up the images from some deep internal well of imagination: a handful of men hunkered over their lunch pails, his father stepping away to glare in frustration at the frozen hands of his battered Timex, the fresh-cut ceiling breaking loose at his back. The town had gathered in horror to watch the body bags trickle from the dark mouth of the mine. But for the busted watch, his father would have been inside one of them.

"Damn watch saved my life," Dad would say. "Dumb luck, that's all it was." But even as a child, Abel sensed that his father attributed his deliverance to something more than luck. He had continued to wear the watch, for one thing, strapping it religiously around his wrist every morning despite the fact that he'd never had it repaired, neither the balky gears that had ground to a halt thirteen minutes short of noon, nor the crystal, which had been cracked by a flying shard of debris during the slate fall. And whenever he told the story—which he did compulsively—he always unbuckled the watch, letting it dangle from his hand as he gazed down upon it with an expression which partook of a variety of emotions—puzzlement, sorrow, even wonder—

but which somehow transcended them all to become . . .
what? Something wholly private and internal, Abel
thought. Awe, maybe. Even reverence.

Abel had felt it, too. They'd all felt it.

That was the crux of it: the almost spiritual veneration
one felt for a religious relic, a fragment of the true cross.
Now, here, in the storm dark with the stunted shadow of
the tree looming over him, Abel recognized that supersti-
tion for what it had really been: a desperate product of the
fearful abyss underlying their everyday lives. He understood his mother's anger, her sense of betrayal, all too
well—and with a depth of insight that transcended his
twelve years he understood something else, too: that her
anger had less to do with the watch itself than with the
man who had worn it, the man she had so often begged to
find a safer profession and who had so often refused her.

Not that any of that mattered. In the end it came down
to a simple truth: his father had prized the watch highly,
and for that alone Abel wanted it.

He groped blindly on his bedside table for the photo he
had snatched from his mother's drawer. He stared at it
through a shimmer of tears, and then, still clutching the
photo, he flopped back on the bed. The watch shimmered
in the cage of shadows printed on his ceiling.

What had she done with it? he thought. What on earth
had she done with it?

6

It was snowing, a cold blustery February morning, by the
time Fletcher Keel stepped off the El and made his way
down to the street. Wedging a battered shoe box under his
arm, he dug a scrap of paper out of the pocket of his jeans
and stared down at it. The address he'd copied out of the
Yellow Pages was two blocks northwest.

Keel folded the paper carefully and slipped it back into
his pocket before he turned up the street. He carried the

box tucked under his arm like a football, his free arm swinging. As he walked, he systematically monitored his surroundings, parsing each block into quadrants and scanning them one by one. The process itself was automatic, habitual rather than purposeful; most of it occurred well below the conscious flow of his thoughts, which were uncharacteristically agitated. Yet he was constantly filing his impressions—of the pedestrians who scuttled past, faces tilted into their collars; of the vehicles moving by him on the street; even of the buildings themselves, a mix of three- and four-story brick storefronts, their security gates rolled back for the day. If necessary, as it occasionally had been, he could reconstruct the scene before him in near-perfect detail. The irony of his situation—present errand included—was that this impressive set of skills no longer served any practical function.

Keel grimaced.

He'd resolved not to think about that. Squaring his shoulders, as much against the relentless press of his own thoughts as against the wind sweeping in from the lake, he slipped past a white-bearded vagrant methodically probing the change receptacles in a bank of newspaper machines. Two or three steps later, a gnarled hand closed over his shoulder. Keel turned, the bum looming up before him, so close that he could see the grime packed into every crevice of the man's seamed and ancient face. He was swatting randomly at something unseen in the air between them, like a man milling his arms through a swarm of insects.

"Microwaves," he was saying. "Goddamn Russian microwaves—you seen these ovens—" He reeled toward Keel suddenly, his eyes clearing, his hands outstretched. "Spare a little change, friend, be a friend now—"

Cursing, Keel pushed him away. Turning, he glimpsed his own reflection in the window of a hardware store. Five years ago, the image would have pleased him. Now he could see beyond the figure's exterior—tall, well muscled, handsome in a fleshless, rawboned way—to an inner core of desperation not entirely unlike that of the vagrant still raving at his back. There was something haunted in the deeply recessed eyes, the thin line of the mouth, something that hadn't always been there. People no longer pointed him out on the street, but Keel didn't have any problem recognizing his own lean features behind the narrow goatee he had grown after the trial. Nor did he have the stomach to look at them, he thought as he hurried past.

Halfway down the block, he found the place. Though he didn't need to—he'd memorized the location with the same natural facility he used to memorize the street around him—he fished out the slip of paper he had written the address on. He stood there, studying it, feeling his heart lurch into a quicker rhythm. What he was about to do was a betrayal—of his father, of his father's ideals, of everything his father had sought to instill within him. Keel scowled. No. The betrayal had occurred six years ago. This was merely its final consequence, the rejection of a legacy he had failed to live up to, maybe even a kind of suicide: the sacrifice of the self he had aspired to be.

Good riddance, too, he thought.

He looked up at the storefront. There was an intercom by the door, with a neatly lettered sign: PLEASE RING FOR ADMITTANCE. The store was otherwise unmarked, the interior invisible beyond the black screen which stood inside the plate glass windows.

Keel pressed the button.

"Yes?"

"My name is Fletcher Keel," he said. "I called yesterday."

"Yes, Mr. Keel. Come in."

There was the buzz of an electric lock. Keel opened the door and stepped inside. After the wind, it was pleasantly warm, an open, plushly carpeted room. Glass display counters crowded the space—an enclosed island of them in the center, and more along each wall, gleaming in the tasteful illumination of recessed spots. But for the handguns under the countertops and the enormous Nazi flag hanging on the back wall, it might have been a jewelry store—it had the same kind of luxurious appointments, the same prosperous hush. The city outside seemed infinitely remote, a faraway hum.

A man in khaki slacks and a finely woven maroon sweater stood inside the central enclosure of display counters, making notes in a ledger. He was at least a decade older than Keel, early forties, maybe older: a thin, compact man, with dark hair that had started to recede. "I'll be with you momentarily, Mr. Keel."

"You Maitland?"

"That's right. Charles Maitland."

Keel glanced over his shoulder at the locked door, thinking of the unmarked exterior. "I guess you don't get much in the way of walk-in traffic."

Maitland gave him a dry smile. "It's not that kind of clientele." He closed the ledger, slid it into a drawer, and came around the counter.

With a little shock, Keel saw that his right arm was missing from the elbow down. The sleeve of the sweater had been pinned up neatly. Keel shifted the box, and extended his left hand. Maitland's grip was cool and poised, firm without any showy exhibition of strength. He seemed comfortable, thoroughly at ease in his own skin. "Most of our customers are serious collectors. They come in once or twice a year, by appointment only. And of course I notify them when something they might be interested in comes my way. We also do a catalog."

"Maybe I'm in the wrong place."

"You said you had some memorabilia."

"Just a few things." Keel lifted the box. "Nothing like this." He glanced around the store. Daggers and bayonets gleamed in the case to his left, medals and pins in the one to his right. Framed recruiting posters—Spanish, German, American, and maybe half a dozen other nationalities—adorned the walls. A collection of combat helmets stood on shelves in one corner, some of them in mint condition, others battered. Keel let his gaze linger on one with a massively spiked crown and the ornate emblem of an eagle on the front.

Maitland noticed his interest. "A Prussian Pickelhauben, World War I vintage, near-mint condition. A bargain at $250." He smiled. "We're not snobby about the size of a collection, Mr. Keel. Most of our stock comes from veterans or their families. Personal items, the spoils of victory, so to speak. You might do very well with just one or two quality pieces. Why don't we have a look?"

Relinquishing the shoe box, Keel allowed himself to be

led to the counter. He watched as the other man removed the lid deftly with his single hand.

"See, this is a very nice piece here," Maitland said, examining the ten-inch dagger that lay inside. "Your grandfather was in the war?"

"My father." Keel swallowed, staring at the knife. The blade was age-stained and dull. "I don't know the story behind it. He didn't like to talk about it."

"It's very good. An officer's blade. Luftwaffe. Made in Solingen by Hoster. See the mark?" He held up the blade. "And the swastika on the pommel is well preserved, which is important." He set the dagger aside, dipped into the box once again, and came out with a pistol. He broke it open, checking the action. "This is good, too," he said, "though it's a very common item, of course. A Luger P08, the standard-issue German army sidearm through '42. Does it work?"

"I haven't fired it."

Maitland raised his eyebrows. "The Walther P38 replaced it. It was a superior weapon, but it certainly didn't have as much style." Putting aside the gun, he said, "What else have you got?"

"Those are the big things, I guess. The rest is just medals and stuff. Some insignia, some badges—I'm not sure what they are."

"German infantry badges, most of them," Maitland said, holding one up to the light. "Good. I can use these, as well." And then, in an offhand way, his attention still on the contents of the box: "Did you do any military service yourself?"

"Four years. Special Forces. Army Airborne."

"Ahh," Maitland said without looking up. He had taken a pad from under the counter and was making notes as he sorted through the box. It was a slow process: pick something up, examine it, put it down, pick up the pencil, make a note, put down the pencil, and start over again. There was something hypnotic in the rhythm of it. "I was in the Marines, myself. Khe Sanh in '68. The arm was my ticket home. When were you in?"

" 'Seventy-five. I missed the action."

"I'm not snobby about that either, Mr. Keel. Would that

we'd all missed it." He lifted out a medal and set it aside. "Some of your father's service decorations seem to have gotten mixed in here, Mr. Keel."

"Yeah," Keel said. And then, "I mean, I know. There's a couple of them. I want to get rid of them, too."

Frowning, Maitland stared down into the box. He combed his fingers through the jumble, lifted a swastika-embossed button, examined it, and placed it back down gently. He'd stopped making notes.

"He died fifteen years ago," Keel said, trying to ignore the scalding voice which sprang up inside his head. *A good thing he did, too,* the voice said. *A good thing he didn't live to see—*

"Still—"

"We weren't close."

"Well, I wouldn't know about that," Maitland said. "The problem is—" He broke off abruptly. Keel felt a weight swing loose inside him when he saw what the other man had plucked from the bottom of the box. Maitland lifted his head, his gaze slowly coming to rest on Keel's face. "The problem is, it's illegal to buy or sell American service decorations." He rolled the medal across his fingers and read the inscription. "I thought you said these were your father's decorations."

"I—" He hesitated, searching for an explanation, but nothing came. "I did."

"John Martin, that was your father's name?"

"Yeah." Keel straightened and put his hands flat on the counter, preparing himself for the question that he knew would follow.

Instead, Maitland said something else entirely. "Do you understand what this is?"

"I do."

"What did he do to earn it, do you know?"

"I don't want to talk about it."

"Are you aware how many of these medals have been awarded?"

"My father made a point of telling me."

"As he should have." Maitland frowned. "I didn't get into this work out of a sense of patriotism, Mr. Keel. I have no illusions about combat heroism. But still—" He nodded at the medal. "You should keep this."

"I'm sure you can find a buyer for it."

"Perhaps." He hesitated. "Almost certainly, in fact. But the question of legality aside, I think you'd regret it in the end." He laid the medal atop the counter and pushed it across to Keel. Keel didn't move. They stared down at it together.

"I'd like to buy the Luger, the knife, and the rest of these items," Maitland said, "but only on the condition that you take your father's decorations and put them in your pocket before you walk out of here. I'll write you a check for a thousand dollars, but I have to see you carry the medals out the door."

They stared at one another in silence. Keel was confident in his powers of intimidation: he was a big man to start with, and his eyes had a steely quality of resolve that most people found unnerving, an attribute that had served him well for years—and one which, like his powers of observation, had ceased to have any professional function. He had spent five years trying to nullify that fact. Just last week he had failed once again, irreversibly this time, and he had done so in a way that would have further disgraced his father. It shamed Keel too, and the shame awakened the anger, and he let *that* show in his eyes as well. Maitland wasn't backing down, though. He simply stood there, staring back at Keel, comfortable with the silence.

"How'd you lose the arm?" Keel said.

"We were pinned down by VC fire and the guy beside me took a round to the throat while he had a live grenade in his hand. It seemed like a good idea to get rid of the grenade before it went off. I came up about a forearm short."

Keel flushed, feeling another surge of self-disgust. He nodded at the medal. "You get one of those?"

"I did not. As I said, Mr. Keel, I've long since lost whatever illusions I may have had about heroism. What I did was purely a matter of self-preservation. Nonetheless, I fully intend for my son to inherit those decorations I *did* receive. I expect he will pass them along to his son in turn. Whatever your father's medals mean to you, they may someday have value to others in your family. Perhaps you didn't hear me the first time: it's illegal to sell them." He waited a moment, and then he added, "It's a point of honor with me," the word—

—*honor*—

—ricocheting like a bullet inside Keel's head. He felt a hot flush mount into his face.

Maitland said, "The question is: How badly do you need the thousand dollars?"

Keel swallowed hard. He stared at Maitland another moment, and then he scraped the medals into his open palm and pocketed them.

"I'll write you a check," Maitland said.

Ten minutes later, Keel was back outside. He glanced up the street as the door swung shut behind him. A white CPD cruiser idled at the curb, its flashers blinking, and as always Keel had to choke back that old sense of camaraderie, of common cause in a worthy enterprise, rising up to reclaim him. He swallowed his instinct to hail the officer inside. Five years. Five long years of struggling to regain that shared sense of purpose, that confidence in his lineage of honor, in his very life—and it was over now. In a moment he'd thrown it all away. He didn't care what Maitland had said.

He didn't deserve his father's medals.

He started toward the El, clutching Maitland's check in one hand. The wind seemed sharper now, blasting in off the lake and slicing through the seams of his coat. He lowered his head, no longer bothering to watch the street before him, no longer caring. And then hands were at his shoulder, clutching at him. He looked up, furious, to find himself staring once again into the ravaged face of the bum. His eyes gleamed above the matted froth of his beard. His breath washed over Keel in a fetid wave. His voice was empty, without affect, a steady unvarying cadence: "—spare me a little change, friend, c'mon now, it's cold today, it's mighty cold, just a cup of coffee, that's all I ask—"

"Here," Keel snapped, digging into his pocket.

He shoved everything he found there at the old man, a handful of change, a crumpled dollar bill, his father's medals. Everything. The whole impossible legacy. He didn't deserve it, hadn't lived up to it. He couldn't bear dragging it around behind him any longer.

The bum took it in his cupped hands and reeled away,

already veering off once again into his litany of grievances against Russian microwaves. Keel was nearly at the corner before the enraged shouts caught up to him.

"You call this change?" the old man was screaming. He waved the medals angrily overhead, the colored ribbons fluttering in the wind. "What the fuck is *this*?"

Keel felt tears starting to his eyes as he turned away.

7

Voices woke him, an incoherent babble in his dreams.

When he had been younger, at the outer cusp of infancy in a world still marvelous and strange, still *new,* Abel's family had shared a party line with the house next door. Even now, he could recall how disorienting it had been, picking up the telephone in the midst of an ongoing conversation, suddenly at sea in the unfamiliar cadences of people who were little more than shadows on the other side of the fence, enthralled by these disembodied echoes of a hidden world beyond the walls of his own narrow house. Now, swimming up through a sodden well of sleep, he felt that same disorienting rush of wonder, as if he'd caught a tantalizing echo of a larger world—

And then he was awake.

For the space of a breath, a single throb of his heart, the voices lingered. He tried to sort them out, but there were too many of them—a hundred, a thousand, maybe more— all of them talking, talking, incessantly talking, taut with urgency, trying to break through—

In the next instant, they were gone, plunging him into silence. Abel sat up. The apple tree outside his window cast a net of shadows across his bed. The snow—which had continued on and off throughout the day, from the time he woke still clutching the photo of his father until he crawled back into his twisted sheets—had finally stopped. The sky was cloudless, stippled with the bright, hard points of stars, and as he leaned closer to the thin pane of the window,

the air felt faintly warmer against his bare skin. The street
had already started melting clear. A black sheen of pavement glimmered here and there through a cloak of molten ice.

The movers would be here in the morning.

And still he hadn't found the watch.

The furnace kicked on downstairs. Abel lay back. He
picked up the photo, studying it in the faint yellow wash
of the streetlight. His father gazed back at him from the
frame of the elevator, his face inscrutable: a moment frozen
in time, irretrievably lost. And as for the voices—well, he'd
been dreaming, that's all.

Yet he felt a persistent little tug of doubt.

He'd heard them once before, after all, the other day in
his parents' bedroom, and that certainly hadn't been a
dream. What's more, there was something else, something
he hadn't quite been able to bring himself to admit. That
half-familiar voice which had floated up out of the babble,
the one that had spoken his name—it had been his father's voice.

Abel punched at his pillow, pondering this. After a moment, he found himself thinking once again of the party
line, those disembodied voices from the house beyond the
fence. His father had passed beyond a kind of fence too,
hadn't he? Beyond the fence and into the darkness on the
other side. Only in this case, the fence was something else.
In this case, the fence was death. Except that the analogy
collapsed at that point. There was no telephone. The lines
were down.

Yet the voices had come through, anyway.

Why?

He cast his mind back, trying to clear away the last lingering cobwebs of sleep. He *had* been dreaming. It came
back to him now: he'd been holding his father's watch in
one hand, the picture in the other, just staring down at
them, pierced by an ache of deep and powerful longing, and
then, suddenly, he had seemed to slip forward, tumbling,
downward and in, the photo scrolling out to envelop him,
expanding first to the size of a television, and then a movie
screen—the big one at the Palace Theater down in Sauls
Run—and finally to the breadth of the world itself, until

he was *inside* it, at the head of the mine, gazing up into his father's face as an enormous cacophony engulfed him, the clank and rattle of the ascendant elevator locking into its frame—

Only what he'd really been hearing were voices, he realized, that swirling chorus of voices. He had rationalized them, worked them into the texture of his dream the way his sleeping mind sometimes worked the clamor of his alarm clock into a dream, or his mother's voice, calling him for school from the head of the stairs. Which led him to still another conclusion, a disturbing one: that somehow, in some way he could not begin to understand, the voices had been a real sound.

He glanced down at the photograph again.

Maybe *that* was the connection—the telephone, the device that opened the line. Both times he'd heard that strange chorus of voices—that afternoon in his parents' bedroom with the watch revolving inside his head like a talisman, and just now, tonight, in his dream—both times he'd been looking at the photograph.

Abel shivered and pulled the counterpane up around his shoulders, chilled suddenly, despite the warm air blowing through the vents. He surveyed his room—the walls stripped of pictures, the boxes stacked by the bureau, the closet door standing six inches ajar on a well of darkness—struck suddenly with a disquieting sense that he wasn't alone. He eyed the closet warily. It was all too easy to imagine someone standing there, just back of the door, maybe reaching for the knob with one cold hand. . . .

He laughed, but it sounded forced and hollow in the silence. The whole thing was absurd, of course—the watch, the voices, the dumb idea about the closet. He should cut this nonsense out, try to get some sleep.

Instead he found himself staring down at the photograph once again, more deliberately this time, trying to test the theory, to evoke that chorus of voices. He concentrated on his father's face—the bony ridges of his cheeks, the sunken eyes—the range of his perceptions narrowing. Just looking at it made him feel heavy; his eyes stung, his throat clotted. Unbidden, his lips shaped the name—

"Dad."

—an almost inaudible whisper rising up into the silence around him, like a signal launched into the dark vault of the midnight sky.

And then, abruptly, he seemed once again to be falling, unhinged from gravity. The bedroom tilted vertiginously, spilling him down and in, the black funnel of the photograph yawning open to receive him. He had a single panicked impulse to try and stop it somehow, to jam a stick into the wheels of whatever process he had set in motion. But he had no idea how, and besides, it was too late. Everything fell away—the stunted apple tree outside his window, the furnace cycling off in the basement, the bedroom itself—and he was there, watching as the elevator clanked to a stop and the figure inside flung back the accordion mesh of the door with a bang—only this time, in some subterranean chamber of his mind, he understood that it wasn't these sounds at all that he was hearing. It was voices, the first faint stir of whispers, urgent, pleading, building toward some awful crescendo.

With that recognition, the world-girdling illusion of the photograph also sheared away. He was in his bedroom— he had been in his bedroom the whole time, he understood that now—but it had grown darker, colder, a bone-chilling ebony cold like the cold of the measureless deeps between the stars, and up through all of that fathomless dark and cold surged an explosive geyser of voices, a clamoring whirlwind of grievance and remorse. He shrank into his covers, closed his eyes, and cried his father's name—

"Dad. *Dad!*"

—hurling it like a harpoon into that cacophony of lamentation. With an almost physical shock, he felt it plunge into something, felt it catch and drag.

As abruptly as it had begun it was over.

The voices disappeared abruptly, as though someone had thrown a switch. Silence filled the room. And yet, somehow, everything had shifted, changed. If possible it had gotten colder still, a blue and numbing cold like no cold he had ever felt. And the silence had a charged and waiting quality. He dared not speak or move, dared not open his eyes. He could barely bring himself to breathe. He simply lay there, freezing under the weight of his comforter, wondering what awful thing he had summoned forth from the whirlwind, too terrified to do anything but listen.

What he heard was an almost subaudible creak, like a hinge badly in need of oil pivoting inside its metal sleeve. *Exactly* like that, actually, and the thought triggered a nightmarish little montage in Abel's mind.

He fought it. A strained, incredulous voice rose up from some remote corner of his mind to protest that it was only his jumped-up nerves playing tricks on his perceptions, that there was nothing there, *nothing*, the closet was empty, he could open his eyes and see for himself—

But another low metallic protest from the hinge cut through that skeptical interior patter like a buzz saw of static, plunging him deeper into cold paralysis. He just lay there, staring blankly at the insides of his own eyelids, frozen in place. And the worst thing of all was that he didn't *need* to open his eyes. The little snippet of cinema playing inside his head showed Abel everything he could ever want to know about what was happening in his gloomy bedroom. It was all right there in vivid Technicolor—the closet door swinging open, its hinges squealing; the shape emerging from the black well on the other side, attended by a sub-zero gust that frosted Abel's breath in the air before his face; the jaundiced glow of the streetlight ascending the shadowy figure as it advanced, to fall at last upon its face—

It was his father.

It was his father, carrying his mining cap in one hand, its crown deeply dented, the lamp affixed to the front shattered and dark. It was his father, wearing the same clothes he had worn in the photograph, the clothes he had put on every workday morning for as long as Abel could remember, the clothes he had died in. Abel didn't open his eyes, *couldn't* open them, not yet, maybe never again, but he could see them anyway, those clothes: the spavined work boots, the jeans grimy with mud and coal, the filthy denim shirt, so often and obsessively laundered that it had at last achieved a kind of neutral vacancy, an utter absence of color, like the skin of creatures too long interred in the deep places of the earth. Like the skin of dead things. Like the skin of the thing that wore it, mottled and torn from the accident, already splotched with gray patches of decay.

Abel squeezed shut his eyes, but it didn't do any good. He could see everything anyway, unspooling on the dark screen inside his mind. A barb of grief pierced him as the thing shambled closer, the heavy work boots scuffing, its sagging face terrible and strange, empty of warmth or recognition, of anything remotely human.

The mattress gave beneath the thing's weight.

Abel cringed from the cold, the absolute zero of the world beyond the fence; he cringed from the noisome stench of decay. But even then—even in that moment of absolute madness and terror—his grief and longing continued to spill through him, carrying the watch endlessly before them, through the deep, covetous wellsprings of his heart.

"Dad," he whimpered.

And then it was leaning over him, its black lips at his ear, whispering its secrets in the cold, dry voice of the grave.

8

On days like today, the psychiatrist sometimes reflected that he might have already retired had he gone into private practice. He was young still, in his early fifties, but the proceeds of such a practice could have been substantial. He had no difficulty picturing the secluded existence he'd have chosen to spend them on: a small ranch somewhere in the wine country to the north, afternoons working with the vines, weekend visits with his grandchildren. He already had one—a fourteen-month-old granddaughter named Casey—and another was on the way. It was easy to imagine them summering at the ranch, absorbing the easy rhythms of the season, getting the earth in their blood.

It was a harmless fantasy, nothing more. In truth, he was more than content with his lot. The school district had given him a supportive network of professional and personal acquaintance; he had a family that he loved and that returned his love. The pay was adequate—he didn't want for anything, certainly—and the work provided other, and more significant, compensations. There were the children.

But that just made the tough ones that much harder.

And this one looked as though it might prove very hard indeed.

He stood at his second-floor window in a wash of golden California light, and watched a maroon Mercedes pulling into the lot below. It was February, and the sky was a lucid and depthless blue. Two hours to the north, the sun would be bathing the fragrant earth, drawing the first green shoots from the nascent vines. A man and a woman got out of the Mercedes. They looked to be ten years his junior, tan and fit. Their clothes were good, tasteful and expensive, without unnecessary extravagance. They were the kind of people he socialized with. Who knows? They might well have attended the same parties, or eaten at the same restaurants. It would be surprising if they hadn't.

He turned to the desk, barren but for a spiral notebook and a manila file folder. The folder contained his notes from several meetings with the boy's teacher. The notebook contained the documents which had occasioned this conference. He thumbed through it as he strolled back to the window, struck once again by the remarkable sophistication of the prose.

And by the even more remarkable violence of the imagery.

The boy might well be a genius of a very limited kind. Certainly he was gifted. Everything about him suggested that he was also deeply disturbed. The psychiatrist called the child's image to mind: his dark, expressionless face, his almost preternatural stillness. Below, the handsome couple were just passing out of his line of sight, into the building.

Ten minutes later, gazing at them across the coffee table, he saw that he had underestimated their age. The man had the look of an ex-jock who'd tried to keep in shape, and was just now starting to lose the battle. He was tall, dark-headed, a little remote, perhaps offended that he'd been called in like this. The woman was petite, shapely, carefully put together: makeup, nail polish, the works. Beneath her shellacked exterior, however, she seemed frayed, a little tense.

The psychiatrist explained why he'd asked to see them. He showed them the notebook and let them look through it. The husband was impassive, the wife nearly so, though he detected a growing tension in the set of her jaw as she flipped the pages. After a few minutes, she closed the notebook and held it on her lap.

They sat quietly.

The psychiatrist watched them expressionlessly. The husband fidgeted, clearly ill at ease; the wife sat rigidly, her hands folded atop the notebook, taking measure of the office—the desk by the window, the informally furnished sitting area he'd chosen for their talk, the play area with its pleasant clutter of toys. Her gaze lingered there for some time, and then it came to rest on him.

"How come his teacher's not here, anyway?" the man said.

The psychiatrist hesitated. He recognized both the hostility of the question and the shame it was intended to disguise, but he forced himself to withhold judgment: both emotions could be measures of the man's hidden reservoirs of affection for his child. Besides, the issue was a delicate one. Normally, the teacher *would* have been there, but in the end he'd elected to host the meeting without her. She was young, she'd been deeply upset by the notebook, and he had sensed the presence of other issues with this particular child—perhaps ones involving race. Her tension would have complicated matters; he thought he stood a better chance of earning their trust without her.

Finally, he said, "Miss Hammond couldn't be here today. Normally, I would have delayed our meeting to accommodate her schedule, but Ben's situation seemed . . . pressing."

"He's imaginative." The man shrugged as he said it.

"Indeed. His facility with language is remarkable. Ben is quite talented, Mr. Prather. Yet the nature of his journal suggests a history of significant trauma which perhaps jeopardizes those extraordinary gifts. I'd like your permission to spend some time talking with him, that's all."

"He's had enough trouble. We don't need the school mucking around in it."

The woman shifted in her seat.

"Well, we don't," her husband said, glaring at her. And then, grudgingly, "We can hire somebody if it comes to that."

"I'd be happy to refer you to someone." The psychiatrist paused. "I'd also like to help him myself."

The man grunted, and stalked over to the window.

"Your son's files indicate that he was adopted when he was five," the psychiatrist said. "Can you tell me about it?"

The man turned. "Is this some kind of race thing?"

"Do you feel that your son's race is at issue, Mr. Prather?" The psychiatrist watched the woman as he spoke. He sensed that she could be an ally, but a direct appeal would merely isolate the husband, feeding his hostility.

"Of course it's an issue. It's always an issue."

And that was no doubt true. The psychiatrist watched the couple, focused on the dynamic between them and how it might have affected their child; yet a small part of his brain had slipped away to his ranch again. He'd spent years constructing it in his imagination, and he could see it clearly in his mind, a rambling structure of stone and wood with high windows and views of the vineyards rolling away to the horizon. He stood at the window and watched Casey cross the green lawn, her small face intent on the still-unmastered trick of putting one foot in front of the other, oblivious to his presence here, smiling down upon her. He ran through the calculations for perhaps the thousandth time, assets versus expenditures, the fieldstone structure of his dreams. A reduction in expenses here, a reallocation of investments there, and who could say, in a year, perhaps two . . .

The woman cleared her throat and shot a glance at her husband. "Frank," she said, "maybe it's time—"

"I thought we'd agreed," her husband said from the window. "The past is done with. He's better off not thinking about it."

Watching, the psychiatrist saw that the woman understood a truth which her husband had yet to perceive: that the past is never done with, never, not if you live a thousand years. It was a hard truth, but not such a terrible thing in the end. He thought of the vineyards, the hazy golden harvest with the grape ripe and firm beneath your thumb, and then the cutting back that followed and the long fallow months with the rain sweeping in from the coast until the season swung round once again and the vines quickened, new life always springing upward from the rich black sediment of years.

"No, Frank," she said softly, "it *is* time," and her husband slumped visibly, the fight going out of him all at once. He crossed the room and sat heavily on the sofa, clasping his hands between his knees. He seemed reduced somehow. The wife took a deep breath.

She looked up. She met the psychiatrist's eyes.

"Let me tell you about Ben," she began.

Two hours had passed before she finished. By the time they left the psychiatrist felt wrung out. He saw them to the door and returned to his office to file the permissions they had signed. Then he slouched in the chair behind his desk. It was late, the shadows lengthening beyond his window. His wife would be worried. Yet he sat there all the same. The man's words kept coming back to him—

—*it's always an issue*—

—but the face he saw in his mind was Casey's face.

He closed his eyes, taking a moment's refuge in his little fantasy of the ranch. He pictured himself walking the rich acres, pausing now and then to test the grapes between his fingers, turning at last in the cool evening to head back to the house. The first lights glimmered warmly in the high windows, beckoning him onward as the purple dusk stole down across the valley.

He stood and collected his keys. He didn't bother with his calculations as he walked down the stairs and out to his car. Casey's perfect laughter chimed in his ears, and he found himself thinking instead of the world he had spent his career trying to summon into being for her.

The vineyard could wait.

9

Maya had gotten his private number somehow—and not the direct line to his office. No, she had gotten his home number, and Ramsey Lomax would have paid a fair sum to know how she had managed it. After all, the evening might have developed unpleasantly had Lomax not picked up the telephone himself.

As chance would have it, however, he did. And he'd known it was her from the first—from the unhurried self-possession of the silence on the line, from the sharp sibilance of her intaken breath. He had heard them both before, and in circumstances far more pleasurable. The word which had followed was the same as well. Only the emotional weight had changed. In the past it had sometimes presaged her imminent climax. Now it presaged . . . what, exactly?

That was the funny thing: Lomax couldn't really say. It didn't forebode the hysterical tirade he might have expected from another woman. It hinted of nothing tearful or recriminating. It was just that one syllable, direct and businesslike after two weeks of silence that he had begun to believe augured a painless break. It was his name, or more accurately, her abbreviated version of it.

"Ram," she'd said—which reminded him of the perverse humor Maya had found in the phallic overtones of the word. In the context, he supposed, it had seemed pretty goddamn hilarious.

It didn't seem so funny anymore, did it?

Lomax snatched a glance at the door to affirm that Sara was still upstairs, dressing for the Foundation Ball they sponsored annually. Not that it would have mattered, exactly. He supposed Sara must have known he was more or less a serial adulterer and had made her peace with it. She wasn't naive, after all, and the tenor of their emotional lives—the endless compromises, large and small, of a marriage conducted largely as an exercise in public relations—had long since become clear to both of them. Still, such an invasion of his home offended Lomax's sense of decorum. And more important than that, his sense of control. So he had acted to reassert both.

"I don't know how you got this number," he had said calmly, enunciating every word, "but if you use it again I will see to it that you lose your job."

Then, without waiting to hear her reply, he cradled the phone. The truth was, however, he had already decided on another, less drastic course of action: a tidy promotion that would send her packing to a facility in another state—Arizona, maybe, the climate wasn't bad there. And then, when the sting had faded, he'd drop her a check in the mail, something generous, a little salve to the wound. He'd done it often enough before, and the moment he'd heard her speak his name he had decided to do it again.

Lomax wasn't even sure why he had ever begun the affair. It wasn't his style. He didn't customarily mess his own nest, for one thing. For another, Maya Underwood hadn't been his type—even before Sara, in the days when his shaven skull and sharply hooked features had been a gossip-column mainstay, he'd tended to gravitate toward statuesque blondes. He hadn't judged celebrity a bad thing, either, at least back then, and if in these later days he'd been forced to sacrifice a public conquest in favor of privacy, there were still plenty of good-looking blondes around, most of them more than receptive to his advances. Lomax didn't flatter himself: he wasn't a particularly handsome man. But power and wealth possessed a certain allure, and when he wanted to turn it on he had charisma to spare.

So when his eye fell upon Maya—an assistant of an assistant, sitting anonymously behind some junior executive during the course of an interminable meeting—Lomax couldn't say what had attracted him. She was small and lean, high-breasted, and perhaps it was only the lure of physical novelty that drew his attention. But he thought it might be the same subtly subversive brand of humor that had led her to highlight the ironic dimensions of his own name. He'd noticed it even that first time, in the occasional glance of wry amusement she shot from beneath a wing of dark hair as the meeting dragged on. Later, pursuing, he'd found her to be self-contained, independent, keenly observant—she'd been more than adequate in bed, confident in fulfilling her needs while plenty attentive to his own, but even there she seemed always to hold some fragment of herself aloof, as if she found even her own human frailty amusing in some sad, all too self-aware way.

Nor had she seemed to harbor any illusions about the nature of their relationship. With Maya, there had been no talk of love, no weighted inquiries about the state of his marriage, no expectation of lavish gifts. As far as he could tell, the whole thing might have been little more than a

pleasant carnal arrangement among friends—and not even
particularly close ones—and a time came when he wondered if perhaps she was using him instead of the other
way around. It was that more than anything else, he supposed, which finally persuaded him to end the thing—a
sense that it was slipping beyond his control, that he needed
Maya more than she needed him, that maybe he always
had.

Which was why the phone call both startled and reas-
sured him. He would not have expected it from her, but it
comforted him all the same: perhaps he'd misjudged the
shifting tides in their relationship. Perhaps she needed him
more than he had thought. It didn't occur to him until
much later that night—after he'd gotten back from the
Foundation Ball and, in a rare fit of remorse, had made a
perfunctory kind of love with Sara—that perhaps what he
had misjudged was the nature of the phone call itself. Perhaps it had been little more than a courtesy—but if so,
what kind of courtesy? The question startled him momentarily awake, and it was still resonating when he finally
drifted off to sleep.

The next morning, Lomax almost picked up the telephone and called her. In the end, however, he contacted
John Harris in Human Resources and arranged for her promotion instead—and if Harris was at all curious about why
the founder and CEO of Eyecom Industries was suddenly
taking a personal interest in such mundane matters of lower
management, he was wise enough to keep his suspicions to
himself. Lomax had nearly forgotten the matter of the
phone call by the time Maya Underwood finished un-
packing her belongings in the high desert of Arizona two
months later.

And when he finally got around to mailing the check—
quite a sizable one, too—he was far too involved in the
pursuit of yet another blonde to notice that no one ever
bothered to cash it.

10

As an adult, Abel would remember almost nothing of the episode with the watch, or how it ended—not the storm and not that geyser of whispering voices in his benighted bedroom, not the give of the mattress as the cold revenant of his father leaned over him to whisper its secrets into his waiting ear. In the end, he would forget even the process of forgetting, the long years of denial during which his innermost self, secret even from his waking daylight mind, labored like an oyster to encase the terrifying memory of those days in layer after layer of oblivion, until at last only the smooth outer surface remained, lovely and impervious as a pearl.

It must have begun that very night, for even then there were things he could not remember. He knew only that he woke, or seemed to wake, from a terrible dream of which he could recall nothing but darkness and whispering voices. And in that strange half-waking state, a bleak urgency possessed him, a black and dreamlike certainty that drove him from his warm nest of sheets into a chill February dark that pimpled his skin into goose bumps.

The watch.

It loomed inside his head as he stole bare-chested through the sleeping house, this too passing as in a dream: his mother's bedroom door and the stairs steep-angled in the gloom and the floor below where everything waited in readiness for the movers, a few last sticks of furniture his mother couldn't bear to part with, the silvery and unblinking eye of the television, the bulging ranks of liquor-store cartons looming over him in the shadows. The watch lured him and led him on, through the kitchen and into the mudroom; it hung before him as he fumbled open the door, leaving it to swing upon its hinges as he stepped into the darkness beyond.

The night unrolled itself to greet him, silent and windy in the aftermath of the storm. The company houses stood tall and close, the ridges looming behind them, more sensed than seen, like the vanguard of an encircling army. Still the watch drew Abel on, through the gated yard and into the alley. His breath frosted the air before his face. His bare feet left prints in the snow. But the cold, if he felt it at all, made no impression upon him. He moved forward steadily, his gaze fixed on the far side of the alley, where garbage bags had been heaped in wild profusion, the cast-off detritus of more than twelve years in the decaying old house at his back.

An observer, watching him, would have thought it strange, the confidence with which he strode forward—a small boy with brown hair, barefoot in the snow, clad only in ragged pajama bottoms—to burrow into that pile of identical garbage bags and surface a moment later, dragging behind him a single bulging green sack. But there was no one to see, only the night and the blank windows of the surrounding houses and the distant points of a thousand stars. Perhaps, far down in his mind, a remote fragment of Abel's waking self remembered the source of the black intelligence which had driven him out into the frozen night; perhaps it lifted its voice in protest—maybe that explained the tears crystallizing on his cheeks, or the pounding of his heart inside its cage of bones. Whatever the case, Abel never hesitated—the fell knowledge which had mastered him won out. Moving like an automaton, he lugged the bag to the center of the alley, where the streetlight cast a jaundiced circle of radiance over the disconsolate stalks of brown grass angling through the snow.

And there, dropping to his knees, Abel tore it open.

Normally, he would have shrunk from the meaty stench rising from the ruptured plastic. Now, seeming to mind the smell no more than he minded the snow soaking through the knees of his pajamas or the cold that pinched his fingers into blue hooks, Abel lunged forward, clawing through the refuse, through the discarded sympathy notes which his mother could not bear to read and the congealed remnants of the lasagna which a sympathetic neighbor had dropped off three nights ago, past a clump of tissue clotted with snot and tears, beyond the deliquescing stalks of the funeral home lilies which his mother had kept on the kitchen table until finally they had drooped and begun to rot and Abel had been forced to dump them himself, draining the foul greenish water into the sink and tossing the disintegrating blossoms into this very bag. He shoved aside a newspaper turned oily and translucent by some nauseating alchemy, dug through a handful of shattered egg shells, and there—just beyond the leathery rind of an orange, curled up on a bed of damp coffee grounds—there, with a glint of cool starlight in the grinning fracture of the face and the hands still frozen thirteen minutes short of noon, as if time itself had stopped in the lost instant of that initial accident, granting Abel's father the right to walk the earth forever, rendering all that had passed in these last days the phantoms of a vile dream—there, lay the watch. With a cry Abel lunged forward, dragged it to his breast, and curled fetal in the snow.

That was how his mother found him thirty minutes later. The noise of the door had startled her awake, and when she came down to shut it, she saw him there, his upturned face already turning pale and blue. Dead, she thought. He has to be dead. The magnitude of the idea, the sheer horror of it, froze her in the doorway, her hand curled before her open mouth. She cried out, a strangled sob, and lurched forward, through the yard and into the alley. Sinking to her knees, she cradled her son, sobbing in relief as she felt his breath warm her cheek. And then she noticed the watch she had denied him, clutched immovably in one frozen claw. Her first thought, rising up through the guilt-choked well of her awareness, was that this was her fault—that her rage and grief might have betrayed her into yet a greater loss. Her second thought was one of wonder and fear. Her gaze flickered upward to take in the mound of trash bags, a wall of them, a mountain of them, twenty of them at least, and maybe half again as many more, who knew you could accumulate so much junk in the course of a life—

Yet Abel had chosen the right bag with his very first attempt, unerringly, as if drawn to it, as if he already knew where he would find the watch. *How?* Perhaps she whispered the word aloud, for Abel's eyes flickered and opened, his gaze unfixed and staring.

"Abel," she whispered. "Abel, baby, how did you know where to look?"

She caught only a fragment of his mumbled response—
". . . told me . . ."

"Who," she asked, leaning closer. "Who told you?"

For a moment, she thought he wouldn't answer. He seemed stunned, lethargic. Then his eyes locked upon her face, and she found herself gazing down into the glare of a bleak and terrible knowing that offered no refuge, no place to hide. He seemed a hundred years old—a thousand—and suddenly she didn't want to hear his answer. She didn't want to hear it at all.

But it was too late. His lips were already moving, forming the words.

"Daddy," he whispered. "My daddy told me."

His eyes fluttered and closed. He slept. Cradling him against her breast, she turned and staggered back through the darkness toward the house, toward the warmth and light emanating from inside. She slammed the door against the night and stripped off their sodden clothes and took her son, still clutching the watch, into the warmth of her own bed, and there they slept until the morning sun broke over the ridges to the east and the movers woke them, hammering on the front door.

If Abel recalled what he had said to her—if he had even known what it was in the first place—he never mentioned it. And though she watched her son in fear and doubt for months, there came a time during the long decade that followed when even she forgot—or could no longer bear to let herself remember—that odd night when she had found him half frozen in the snow.

Yet perhaps the memory wasn't utterly lost.

Years later, when Abel was grown, some watchful unforgetting self hidden deep in the cellars of his mother's mind wondered if perhaps there wasn't some odd echo of those words—

—*daddy my daddy told me*—

—in the strange and public life her son had chosen—a life as distant from Copperhead, West Virginia, as Abel had ever dared to dream in those long nights of staring into the shadowy net of branches over his bed. Abel's mother was a practical woman, a realist. She had no sympathy for psychics or palm readers or anything of the kind. She called such people frauds. She called her son a fraud, too—and she called him worse, a vulture preying upon sorrow and grief, and one who should know better, having had such a bitter draught of both in his own life. She was ashamed.

But that deeper, hidden self remembered—and wondered.

11

Through all that long winter and into the years that followed, Dreamland drowsed, waiting with a patience only concrete and stone can know.

Strange vapors breathed from its open drains, wafted up from the sewers buried far beneath the streets, and even on the hottest days, a thin viscid fluid, almost organic, wept from the dank blocks of its interior. It stank of mildew and urine, of fly-swarmed trash stewing in damp corridors, of spent gunshots. It stank of blood. At night, when darkness clamped down upon the city like the lid of a pressure cooker, packs of young men roved its corridors and courtyards, driven by hungers they could neither name nor sate.

And there was worse: rumors that deserted apartments were not always empty. That some cold intelligence drowsed in the empty places of Dreamland, in the moldering trash-heaped dark of the subbasements and the black vacuum of the empty elevator shafts. That occasionally it heaved itself into wakefulness, and unlidded its terrible eyes. Many who lived inside Dreamland's walls discounted such tales—too mired in the mundane tragedies of hunger and drugs and lost children to countenance such horrors. Others fled the place, avoiding the sidewalks outside its gates, unwilling to endure even its shadow falling across them.

There are places on the earth so scarred and mutilated,

so drenched in the blood of human suffering, so saturated with misery and pain, that the very stones cry out. Even years later you can sense it in the air. The stench of the ovens lingers in Auschwitz. At sunset, the killing fields of Cambodia still run with blood. There are such places here as well. We have our Shilohs, our Oklahoma Cities. A sleeper in the shadow of the Alamo may still suffer unsettled dreams, and on a quiet morning in New Orleans, a pedestrian on Canal Street may yet hear the bark of the auctioneer's gavel from the slave market that once thrived just blocks to the west.

No one can say for sure when such a place stirs to consciousness, or why. Perhaps there are spots where the very fabric of reality grows thin, where the endless void without presses too hard against the fraying margins of space and time, and those rare few who have ears to hear them can detect the sound of titanic intelligences at work in the outer dark, drawing their plans against the sunlit regions of the world. Or it could be that a house, a street, even a sprawling hive of towers like Dreamland, takes on the inner hue of the people who inhabit it, that too much misery and hatred and bloodshed can awaken a furtive darkness in even the brightest place. Or it could be that haunted places arise through some fraught intersection of human misery and geographic chance. Maybe the darkness in our hearts and in our acts calls out through the thin margins of the world to the greater darkness that presses ever upon them, misery to misery, hatred to hatred. Maybe such places and their inhabitants become doorways for whatever powers and dominions reign in the fathomless vacuum without.

In any case, Dreamland stirred slowly toward full awareness, reaching out now and again to probe and to test its powers. Once already, in the years before that difficult winter, it had roused itself from slumber and the eyes of the world had turned upon it, transfixed by the sound of snipers' gunshots. But the public eye is fickle. Soon the bright television glare turned elsewhere, distracted by the prospect of fresher carnage. Dreamland sank once again into the realm of fitful rumor, largely forgotten by the world. Now and again stories appeared in the papers or on local television, but not many of them—violence was too common there, death routine.

And besides, the victims were black.

It wasn't until years later, when Abel Williams stood on the verge of achieving his dubious fame and the sole survivor of that first catastrophe had grown into a troubled maturity, that the TV cameras returned. Ironically enough, it was another boy, this one a mere five years old, who caught the world's attention. Hurled from the cold heights of Dreamland, Dante Morris had plunged eighteen stories to the crumbling plaza below. And even that would not have been enough—such falls were common, after all—had not the perpetrators been so young, nine and ten years old, mere children themselves, though the police who interviewed them afterward said that their eyes were as weary as the eyes of old men. If you had inquired further, if you had earned the trust of the grizzled uniformed officers who arrived first on the scene, who saw the child's shattered body and his killers staring down from the roofline high above, you might have learned something that the reporters and the TV cameras never learned, something that even the people of Dreamland spoke of only in whispers; you might have learned that there in the immediate aftermath, the eyes of the killers looked barely human at all—that staring into them was like staring through ragged holes into the hot glare of eternity itself. And had you wormed your way into the innermost thoughts of those men, where they held secrets even from themselves, you might have learned what they had never said even to each other: that they had glimpsed something else far down in the incandescent pits of those eyes, some cold intelligence peering back at them.

But no one ever learned that.

The nation's attention held. From plush offices and marble porticoes half a continent away, politicians railed against the inhumanity. Men of God wept in their pulpits and passed the collection plate. Deep in the bowels of the Housing Authority, plans for Dreamland's destruction were drawn up. Then the public's attention swerved, distracted by some new calamity. The cameras went away. For a time, the plans were forgotten.

Dreamland subsided once again into sleep, or what passed for sleep. It abided anyway, and if occasionally it stirred from its long stone thoughts to some small act of malice—like the time Robert Johnson poured boiling water in the face of his screaming baby, or the day Letitia Rayfield pushed her little sister down the north stairwell, breaking her arm—no one could say for sure that these weren't acts of merely human cruelty, and even those who suspected otherwise said nothing, or only whispered it among themselves. For its part, Dreamland stood patient and unchanged, a circle of featureless slabs, as mute and inexpressive as a ring of stone megaliths erected in supplication to some bloodthirsty Neolithic god.

Invitation to

Dreamland

THE PRESENT

1

But for the happenstance of a Ouija board and half a case of Budweiser, Abel might never have stumbled across Dreamland at all. The Ouija board belonged to Greg, his sophomore roommate at WVU; the Budweiser belonged to the roommate's tearful ex-girlfriend, Susie—and had Greg been present when she arrived, Abel's life might have taken an utterly different path. As it happened, though, Greg, exhausted by Susie's near-daily assaults on his apartment, had fled home to Parkersburg, leaving Abel to fend for himself. So it was that Abel, who should have been studying for a psych midterm, spent that Saturday night knocking back pilsner with Susie instead—and when Susie's eyes happened to light on the Ouija board jammed under the television stand, he was three beers too far gone not to play along.

Ten minutes later, Abel found himself hunched on the threadbare carpet, staring blearily at the lettered board by the flickering light of a single candle. Several things quickly became evident, among them the fact that Susie was a breathtakingly ordinary girl. Neither her questions nor the responses she sought from the "presiding spirits" (her phrase) showed the faintest sign of imagination. But the answers themselves—answers which Abel dutifully manufactured, picking them out letter by solitary letter ("u will find luv") through the nearly invisible exertions of his fingertips atop the planchette—seemed to gain authority through the agency of the Ouija board. It was a lesson in human nature far more useful than anything he could have learned poring over his psych book, and by the end of the night—when Susie fell enthusiastically into his bed, her avowed passion for his absent roommate temporarily forgotten—Abel had taken it thoroughly to heart. What people said they wanted and what they really wanted were two entirely different matters—and someone willing to exploit that division could occasionally accomplish something of merit. In this case, for example, Greg no longer had to dodge his ex-girlfriend's kamikaze assaults upon his apartment, while Susie, who thought she had come in search of reconciliation, departed instead with a measure of the revenge she had truly been seeking. From Abel's perspective it was nearly a perfect resolution—and he got laid to boot.

It was a classic case of doing well by doing good, and one he would not soon forget. By the time he graduated, the paranormal had become a lucrative hobby for Abel. A few parlor tricks and an increasingly sharp eye for what people *really* wanted garnered him a pretty fair campus reputation; that, in turn, gleaned him invitations to the best parties and, even better, an occasional tryst with a girl who would otherwise be out of his league. They were usually on the rebound from one disastrous affair or another, true, but as far as Abel was concerned the temporary nature of these liaisons merely contributed to their appeal. Variety, after all, was the spice of life.

Three years later, jobless and adrift in the Midwest, Abel decided to try parlaying the same set of skills into a living. In a culture defined by sitcoms and office cubicles, he reasoned, the secret to success might well be to demystify the paranormal, to work it into the fabric of mundane existence. So he placed an ad in the Yellow Pages, scraped up the cash to lease a strip-mall storefront, and jettisoned all the hoary supernatural clichés—the crystal balls, the Tarot cards, even his precious Ouija board—opting instead for the bland professional decor of a psychotherapist: a sofa, a couple of comfortable chairs, fresh flowers on the table. Six months later he had a thriving clientele. A year after that people were flying in for consultations from around the country—a heady brew of grief, redemption, and cash, well spiced by an occasional squeeze from the odd good-looking widow.

Abel might have been content, but for a call from a television producer named Gale Parker. As Parker talked, he found himself staring once again into that net of branches printed on the ceiling of his boyhood bedroom. The old dream of glamour stirred within him. He knew he would say yes ten minutes before she finished her pitch.

The program, *Messages from Beyond*, proved to be another landmark on the long road to Dreamland. Over Parker's objections, Abel vetoed spooky mood music, atmospheric camera angles, and horror movie sound effects. He kept the show as familiar and nonthreatening as that strip-mall storefront: a studio audience of the bereaved, an occasional celebrity guest, and of course Abel himself, strolling back and forth across the stage, his brow furrowing as he plucked messages out of the ether. The show's real drama, he argued, ought to come from within—from the interaction between Abel and the audience, from the tears of relief and reconciliation, from the heartfelt testaments to Abel's accuracy that would close every show. His sole concession to Parker's sensibilities was the opening montage of photos, a gallery of the dear departed as submitted every week by members of the studio audience. Just watching it sent a strangely disquieting shiver up Abel's spine.

A year later *Messages* had become a morning staple, sandwiched somewhere between *Regis* and *Oprah* in just about every television market in the nation. In the two years following that, he landed a book deal and a contract for a sequence of self-help tapes. Abel's agent opened negotiations for a prime-time slot on FOX, and for the space of a single glorious summer Abel's face seemed to peer out of every magazine cover in America.

Then, almost as quickly as it had risen, Abel's star faded. The book tanked. The tapes sat on the shelves unsold. The promise of prime time waned. The syndicated show limped on for another season, but ratings slipped. Cancellation loomed.

And then came the murder of a south-side volunteer named Theresa Matheson. The details of the crime alone—a six-hour ordeal of gang-rape and torture conducted in the abandoned lobby of Dreamland's Tower Number Three—guaranteed a modicum of coverage. Matheson's personal profile—she had been eighteen, attractive, socially committed and, most important of all, white—sent the national media into paroxysms of indignation.

When Abel got to the studio the next Monday, he found

a message from *Hard Copy* waiting. A week later, he accompanied a reporter, a camera crew, and a handful of Theresa Matheson's friends on an expedition into the decaying lobby where she had died. Abel would have preferred family—family were easier to read, and they could always be counted on for a sympathetic tear—but Matheson was fresh out of blood relations. Her mom had died of breast cancer a year previously; her dad had died in a car crash two years before that. In a week of frenzied research, Abel hadn't been able to locate so much as a single distant cousin.

Nor did he have any great love of Dreamland itself. The whole complex gave him a genuine case of the willies. The sketchy history provided by *Hard Copy*'s producer was part of it. She filled him in on the drive over, describing both the rooftop plunge of Dante Morris and the twenty-six-year-old police raid in which six people had died—seven if you counted the first victim, gunned down at random from an upper-story window. "Kind of creepy, all that happening in one tower, isn't it?" she said, with a gusto that seemed tasteless given the wide-eyed presence of Theresa Matheson's friends. The perverse brilliance of the move—she'd been laying the groundwork for the emotional reactions she hoped to catch on film—hadn't struck Abel until later, and even then it was shot through with a spasm of self-loathing. Were they really that different, after all?

He knew what his mother would say.

But that was only the start of it. For one thing, the cratered moonscape of the projects—a desolation of abandoned cars and crumbling streets—reminded him oddly of his boyhood, the polluted industrial wreckage of the coal fields. For another, the place itself, Dreamland, projected a sense of disturbingly sentient awareness. Abel felt it the moment he climbed out of the van and looked up at Tower Three, lifting its cold facade eighteen stories into the sky. Even on that sunlit July day, it seemed shrouded in darkness, a sensation produced not so much by any literal gloom—the morning sun fell in a golden wash against the bleached concrete surface of the upper stories—as by . . . well, what, exactly? And that was it: he couldn't really say. All Abel knew was that the place simply *felt* dark. Every time he caught a glimpse of it, jutting unexpectedly into his angle of vision, he felt a cold knot of tension in his guts.

Leaving Matheson's friends huddled nervously around the van—it wouldn't do to be seen cozying up with them—Abel trailed the producer and her team into Tower Three. His uneasiness only grew inside. The glass entrance doors had been shattered, and beyond the bright space of the vestibule the lobby receded into shadowy dimness, unrelieved except for the distant red glow of an exit sign. Two elevator banks stood on the far side of the room, one set of doors sensibly closed, the other yawning open upon a well of darkness. A stench of urine and rotting trash shimmered palpably in the heat.

"So this is where it happened," the producer said, almost reverentially. And then, looking up at the cameraman: "I want to shoot Abel's reading here."

The cameraman surveyed the room with narrowed eyes. "Gonna have some trouble with lighting."

"Screw the lighting. This is where she died."

The cameraman snorted. "Let me get a meter," he said. He kicked an empty liquor bottle toward the black mouth of the elevator shaft as he turned away. Abel watched in a kind of fascination as it skidded across the metal lip and into the void beyond. A numb instant of silence followed, and then the sound of shattering glass came rolling up at them, doubling and redoubling in the echo chamber of the empty elevator shaft.

"Asshole," the producer muttered, but Abel barely heard her. He was listening to the odd reverberations even now dying away into stillness. They had almost sounded like voices, a swirling chorus of whispering voices rising up out of the darkness—

His bowels cramped. For the space of a single heartbeat, a ghost of memory hovered at the edge of his awareness. The next instant, it was gone.

Abel turned away, suddenly anxious for the touch of the July sun against his skin, realizing too late that one of Theresa Matheson's girlfriends—a lanky brunette with an oval face—had followed them inside. That was the instant, he would later think, that killed his career. It was not merely that the girl had overheard the exchange between the pro-

ducer and her half-witted cameraman—though God knew
that was bad enough. It was that she had seen that flicker
of unease in Abel's eyes. Her face closed like a fist. Watching her, Abel was struck by a sudden further insight: people
knew he was a fake, they wanted him to be. If they *truly*
believed he could speak with the dead—believed the way
they believed in Toyotas or telephone bills—they would be
terrified of him. Three hundred years ago they might have
burned him at the stake. That thought triggered another
ghostly flutter of memory. His mother's face loomed momentarily in his mind—

—who told you how did you know—

—and then it flickered and disappeared, driven out by
the clatter of heels against the concrete floor as Theresa
Matheson's friend turned away.

"Wait—" Abel said, but the door swung shut behind her.

Which was just as well, he supposed. What would he
have told her, after all—*Don't worry. I really* am *a con
artist?*

Besides, the reading had already been spoiled.

It worked out pretty much as Abel had feared. The producer took her time dressing the scene, arranging and rear-
ranging several massive displays of bouquets and candles
around dramatically enlarged photos of Theresa Matheson's face. Another hour passed while the camera crew
worked out the lights. By the time everything was set, the
oval-faced girl's tension and resentment had communicated
themselves to her friends. The whole crew of them sat rigidly before Abel while the cameras rolled inexorably, catching every minute of the disaster on tape.

There had been only one incident that was the least bit
memorable—and even that could hardly be counted a success. Abel had been doing his standard shtick—pacing,
wrinkling his brow, studying his audience for even the tiniest reaction as he worked to refine a mix of generic patter
and careful guesswork into something they hoped to hear.
Given the amount he already knew about Theresa Matheson's death, it should have been easy. But Matheson's
friends merely sat there, mute and uncooperative. The
reading was already going badly when, turning, Abel happened to catch a glimpse of Matheson's candlelit photo.
The temperature seemed to dip, and he paused, transfixed,

as a chorus of whispers swirled around him. A panicked phrase—

—*please no please*—

—rose up out of the babble, and suddenly the air before him shifted and parted, like stage curtains sweeping back to reveal the scene beyond. For a single terrifying moment, he saw, or imagined he saw, the whole thing: the shadowy lobby and the ring of jeering black men and Theresa Matheson herself, flung at an angle across a rickety table, her battered face twisted in agony and her skirt bunched around her thighs as a thickly muscled kid in a battered Cubs cap worked himself steadily between her outflung legs.

"Jesus," Abel gasped.

Even as the word slipped unbidden from his lips, the scene faded. He snatched a final desperate whisper—

—*no help me please*—

—from the whirl of sound, and then that too was gone. The world was the same world it had always been.

He caught his breath and turned away. "I'm getting a strong sense of peace," he said, but it was already too late.

The reading was a disaster. *Hard Copy* never used the footage—which was a blessing in disguise, he supposed—and his star continued to fall. Abel chalked up the rest of it—the chorus of voices, the glimpse of Theresa Matheson's rape—to stress and an overstimulated imagination.

Messages from Beyond got canceled six months later.

Abel drifted for a year or so. He didn't go hungry—he had a reputation, after all, and he could subsist on private readings for years to come. But he missed the glare of the spotlight, the glamorous life he'd always longed for.

He had almost reconciled himself to the fact that it was over when Ramsey Lomax called. Though Abel knew the name—he'd had plenty of money to invest over the last couple of years and telecom stocks had been good to him—he wasn't particularly impressed. He'd grown accustomed to celebrity readings by then. But Lomax didn't want a reading.

"What *do* you want, then?" Abel asked.

"I want you to spend two weeks with me," Lomax responded. "I want you to come to Dreamland."

2

Lomax would make several such communications over the weeks that followed. Lara McGovern's came indirectly, in a meeting with Dan Sutherland, the Chief Resident of Mercy General Hospital. Sutherland was tall and lean, with rheumy blue eyes and a thatch of unruly red hair that receded sharply to either side of a narrow widow's peak. Despite the red hair, however, Sutherland seemed to have no temper; what he possessed instead was an apparently endless reservoir of melancholy. His charges, Lara among them, feared error less out of self-interest than from a desire to avoid further burdening their boss. Indeed, when Sutherland had suspended her privileges two months ago, Lara had found herself in the strange position of wanting to comfort him. Now, looking at him slumped on the other side of his desk, she had to choke back the same maternal impulse.

"No, I'm *not* saying you're finished at Mercy, Lara," he was telling her. "What I'm saying is I can't reinstate you until the review board finishes its investigation."

"What's there to investigate? I've already admitted fault."

Lara's voice was steady as she made this admission. It hadn't been so strong the first time she had said it, to Katie Wright's family, nor the second time, in the office of the staff psychologist. But it had grown stronger by the time she made the same statement to the hospital's general counsel, and it was steadier still now. She liked to think of this as progress.

Sutherland sighed. "I know you've admitted fault. The board knows you admitted fault. Katie Wright's parents know you've admitted fault. Everyone knows you've admitted fault. That's part of the problem, isn't it?"

Lara said nothing.

Sutherland leaned forward, propped his elbows on the cluttered desk, and stared at her from the cradle of his palms. "Did you ever stop to think about the liability issues involved here?"

This time she didn't have to monitor the steadiness of her voice. It came out filled with a cold fury that drove any consideration for Dan Sutherland completely out of her head. "I haven't thought about much of anything else for the last two months," she said, and the ghost of Katie Wright hovered briefly in the room between them.

Even Sutherland seemed to feel it, for he sat back, frowning, steepled his long fingers under his nose, and stared over them at her. He seemed abruptly sadder, his customary mien shot through with something deeper and more authentic, something personal; watching him, Lara was reminded suddenly of all he had done for her in these last years. Sutherland was the one who had recruited her to Mercy in the first place, and he'd stood by her without wavering long after everyone else had written her off. She had to swallow an impulse to apologize.

"I know that Lara," he was saying, but she cut him off with a wave of her hand.

She shook her head, fighting back tears.

"Maybe you don't understand," she said. "This is all I've ever wanted. It's all I've dreamed about since—" She broke off, not wanting to utter the name—

—*Lana*—

—not wanting to summon up all those years of grief and sorrow. "Since I was a little girl," she said finally. "It's all I was ever good at. I didn't want this to happen. I mean, Jesus Christ, Dan, I hadn't slept in thirty-six hours, it was just a mistake, and now"—she shook her head ruefully—"now, I can't sleep at all. Every time I close my eyes, I see her face. If I can't get back to work soon, I'm going to go crazy. I don't know what's going to happen to me—"

"I know," he said. "That's why I called you in."

"You just said you couldn't reinstate me."

"I can't, not while the Review Board is dragging its feet. And I think we both know they're waiting to see which way the wind blows. If the hospital can get a settlement, maybe I can do something for you. If it goes to trial . . ."

He didn't finish the statement, but he didn't need to.

Lara could still see the anger on the general counsel's face when she had told him what she had said to Katie's parents. *Christ,* he'd snapped, *of all the stupid things you could have done.* And then, turning abruptly away from her, as if she no longer merited his consideration—as if she no longer even existed—he'd looked at Dan Sutherland. *Cut her loose, that's my advice. Take the hit and cut our losses.* Sutherland had stood by her then, but they both knew he didn't have the power to protect her if the case went public. Lara sat back, the events of the last two months weighing leadenly upon her. She felt tired. She felt so tired.

"But there's something else," Sutherland said. "I had a phone call from a gentleman named Ramsey Lomax."

Lara looked up, puzzled. "The telecom guy?"

"That's right." Sutherland hesitated. "He called me himself, Lara. I don't know how he found out about this . . . situation. But he wants to intervene."

"What do you mean?"

"He's willing to offer a financial settlement to the Wrights. I don't know how much, but—"

"They don't *want* money. They want their daughter—"

"I know, but listen: if they'll agree to let you off the hook, he's also promised to endow a foundation in Katie's name. We're talking a major research initiative to study medical errors and their prevention—"

"Where?"

"Here. Right here. At Mercy General. But the whole deal is contingent on your finishing up your residency. If you're denied that opportunity"—Sutherland lifted his hands—"the money goes away."

Lara, shocked, didn't move. The silence in the office seemed suddenly unbearable—each tick of the clock as loud as a bomb, the rise and fall of Dan Sutherland's respiration as steady and mysterious as the sea.

"But . . . why? What does he want?"

"That's just the thing, Lara. He wants you."

3

At that very moment, in a San Antonio bar more than one thousand miles to the south, another speaker had dropped virtually the same words—*Mr. Lomax wants you*—into the smoky midafternoon stillness.

"Me?" Fletcher Keel said. "He wants me?"

"That's right," the stranger said. "He wants you."

Fletcher Keel took a sip of beer and wiped his mouth with the back of his hand. He glanced up at the television, where a late-summer Rangers game was playing, and then out the window. Two or three cars swept by in a blur of colors, there and gone again, the street empty. A woman in a yellow blouse walked past carrying a paper shopping bag. A whole world full of people, Keel thought, sunlit and busy, slipping by untouched. Yet despite the buttery slabs of bright southwestern light that lay against the pavement, it seemed suddenly a darker place. Keel turned away. The bar was nearly empty. A man and a woman huddled whispering at a corner table, their drinks forgotten. The bartender stood by the register, polishing glasses.

The stranger—Klavan, he had introduced himself— stared up at the television. "Rangers are for shit this year."

Keel grunted.

"Me, I've always been a Cubs fan," Klavan said.

"You would be, I guess."

"Just a hometown boy. Much like yourself, John."

"Don't call me that. That's not my name."

The man shrugged, unmoved. "You're the boss."

Keel felt a flush of anger, but he let it ride. He stared at the liquor bottles standing in jeweled ranks on the other side of the bar and took a deliberate pull off his beer. One swallow, two swallows, three. Yet his heart still hammered inside his breast. It felt like it might tear itself loose and plunge, still wet and pulsing, into his lap.

"Let's have something a little stronger," he said.

Klavan shrugged again and crooked his finger. The bartender set them up in silence—two double shots of Maker's Mark and a fresh round of Sam Adams—and then went back to polishing glasses. Keel picked up his shot glass, studied the light swimming in the amber depths of the bourbon, and tilted it to his lips. It went down smoothly, drawing a line of fire that detonated in his stomach. Keel's heart slowed. He held himself still, basking in the calming glow of the liquor.

Klavan's shot stood untouched by his beer. Keel stared at it.

"Dreamland," he said at last.

"Changed a lot since your day on the force," Klavan told him. "Housing Authority took the wrecking ball to it a while back. But it was mostly abandoned by then anyway. It's nearly gone now. Tower Three is the only one still standing, and that would have gone too if Mr. Lomax hadn't intervened. You remember Tower Three, don't you . . . Fletcher? A lot of bad shit happened in Tower Three."

A lot of bad shit indeed, Keel thought, and for a moment—just a moment—he felt it all trembling at the lip of some crumbling internal dike: the trial, the publicity, the wrenching agonies of shame. But most of all he remembered Dreamland itself, the looming weight of the place, the—

He took a slug of his beer.

"That girl was raped there," Klavan said, ticking points off on his fingers, "and that kid Dante Morris took a header off the roof—a terrible thing, that one—and of course you remember the—"

"Shut up."

Klavan shrugged. It seemed like the only gesture he was capable of. "Whatever you say. Course that's just the stuff that made the papers. Dig deeper—and Mr. Lomax has—you'll find a world of nasty shit. You don't know the half—"

"What's he want?"

"Lomax?"

Keel nodded.

"Two weeks of your time, that's all."

Two weeks in Dreamland, Keel thought, and once again he felt the subterranean lure of the past, deep buried, but never quite forgotten. "To do what?"

Yet another shrug. "Eat, breathe, sleep. Whatever. Protect Mr. Lomax if it comes to that."

"Protect him from what?"

Klavan didn't answer. He simply sat there and gazed back at Keel. He had the look of a cop, Keel thought. There was something in the economy and grace of his movements, a certain watchfulness in his eyes. It was a little like looking in a mirror—or, better still, through a window in time, into the face of an alternative self, the man he might have become.

"I'm surprised he didn't hire you to do it," Keel said.

"So am I, frankly," Klavan said. "But he seems to want you."

"And if I go, what's in it for me?"

This time Klavan didn't shrug. He reached into the inner pocket of his sport coat and pulled out a pen. Dragging a napkin close, he scratched out a figure with a series of broad confident loops: zeroes—a lot of them—and one sharp downward slash. There must have been some moisture on the bar because the ink bled. Even as Klavan drew his hand away, the lines were spreading, losing definition, fading slowly into illegibility, until finally nothing but a soggy Rorschach blotch remained. It was like watching a mirage loom on the horizon—a shimmering promise of green-dappled shade and a pool of thirsty blue, the answer to all your dreams—only to see it dissolve into a wasteland of sand and broken stone.

Keel looked up.

"It's exactly what you think it is," Klavan said.

His fingers dipped into the pocket and emerged yet again, this time with a plane ticket. "That'll get you home," he said, and once again the blunt fingers moved toward the pocket, Keel watching mesmerized as they emerged clutching a thick roll of bills, folded in half and secured with a rubber band. Klavan removed the band, licked his fingers, and counted out twenty one-hundred-dollar bills. "That'll get the debtors off your back for a little while," he said. He counted out another ten. "And that's for you. Call it a down payment."

Klavan folded the rest of the cash, banded it once again, and slid it back into his pocket. He stood, smoothing his slacks. When he let his gaze fall on Keel at last, his eyes glinted with disdain.

"Use it to get yourself sobered up," he said. "Otherwise don't bother coming at all."

And then he was gone.

Keel sat there for a long time afterwards, staring down at the cash fanned on the bar before him, at the splotched black promise of the napkin.

Dreamland, he thought.

When he reached out for Klavan's untouched shot of bourbon, his fingers were trembling.

4

For Benjamin Prather it began—or, more accurately, it began again—in the comforting nest of his home office, where he worked in a flood of almost subaudible jazz from corner-mounted speakers, among a forest of ferns glistening in the brightly moted shafts of California sunlight that lanced through the slatted blinds. Hunched in front of his keyboard, his fingers flying as he chased the blinking cursor of his thoughts, Ben almost didn't hear the telephone. Almost. In the months that followed, he would have occasion to wonder how things might have turned out differently if the ring had passed unnoticed.

It didn't though.

Startled, Ben stared blankly at the screen, readjusting himself to the tactile reality of his surroundings: the hum of the hard drive and the understated tinkle of piano keys which he had tuned out almost the moment he plugged the CD into the changer, the faintly humid scent of the ferns, the line of sun-fired dust on the lip of the monitor.

Then the shrill banshee shriek of the phone. Again.

Ben lifted the receiver and punched the button. "Prather," he said, more than half expecting the gruff complaint of his editor in response. He was already framing his defenses when he realized that the smoothly professional voice emanating from the earpiece belonged to someone else entirely. A female someone.

"Benjamin Prather?" she was saying.

Cradling the phone with his shoulder, Ben started typing again. "That's right. Is there something I can do to help you?"

"I hope so. My name is Sara Havilund."

The fingers stopped. "Did you say Sara Havilund?"

"That's right. I'm Ramsey Lomax's per—"

"I know who you are," Ben said. "This is a joke, right?"

"Would you feel more comfortable if you called me back, Mr. Prather? The number—"

"I'll find the number myself. You're at your office?"

"I am. I'll see that you get through," she said, and the line went dead in his ear.

Ben put down the phone. He stared into the monitor, his thoughts buzzing, before he saved his changes and backed up to disk. Then, still staring at the empty screen in front of him, he picked up the phone and dialed a friend at the *LA Times*.

"Shirley," he said. "Any chance I can get you to run down a telephone number for me?"

"Sure, Benny. That's why I'm here: to serve the needs of freelancers everywhere. What do you need?"

"The number of an attorney named Sara Havilund. She's in Chicago."

"You got some legal troubles, Benny?"

"Just getting tired of your sex talk, Shirley, that's all."

The voice at the other end made a rude noise. "You want me to call you back with that?"

"I'll hold."

"It's your dime."

She punched a button, dropping him into the faint purgatorial hiss of the open line. Tilting his head against the back of his chair, Ben took his glasses off and pinched the bridge of his nose between his thumb and forefinger. He tried to concentrate on the delicate stream of notes pouring from the speakers at his back, but Ramsey Lomax's sharply hooked features and clean-shaven skull—once gossip-column mainstays—kept breaking into his thoughts. Lomax hadn't spoken to the press in almost two years—not since his abrupt divestiture of EyeCom Industries, the telecom firm he had started with a single radio station five decades before. Ben's reputation as a journalist—however ascendant—would hardly have been sufficient to sway him.

Besides, Ben hadn't even asked for an interview.

A minute passed, then another. Ben drummed his fingers on the desk.

Shirley came back on the line. "You know who Sara Havilund is?" she said after Ben had scrawled the number on the back of an envelope.

"I know."

"You on to something, Benny?"

"I suspect somebody's putting me on, actually," he said. "And don't call me Benny."

He broke the connection and dialed the number on the envelope. Circuits clicked and fell into place. Half a continent away, a telephone began to ring. To his surprise, it didn't look like a prank after all: the receptionist seemed to be expecting him. The minute he identified himself, she put him through.

"Ah, Mr. Prather," Sara Havilund said when she came on the line. "I trust you satisfied yourself as to my authenticity?"

"It never hurts to double-check, does it, Ms. Havilund? So what can I do for you?"

"I don't think I'm the right person to answer that question. Hold for Mr. Lomax, will you?"

Before Ben could answer, there was another click, and then a new voice was speaking in his ear. "So tell me, Mr. Prather," Ramsey Lomax said. "Do you believe in ghosts?"

5

When he hung up the phone half an hour later, the question was still echoing in Ben's mind. His immediate impulse was to call Paul Cook, who had been more of a father to him than either of his real fathers—certainly more than the anonymous one-night stand who had surrendered up his half-measure of Ben's genetic heritage before disappearing forever, into one of the myriad unhappily-ever-afters that awaited black men of his station. And more too than the white man Ben had grown up calling Dad—though Ben supposed even he had done his best in his strangled and conflicted way.

But Paul—Paul Cook had saved him. Paul had rescued him from himself. Paul had revealed to him a past which even now Ben could not truly remember—a past which Ben's adoptive father had never permitted himself to discuss, as though merely acknowledging Ben's true parentage would somehow unman him—this despite the different colors of their skin.

No, it had been Paul. There in that unassuming second-floor office where Ben had continued to go for weekly therapy sessions years after he left Murrow Elementary School, it had been Paul. Paul who traced the contours of the trauma—in Ben's need for solitude, in his love for the orderly cadence of words, like ripples in the still water where a stone has dropped. Paul who showed him how to start the healing—who helped him turn the writing from compulsion (writing as self-medication, he had called it) into vocation. Paul who phoned him weekly while Ben was away at UCLA. Even years later, after Paul had retired and Ben himself had gone on to launch a career, a life, Ben had found himself drawn irresistibly back to the man—through letters and email, by telephone, in visits—returning time and again to bask in his simple kindness and uncomplicated love, as a flower will turn its face always to the sun. But Paul had died five long years ago—three years after the auto accident which had claimed Ben's mother—and now no one remained to Ben but his adoptive father. And the subject of Ramsey Lomax's phone call was the one subject Frank Prather had never been able to bring himself to discuss.

The subject of Ramsey Lomax's phone call was Dreamland.

"So, tell me, Mr. Prather," he'd said, "do you believe in ghosts?"

And the sheer unexpectedness of the question—the sheer

absurdity of it—had surprised Ben into laughter. "Why? Are you planning to go on a ghost hunt?"

"As a matter of fact," Lomax had said, in a voice empty of levity, "I am."

Ben sat up straight in his chair and reached for a notepad. "Where?"

"Are we off the record?"

"Sure."

"Dreamland."

A single word—two syllables, that's all—and it rocked Ben like a blow. He dragged in a long breath. "The housing project?"

"That's right."

Silence followed, a silence that spun itself out in a dialogue of bass and tenor sax from the overhead speakers, a silence in which Ben felt his whole world shifting into a network of new relationships, a silence in which Ramsey Lomax's question—

—*do you believe in ghosts*—

—took on an added complexity.

It was simple enough on the face of it. But peel back the surface, and what did you see? Wheels inside of wheels inside of wheels, all of them spinning at once. There were ghosts, Ben thought—Hollywood spooks and specters. And then there were ghosts. Inside every cheesy ectoplasmic phantom lay the dizzying abyss of memory and regret—and inside that, the hollow echo where memory failed. Ghosts— *real* ghosts—were in your head, and just when you thought you had forgotten them—just when you thought you had escaped them forever—they could loom up and seize you once again. They could possess you.

Dreamland, he thought. And what he saw was not the place itself. What he saw was a panoply of grainy black-and-white newspaper photos projected in the merciless glare of a microfilm reader.

How old had he been? Ten? Maybe eleven?

Even now Ben could remember the afternoon hush of the Santa Monica library. Paul Cook had been the one who brought him there, driving him across town in his sagging old Volvo, and Paul had been the one who stood behind his chair with the comforting weight of his hand draped across Ben's shoulder as Ben gazed down and down into the glowing well of the microfilm reader and felt the entire weight of the unremembered past settle over him like a shroud—the endless nightmares and the panic attacks that gripped him like a vise and the dark compulsion that had unleashed that flood of violent imagery, that deluge of words like poison from a freshly lanced wound. *Seven die in hostage stand-off*, the headline read, and below that the subhead: *Three-year-old survivor catatonic*. But it was the photographs that had mesmerized Ben: the aerial shot of Harold P. Taylor Homes—of Dreamland—like a snapshot of his dreams. And below that the gallery of victims. The cop, resplendent in his dress blues; the two shooters, and their first victim, shot dead on the plaza; the family last of all: the woman, her two daughters, and the sole survivor—a three-year-old boy who might have been Ben's younger cousin, but wasn't.

No indeed, Ben had thought, staring down into the child's eyes. Not a cousin at all.

"You there, Mr. Prather?"

Ben swallowed. "Right here," he said. And then, with more force: "I thought they tore it down. After that girl died, I—"

"Theresa Matheson," Lomax said. "Her name was Theresa Matheson."

"Right." Ben took a deep breath. "I thought they tore the place down."

"Oh, they started to," Lomax said. "And they'll finish the job, too. But not yet. Seven of the towers are down, but number three is still standing. I've seen to that."

"Why?"

"Curiosity," Lomax said. "Simple curiosity, Mr. Prather. If you accept the premise that hauntings are byproducts of human violence, then Dreamland is, well, a researcher's dream. Can you imagine the quantity of blood that's been spilled in that place?"

Ben, still grappling with his own internal turmoil, hesitated. He could imagine all right. He had no problem on that score, no problem at all. Then, simply to fill the silence, to keep the conversation going, he asked another question, the first one that came to mind. "Do you have— I mean— Is there any evidence?"

Lomax laughed. "Evidence? Of course not. Just tantalizing clues: the residents of Dreamland abandoned Tower Three years before they gave up on the rest of the complex, did you know that? Three years. No one quite knows why—it's not the sort of thing people are comfortable talking about. But if you ask around long enough you'll hear rumors. Plenty of rumors. Bad dreams, disembodied voices. A sense that there was something unwholesome about the place. Street people avoid it like the plague. Street people! All those empty rooms, and they stay away. They say it has a way of turning suddenly cold inside, even at the height of summer. They say that sometimes you can hear the elevators running, though the building hasn't had power in years. They say that once in a while someone wanders inside and simply disappears. No one ever sees them again." Lomax laughed again, more quietly this time, and without any real humor. "They say. But they're street people, right? Who's going to notice if one of them disappears? So no, there's no evidence at all, not a shred of it."

"What do you have in mind?"

"I'm going to live there two weeks, that's all. I'm going to see what happens. Nothing to prove. No scientific crap, no Rhine Institute investigation, no truckload of instruments, none of that bullshit. Just personal curiosity, that's all. I'm just going to live there and see what happens for myself. And I'd like you to come with me."

Now, remembering, Ben felt sweep over him the same depthless wave of apprehension he'd felt at the time, a suffocating breaker of dread through which he had managed to squeeze only one final inconsequential question. "Why me?" he'd asked.

But he knew why, didn't he? He'd known the minute he'd uttered the words.

And Lomax knew as well. He had waited a beat, and then he had said, very softly and with the faintest undercurrent of amusement: "Do I really have to answer that question, Mr. Prather?"

No, Ben had thought. No you don't.

Now, glancing down into the monitor of his computer, Ben had another nasty little shock. Lomax's question—

—*do you believe in ghosts*—

—glimmered patiently up at him from the screen. He had written it himself, hadn't he? Just like old times—the self-medication of prose, obsessive and all unconscious, more than a little terrifying. He had no memory of the act, but the muscles in his hands still tingled with its neural echo.

Ben stabbed the delete button, erasing the words letter by letter until finally nothing remained but the pristine void of an empty screen. But even then the question lingered.

Tell me, Mr. Prather. Do you believe in ghosts?

Ben couldn't answer the question—not really—but he knew one thing: he was haunted. What had happened in Dreamland—whether he could remember it or not—had shaped everything that he had become.

Now, listening to that name—

—*Dreamland*—

—reverberate in his thoughts, Ben recalled Lomax's closing words.

"There's probably a book in it for you," he had said. "Probably a nice chunk of money."

But Ben wouldn't do it for the money—there wasn't enough money in the world to coax him back into that place. And he wouldn't do it because he wanted to. He didn't. Every fiber in his being resisted it. He would do it because he had to—because he had no choice in the matter.

Once, years ago, Ben had done a story on radio astronomy: the giant radar dishes you sometimes saw sprouting like enormous mushrooms along the edge of the highway, the scientists who staffed them. He'd been fascinated by the singular focus of the men and women he had interviewed—men and women who had dedicated their professional lives to studying the ghost of an event they could never truly observe, to isolating amid the cosmic aftermath of catastrophe the outward and expanding arc of the Big Bang itself.

Now he understood. *This* was how it began: the quest for the defining moment, origin and end, alpha and omega, forever sundered in a single moment of cataclysmic violence.

He would go back to Dreamland.

If it came to it, he would do it for free.

6

They made their preparations over the months that followed—Abel and Fletcher Keel, Lara, Ben; Ramsey Lomax most of all. Abel worked the phones as the summer faded, cultivating his contacts in the industry. He guested once or twice on the local morning shows, keeping silent about Ramsey Lomax's plans for Dreamland (what little he knew of them); he did readings in the afternoon. Aside from his absence on the airwaves, his life continued outwardly unchanged. Inwardly, his doubts and ambitions hung in delicate balance, and that spectral glimpse of Theresa Matheson haunted his dreams.

By the end of September Keel had gotten himself into Alcoholics Anonymous, and by the time jack-o'-lanterns began grinning from the windows of San Antonio, he was celebrating nearly two weeks of sobriety. Fortified by the splotched promise of the bar napkin he kept folded in his wallet, he started going to the gym. As he gradually recovered the sleek musculature he'd let slip away over the years, his fears of Dreamland faded.

Lara, too, had returned to a physical regimen which the long hours of her residency had rendered impossible. For a time, she feared she'd have to find some temp work to keep herself afloat until the situation at Mercy General resolved itself. But then a letter from Ramsey Lomax arrived—a brief note naming a date, and a check drawn to her name. A sizable check. *No strings attached,* the note had added, though she was wise enough to know that there were always strings attached. After a pensive afternoon staring at the bills spilling across her battered kitchen table, she cashed the check anyway. And in the mornings that followed—mornings she normally would have spent in the ER—she ran along the lake shore, replaying the events leading to Katie Wright's death until they burned in her memory.

In between freelance gigs, Ben started delving into Ramsey Lomax's plans for Dreamland. A friend of a friend of a friend managed to shake loose a copy of Lomax's lease with the Housing Authority. Ben gasped when he saw the numbers. Much of it was boilerplate—insurance, liability, and so on—but the numbers were anything but standard. Twelve million in redevelopment funds had been necessary to halt the scheduled demolition. Six million more had bought him a six-month lease, September through February. In the emerald gloom of his fern-thronged office on the coast, Ben stared into his monitor and pondered the figures. A million dollars a month. Eighteen million dollars total. Doubtless hundreds of thousands more in insurance and attorney fees, security, renovations. And all of it to buy two weeks inside a slum any sane person would have paid half again as much to escape.

Why? he wondered. What was Lomax really after?

Half a continent away, where Dreamland drowsed beneath a pristine October sky, the diesel roar of destruction had dwindled. The demolition crews withdrew and eighteen-wheelers rumbled down the narrow streets to haul away the bulldozers and the enormous earth-moving trucks, creaking in their nests of chains atop a fleet of flatbed trailers. The next day a square mile of fence went up, enclosing the entire compound inside twenty-five vertical feet of heavy-gauge chain link surmounted by coils of razor wire. Inside, Tower Three alone still stood upright. Two weeks passed, and then another wave of contractors arrived, climbing down from their pickups and riding the sole functioning elevator to the fifth floor. Refuse was hauled away by the truckload. Walls came down amid clouds of dust. As winter closed in, the din of power saws and hammers rang across the broken plaza.

For Ben, as for Lara and the others, those months passed in a fog, a grim limbo of formless apprehension and uneasy dreams. In November, as instructed, Ben dispatched several boxes of personal effects—clothes and books, a few photos, a portable stereo and half a hundred CDs: classic Motown, a healthy sampling from the Blue Note catalog of the fifties and early sixties, a handful from the classical canon. It was like packing up for the dormitories at UCLA all over again, and with a similar mixture of anticipation and dread.

The next week, two moving vans pulled up to the shattered compound from which Tower Three jutted like an accusing finger. A platoon of men hopped down from the warmth of their cabs to wrestle furniture and appliances and load after load of cardboard boxes through the lobby where Theresa Matheson had died.

Christmas came and went, and in the bleak dawn of a new year they began to gather at last—Keel winging his way in from San Antonio, Ben from LAX. On the appointed day, Lara woke up late and ran for hours along the lake shore, until the breath clawed in her lungs and the muscles in her legs screamed for mercy. At home, she showered and dressed. It was already late in the afternoon by the time she strode out of her apartment and caught the El across town. Abel cabbed over, hunched and shivering beneath a lowering January sky as he paid the driver and lifted his eyes to Lomax's luxurious penthouse apartment, warmly ablaze in the gray air.

Upstairs, Lomax greeted them one by one.

Introductions were made, pleasantries exchanged. And in the tense silence that followed, each of them sensed the wary scrutiny of these strangers, their companions for the weeks to come.

"So," Lomax said. "Shall we go?"

They went, descending in his private elevator to the cavernous basement garage, where his limo awaited them. By the time the car emerged at street level, the sun was falling in the west. A thin, angry snow had started pelting down.

Arrivals

1

Ben gazed out the window as the car motored through the winter-swept streets, watching the city slip by, the glistening apartment towers, the broad avenues and acres of gleaming sidewalk. And then the limo swung beneath an underpass. In the flickering span of darkness before they emerged once again into the thin January twilight, the city's geography changed. As always, Ben was struck by the abrupt juxtapositions in American life, the narrow margins between black and white, poverty and prosperity. The chic department stores gave way to pawn shops, the marble-fronted banks to check-cashing stores, their interiors dim beyond steel security gates. The pedestrians were fewer here, their complexions darker. They hurried by, hunched and hooded against the cold, their faces downcast, clutching packages against their breasts. Young men lounged on the corners, hooting at the limo as it passed.

The car stopped at a traffic signal, and then, when the light changed, turned left. Cramped three-story houses crowded the sidewalks, their wind-blasted facades grim and colorless. Wind-blown debris and drifts of ashen week-old snow had collected in the corners by their stoops. Rusty cages enclosed their street-level windows. Here and there, Ben caught an occasional flash of color—a freshly painted door or a glimpse of bright curtains in some upper-story window—but in another block or two even these paltry gestures of defiance dwindled. The street simply gave up. The asphalt was pitted and broken. Cannibalized cars lined the sidewalks, flaking slowly into rust. Most of the houses had fallen into active disrepair—broken glass and boarded-over windows, looping scrawls of graffiti, front doors swinging lazily in the wind. Others existed only as burned-out shells. A child, frail and under-dressed, his brown eyes solemn and enormous in the dark setting of his face, stood on the sidewalk and watched them pass. Ben felt the doctor—Lara, he thought, Lara McGovern—stiffen at his side.

"Any minute now," Lomax said, his voice tense with anticipation.

Even as the words died away, the limo swung to the right. The last of the houses fell back, and an arid wasteland opened before them. At first Ben didn't see it—he saw nothing but the high, curving arc of the fence line, glittering in the last rays of the sun, and the bombed-out desert beyond, the gaping mouth of an empty foundation, the jagged heaps of broken masonry and twisted steel. Then Lara McGovern touched his arm. Startled, Ben glanced over at her, the strong almost masculine line of her jaw and the washed-out denim of her eyes and the sense of bones just millimeters under her lightly freckled flesh. She smiled, tentatively, and the spare lines of her face—the harsh, angular bone structure of someone who works out too much—softened.

"There," she said.

Ben looked, uncertain what she was pointing at. In the same instant that his eye at last isolated a boxy pinnacle edging above the nearest mound of wreckage, the limo made its final turn. The debris field drew back and it was there, Dreamland, squarely before him in the windshield of the limo, wounded, dismembered, arrogant, looming high above the rubble of its toppled siblings. Mesmerized, Ben gazed up at it, feeling nothing, hardly thinking, everything slipping by him as effortlessly as in a dream, the air bluing off toward night and the unremembered past and the limo so noiseless and smooth that it seemed hardly to be moving at all, it seemed to be standing still, it was the building that was moving, it was Dreamland, languorous and arrogant, gliding closer and closer until it towered over him, rearing its crushing height story after story into the cold January air, up and up and up, obliterating everything else, the limo and the heat of his companions and the distant towers downtown, until at last it blotted out even the sky—

He took a breath, and wrenched his gaze away, abruptly conscious of the doctor's attention. No one else was paying

him any mind. They were staring out the windows at the
building or into their laps or blankly into the air before
their faces, like passengers on a bus.

The limo coasted to a stop.

The driver punched a button. The great automated gate
rolled back, and then they were moving forward again,
through the gate and past tumbled dunes of shattered concrete, the building drawing inexorably toward them. The
driver touched his brakes and parked, idling.

"Well, then," Lomax said. "Shall we?"

Ben fumbled with the latch and stepped out, the air sharp
against his face. He glanced back toward the fence line
three hundred yards away, and then he turned to survey
his companions. They stood gazing at the building as one,
breath frosting the air before their faces.

The driver popped the trunk and lined their bags up
along the edge of the crumbling plaza. "Anything else,
sir?" he asked Lomax.

"No. You can go, Tyler."

The driver nodded, and slid back into the car. It swung
around and accelerated smoothly back toward the fence,
its brake lights flaring through thin, hard snow as it ap-
proached the gate. It paused there, pouring gray exhaust
into the air, and then it was gone, slipping silently into the
devastated streets beyond. The gate rolled closed with a
metallic clank that echoed in the stillness, reminding Ben
suddenly of a story he'd done on death row inmates at San
Quentin, the fatal clash of all those electric gates sliding
irrevocably home behind you, one by one by one.

Abel Williams' thoughts must have been running along
the same lines. "What if somebody gets sick or something?"

"That's why we have the doctor," Lomax said.

They stood there a moment longer, staring at the poured-
concrete facade of Tower Three, monumental and aggres-
sively utilitarian, its shattered doors—they must have been
glass once—patched with splintering, graffiti-smirched panels of plywood.

Lomax shivered. "It's cold out here," he said. "Let's go
in."

2

Fletcher Keel slung his battered duffel bag over one shoulder and followed the others toward the doors with a confidence he didn't really feel. He'd had a bad moment on the plane that morning, somewhere back there in the thin air 37,000 feet above the frozen cornfields of Iowa. One minute everything had been normal. He'd been dozing even, lulled by the white roar of the jet engines and the subdued chatter of the flight attendants as they trundled the service cart up the aisle behind him. The next instant the plane had taken a sickening lurch, and Keel had jerked awake to find himself gripping the armrests so tightly that his knuckles blanched. A dream voice was still echoing inside his head.

And not just any voice. No indeed.

It was his father's voice —and how long had it been since he'd heard his father's voice? How long since he'd managed to pour enough booze and pills down his throat to drown that voice for good? Fifteen years at least. When he'd sobered up, it had been the return of that voice that Keel had feared most of all. But until that moment on the plane, he'd managed to dodge that particular blast from the past. Until that moment on the plane he'd had nothing but blessed silence.

Honor, his father had said inside his head. *Honor and integrity, and look at you, look at what you've become, you think you're good enough—*

And those words, that phrase—

—you think you're good enough—

—triggered a flash of memory so visceral that the narrow fuselage of the plane seemed to sheer away before him. For a moment he had been there, *there* in the humid gloom of a past twenty-seven years lost, there in Dreamland—

"No," Keel had whispered.

That's when he'd realized that the service cart had rolled

to a halt beside him. The flight attendant leaned over him in a floral-scented cloud, the tantalizing swell of her breast at his cheek.

"Something to drink?"

The plane bounced again, rattling a handful of shot-sized liquor bottles in one metal drawer. For the space of a single heartbeat the memory of bourbon bloomed in Keel's mouth: the ashen taste of the stuff, its heat in his throat. His hand was halfway to his wallet before he managed to check the impulse.

"No," he said again. And then, more strongly: "No thanks."

She gave him an empty smile and moved on, her ass swinging as she leaned over the seat in front of him. Keel leaned back and closed his eyes, trying not to think of the glint of those little whiskey bottles just visible beyond the tempting curve of her hip. Trying not to think of anything at all.

But his father's voice had lingered in his mind.

He could hear it even now, all these hours later, as he stepped over the threshold—

—last chance, John—

—and as the doors of Dreamland swung shut behind him, iron bands seemed to close around his chest.

Ramsey Lomax flipped a switch and maybe a third of the fluorescent tubes overhead flickered to life. As soon as Keel saw the place—really *saw* it, with his eyes instead of his mind and memory—he felt a weight slip off his shoulders.

What was there to fear?

Dreamland was nothing but a derelict shell: unheated and uninhabited. Despite islands of cast-off furniture—a handful of rusty folding chairs, a broken wooden school desk, a spavined sofa that stank of urine even from here—it projected a sense of cavernous abandonment. It was empty: empty of human habitation, of voice or personality, empty even of memory. Definitively, irredeemably, and irrefutably empty.

Keel studied the ornate scroll of graffiti festooning the dank cinder block walls, the gloom lurking in the empty stairwells—

—not the stairwell—

—the paired elevators, one set of doors sensibly shut, the other gaping on a black pit. A wall of blank mailboxes turned their copper faces to him; his own cloudy reflection gazed back at him from the pitted glass box of a reception area. Otherwise nothing. Nothing, nothing, and nothing, he thought, and the bands at his chest loosened. He drew a deep breath, laden with the stench of mildew, damp concrete, and sodden acoustical ceiling tile. He nearly laughed aloud.

He would have if the black guy—Prather—hadn't started speaking first. "So this is where the girl died?" He turned slowly, surveying the room, his bag draped over one shoulder.

"What girl?" Lara McGovern said.

Prather looked at her. "The social worker—"

"Theresa Matheson," Lomax said. "Her name was Theresa Matheson. And to say she died is something of an understatement, isn't it?"

"What do you mean?" Lara asked.

"She was tortured," Lomax said. "Gang-raped and tortured for something like six hours right here in the lobby."

"And nobody stopped it?" Lara said, a faint disbelieving edge in her voice. "Nobody reported it?"

"No," Lomax said. "Nobody did anything at all."

In the stiff, uncomfortable silence that followed, Abel Williams drifted away, a faraway look on his face. Keel, looking on, caught another glimpse of the south stairwell. He felt his guts twist—

—*something there*—

—a disconcerting twinge of not-quite-memory, there and gone again in the space of a breath. But it was nothing, nothing at all, and if he felt as green as Abel Williams *looked*—standing twenty feet away, his expression distant— well, that was purely a matter of chance. Not his father's warnings and not the paralyzing shame which had driven him to drink, most of all not the humiliating knot of dread rising into his throat—

He shut off the tumbling freshet of his thoughts. Took a deep breath. Turned away from the shadowy reaches beyond the doorway.

There was nothing there. Period.

"You okay, man?" he said to Abel.

Abel Williams looked up, startled. "What?"

"You seem . . . distracted." Keel shrugged. "I thought you might be having a vision or something."

"It doesn't work that way," Ben said. And then, when no one responded, "Does it, Abel?"

"No," Abel said. He looked around at them, surveying their faces as if surprised to find them there. As if surprised to find *himself* there, actually, and a little uncertain how it had come to happen. To Keel, he looked like a man waking abruptly from a deep and unpleasant dream. "No," Abel said once again, his voice hesitant, uncertain. "It doesn't work that way."

"How *does* it work?" Lara asked, lifting her eyebrows.

"It's . . . energy, that's all. It's a matter of sensing energy." Glancing around once again, he turned to join them, his voice gaining strength and confidence. "It's hard to explain."

"I'll bet," Ben said.

"Well," Lomax said, "putting aside the issue of *how* you do it, why don't you tell us *if* you're doing it?"

"Now?"

"Now."

"Like I said, it doesn't work like that." He hesitated again. He looked around at the shattered lobby, that faraway expression stealing across his face. "I mean, I'm getting some vague impressions . . ."

"Such as?"

"There's clearly been a great deal of misery here, a great deal of pain and unhappiness."

"You don't have to be psychic to see that, do you?" Ben said, and that was a sentiment Fletcher Keel could heartily assent to, yes indeed. The misery the place had seen was palpable—in the empty bottles of MD 20/20 and Wild Irish Rose and Colt .45 scattered among the debris, in the sagging piss-stained cushions of the sofa and the overstuffed garbage bags rotting in one corner, in the sour reek of an abandoned refrigerator propped doorless against one wall, a flat, faintly organic stench, like garbage that had been broiling inside a metal trash barrel the length of an August afternoon.

Or like the air inside a freshly opened grave.

He glanced at Lomax. "The whole place this bad?"

"Never fear, Mr. Keel. You'll find your accommodations acceptable."

Grunting, Keel gave the room a last once-over. "We'll see, I guess," he said. Hiking the strap of his duffel bag higher on his shoulder, he started toward the elevator. It wasn't until he was inside the car with the rest of them, clutching the waist-high hand rail as the metal doors rolled closed before him, that he let his gaze slide once again toward the black mouth of the south stairwell. He thought he saw something stir inside the open doorway, a deeper shadow coalescing from the gloom. In the same instant, he sensed something staring back at him, something diffuse and cold and infinitely patient. *You shouldn't have come back,* his father said inside his head, so clearly that Keel thought the words must have been spoken aloud. He felt a choking wave of shame and resentment. *You would have,* he thought. *You weren't afraid of anything, were you, Dad?*

I wouldn't have had to, the voice said.

And there was no answer to that, was there?

There never had been.

Sighing, Keel stared resolutely into the dark interior of the south stairwell. He was still looking at it when the doors slid shut before him.

3

The elevator jerked into motion.

They rose slowly through the heart of the building, alone in the brittle silence of their thoughts. There would come a time when Abel, Lara, and even Keel himself would wonder if that had been the moment when it began, if as the doors slid shut and the elevator's gears engaged with a clunk, something buried deep and sleeping in the twisted entrails of Dreamland had not stirred itself to waking and, in waking, speech. For Keel, it was what he perceived taking shape in the formless dark of the abandoned stairwell—the memory of a past that would not die, the disembodied

contours of his own worst fears. For the others, for Abel
and Lara, it was what they heard or thought they heard or
anyway imagined that they heard—the merest stir of whispers, the falsetto laughter of a child.

Keel, bracing his feet as the battered elevator rocked
beneath him, shook his head as a horse will shake at the
flies clustering around his nostrils and eyes. Nerves, he told
himself. Imagination, nothing more.

Lara McGovern, trained to the skepticism of a scientist,
arrived at much the same conclusion.

None of them believed.

Not Ben, and not Abel Williams, despite the faint mina-
tory rumble of memory—

—*father, father*—

—triggered by that chorus of competing whispers, like
the rustle of dried leaves swept up in a whirl of autumn
wind. An image of his childhood bedroom—the quilt his
grandmother had made, the streetlight outside and that
Rorschach cage of shadow on his ceiling—sprang into
Abel's mind with such vivid clarity that he almost gasped.
He hovered at the edge of revelation, his right hand stealing unbidden toward the watch he wore on his left wrist;
then his outraged mind beat the memory back.

None of them believed.

Not even Ramsey Lomax.

He stood alone at the back of the elevator, his face upturned like a penitent's as the numbers over the doors
flared one by one, his shaven skull gleaming in the flickering and fly-specked light.

4

"The original floor plans called for twenty-four units on
every level," Lomax said as the elevator came to a stop on
the fifth floor. "My intention was to leave things as I found
them on the principle that the force or forces that inhabit
Dreamland—if there *are* such forces—would be more likely

to manifest themselves in familiar circumstances." He smiled. "As you'll see, however, my dedication to the spirit of scientific enterprise extends only so far."

The doors rumbled aside.

Stepping out of the elevator was a little bit like stepping into another world, Ben thought. The twelve-by-twelve square of the elevator alcove was furnished as a sitting area. The broad corridor beyond had the bland luxury of a Hilton. Wall-mounted sconces printed tastefully alternating parabolas of light and shadow on the plush carpet. An almost subliminal hum of climate control filled the air, wafting to him the faint odors of new construction—fresh paint and carpet, the woodsy scent of sawdust.

"Our suites—bedroom, sitting room, private baths—are located at either end of the hall," Lomax said, leading them out into the corridor. "I've closed off the wings on this level—it's not like we need the space—and gutted the central corridor. Mr. Williams and I will occupy apartments at the south end. The other three units are at the north end." He turned back toward the elevators, pointing. "Common areas are in the center, radiating outward from the elevators. A basic gym—a couple of treadmills, a weight machine—to the left of the elevator, kitchen and dining room on the right. And then there's the lounge."

He crossed the hallway, stepped through an arched entryway, and flipped a switch. Overhead lights flickered on, revealing a long space furnished with sleek art deco furniture—all chromed metal and supple leather. A pool table stood at one end of the room. Books had been shelved along the facing wall.

"No television?" Keel said.

"Alas, no, Mr. Keel. No television, no Internet, no telephones. As you all agreed, of course." Lomax surveyed them as a group. "My hope is to confront whatever might exist here directly, face-to-face and on its own merits, without mediation. Have you any idea how rare unmediated experience *is* in today's world?"

Lomax snapped off the light and ushered them back into the hall without waiting for an answer. "We'll need to figure out a rotation for the cooking and other chores," he said, leading them through a double-hung door, "but I think you'll find the kitchen facilities more than adequate."

Ben, following, took an involuntary step backward as the lights came up, dazzled by the radiance glaring back at him from every polished surface: the gleaming expanses of tile and stainless-steel countertops, the glossy mirror of the stove, the massive chromed shield of the refrigerator. "Wow," he said.

"I believe in comfort, Mr. Prather," Lomax said crisply. "I can afford it." He pointed. "That's the utility room to the left, including breakers for the renovated floor space and the one functioning elevator, plus a master switch that shuts down the entire building. The dining area is to the right. The walk-in freezer contains substantial stocks of meat and seafood. Canned and boxed goods are in the pantry. We also have two weeks' worth of fresh fruits and vegetables, dairy supplies, deli meats, and bread. Starving is the least of our worries." He turned to face them. "Booze might have been. That's why there isn't any. After you've spent a few days here, I think you'll understand why it's in our best interests to stay sober."

He snapped off the light and led them across the hall to another room—a standard doorway, this time, with a lock in the doorknob.

"Last but not least, the infirmary, outfitted as you requested, Doctor."

Lomax switched on the light, and Ben saw that this room too was sterile and cold. It looked pretty much like a standard examination room, minimally furnished: a reclining table, a sink and a few feet of counterspace, a computer workstation. Locking cabinets lined either wall. Lomax pointed to a wall-mounted telephone, naked without its keypad. "This is a dedicated line to the Mercy General Emergency Room, a seventeen-minute trip by ambulance. It's also the only functioning telephone line in the building."

"Kind of an elaborate setup for a two-week stay," Ben said.

"True. But given our experiences during the renovation, Mr. Prather, it seemed only prudent."

"Why is that, exactly?"

"People have a penchant for injuring themselves at Dreamland, often badly," Lomax said, shutting off the light. "And a lot can happen in seventeen minutes."

5

Alone in her suite, Lara lowered her overnight bag to the floor. She stood in the gloom, letting the stress of the day—the ravaged lobby, the fault lines among her companions, Ramsey Lomax's penchant for ominous little pronouncements most of all—settle over her. Then, without being entirely certain why she was doing it, she turned and slid the tongue of the deadbolt home behind her.

Feeling better, she turned on the lights.

The suite wasn't bad at all—considerably better, actually, than the rundown walk-up she'd leased for her residency. At the time, the place hadn't seemed like a bad idea: a chance to save a little money—God knew she needed it—without undue hardship. After all, she'd reasoned, how much time would she actually be spending there? She hadn't been naïve about the hours a residency required—shifts that routinely ran thirty-six hours, work weeks that sometimes totaled more than a hundred and twenty. She thought she had been prepared.

Now, surveying the generic comforts of the suite that would be her home for the next two weeks—a suite that might have been lifted entire from the nearest Sheraton—Lara uttered a rueful laugh at just how unprepared she really had been. The stress had been all but shattering, the workload crushing, the fatigue unbearable. As for the difficulty of making rational decisions in that fog of weariness—well, that had been something else altogether.

And just that easily, the memory of Katie Wright—her thin fevered face and the damp blond curls matted against her forehead—loomed up in Lara's mind.

There was no escaping Katie Wright, was there?

She waited at every turn of thought.

And considering Katie's present accommodations—a wooden box roughly six feet long and half as wide, and dark, unendurably dark—there was something obscene about the pleasure Lara found herself taking in these unexpectedly luxurious digs.

That was the thing of it. You wanted the world to stop in its tracks, to acknowledge your tragedy—

—*except it isn't your tragedy, Lars,* a voice whispered inside her head—

—but the world kept steaming full speed ahead. The earth still turned on its axis, the stars swung by in their unvarying arcs, and come dawn, when you woke from the brief oblivion of sleep, the morning light fell through your window with the precise clarity and weight it had always possessed, firing each floating scintilla of dust with a beauty that would not yield even for an instant to the primacy of some merely human sorrow.

And even that wasn't the worst of it.

No. The worst of it was that there came a time when even your own body betrayed you. It didn't take long either. An hour, two hours, maybe three if you were lucky, and you felt the world summon you back. You felt the pressure of a full bladder or your mouth went dry or somebody told you to get some rest, and suddenly you were back in the world again. The old imperatives of flesh possessed you, sleep and food and sex in their eternal round, and there was nothing you could do to mortify them out of you. You could run for hours along the lake—you could run until the world dissolved like celluloid on the fevered lamp of your exhaustion, and when you surfaced from unconsciousness at last, the world would still be there. And you would still find pleasure in it.

Katie Wright was gone. She would always be gone.

But you—you could still take pleasure in the overripe aroma of magnolia pushing out from the open door of a flower shop, or the new-minted coins of sunlight dazzling the rippled surface of the lake during your morning run. Or even, God help you, in the bland luxury of a hotel-quality suite. That was the horror of it.

In the end, you grieved because you could no longer grieve.

In the end, you strangled yourself with guilt.

And maybe—maybe—you ran away.

Is that why you're here, Lars? a voice inquired inside her head, and Lara laughed, for she knew that voice, didn't she? She knew it all too well.

Shouldering her bag, she walked into the bedroom. The boxes containing her personal effects waited at the end of the bed. It didn't take long to find the photo—Lana and Lara, Lara and Lana, leaning together to blow out the candles on an enormous birthday cake, their seven-year-old faces joyfully oblivious to everything that lay before them.

One golden moment.

You grieved because you could no longer grieve.

Life went on, that's all, and the dead fell behind.

Lara sat on the bed. Brushing the hair from her eyes, she stared down at the photo, and what came to her mind was Lomax's grim little speech about Theresa Matheson, raped and tortured to death over a span of six hours in the lobby below. What came to mind was the sound she had imagined as the elevator doors rumbled closed before her. The faintly mocking laughter of a child.

Is that why you're here, Lars? Lana said again, and this time she didn't wait for an answer. This time she just plowed on ahead. *You think you can just run away? Cause I gotta say that doesn't seem all that wise, you being the only game in town as far as female companionship goes—not unless you want to wind up like that chick in the lobby.*

"Shut up, Lana."

Leaning over, Lara propped the photo on the nightstand. Then she stood, smoothing her slacks, and shut off the light. She walked to the window and leaned there, looking out. The night hung in velvet folds beyond the glass, stippled with city lights.

She was here because she wanted it back. The thirty-six-hour shifts, the endless paperwork, the adrenaline rush that jolted through you whenever a trauma came rolling through the doors. That most of all, she supposed. She wanted her life—a life that mattered—back.

That's what Ramsey Lomax had offered her. All he wanted in return was two weeks of her time. It didn't seem like too much to ask.

"Right, Lana?" she said. "Right?"

She waited in darkness for a long time afterward. But Lana didn't answer.

6

"So what happened during the renovations?" Lara said over dinner.

They sat over plates of fettuccini and grilled chicken—Ben had cooked it—in the gleaming, overbright industrial kitchen, Lara and Ben on one side of the long trestle, Abel and Keel on the other, with Ramsey Lomax peering down from the head of the table like some bizarre family patriarch.

Lomax dabbed his lips with a napkin. "There was an accident," he said. "There were a number of accidents actually, minor ones, but one in particular that persuaded me we should have medical facilities—and someone capable of using them—on site."

"Accidents happen," Keel said.

"Indeed, yes, Mr. Keel, all the time I'm afraid, especially in construction. But this one . . ." He shook his head. "There was an enormous amount of work to do, just in renovating this one floor. The place was built on the cheap in the early sixties." He shook his head. "The Great Society. What a ridiculous notion that turned out to be. Such naïveté."

"Naïveté wasn't the problem," Ben said.

"No? What was it then?"

"Corruption. I've seen the plans of this place—the original plans, I mean. What it was supposed to be, what it could have been. The money was there, too. But it had a way of disappearing in the Housing Authority, didn't it, so they built the place on the cheap instead."

"Well, what would you expect, Mr. Prather? Corruption's everywhere. Failure to anticipate it—that's just naïveté." Lomax shrugged. "The point is, there wasn't enough money from the start, and as time went on the situation worsened. Reagan made cuts in the eighties. The Democrats gave us welfare reform—such as it was—in the nineties. There had been no routine maintenance here for years, maybe even a decade—no painting, no repairs, nothing. The elevators didn't work. Neither did the plumbing, the heat—the list went on and on. So there was a lot to do just to make the place livable, not to mention"—Lomax swept his hands around in a gesture that encompassed the elaborate kitchen, the neighboring lounge, the entire floor beyond— "the renovations."

"A lot of people found it livable for years," Ben said.

"Perhaps so. But I'm not inclined to make the sacrifices they were forced to make. Nor, Mr. Prather, to subject my companions to such conditions. Seeing as all of you—even you, Mr. Prather—have lived substantially more . . . comfortable lifestyles."

There was a faintly mocking edge to this last. In the stiff silence that followed, Ben leaned back, crossing his arms over his chest.

"You said there was an accident," Lara said.

"Oh, yes," Lomax said, smiling. "Yes indeed. If you want to call it that. When we first started the work, we established a buddy system to keep people from being alone in the place—things have a way of happening here when you're alone, something I'd suggest you keep in mind."

"We *live* alone," Keel said darkly.

"True. But I think the . . . power, if you want to call it that . . . I think the power of the place—in this renovated corridor anyway—has been considerably weakened."

"Why is that?"

"We've inhabited it, haven't we? *We've* possessed *it*, if you will. Nothing of the original structure remains here, not even the walls." He leaned forward. "Let me tell you: the first time I came here I could *feel* something in the air, something"—he waved a hand—"watchful, I guess. Elsewhere in the building, I can feel it still—I felt it in the lobby today. But here . . . nothing." Lomax shrugged, eyeing them over his fork. "Besides, much as I'm sure I'll come to like you all, I have no desire for a roommate. Do you?"

No one had an answer for that.

"So, the buddy system," Lara said into the silence. "What happened with that?"

"It didn't quite work out as planned."

"Why not?" Keel said.

"People didn't want to work here for one thing, despite an unusually generous wage. They'd be enthusiastic enough at the start. They'd put in a day or two, and then"—he shrugged—"they would just quit. Sometimes they'd have an excuse, other times they'd just stop showing up. I suppose we should have expected it. Pretty much the same thing happened with the residents in the early nineties—a mass exodus. People just wouldn't live here anymore. By the time Theresa Matheson was raped and murdered, Tower Three was essentially abandoned."

"What was she doing here, then?" Lara said.

"She was headed for one of the *other* towers—there were eight of them, remember, most of them at least still half full. Tower Three—for whatever reason—seems to be the nexus of . . . whatever was happening here."

"That still doesn't explain how she wound up here."

"No. Nor does it explain how her assailants—most of them residents of the surrounding towers—ended up here that day either. They can't explain it themselves."

"They *won't* explain it, you mean," Keel said.

"What do you mean?" Lara said.

"It's not rocket science, Doc. You got an abandoned building in the middle of an area known for intensive gang activity. You bet those guys are going to use it."

"Maybe so," Lomax said. "Though our interviews with the city's gang units suggest otherwise. According to them, Tower Three had been universally abandoned by the mid-nineties. Gangs included."

"So how did they come to be there, then?" Ben said.

"I don't know. Perhaps—" Lomax hesitated. "Perhaps Tower Three summoned them."

"What?"

"Summoned them, Doctor." Lomax looked around at them. "Summoned her assailants anyway, and then used them to lure Miss Matheson into the lobby, into the shadows there, where passersby—if there were any—wouldn't notice."

Keel shifted in his seat. He snorted and shook his head.

"Laugh if you wish, Mr. Keel," Lomax said. "You

needn't worry about offending me. But I believe this place *can* summon people, in some cases. I believe it calls out to them. I believe that's what happened to our glazier."

"Your glazier?" Ben said.

"Our accident victim. If you want to call it an accident. Ironically, he *had* a work partner—but people get sloppy, don't they? People *always* get sloppy."

"So what happened?" Lara said.

"Like I said, the further we got with the renovations, the more comfortable everybody became. The partner stepped out to use the rest room, and rather than buddy up with somebody else, the glazier stuck around to finish something else—an interval of perhaps ten minutes, that's all, yet he managed to cut himself quite badly and nearly bled to death before his partner got back. An accident, that's what I chose to call it and I paid accordingly out of pocket, I should add. The workman's comp adjuster denied the claim."

"Why is that?" Keel said.

"If it was an accident," Lomax said, "the man managed to slash both wrists with the same piece of glass. Nor did the injuries appear to happen simultaneously, as they might have had he lunged to catch a pane of glass that had slipped out of its frame or whatever. They ran longways"—Lomax drew a finger along his forearm—"and they were quite deep, a consistent depth the length of each incision. And if the fingerprints on the glass—some of them bloody—are any indication, he managed to use both hands in the process. You're a seasoned investigator, Mr. Keel. What does the evidence suggest to you?"

Flushing, Keel pushed his plate away. "He did it himself, that what you're saying?"

"That's what the insurance adjuster said. The glazier was fortunate that his friend was quick-thinking. He managed to get tourniquets on both arms, which enabled the ambulance to make the full round-trip from Mercy General and back. Thirty-four minutes."

"And?" Ben said.

"And what? He'll never work again, not with his hands anyway. The nerve damage was fairly extensive."

"No. What did he say about it?"

"Nothing, Mr. Prather. Much like Theresa Matheson's

assailants, actually. He says he remembers asking his partner to bring him some bottled water from the cooler in the
corridor. And then he just blanks out, like a spot missing
in a cassette tape. The next thing he remembers is
screaming—that was his partner—and he realizes that he's
on his knees, that he's wet. You should hear him tell it,
he's quite eloquent on the issue. 'I thought I must have
pissed myself at first.' That's what he told me." Lomax
shook his head. "He realized it was blood soon enough,
though—it must have taken a second or two, that's all. I
suppose he must have gone into shock almost immediately.
Right, Doctor?"

"It happens pretty quickly."

"The next thing he remembers is the emergency room."

"They must have done a psych consult," Lara said.

"Oh, yes. They admitted him for observation, did a full
battery of tests, the works."

"And?" Ben said.

"He was fine. No suicidal ideation. No personal problems
of any real significance. His marriage was solid, his health
was good, his finances were sound." Lomax shrugged. "He
was fine."

"Except for the slashed wrists," Keel said.

And Lomax smiled. "Indeed, yes, Mr. Keel. Except for
that."

7

"So what do you think of him?" Fletcher Keel said.

He chalked his cue, leaned over the table, and sank the
five in the corner pocket. They listened to it rattle down
through the bowels of the table, and clatter into the return
tray at the other end.

"Who?" Ben said.

Keel took his time answering. He moved around the
table, poker-faced as he considered his next shot. Then,
without looking up—though he projected a kind of taut

peripheral awareness—he said, "Three in the side pocket." He took the shot with unstudied grace: a single confident stroke with the cue, the sharp crack of the cushioned tip against the ivory. Ben watched as the ball zipped silently over the felt, a red blur on a green field. It rattled around the rim of the hole and dropped, snicking against the balls already waiting in the tray.

Keel looked up, smiling, a lean blue-eyed man with long muscles and a deeply scored face. There was something paradoxical about him, a youthful grace that belied the gray in his neatly trimmed goatee. Even in repose—pausing to study his next shot—he radiated an aura of contained energy, a coiled potential: like a spring, or a snake. He seemed deeply at home inside his flesh, in a way that seemed, to Ben, who'd always been clumsy, both mysterious and faintly miraculous.

"Mine host," Keel said. "That's who."

"Lomax?" Ben said.

"Yep."

"Gosh, I don't know."

Keel gave Ben a raspberry and turned back to the table, pointing his next shot with the tip of his cue. It went a quarter inch wide, caroming off the rail and shaking up the balls in the middle of the table. "Hurried that one," he said under his breath, and then, looking up, "Come on, you've got to have an opinion."

Ben studied the table while he pondered how to answer the question—or whether to answer it at all. Keel wasn't bad, there was no question about that. Ben's only unimpeded shot ran the length of the felt. He chalked his stick. "Nine ball in the corner." He leaned over the table, sighted down the cue, drew it back, and took the shot. He could see right away that he'd misjudged the angle. The nine rebounded off the corner of the pocket and coasted to the center of the table.

Keel sank the seven and four in quick succession.

"Well?" he said.

"Well, what?"

"What do you think of the man?"

"I'm a journalist. I'm not supposed to have opinions."

"Everybody has opinions. You just try to disguise them— which is far more insidious. Six in the side." He leaned over the table and banked the ball off the far rail. It dropped neatly into the pocket. "Besides," he added. "It's not like you're writing an article."

"No. But I might. I really am trying to withhold judgment."

"Not me," Keel said. "The guy's a loon."

"You think?"

"Ghosts, Mr. Prather?"

"Ben."

"Well, Ben, do you have any opinions on ghosts, or would that compromise your objectivity too much?"

"I'm inclined to disbelieve in them, I guess."

"Well, that's something, then—"

"On the other hand, I don't think that makes Lomax crazy."

"No?" Keel lifted his cue. "Two in the corner."

But this time, he'd misjudged. The ball came off the rail hard, leaving Ben a gimme on the ten.

"So what do you mean, then?" Keel asked.

"Just . . . that . . ." Biting his lower lip, Ben leaned over the table. The ten went down with a satisfying clunk. Which left him, what, six balls behind? He looked up. ". . . people believe in lots of things they can't see."

"Such as?"

"God for one thing."

"Yeah, well, that's different."

"Is it?" Ben looked at the table. The upside to being so far behind was that there was nothing left in his way: the table was, literally, wide open. He pointed out the fourteen, leaned over, and sank it. His next shot—on the eleven—rolled wide.

"Here's another thing," Keel said. "Why us?"

And Ben, though he suspected at least half the answer, though he knew or thought he knew why Ramsey Lomax had recruited *him,* anyway, only said, "What do you mean?"

"I mean the four of us: you, me, the doctor. Abel Williams."

"Well, Abel seems pretty obvious."

"If you believe all that," Keel said, pointing with his cue. The two ball rattled home. He straightened and looked at Ben. "Still, the whole thing's pretty strange, when you think about it. Where did you say you're from? LA? Me, I've been living in San Antonio—"

"So?"

"So why us, from halfway across the country? Or why not a real doctor—"

"She is a real doctor."

"She's a resident. She's still in training. You think Lomax doesn't have his own personal physician?"

"Maybe he wasn't interested in coming along for the ride."

"And Lara?"

Ben shrugged. "You think he has some leverage over her?"

"My point exactly," Keel said. "Which raises a question: what's his leverage over you?"

"Or you, for that matter," Ben said.

They stared silently at one another.

Fletcher Keel smiled. "Eight ball in the corner pocket," he said. He leaned across the table, splayed his left hand atop the felt, and leveled his cue in the fleshy dip between his thumb and forefinger. He drew it back and swept it down in a single graceful gesture. The cue ball snapped forward. There was a sharp concussion as it collided with the eight, and then it spun backward, a white blur. The eight ball drained into the corner pocket. "Game," Keel said. "Care to have another go?"

"Why not?"

As Keel racked the balls, Ben wandered over toward the books, his mind churning. Maybe—probably, he decided—Lomax was a little crazy. Perhaps more than a little. But that merely begged the larger—and, to Ben, more interesting—question. Specifically *how* was he crazy? And why? And what role did Dreamland play in his psychosis? What did he hope to accomplish here? Because the cost-benefit ratio of this little expedition didn't quite add up, did it—not to Ben's mind anyway. And Lomax's explanation—simple curiosity—seemed altogether too facile for a man of his sophistication.

Ben gave the books a cursory glance—bestselling fiction mostly, much of it recently remaindered—and turned away, dragging one finger along the ranked spines. That was when he noticed the painting mounted on the far wall. Only—

Ben stepped closer.

—it wasn't a painting, was it?

It was a photograph, an aerial shot of Dreamland, taken in the shining moment of its conception, just before everything turned sour. It looked new, a diminished thing compared to the architectural renderings, certainly—eight squarish towers in lieu of the glass spires that had been planned, a concrete plaza that might have been a park— but still scrubbed and fresh-looking, awash and hopeful in bright morning sunlight. Unstained by the darkness to come. Yet there was something faintly unsettling about it all the same. Maybe he was projecting it on the picture himself—almost certainly, in fact, considering both his apprehension about the place and Lomax's little penny dreadful over dinner. Still . . .

There was something foreboding about it. Some chance juxtaposition of elements. Something about the towers themselves. Something about their placement around the plaza . . .

What did it remind him of?

Ben lifted his hand, his fingers outstretched—

"Weird, isn't it?" Keel said.

Startled, Ben looked up. Keel stood at his shoulder. He must move like a cat, Ben thought uneasily.

"It looks like one of those places in England," Keel said, nodding at the photo. "Stonehenge or something."

And that was it exactly. Stonehenge.

Or something.

A circle of ancient standing stones. It creeped him out a little.

Keel laughed. "Let's go," he said. "You can break."

8

Lara was almost done with the dishes before she noticed the watch.

Really noticed it, that is.

Sure, she'd seen Abel loosen the catch, slide it over his wrist, and put it out of harm's way on the countertop—it was the first thing he'd done after he had volunteered to help clean up the kitchen. But there was nothing unusual about that. Indeed, as far as she'd been able to tell, there was nothing much unusual about Abel Williams at all.

Lara wasn't sure what she had expected. She'd caught his show—bits and pieces of it, anyway—on the television mounted high in one corner of the ER's waiting room. Once or twice, at home in her apartment, flipping through the channels when the adrenaline hangover from trauma duty kept sleep at bay, she'd even watched it all the way through. But she'd been far more interested in the dumbfounding gullibility of his audience than in the phenomenon of Abel Williams himself. She'd written him off as a con man from the very first.

Her ER rotation had taught her far too much about the frangible realities of the human condition to accept him as anything else. The truth was, the line between life and death was exceedingly narrow even at the best of times. Everyone stood a scant heartbeat from the abyss. It didn't take much—a slip of the foot, a blink on the highway—

—a single stroke of the pen—

—to push them over the edge. And what a step it usually turned out to be—messy, smelly, all too often agonizing. You didn't have to see too many torn aortas or gutshot teenagers to get the point: the body was a fragile mechanism, strung together with chicken wire and bone, and God, if God existed at all (she had more than a few doubts on that score, too), had one sick sense of humor. If nothing else, the ER assaulted you with the organic reality of human existence, its meaty physicality—with the mingled stenches of vomit and urine and blood, with the fine grit of particles in the hamburger that used to be a spilled motorcyclist's leg (donorcycles, they called them in the ER) or the shocking white grin of exposed bone.

In the context, spiritual survival—the ghost in the machine—seemed like a long shot. Which had made the gullibility of Abel Williams' petitioners all the more unfathomable. Yet Lara had seen the same kind of denial in the ER, survivors clinging to hope long after all hope had realistically been exhausted.

Hang the paddles and pronounce the patient, as one of her med school professors had been fond of saying. Human beings just didn't last, and Lara couldn't understand how anyone could believe otherwise, even for the thirty-minute span of a television program.

Ergo: Abel Williams was a fraud.

But she'd reached that conclusion before she had ever talked with the man—before she'd seen him in the flesh instead of as a presence on the screen. In person, divested of the mannered theatricality of performance—the portentous little pauses, the wrinkled brow and puzzled frown of concentration—Abel seemed essentially normal, friendly and handsome in an unthreatening way, with his blocky face, his head of close-cropped brown hair and his washed-out green eyes. So normal in fact that you could forget his penchant for sententious little pronouncements from the dead.

She had, anyway.

"Come on, surrender the sink," he'd called playfully no sooner than the door swung shut behind Lomax and the others. "Move aside. I hate to dry."

Lara, already filling the oversized basin with iridescent mountains of suds, just shook her head. "Too late."

"It's never too late," he said, rolling back his sleeves. Unsnapping the catch on his watch, he worked it over his hand and set it aside. He cracked his knuckles ostentatiously. "See? I'm ready. Come on, scoot. You wouldn't want an unsightly case of dishpan hands."

"I'll risk it," she said, laughing in spite of herself as she tossed him a dish towel.

But that little negotiation—*though it was really more of a flirtation, wasn't it?* Lana announced inside her head—had served to sweep away the worst of the awkwardness between them: the accumulated tension from dinner, from Ben Prather's wounded touchiness and Lomax's horror story about the glazier—a performance worthy of television in its own right, she realized. What she *hadn't* realized—not immediately, anyway—was that Abel Williams was putting on a performance, as well. She hadn't even noticed, had she? He was that good.

"So you always been this domineering?" he said as he loaded a freshly rinsed plate into the dishwasher.

"From day one."

"Yeah? And where was that?"

"Where was what?"

"Day one."

"Wilmington, North Carolina," she said. "I'm a Tarheel by birth. What about you?"

"I grew up in Pittsburgh," he said. "Mostly, anyway."

So it went, light and quick, through the plates and silver and into the pots and pans, which she scrubbed by hand. A flirtation Lana had called it, and Lana—as she usually turned out to be—had been right. By the time Lara finished wiping down the countertops and started helping him stow the final odds and ends in the cabinets, she had grown so comfortable that she almost told him the truth when he asked why she had become a doctor.

Almost.

In fact, Lana's name was already on the tip of her tongue when two events occurred simultaneously. The first event—which happened entirely inside her own head—was an abrupt realization about where the flow of this conversation was taking her. The natural follow-up to Abel's query was a simple reversal of its direction: how had *he* wound up in the profession he had chosen? Except, given the nature of the profession he had chosen, she couldn't think of a way to phrase the question that wouldn't betray her bone-deep skepticism about the entire enterprise. And this simple reminder of what Abel claimed to be spurred yet another, more disturbing perception—how easily she had been drawn in, how willing to surrender to him the most intimate details of her past, details she hardly allowed herself even to *think* about on any truly conscious level, let alone discuss aloud, and with a total stranger. Perhaps *that* was the secret of Abel's success—he had the seductive charisma of a good therapist. You *wanted* to trust him. You *wanted* to believe him. And if you weren't careful, you'd wind up telling him far more than you had ever intended—maybe more than you were even aware of yourself.

In the same moment that these thoughts were passing through her mind, Lara happened to notice Abel Williams' watch. *Really* notice it this time. She'd been leaning over the counter on her toes to slide a colander onto a high shelf, and just as she settled back on the soles of her feet, she caught a glimpse of it, curled atop the Corian beneath her. At first she mistook the flaw in the crystal for the shadow of the overhanging cabinets. A closer examination revealed it as a jagged fissure in the glass. For a single irrational moment she thought *she* might have broken it somehow—maybe she had jarred it in leaning over to get at the shelves above.

But that was absurd, wasn't it? Because there was no way she could have been responsible for the rest of the damage—the other chip in the face or the peeling silver laminate on the battered metal band or the frozen second hand—not unless she had dropped the entire colander on the thing—and she knew that hadn't happened. Besides, the watch had obviously stopped working some time ago. It had to be getting on past eight now, and the hands seemed to have frozen up almost ten minutes short of twelve.

"Lara?"

She responded without looking up, her voice distracted. "Yeah?"

"You were telling me why you decided to become a doctor."

In that moment, with the name of her long-dead sister hovering unspoken on her lips, Lara McGovern had a sudden change of heart. Abel Williams was performing, too, she thought, and his normality was *part* of the performance, maybe the key part. That was how he did it to you. His everyday facade, his utterly unremarkable averageness, ran so counter to your expectations that he could charm the truth out of you and feed it back piecemeal, and you would never even notice that you'd been had. She had a sudden sense of herself surrounded by performers—by Lomax and Benjamin Prather, by Fletcher Keel and Abel Williams, too, all of them moved by barely concealed agendas to push and probe at one another, working for position in some kind of macho game she hadn't even known was going on. It was like standing in a hall of mirrors, like stumbling among the revelers at a masquerade ball.

Lana was right: what on earth had she gotten herself into?

And just like that, as swiftly and neatly as a cartoon frog darting out his tongue to snatch home a cartoon fly, Lara drew in a breath and swallowed down her dead sister's name, taking it safely back inside herself, where she had kept it all these years, nursing it like a stone. She felt violated, angry.

But she didn't let it show. Oh, no, she thought. When in Rome . . .

She could be an actress, too.

She let surprise creep into her voice, the faintest note of concern. "Hey!"

"What?" Williams said.

"Your watch." Lara shut the cabinet and picked up the watch. Now, examining it in the even glare of the overhead lights, she saw that it was older than she'd thought—not merely battered, but old. *Really* old, decades even, to judge by the greenish crud that had accumulated in the joints of the band. Moisture must have seeped through the cracked crystal at some point. The age-jaundiced face was slightly wrinkled, the figures of the five and six blurrily adrift in the deeper yellow lagoon of a water stain. Some kind of black gunk clogged the pin from which the hands radiated.

"Oh," Williams said. "That."

"Was it like this when you took it off or is it, like"—she tried to resist the joke, she really did, but given the context, it was just too easy—"oooh, the haunted watch?"

She looked up, laughing, but Abel Williams didn't seem to find it funny. He stepped toward her, and lifted the watch firmly out of her hand. "Yeah, right."

He was halfway to the door before she realized he was angry.

"Hey, wait," she said, but something in the obdurate set of his shoulders told her it was too little, too late, and that was a shame because she couldn't exactly afford to alienate anyone here, could she? The circumstances hardly provided for a generous circle of acquaintance—

But Abel Williams paused.

"Really," she said. "I didn't mean—"

"I know." Turning, he lifted his hands. The watch dangled between his fingers, glinting. He smiled sheepishly. "I know. I'm being ridiculous. Look, the watch—it was my father's—"

"I'm sorry," she said, her hand moving unbidden toward the neck of her blouse, where the locket—Lana's locket—

nestled unseen between her breasts. She felt like a complete ass.

"—it has a lot of sentimental value," Abel finished.

They stood there, staring at one another in the silent kitchen.

Abel swallowed. "He was wearing it when he died. In the coal mines, back home in West Virginia."

"I thought you were from Pittsburgh."

"We moved there. After Dad died. I was just a kid." He hesitated. "Anyway, I've worn the watch ever since. It's kind of a superstitious thing, I guess."

It was only then, ten seconds too late, that his words—

—*he died in the mines*—

—managed to penetrate her thick skull. A coal mine, to be exact. And suddenly the significance of the time dawned on her—those hands frozen forever a few minutes short of noon and the jagged crack in the face and the black gunk clogging up the works. Everything.

She felt herself flush, the heat rising in her face.

"That—" She swallowed. Took a breath. "That must have been really hard."

"Yeah," he said. "Death's hard."

Nothing more, and just like that they had passed over some kind of weird border and into foreign territory. Into *his* territory, actually—into the Twilight Zone, where the dead had voices.

Like this place, Lars, Lana intoned inside her head, her little-girl voice pitched unnaturally low in a strained imitation of Rod Serling's best sepulchral tone.

Except there was nothing funny about it, was there? Nothing at all. The truth was, death *was* hard—as this Hallmark moment in the kitchen, this awkward little epiphany made all too abundantly clear. Because let's face it, Abel Williams' father must have died years ago, decades even, but the wound was obviously still fresh. Some wounds just never heal, that's all—no one knew that better than she did. Maybe everyone staggered through life this way, enchained by their promises to the dead.

The idea cast a new light on the phenomenon of Abel Williams, didn't it?

Not that she believed he could really do what he claimed he could do—death was death. Death was another country.

The borders were closed and the lines were down. There was no passage between. But that didn't make Abel Williams a fraud, not if *he* believed he could really do it. And maybe he *did* believe it.

Maybe he had to.

She stood there looking at him without really seeing him, her face masklike, as these thoughts passed through her mind in a kind of half-conscious blur.

"You okay?" he asked.

She looked down to find her hand curled at her breast. She forced a smile. "Yeah," she said. "I was just thinking about what you said. About . . . how hard it is."

He nodded.

"Anyway," she said. "That was totally insensitive of me."

Abel Williams shook his head and smiled. He had a nice smile, she thought. A slightly lopsided smile, with teeth that were a shade less white than most television teeth. It was all part of his charm—as was the ease with which he passed off her discomfort, saying, "There wasn't any way you could have known. Let's just forget it, okay?"

"Yeah, okay."

He smiled again, that same average and reassuring smile, and as he turned to go, a sudden impulse rose up inside her.

"Abel—"

"Yeah?"

"It happened a long time ago, right?"

"Twenty-one years," he said.

"And the watch . . . it still bothers you?"

It was the kind of question Lana might have asked: blunt and direct, because she wanted to know the answer, without consideration for the social niceties. Lara wasn't sure what kind of response she intended to elicit by it, either—only that his feelings about the watch seemed to strike some answering chord within her.

Abel didn't seem to take offense—maybe they had moved beyond that—but he took a long time answering. He slid the watch over his wrist and closed the catch, his expression faraway. Then he looked up and for a moment she was certain that he was going to fetch back news out of all that hazy distance. She could feel the certainty chime inside her, she could feel it humming in her bones.

But he only shook his head.

"It's not the watch that bothers me," he said. "It's the death."

He nodded and went out, and it was only afterward, bereft in the sparkling and silent kitchen, that Lara recognized what she had been hoping to hear—the same frail hope all of them must have brought to lay at his feet, the petitioners who waited in line for hours just for the privilege of sweating under the hot lights of Abel Williams' studio. Not anything as simple as knowledge or understanding, not by a long shot. What they wanted—what *she* wanted—maybe what everyone wanted—was absolution from the dead. What they wanted was the assurance that someday the burden would be lifted—that someday the awful weight of guilt and terror and grief would pass away—that someday please God it would be over.

But the truth was, it never would be.

The truth was you carried that freight of sorrow to the grave.

9

Night closed in.

The cold plummeted past zero, and the snow quickened, whipping in sheets through the shuttered downtown canyons. The lake turned its wind-frothed mirror to the sky, standing water crackled into glossy obsidian panes of ice, and the city, boisterous, broad-shouldered, subsided into stillness. In the broad tree-lined avenues of the Gold Coast—where luxury apartment towers with uniformed doormen reared up alongside the immaculate brownstones of millionares—brokers, bankers, and executives, snug in their security-monitored bedrooms, drifted off with Leno on their sleep-timed televisions. In the streets outside, patrol cars whispered past.

A dog barked, and somewhere in the darkness a bus slowed with a woosh of air brakes. And still the snow came, down, down, down, a silent ministry of frost, covering the streets and curbs, the gutters and alleys in the fine white fabric of a dream.

In the shadow of the El, huddled among his companions along that borderland where the Gold Coast turns to iron, a homeless man shivered under a threadbare blanket. He grumbled in his sleep as a train screamed overhead, showering sparks and cinders upon his shoulders. The lights flickered across his seamed and stubbled face, and amid the flying shadows, you could not say for sure whether he was black or white.

There was no such uncertainty in the dying streets across the elevated rails. There, where a single slat-ribbed rat nosed disconsolately through the spilled wreckage of an overturned Dumpster, and the smoke-grimed storefronts sagged wearily behind their steel security gates, made momentarily beautiful by weather, all the faces were black, or anyway what passed for black: a wild profusion, actually, of walnut and mahogany, chocolate, cocoa, tan, and a café au lait so pale and milky yellow brown that it was right next door to white. They too were sleeping, most of them, in crowded second-floor efficiencies and decaying rowhouses, in the gang-infested hives of the projects, in basement apartments with miserly window-wells that hoarded coins of barred and jaundiced sky.

It fell beyond that, too, the snow, indiscriminately, in the dead lands.

The dead lands, where the streets gave way to shattered pavement and the chitinous husks of burned-out cars, like the shucked hulls of gigantic insects. Where fire-gutted houses presided over lots bereft of anything but broken stone.

Where Dreamland, blinded, lifted its shoulders like a crippled king.

Only now it was alight.

Fenced in, walled up and more than half-unmade, rising in ghostly stone from the snow-drift rubble of its seven tumbled sisters. But alight.

For a time—an hour more, maybe two—a handful of yellow beacons glimmered almost halfway up the tower's central facade. Then footsteps retreated down a hallway. A door slammed. A toilet flushed. And, as the night tipped imperceptibly toward dawn—one, two, three minutes past midnight, the toll of a distant church bell still shivering the air—the fifth-floor lights began to blink out.

In the kitchen, the counters gleaming—out. In the lounge, the pool cues at attention in their racks—out. In Ramsey Lomax's room, and in those of Abel Williams and Lara McGovern, too—out, out, out.

The night deepened. Still, the snow fell.

Dreamland, dark, loomed against the sky: eighteen stories of formed and molded concrete, of empty hallways and abandoned apartments; eighteen stories of shattered doors and vacant eyelike windows. Outwardly unchanged, after all, the lights a mere illusion—or so it might have seemed, had anyone been out there to see, beyond the fence, in the devastated street, in all that dark and snow: Dreamland, unchanged. Dreamland: derelict, diminished, delimbed, its decaying arms outstretched.

But not dead.

Oh, no.

Behind a locked door, in a dark room off a renovated hall where light fell dim and orderly in overlapping parabolas, Benjamin Prather hunched closer to his computer, face slack, fingers flying, his skin sallow in the ghostly blue backwash from his monitor, the wire-rimmed glasses sliding down his nose dizzy with reflection.

That observer, looking closer, might have seen it—

Dreamland in darkness, shrouded in snow, an ethereal light guttering at one high window. Like the film of thin blue flame that hovers over dying embers, fluttering, fluttering, unless some chance draft should fan it once again to life. Like a ghostly pulse.

Or a faltered heartbeat, catching.

10

In the deepest trough of morning, when the snow had stopped and the clouds had drifted further east, disclosing a limpid shield of sky from which a crescent moon gilded the Gold Coast and the dead lands alike, Fletcher Keel came suddenly awake, his heart booming in his breast. He stared disoriented at the strange ceiling, memory coming back in shards: the smudged and crumpled promise of a barroom napkin, the long plane ride home, and that strange stir of presence in the south stairwell.

Everything but the dream that had startled him awake.

He lay very still, trying to recall it, until sleep carried him away at last.

11

In Dreamland, no one else dreamed, all the rest of that night.

A Tour of the Ruins

1

KATRINA SUKS COCKS, the words said, staggering in jagged foot-high letters across an otherwise unmarred wall of unpainted cinder block. As the others drifted down the hallway toward the twelfth-floor elevator, Lara paused in an empty doorway, staring in at those words and thinking not for the first time that maybe it had been a bad idea, this little tour. That was Ramsey Lomax's word, not hers—the word he'd used when he had proposed the idea over lunch, in the same tone he might have used to suggest a stroll in the park or some other lark. And to Lara, that's exactly how the whole thing had felt—like a tour, appallingly so, in fact: a lazy hike through floor after devastated floor, apartment after wrecked apartment, accompanied by Lomax's incessant commentary—a fourteen-year-old girl raped and left for dead in a utility closet on seven, a thirty-seven-year-old grandmother—

"Thirty-seven and a grandmother!" Keel had marveled.

—gunned down in the hall on nine—horror after horror after horror, all of it narrated with the same blithe indifference to the incredible cost this place had exacted, the unbelievable human toll. No wonder Benjamin Prather's expression had begun to curdle half an hour into the excursion, she thought. No wonder she had found herself drifting farther and farther behind the other four, until at last Lomax's voice faded to a distant quacking.

Anything for a moment of silence.

She looked up, watching the others as they neared the intersection with the central corridor. The red glow of a still-functioning exit sign, mounted over the door into the stairwell, momentarily illuminated them, and then they turned the corner, apparently unaware of her absence.

Which was fine with her.

She turned her attention back to the apartment. The words—

—*Katrina suks cocks*—

—were still there. Looking at them, she felt something turn over inside her. It wasn't the sentiment itself that shocked her—God knows she'd heard worse in the trauma rooms at Mercy General. It was the location: here in a room that had once been someone's home.

That was the thing you had to remember, the thing Lomax—and Keel, too, and maybe even Abel Williams— apparently found so easy to forget—if they'd ever really understood it in the first place. People—real, live human beings—had lived here, *here*, in this . . .

Lara sought for the word, but everything that came to mind—slum, ghetto, whatever—seemed somehow inadequate.

Hell might do it justice.

In the depleted gray light admitted by the sole window— a tall, narrow aperture more like an arrow slot than a proper window, an arrow slot sporting shards of broken glass like teeth—the word seemed close enough. Good enough for government work, as her father used to say— which, come to think of it, Dreamland had been. Your tax dollars at work.

Ha, ha.

Lara scanned the room once again: narrow and airless, with flat cinder block walls, a floor of peeling linoleum, and a swaybacked sleeper sofa the color of phlegm, its cushions canted back to reveal the thin mattress underneath.

Maybe right there, Lana said inside her head.

Right there what?

Katrina. You know . . . Maybe Katrina suc—

Right, Lara thought.

But from the look of the mattress, yellowing and mysteriously stained, it seemed like more than a remote possibility. It seemed like a probability, actually. Standing there in the empty doorway (which raised another question: what had happened to all the damn doors in this place?), the scene was all too easy to imagine. And as much as it bothered her—the idea of some strung-out black kid named Katrina working a stranger to joyless spasm on that sagging, piss-stained mattress—as much as it bothered her, it didn't bother her quite enough, did it?

Not as much as Lomax's story about Theresa Matheson had bothered her. Not as much as that story *still* bothered her. Which said what, exactly, about her character? Something she didn't want to think about, that much was certain.

Just then, the wind kicked up, drawing a mournful keening harmonic across the saw-edged teeth in the window. Lara shivered and crossed her arms over her breasts, mindful suddenly of the forsaken arcade at her back, the echoing emptiness of the floors below. Turning, she gazed once again down the hallway, so unlike the renovated hallway seven stories below that they might have been in entirely different buildings—or entirely different worlds, for that matter. She stood at the far end of the southern wing, at the door to the next-to-last apartment in line. The corridor stretched away before her, uncarpeted concrete cluttered with still more cast-off furniture—a broken bar stool, another battered sofa. Two or three doorways at the other end of the hall radiated that same wan exterior light—more arrow slots, she supposed—and the exit sign continued to shed its faint cherry glow, but otherwise the gloom was unrelieved. And it stank. Even in subzero weather, with the wind pouring through half a dozen or more broken windows, the place stank. Come August it must have been intolerable. Lara took a long breath and let it whistle between her pursed lips, clouding the air before her.

Not a good place to be alone, sis, Lana said. *Remember what the man said.*

"Shut up," Lara said softly.

Something had started banging down the hall, a rhythmic clapping. The wind, she told herself. Another broken window, maybe a shutter or something. Except people didn't exactly install shutters in places like this, did they? They had more pressing concerns. Like not getting shot.

In the next moment, the wind died away. The clapping died, too, along with that awful keening. Thank God for small favors. But that left the silence, which seemed deeper now, more pervasive. It welled up around her, spilling out of empty apartments, through doorways, in windows, and suddenly she found herself longing for the sound of human voices, even Ramsey Lomax's endless quacking.

She took a first hesitant step, and then another, and then, without intending it, she found herself hurrying down the crepuscular hallway at a quick walk, snatching glances into open apartments on either side.

"Guys?" she said. And then, louder, hating the way it sounded, the weakness: "Hey, guys, wait up!"

She barked her shin on a discarded chair, cursed under her breath, and kept moving—faster now, pumping her legs in something just short of a jog as she took the corner.

There.

Lara checked her progress mid-stride. She'd caught a glimpse of something—movement, a flash of yellowish white—through a half-open door.

"Very funny," she started to say as she swung toward the apartment, brushing back the door—this one actually had a door—with one hand.

The words died in her throat.

The apartment was empty: dank cinder block walls strewn with graffiti, that same scarred linoleum, a faint lingering reek of urine, the smell of it reminding her suddenly of the ER, its complex melange of odors: urine, sweat, the omnipresent ammonia burn of disinfectant.

How much she missed it.

In the same moment, she once again sensed movement, an ivory blur hurtling toward her from the absolute limit of her peripheral vision. Lara gasped, a sharp little blurt of surprise—more like a squawk than a real scream—slipping out before she could choke it back. As she turned, a cold draft lifted her hair—

And then a bottomless wave of relief buoyed her.

Laughter, bright and glassy, burbled in her throat. A window shade—a ragged age-yellowed *remnant* of a window shade, actually, the plastic roll-up type—that's all it was, all it had ever been. And as she stood there, listening to that odd, disturbing little laugh die away, the wind picked up again, hurling itself in a chill blast through the shattered hole of the window. The shade bellied outward, its weighted bottom smacking the wall—a hollow *thwacking* sound, like an irregular drumbeat—with every fresh gust.

Lara laughed again, real laughter this time.

And you call yourself a scientist, Lana said inside her head, and that only made her laugh harder. She was still laughing when Abel Williams appeared in the doorway.

"You all right?" he said, and for some reason that set her off again.

"What?" he said. "What's so funny?"

"The window shade," she managed to gasp. "It scared the shit out of me."

"The window shade?" Abel said incredulously. He snorted, and she couldn't help herself, she snickered in response—then they were both laughing, a wild, rising gale of hilarity that kept renewing itself every time one of them tried to speak, until finally, abruptly, it burst, leaving them wrung out, breathless.

Still gasping, Lara shook her head. "Where the hell were you guys? That window shade could have killed me."

Abel laughed once again—a single sharp bark, like an explosion—and then he drew himself upright. "At the elevator," he said, with an air of injured dignity. "Waiting for you."

2

By the time Lara and Abel swung back through the doors of the waiting elevator, their pale faces highlighted by rosy patches of color, the nature of Lomax's little "tour"—not to mention the climax he clearly had in mind for it—had become all too evident. Just thinking about it, Ben felt the knot of tension in his chest grow tighter.

It had been there all morning, that knot, from the moment he woke unrested just after nine o'clock, his eyes burning with weariness. Lomax's leisurely pilgrimage through the blasted warren of Dreamland hadn't helped any. By the time they had reached the tenth floor, it had begun hardening into resentment. "By the mid-eighties, gangbangers, the Conservative Vice Lords, were pretty much running this place," Lomax had said, staring into a vacant bedroom where a gaping hole had been punched through one wall, providing access to the neighboring apartment.

An enormous black-and-gold graffito had been painted on the cinder block wall opposite—a top hat, a glove, and a cane, all of them superimposed atop a gigantic pentagram, like a coat of arms, faded now, but far more proficiently executed than anything Ben had seen elsewhere in the building. Sheets of rain-warped plywood covered both windows, but the smoky faraway light of the winter sun bled around the edges and streamed in glittering spokes through splintering holes in the panels—bullet holes, Ben suspected—suffusing the room with an ethereal undersea glow.

Lomax turned, his hawklike profile momentarily illuminated. "This was one of their safe houses," he said. "They'd set them up in vacant apartments and tunnel through the interior walls to set up escape routes."

"Jesus Christ," Keel had muttered.

And the other men in the room—the *white* men, Ben couldn't help thinking, one of whom had never been short so much as a single dime in the last thirty years—stood there sober as deacons, shaking their heads in agreement: unbelievable, these people. Ben, watching from the doorway, felt the knot tighten another notch.

The doctor, at least, had dissented.

"It's not like they had a lot of choices," she'd said.

"People *always* have choices, Doctor," Lomax replied crisply, and that had been that, the final word, delivered with a steely edge: the chairman quelling an insurrection in the boardroom. Or—more appropriate, given the context— the master delivering a stern warning to some uppity darky. That cultured voice, that whiplash smile.

Except the only darky in the room is me, Ben thought, and the old sense of being somehow an interloper loomed up inside him, the all-too-familiar awareness that his was the only black face among all the white ones staring back at him—that no matter how much he liked to pretend otherwise, he remained after all these years an envoy from a different and a darker nation. The shadow nation. You're invited to the party, but don't expect to dance.

It was like living your life behind a pane of glass.

He felt the knot draw tighter, the resentment shading into anger.

By the time the doctor pulled her little disappearing act on twelve, it had drawn so tight that it took an active effort of will even to breathe. And by the time Abel retrieved her, the anger had gotten the upper hand. Ben cleared his throat, determined suddenly not to play along with Lomax's charade. Both of them knew why he had come here—hell, for all Ben knew, maybe everyone was in on his little secret. That didn't mean he had any obligation to pose as Exhibit A.

"You really intend to inspect every floor?" he said, uncertain what exactly he expected to accomplish by this statement. He supposed that some small part of him, that terrified inner self who held the secrets of his past, had hoped to engineer some kind of last-minute reprieve. If so, he'd miscalculated badly.

Lomax smiled coldly. "We can do it any way you want, Mr. Prather." He lifted his finger to the control panel and punched a button. "We can go straight up to eighteen," he said. He held Ben's gaze as the doors slid shut and the elevator lurched into gear, steadied, and began pulling itself laboriously higher. And then he turned away. "Eighteen saw the worst of it," he said to the others. "I'm a little rusty on the dates, though. That was—when, Mr. Prather?"—flinging this last over his shoulder, as he might have flung a table scrap to a dog.

But Ben never got a chance to answer.

"Eighty," Keel said. "Nineteen-eighty."

"Ah, yes, Mr. Keel. Nineteen-eighty. Practically a lifetime ago."

That phrase—

—*practically a lifetime ago*—

—ricocheted around inside Ben's head like shrapnel. Now that the elevator was climbing, moving inexorably toward a rendezvous with the past, he could hardly breathe, much less think. He leaned back, clutching the cool metal railing that ran waist-high around the elevator's interior. Decades-old newspaper headlines swarmed the air before him, blurry newsprint photos of faces he'd seen a thousand times in his dreams.

"It started with a sniper," Lomax was saying. "Picking

people off in the plaza. He wounded one man, and shot another one dead, a seventeen-year—"

"They," Ben said, dredging the word up the dry funnel of his throat.

He felt the cumulative attention in the car shift, its weight on his skin. His voice seemed unnaturally loud, the air dense with the heat of their bodies. And still they rose upward—thirteen, fourteen, fifteen, each number flaring momentarily orange above the doors. Blood sang at his temples. He dragged in a long breath, and lowered his gaze. Lomax was staring at him the way a man might stare at some chance oddity he'd discovered in the grass. An insect, or maybe a spider. Something loathsome anyway, and possibly deadly.

"There were two of them," Ben said.

Above the doors, another number flared. Sixteen.

"That's right," Lomax said. "No one knew that at the time, of course. Otherwise things might have turned out differently."

Seventeen.

"What happened?" Abel asked.

Lomax lifted his eyebrows. "Perhaps you'd like to tell it, Mr. Prather," he said, but Ben said nothing.

The elevator dinged. The eighteen—what was left of it, anyway—lit up. The eight glowed evenly, but the upper half of the one had gone dark. Its base flickered intermittently, a washed-out, sickly orange. Staring at it, Ben felt a wave of dizziness swamp him. The elevator doors drew back, disclosing the tee of another decaying foyer, the corridor receding in shadow to either side. A heap of damp carpet remnants mildewed in one corner, and a moist organic stench hung like a curtain in the chill air. Water dripped somewhere faraway.

"Jesus," Abel whispered, kicking at a discarded beer bottle, and Ben, fuming, felt the knot draw tighter.

"You tell it," he told Lomax. "You seem to have all the answers."

"All right, then," Lomax said. "It turned out to be a home invasion. Apartment 1824. A woman and her family, three kids. The woman managed to make a 911 call before one of the snipers yanked the phone out of the wall. That

was it for a while. The police got their own marksmen
into position on the neighboring buildings, shut down the
elevators, put SWAT teams in the stairwells."

They were moving toward the far end of the corridor
now, where it hooked toward the south wing. The wind
had picked up again. Ben could hear it sobbing through a
broken window somewhere. He tried to focus on that—the
wind and the graffiti scrawled on the cinder block walls,
the occasional bare lightbulb casting down its jaundiced circle of radiance. Anything but the sound of Lomax's smug
little monologue. Anything but the weathered numbers
painted beside each apartment door—1810, 1811, 1812—
as they drew inexorably nearer and slipped by him, into
the shadows.

"The SWAT teams moved in when the shooting started
again. They took down the first shooter—the *only* shooter
so far as they knew—right away."

They turned the corner then, into the south wing, the
corridor stretching out before them. Ben glanced at the first
door on his right—1818—and then let his gaze slip ahead,
farther down the narrowing perspective of the hallway,
counting doorways. Twenty, twenty-two . . . twenty-four.
1824. So Lomax had said, but he needn't have bothered,
not for Ben's sake, anyway. Ben had been knowing that
number for years—all his life, it seemed—knowing it, longing for it, dreading it, even dreaming of it, and here it was
at last, scant yards away—twenty feet, thirty at the most—
the door standing open, a rectangle of ashen light in the
deepening gloom, like a gateway into the past.

"And then?" Lara asked.

"And then the second one came through a bedroom
door. In the shooting that followed, six people died."

"Christ," she whispered.

"Cops killed five of them," Ben said.

The words slipped out without his volition, his voice low
and tense. He felt their attention shift to him once again,
the entire group—Keel and Lara and Abel Williams, Ramsey Lomax, too—slowing to gaze back at him, mere shadows, silhouetted against the gray aperture of that doorway,
1824, their faces unreadable.

How had he fallen so far behind?

"What?" Lara said.

"The cops. Six people died, seven if you count the one the sniper shot on the plaza. The cops killed five of them."

"He's right, I'm afraid," Lomax said. "When the second sniper burst in—"

"The snipers, sure," Ben said. He drew closer to them, ten feet, five, closer still, until he could see them, summoning their pale features out of the shadows. "They killed the snipers, all right. Not to mention one of the two little girls inside the apartment—the eleven-year-old. Also the girl's mother—"

"Wait a minute—" Keel said.

"She was thirty-seven. Their *mother*," Ben said, shooting a glance at Keel. "*Not* their grandmother. They even shot a couple of other cops. One of them died, too."

"Don't blame the cops," Keel said. "Listen to the man's story, why don't you. Your two gangbangers there started—"

"*My* gangbangers?" Ben said quietly.

Fletcher Keel fell abruptly silent. No one said anything. They just stood there, listening to the wind slowly die away, leaving only the regular cadence of their respiration to fill the silence, and that drip of water, close now, and steady, like something else in the darkness with them. Breathing.

"I'm curious," Ben said. "I want to know: how do you figure they're my gangbangers? Because of the color of my skin, is that what you had in mind?"

Keel shifted on his feet. "That's not fair. That's not what I meant at—"

"What did you mean, then? Explain it, why don't you? I'm all ears."

"Listen," Abel said. "Everybody just calm down. Nobody wants to—"

"I do," Ben said. "I want to."

The silence spun itself out in the agonizing intervals between each *plink* of water. Ben stepped closer to Keel and stood there, staring up at the bigger man, his shape bulking large in that strange swimming light. Blood hammered at his temples. The knot in his chest pulled tighter and tighter still.

Keel, looking down at him, laughed softly. "Shit," he said, and turned away. He took a step, and then another, moving swiftly, and then his foot came down with a splash in the center of a puddle, the water dripping from a pipe that had burst overhead—Ben saw it now—dripping steady and cold to pool there in a shallow depression in the concrete.

"Shit," Keel said again, louder this time, and turning back to them, he kicked savagely at something. Water arced up in a glittering spray, and an oblong brown shape skidded across the concrete to stop at Ben's feet. A football—that was his first incoherent thought, and then looking down at the thing, he saw it for what it really was: a sodden rat the size of a dinner plate, its vacant eye upturned, black and staring. Water clung in silvery droplets to its matted fur. Blood clotted its whiskers. Its tail curled out behind it, prehensile, naked, somehow obscene.

Ben prodded it with his toe. He looked up.

"People lived like fucking animals," Keel said.

"You ought to listen to yourself," Ben said. "All of you, you ought to listen to yourselves, touring this place like it's some kind of zoo, like the people who lived here weren't even people at all, like they were animals in some kind of cage, and you never even bothered to think about who put them there."

"I think Mr. Williams was right," Lomax said. "I think we all need to calm down."

"Calm down? What does that mean? Have you even been listening to the words coming out of your mouth? You're the worst of the bunch, marching around here like a tin-plated God, passing judgment on everything you see. These people, most of them, they never had a chance—"

"That's bullshit," Keel said. "They had as much chance as anyone else,"

"Did they? You grow up in this kind of environment, Fletcher? What color is your skin?" Ben looked around in disbelief, from face to startled face, settling at last on Lomax. He laughed humorlessly. "You know who you remind me of? That mayor, Jane Byrne. Moved right into Cabrini-Green, said she'd had enough of the killing. People said she was brave, but there was nothing brave about what she did. How much courage does it take to live in a place like this when you got a whole entourage of cops and body-guards to take care of you? Especially when you know you can leave any time you take a notion to. You know how long she stayed, Fletcher? How about you, Abel, you got any idea how long she stayed?''

"Three weeks," Lomax said. "She stayed three weeks."

"Seems to me that's about how long *you* were planning to stay," Ben said. "And in the meantime, you've done exactly what she did, down there on the fifth floor. You brought a little piece of white America with you."

He hesitated, wanting to say more, knowing that there was nothing more to say. And even if there had been, he couldn't say it, could he? Couldn't find the air to give it voice, couldn't squeeze the words past the obstruction in his chest, that Gordian tangle of fury and resentment and—

And what?

Fear, of course.

Ben saw it now, felt it in the hollows of his bones. Fear of apartment 1824 and fear of a past he could not remember. Fear of the terrified child who still lived inside his flesh, drowning in words. That most of all, maybe. He glanced around at them, at Keel and Ramsey Lomax, at Abel Williams, at Lara, her hand outstretched as if she wanted to comfort him—

He glanced down at the rat which lay dead at his feet.

Blood glistened on its snout, in its whiskers, on the curving yellow blades of its teeth. It stared up at him from the dizzy abyss of one glossy black eye, empty of everything but the dumb enormity of its own death.

Suddenly he wanted to cry.

"Screw this," he said. "I'm going downstairs."

"Wait, Ben—" Lara said, but Ramsey Lomax interrupted.

"Mr. Prather," he said. "I'm serious about this: it's unwise to be alone here."

Ben, already moving in the direction of the elevator, didn't bother looking back. "I think I'll risk it," he said.

3

Ben came unglued in the elevator.

An observer might not have noticed, but that was the word for it all the same: unglued. His hands shook. His eyes watered. And as the elevator carried him down, unspooling the floors until at last the doors swept open, delivering him into the womblike comfort of the renovated corridor, he thought he might be sick. He stood in the foyer, waiting for the nausea to retreat; then, calmer, he made his way down the hall to his suite.

Inside, the door secured at his back, Ben stood in front of his laptop, still anxious for the comfort of words after all these years. What would Paul Cook make of him now, he wondered: thirty years old and still unattached, with nothing but his words to console him? What would Paul say about *this*, his decision to come—

—*home*—

—*here*, to Dreamland, to try piecing together a single moment in time, twenty-seven years lost? And wouldn't it be nice to ask—to have just an hour with the man, a chance to talk things over? Maybe he could talk to Abel Williams about it, see if he could arrange a person-to-person call with the dead.

Ben laughed, imagining the scene—How am I doing, old friend? Inquiring minds want to know—and then he turned on the computer. While it booted up, he slipped a Chet Baker disc into the CD player. He'd always identified with Chet, Chet Baker and Dave Brubeck, Bill Evans, all those white men stranded in the black, black world of jazz, like photo negatives of his own life.

Back at the desk, the spare trumpet line snaking through his thoughts, he opened the previous night's work and began scrolling through it, ten pages or so: impressions of

his companions mostly, descriptions of their first evening
in Dreamland.

Halfway down page six, his eye snagged.

Ben felt something sodden and inert settle in his guts,
and unbidden his mind served up an appropriate image:
the dead rat, its black and staring eye.

It was a typo, he told himself. It had to be a typo. Yet
he knew even then that it was no typo. It appeared near
the bottom of the page, two words centered on an empty
line, square in the middle of an otherwise unremarkable
sentence—a sentence that resumed uninterrupted on the
very next line. He read through it again:

> I wasn't prepared for the remarkable level of
>
> *do you*
>
> destruction. I should have been, I know; yet the
> physical reality of the place surpassed

The words—
—*do you*—
—jumped out at him. Ben stared at them, his breath
suspended, then scrolled further down. The phrase re-
curred at the top of the very next page—

> .   *do you*

—and again two-thirds of the way down, each time
breaking the flow of another sentence. Ben's interior chill
deepened, dipping into the glacial abyss on the far side
of zero.

His fingers jockeyed with the track ball, faster now. Page
seven, four broken sentences, the same phrase repeated
four times. Page eight, five times—no, six, for there toward
the bottom of the page, just before it broke, he saw the
phrase once again, this time with an expansion of the
formula—

> *do you believe*

—the sentence once again continuing despite the interruption. Ben scanned it without real comprehension. Something about Fletcher Keel, something familiar about his eyes as he had stepped into the lobby elevator—

Screw it, though.

A buzzsaw of static cut through his thoughts. It was all he could do to make sense of the words. He wanted to shut down the computer and make his way to the elevator, to walk out the front doors of Dreamland and never look back. He sat still instead, numb, his fingers working, summoning page nine into view. A pixilated column of repetition—

do you believe
do you believe
do you believe

—marched down the center of his screen. The column broadened toward the base, the sentence—a question actually, his stunned brain surmised—expanding once again to echo the first phrase he had ever heard Ramsey Lomax speak—

Do you believe in ghosts?

And even that was not what really terrified him. What terrified him, what set his pulse racing and sent raw panic clawing up the knuckles of his spine was not this mindless pattern of repetition and expansion, but the *other* lines on the page, the three or four lines of conventional prose, each separated by as many as ten or twelve iterations of that same rote phrase. Each time, the broken sentence recovered its rhythm with nary a stumble, hauling itself forward with the familiar cadence of his own voice. As if nothing at all had intervened, not a single line. As if the personality that had written and rewritten and rewritten yet again that same rote line had nothing whatsoever to do with him.

Do you believe in ghosts? read the final line on the page. Against his will, Ben's finger slipped once more over the track ball, summoning up the final page. A single sentence glimmered mockingly at the center of an otherwise empty screen:

You should.

He was still staring at it when someone knocked on his
door.

4

It was the doctor. Lara.

"Hey," she said.

Shaken—more shaken than he wanted to admit—Ben
stood in the doorway before her. The CD came to an end,
Baker's last plangent notes falling away into silence. In the
stillness, the phrase he'd seen on his computer screen—

—you should—

—seemed to reverberate endlessly, frightening not so
much because of what it said as because of what it implied
about his own hard-won equilibrium. He didn't believe in
ghosts, couldn't imagine *ever* believing in ghosts, even if
Ramsey Lomax whipped up a thousand spook stories over
the next two weeks. But the prospect of some kind of emotional collapse seemed suddenly all too plausible.

He shouldn't have come back here.

"Earth to Ben," Lara said. She snapped her fingers.
"You there?"

Ben forced a smile. "Sorry. I'm distracted, I guess. I was
trying to write." Which wasn't entirely a lie, anyway.

"Oh. Hey. I can come back if—"

He waved a hand dismissively. "No. It was for crap anyway. Trust me. I could use a break."

Inside, she sat on the love seat. He reversed the desk
chair in front of her and lowered himself into it, crossing
his arms across the back. Looking at her, he was struck
once again by her appearance: a sinewy fitness that seemed
somehow willed into being, a deliberate front for some
deeper vulnerability. She gazed back at him frankly, her
eyes a washed-out blue in her too-thin face. The heat
kicked on, wafting to him a faint lilac hint of her perfume.

"So to what do I owe the pleasure?"

"That scene upstairs." She made a face. "What a mess. I'm sorry that happened, Ben."

"You don't need to apologize for them."

"Yeah, well, maybe, maybe not. Still. You okay?"

"You get used to it. I've been writing professionally for nearly a decade—I've published in *The New Yorker*, *Esquire*, *Harper's*. And you know what? I'm still a 'black' journalist. No matter what I do, that's always the deciding factor. The color of my skin. Like I said, you get used to it." He shrugged. "The horror show go on after I left?"

"For a little while, anyway. You didn't miss much."

"No?"

"The roof," she said. "You missed the roof."

"Ah. So you got to hear the story of Dante Morris, then?"

"I got to hear it, all right."

"How old were the kids that tossed him over the side? Do you remember?"

"Nine," she said. "Nine and ten. That's what Lomax said."

"Right. And to listen to him tell it, you'd probably think black kids around here routinely chucked five-year-olds off roofs." Ben shook his head. "You know what really gets to me, though? You put a bunch of white kids in a place like this, the same exact things are going to happen. But people like Lomax, they're never going to believe it."

"Yeah. Well." She pursed her lips, hesitated, and then looked up at him. "Anyway. I just wanted to see if you were okay."

"I am. I'm fine."

"You sure? Because you know what, you don't look so hot, Ben."

"Is that your medical opinion?"

"Nope." She lifted her hands. "Just that of an interested acquaintance."

"Well, I appreciate that. But you needn't be concerned. I'm fine. Really, I am."

"Okay."

At an impasse, they retreated into silence—a fraught, uncertain silence. Ben's thoughts circled relentlessly back to the phrases floating on the computer screen at his back.

What would Lara think if she could see them? Or better yet, what would the doctor Lara had trained to become think of them? He probably didn't want the answer to that one, did he? Still pondering that, he looked up, back into that narrow face, its blue eyes intent.

They spoke at the same time.

"What are you writing?" she asked, the question tangling with one of his own—

"What brings you here, anyway?"

They laughed together, but to Ben's ears there was something strained about it. There was in his case anyway, because, let's face it, her question cut a little too close to the merciless arc of his own anxieties. So he smiled, and said, "Nothing, really. Finger exercises, just trying to keep the muscles toned. I'm not even working on a story"—and if she detected the lie, she wasn't letting on. "Really, though," he added. "I have to admit, I'm curious. What made you decide to tag along on this little expedition?"

Now it was her turn to smile, and there *was* something forced about that. "It's boring," she said too abruptly, clearly wanting to move on.

But Ben had been a journalist too long to let anything die that easily. "Let me be the judge of that."

Lara didn't bother disguising her feelings this time. Her smile withered. Her face closed like a safe. "Trust me. You don't want to hear about it. It's brain-numbing, it's so boring." She stood, smoothing her jeans over her thighs.

Ben got to his feet after her. "You leaving?"

"Yeah. I got a lot to do," she said from the door, the bald falseness of the statement—the utter inadequacy of the lie—momentarily paralyzing them both. For the truth was, none of them had much of anything to do, not for the next two weeks anyway. And both of them knew it.

Ben, weighing his options, decided to let it ride. For now anyway. "Well, thanks for coming by," he said.

Another smile, this one almost genuine, broke through the china-brittle set of Lara's face. "You bet," she said. "I'm glad you're okay."

5

After the door closed, Lara stood in the corridor, her shoulders aching with tension. Ben's footsteps retreated on the other side, and then music came on: the portable stereo in the corner, a tangle of horns, the steady throb of a bass line, unstructured, almost tuneless. It was meaningless to her. Her musical interests—such as they were—didn't extend much beyond whatever happened to be playing on the car radio. She couldn't remember the last time she'd actually bought a CD. Ben, on the other hand, seemed to have dozens of them, in stacks on the coffee table and the spare cushion of the love seat, a precarious tower of them on the floor by the desk. Thinking of that, she had a glimmering of the gulf yawning between them, an ocean of difference, a universe of it, far transcending mundane matters of musical taste: gender, profession, race most of all; the colors of their skin, black and white, the insurmountable and opaque barrier of the other.

Whatever had possessed her to try bridging that gap?

Lana would have known the answer. *You're the maternal one. You're the one likes to take care of everybody.*

Right. And what a goddamn disaster *that* life strategy had turned out to be.

Sighing, Lara studied the hallway. To the right, it lengthened in narrowing perspective, carpeted, well lit: the elevator bay and the cluster of common rooms, the distant suites belonging to Abel and Ramsey Lomax. To the left, it terminated abruptly in a slanting wall with a metal fire door, the dividing line between Lomax's comfortable living quarters and the unrenovated wing beyond. Two hallways, two worlds, she thought, and Ben's words came back to her: *You brought a little piece of white America with you.*

Shivering a little, she stepped closer, angled one hand over her eyes, and peered through the wire-reinforced window set in the center of the door. Everything beyond was shadowy and desolate, obscured by the tempered glass and the gloom on the other side. What little she could see—a rusting kitchen range, an ancient set of box springs leaning precariously against one wall—looked pretty much like every other square inch of Dreamland: a blasted and hopeless ruin. Why on earth had Ramsey Lomax come here? Why had she? Which, come to think of it, was more or less what Ben had just asked her.

Secrets, she thought. Everyone here had secrets.

Even her.

6

Alone in his suite, Abel Williams was nursing a secret of his own:

He'd been hearing things.

His hardcore clientele—the true believers who had watched *Messages* with a near-religious devotion, had actually bought his book, and who even now, in this brave new post-celebrity post-*Messages* era, waited months for his high-dollar consultations—might not have been surprised. Yet to Abel himself, this new sensitivity came as a hard trial indeed. His professional life, if he was to look himself in the mirror every morning, required him to hold two contradictory ideas simultaneously in mind: the certainty that he could not actually do what he claimed to be able to do, and an equivalent conviction that he was not exploiting his customers. In Abel's view, it was Susie all over again. He returned solid value on the dollar: his clients heard what they needed to hear. Ergo, he wasn't a con artist.

But he never—*never*—believed he could speak with the dead.

Someone—Fitzgerald, maybe? Keats?—had called this kind of conflicted thinking the mark of genius. If that was the case, what did it mean when the paradox unraveled?

Abel had a sneaking suspicion that Fitzgerald, the crafty old drunk, might have called it insanity.

And he might have been right.

Standing, Abel moved across the room toward the window. The suite was spare, neat, impersonal as a hotel room—no books, no knickknacks, no photographs. His presence had left no mark here. Unlike the others, Abel had shipped almost no personal effects to Lomax, partly from a desire to protect his privacy, mostly because he knew that success in this little enterprise hinged upon his absolute focus on the problem at hand: deducing Ramsey Lomax's reasons for coming to Dreamland.

Everything—the stage he longed to reclaim, the glare of klieg lights, the applause of millions—was riding on his success. Oh, Lomax was paying him, and well—Abel wasn't naive about money. But he knew himself well enough to know that money wasn't what he really wanted. What he wanted—what he'd *always* wanted, from the moment he had opened his eyes and stared for the first time into that cage of shadows above his boyhood bed—was the romance of celebrity. And Lomax—with his connections in the industry—could give it all back to him. All Abel had to do was find the key and fit it to the lock of Lomax's needs. It was that simple: the tumblers would fall into place, the safe would swing open, and all the treasures of the world—the life he had lost—would be Abel's for the taking. The last thing he needed was distractions.

The voices were a distraction.

Brushing aside the curtains, he stared out the window. His suite faced the plaza—or what had been the plaza. Gazing out into the blighted twilight, he tried to imagine the plaza as it might have been, a bucolic pocket in the heart of the city—or failing that, to envision the place it had finally become, a wasteland of cracked and weed-blown asphalt, abandoned cars, the limbs of a dismembered jungle gym jutting like a praying mantis above the pavement. But even then, at its worst, Dreamland had been a human place: a place where children played beneath the watchful eyes of nervous mothers, where laundry flapped from open windows, drying in the arms of the August sun. But it was human no longer. Now it was a maze of sundered girders and shattered concrete, here a tumulus of debris, there the gaping socket of an abandoned foundation, like a blinded eye, aswim in dregs of ashen snow.

Dead. All dead.

Just like the voices.

He'd been able to ignore them at first—to attribute that first echo of Theresa Matheson's death—

—please no—

—and the accompanying glimpse of the black kid working himself between her legs, to an overactive imagination: the stress of a difficult situation, the pressure of an unfamiliar environment. But yesterday, in the lobby with the others, he'd felt yet another whisper of energy. And as the elevator doors slid closed before him, he thought he'd heard voices—faraway, nearly inaudible, an incoherent babble like the disembodied echo of a badly tuned radio station, but voices all the same. Last night, adrift in that paralyzed half-dreaming state that is the near frontier of sleep, an assembly of whispers had contended with his thoughts; and though, as the night deepened, he had fallen into a deep and dreamless slumber, he had woken late and unrested, his ears attuned to that odd vacuum that is the aftermath of sound. And it seemed to Abel in that moment fuzzy with sleep, that someone, or something, must have spoken his name, and it was that which had awakened him.

Remembering that eerie certainty, he clutched the window ledge with whitened fingers. He stared out into the darkening plaza for another moment, and then he turned away, letting the curtain fall back into place.

This afternoon, during Lomax's little tour, things had taken a turn for the worse.

No one had noticed; Abel could be thankful for that much. But that didn't alter the basic fact: something had happened in apartment 1824, and not just a twenty-seven-year-old police raid either. Abel knew about that, of course—that and Theresa Matheson's death in the lobby and Dante Morris' fatal plunge and half a dozen less-publicized horrors. He'd long since learned the value of preparation. But he'd been listening to Lomax anyway, less out of interest in the events themselves than in what the telling of them might reveal about his host.

Yet in apartment 1824, not long after Prather's melodramatic little exit, Abel's attention had drifted. It was a mystery to him. One minute, he'd been utterly focused—Lomax had been saying something about the second shooter, hiding in the bedroom during the opening salvos of the firefight. In the instant that followed, Abel found his gaze drawn back to a drift of debris he'd hardly noticed in his first quick glance around the room: a rat's nest of shredded newspaper, rusting beer cans, and something else, something it had taken his brain a moment to process. What was it?

He stepped closer.

Then he saw it: an old photograph, one corner peeking from underneath a crumpled Big Mac wrapper. Hunkering down, Abel brushed the grease-stained wrapper aside, and plucked the picture out of the morass. It was water-stained and blurry, bleached almost to illegibility: a washed-out snapshot of a black kid, a girl of maybe nine or ten, suspended forever in that awkward moment of transition between childhood and adolescence. He lifted it higher, scraping at a patch of dirt with his thumbnail, only half-listening to Lomax—

". . . almost the whole family died in the cross fire. Only the little boy survived unscathed. . . ."

That's when it had happened: a voice inside his head, a moment of stark and heartbreaking clarity, like one of those trick atmospheric acoustics that sends an AM radio signal bouncing halfway around the world, so that for the space of a startled breath, spinning down a dial on the far side of the planet, you catch a fragment of some utterly enigmatic transmission bearing down upon you from the black, black sky—a single haunting phrase, or a melody of such surpassing beauty that you despair of ever hearing its like again. It was like that, or like a garbled broadcast from the stars, snatched by chance from the background crackle of the universe. It was like a voice on a party line, overheard by chance, and what it said was,

I'm here, Abel.

And in that moment, Abel knew without the faintest shadow of a doubt that it was the voice of the girl locked inside that photograph, and that she had been speaking from the world beyond the fence.

That was when Lara had touched his shoulder. "What'd you find?"

Somehow, Abel had managed a shrug. "Nothing," he'd

said, holding it out for her inspection. "Just an old photograph." Yet when Lara had turned away, he hadn't discarded it, had he? No, he'd tucked it into the pocket of his jeans, and as he had ascended the steep and winding metal stairs to the roof, apartment 1824 falling away beneath him, that phrase—

—*the world beyond the fence*—

—had echoed in his thoughts.

Yes, and it came back to him again as he crossed the room and sat down on the love seat. The world beyond the fence. What the hell did it mean? he wondered. And why did it make him think of his father?

Such were his thoughts as he sat there among the slow-encroaching shadows, staring down at the hands twisting in his lap as he might have stared at a stranger's hands, fearing that at any moment one of them might creep inside the pocket of his jeans and pull the photo out where he could see it.

Working Out

1

In the long restless hours before dawn, Fletcher Keel dreamed of women.

There had been a time when he had not lacked for female companionship. He'd had more than his share during his army years. At twenty-three, he had almost married. The girl—and that's what she had been, a girl, both of them hardly more than children, really—had been a honeyed blonde named Lisa. They had met of all places in a bar at JFK in 1979, Lisa headed home from Columbia for the holidays, Keel just headed home, his four-year stint in the service behind him. After a pleasant half hour's flirtation, Keel paid for their drinks and struck off to find his gate, suffused with a dreamy ache of nostalgia for an imagined life with a stranger he would never see again.

Forty minutes later, stowing his carry-on in the overhead bin of a crowded 737, he caught a glimpse of honeyed-blond hair ten rows back. Negotiations with a flight attendant ensued: a change of seat, a moment of shared laughter at the coincidence, another drink. By the time they began their descent, Keel had coaxed free her number. By year's end he'd managed a date. And during a stolen weekend in April, she had accepted a ring. Summer arrived at last: Lisa graduated, plans for the wedding commenced in earnest.

And then, in a span of seconds on one steaming August afternoon, Keel's dreams came apart around him. Like everything else in his life—like his career and his self-image, like his father's legacy of honor—the relationship disintegrated during the long months of investigation and the trial that followed. By the time he emerged from the process a free man, paralyzed by shame, Lisa was gone.

There had been other women in the months and years that followed: a plethora of brittle moths attracted by the flame of his notoriety to start with, and then, during his aimless drift south and west, a series of women he picked up in bars, a calculating, aging, bitter lot for the most part, gaunt with drink and desperation, distaff mirrors of his own ener-vated soul.

Somewhere along the way, he lost interest in the entire enterprise of sex. The frequency of the one-night stands dwindled, replaced at first by occasional dalliances with women one step short of prostitutes—backseat blow jobs in exchange for a dime bag, massage-parlor hand jobs—then by his own practical ministrations, at last by nothing at all.

He didn't miss it.

He drifted from city to city, job to job—mall security guard in Omaha, bartender in Santa Fe, bouncer in Austin—hanging on in each place until the booze and pills caught up with him. By the time Klavan bought him that shot of Maker's Mark in San Antonio, Keel doubted he could have gotten it up even if he'd wanted to.

Susan Avery changed all that.

He met her at his first AA meeting: a lean no-nonsense forty-something with graying hair tied in a loose ponytail and teeth yellowed by years of nicotine, coffee, and booze. Five years sober, she'd sworn off everything but the coffee, and though she was nothing to write home about in the looks department, Keel, studying her across the circle, couldn't help reflecting that it wasn't as if he had a home to write to anyway. Besides, something in the smoky ring of her laughter reminded him of Lisa. And how long had it been since he had known someone to whom laughter came so easily?

He struck up a conversation after the meeting. The con-versation led to coffee in a diner down the street, and that led to lunch later in the week. In the days that followed she became his sponsor, and ultimately more than his spon-sor: a friend. It had been a long time since he'd had one of those, too, and maybe that's where it came from, the growing attraction he sensed between them: the product of her simple kindness, and nothing more. Things had come to a head one night toward the end of November when he dropped her off at her apartment after dinner. She had leaned forward to collect her purse, and somehow—how?—he found himself brushing her cheek with one hand, tilting her face to meet his own. The kiss lasted maybe thirty seconds, a minute at the most. The kiss lasted a lifetime. And when she drew away, Keel felt an erotic jolt charged with nearly three decades of loneliness and yearning shudder through him.

Susan had smiled sadly, her eyes glistening in the dim interior of the car. She touched the back of his hand, still cupped along the line of her jaw. She brought it to her lap and clutched his fingers. "Me, too," she said softly. "But you're only two months sober, Fletcher, and we can't risk complicating that. Not right now."

"But—"

She laid a finger against his lips. "Shhh," she said. "There's plenty of time for that. We've got the rest of our lives." She leaned forward and kissed him once again, on the forehead this time.

Then she got out of the car.

Watching her walk away, Keel felt as a castaway might have felt, watching a distant ship drop unhailed over the rim of the world. Yet his libido, newly awakened, could not be so easily assuaged. In the gym where he'd started working out, he took a fresh interest in the Lycra-encased flesh gyrating beyond the glassed-in wall where the aerobics classes met. And at the restaurant where he washed dishes, he suddenly found himself more tempted by the mid-afternoon crowd of sleek professional women in business suits than by the liquor bottles stacked in shining rows along the mirrored backboard of the bar. His breath caught at the rounded pressure of a breast against the silken blouse containing it, or a wisp of perfume wafted to him by some vagary of air.

And so he dreamed of women—of Susan, of Lisa, of the uniformed attendant on the flight that had ferried him back to Dreamland, cocking the alluring arc of her hip at him as she bent to take a drink order; and, yes, of too-thin Lara McGovern as well, her boyish frame, her smooth white flesh. He dreamed of women, a kaleidoscope of shining eyes and slanting veils of hair, of lipsticked mouths, of buttocks and breasts. Lips that met his lips, painted nails against his stomach, the slippery lubricity of passage.

Outside, the sun heaved a fiery red crescent above the horizon, bathing the ruins of Dreamland in blood. Keel cried out in his sleep as a wave of pleasure wracked him, and Susan Avery's husky voice echoed through his dreams. *Get away from that place, Fletcher,* it said. *Get away before it's too late.*

2

Prather was in the gym when Keel got there just after ten.

Keel hesitated in the doorway when he saw him. He had woken after nine from dreams that once again eluded memory—though judging from the evidence they had been considerably more pleasant than the dreams that had sent him surging out of sleep that first night at Dreamland. Yet he felt strangely disquieted all the same, an uneasiness that pervaded his thoughts as he breakfasted alone on cereal and coffee at the table in the kitchen.

Sweat it out, that had been Susan's advice—advice he had more or less lived by in those first difficult weeks of sobriety, sometimes spending four or five hours a day at the gym, pumping iron or running the endless looping circuit of the indoor track until his muscles burned and fatigue closed around him in a gray fog. Whatever it took. The fog of exhaustion was preferable to the fog of inebriation: at least he could sleep.

Only sleep seemed to be the problem just now, didn't it? he thought, rinsing his dishes and loading them into the dishwasher. The exercise would help that, too, though. That's what Susan would have said, anyway. And the truth was, he agreed. Sober, Keel had felt reawakening the long-dormant love of discipline that his father had sought to instill in him, and that his military and police experience had reinforced. Order, discipline, integrity—those had been the touchstones of his father's life. Keel's too, or so he had thought. Before Dreamland. Before everything came crashing down around him.

Keel grimaced. *That* was the true touchstone of his life. That and the unbearable weight of betrayal, the shame his father had not lived to witness.

God knows he had tried to redeem it. For five long years, he'd tried. But in the end he just couldn't do it. The shame was there, woven into the fabric of his bones.

And not all the exercise in the world would ever sweat it out.

In his room, he threw on a pair of sweats and a San Diego State tee shirt with the sleeves hacked off. Draping a towel around his shoulders, he strode down the corridor to the gym—and that's when he saw Prather, flat on his back at the weight machine, doing bench presses. Keel's immediate instinct was to turn away. His second impulse— the one Susan would have endorsed—was the better one: make peace. There were days to go here, after all. They couldn't dodge each other forever. Besides, he'd never meant to offend the guy.

So he stepped inside, nodding a brisk acknowledgment. The gym wasn't much—a secondhand Nautilus machine, a couple of treadmills—but it was adequate. And just being there, even with Prather present, took the edge off Keel's anxiety. The regimen of the gym appealed to him: the comforting repetition of the exercises, the sharp odor of perspiration, the tinny blast of muscle-head music—testosterone-charged stuff like AC/DC and Metallica—on the sound system. It was as close as he'd ever come to recapturing the camaraderie he'd known in the army and during his brief career as a cop: that sense of men united by shared goals, with the skills and resolve to achieve them.

He should have done this yesterday, he thought, slotting the pin high in the stack of weights. He warmed up with a set of light curls, watching Prather on the weight bench.

"You got too much weight on there," he found himself saying when Prather finished.

Prather, sitting up, exhaled slowly. "What?"

"You're fighting yourself. It's counterproductive. Here." Keel circled the machine and knelt to readjust the pin. "Try that."

Prather lay back obediently, took a breath, gripped the bar. "Slowly now," Keel said. "Watch your form."

Prather did ten reps, breathing evenly. The weight moved steadily, the braided steel line singing in its reel. He sat up and wiped his forehead with the back of his hand. His brown skin glistened with perspiration. "It doesn't feel like I'm doing as much, though."

"Doesn't matter." Keel sat on the facing bench. "Form is everything. Plus, a guy like you, you're not looking to bulk up, am I right? What you want to do is use light weights, lots of reps."

"You sound like an expert."

Keel shrugged. "Just trying to help."

It came out more abrupt than he intended. Uncertain how to undo the impression, he moved to the other side of the Nautilus, readjusted the weight, and did another set of curls. He could feel himself relaxing into the rhythm of the exercise, the hypnotic cadence of his breathing, the pleasant ache of muscles surrendering their poison. He did another set, moved to the next station, and began to work his lats, the knots in his shoulders unclenching. It was like drinking or pills or sex, exercise—the same sense of tension abating, the relentless rush of his thoughts dropping away into the simple physicality of the moment. Like Zen or something. He understood the role of endorphins in the process, but it felt like more than a glandular process, purer, almost spiritual.

Prather broke his reverie.

"How long you been working out?" he said.

Keel extended his arms and released the bar, letting the line spin over the pulley. The weights clanked into place. "Years, I guess. I used to be into it pretty heavy. I laid off a long time, though."

"You wouldn't know it."

Keel looked up, searching the phrase for some hint at reconciliation—a move, however awkward, to paper over the incident upstairs. "Yeah, well," he said. "Some things just come natural. Like you. You've been writing all your life, I bet."

Something—it was hard to say exactly what—passed over the other man's face. "Yeah. You could say that."

"You always lived in California?"

Prather hesitated. "I was born here. I grew up in Santa Monica."

"No kidding. Santa Monica, huh?"

"Yeah."

"I spent some time in California. Long Beach, working on the docks. The late eighties, it would have been."

"I thought Lomax said you'd been in law enforcement."

Keel shook his head. "I was an MP in the army for a while and, then, when I got out, I worked for a year or two as a cop. That was a long time ago, though."

"Yeah? How long?"

"You'd have been a kid then."

"What happened?"

"It wasn't for me, that's all." His voice held steady as he said it, but even after all these years, the sentiment rankled.

"So what have you been doing all this time?"

"This and that. Tending bar, construction, some private security now and then."

"This was all in California?"

Keel forced himself to keep calm, forced himself not to think about how little of the last two decades he could even really remember. "I lived practically everywhere," he said casually. "California, Texas, New Mexico. Even Vegas for a while. Vegas was a kick."

It had been, too—until the booze caught up with him the way it always did. He'd landed a gig at one of the casinos and had managed to keep himself reasonably sober for a couple of months. He'd actually started to think he might be able to turn things around this time, and then, boom, one night he took a drink and fell off the edge of the world. When he showed up at work a week later, still shaky from the binge, his boss, this beefy kid half his age named Frank, had merely shaken his head. Don't get me wrong, he said, I like you fine, but the man says you got to walk, you got to walk. Nothing personal.

But it was always personal, wasn't it?

"So what," Ben said, "you're telling me you just drifted for the last twenty years?"

But it hadn't even been drifting, had it? Most of the time he'd been running—from the past, from the charges still pending back home, from fresh trouble brewed up in booze-soaked binges. And that reminded him of why he'd finally left Vegas. That reminded him of—

Keel shook his head, refusing the thought. He looked up, forcing himself to smile. "Got those wandering feet, I guess." He did a self-mocking little soft shoe, surprising a laugh out of Prather. "A man's just got to move." Then, as if to prove his point, he walked to the next station—leg presses—and sat down. "What about you?" he said. "How come your family headed west?"

"It was just me. I was adopted, actually."

"No shit? You know, there's something I've always wondered about that. You mind if I ask you?"

"What's that?"

"Did you know you were adopted your whole life or did your parents just up and tell you one day, or what?"

Prather laughed again. "It wasn't really an issue."

"No? How's that?"

"My parents are white."

There was a showstopper for you, Keel thought: the very thing they'd been dancing around all day yesterday, and here the guy just heaves it up on the table in front of him, like a sackful of anvils. "Oh." Keel leaned forward to adjust the pin in the stack of weights, the faint gunmetal scent of the mechanism rising to his nostrils. Something—he couldn't say for sure what—compelled him to continue. If Prather could talk about it, why couldn't he?

"About yesterday," he said, without looking up.

"What about it?"

"I didn't mean to offend you."

Prather didn't answer right away. When he did speak, his tone was cool: "Yeah, I know. That's part of the problem, isn't it?"

Keel leaned back. He positioned his shoes on the footrests, took hold of the handles jutting up at either side of the seat, and gave the press a tentative push, lifting the stack of weights an inch or so before he let it settle back into place. "What do you mean?"

"It's so deeply ingrained most people don't even realize it's there."

"What is?"

"The whole race thing."

Lightly, Keel said, "You calling me a racist?"

"Who isn't?"

"What's that supposed to mean?"

"Let me put it this way. You were a cop, right? You see a black guy in a nice car, a Lexus, a BMW, whatever—what's your first thought?"

"Oh, come on," Keel said.

He stared at Prather for a moment, and then he shook his head. Taking a deep breath, he did a set of leg extensions, concentrating on his breathing. The muscles in his thighs and calves burned, but the exercise brought none of its usual clarity. Nor did it dispel the hostility Keel felt welling up inside him. The nerve of these people. It was nothing he hadn't seen before—hell, you saw it every day, didn't you? Nothing was ever good enough. More than a century later and every white man on the planet was still somehow personally responsible for slavery. Grunting, he clenched the handgrips and shoved himself back against the seat, muscling the weight to its highest point. He held it there a moment and let it drop with a crash, aware of the constant pressure of Prather's scrutiny.

"What?" he said.

"The only reason you're angry is you know I'm right."

Keel stood, reaching for his towel. "Bullshit."

"Why don't you answer the question, then?"

Keel turned to face him. "I've got an idea. Why don't you answer a couple questions instead?"

"I don't have anything to hide."

"How old were you when you were adopted?"

"Four. I was four years old."

"You pretty much lived in Santa Monica your whole life, then?"

"So?"

"Well, it's not exactly the 'hood is it?"

"What are you trying to say?"

"What about your dad, he a lawyer or something?"

"He was—he *is*—a stockbroker."

Keel snorted in disgust. "See, that's just exactly what I mean. You know what my dad did? He went to Europe in 1944 and got his ass shot off in the Ardennes Forest. And then he came home and he took a job pushing a broom around a factory for the next thirty years 'cause that's all he was able to do. And he never complained, not once until the day he dropped dead of a heart attack, right there with the broom in his hand. The man *never* complained."

"So what's your point?"

"My point is, you walk around this place slinging all this crap about solidarity with your brothers and the man keeping your people down, but you had everything handed to you. Everything. Nothing personal, you understand, I'm just saying."

Keel stopped abruptly, out of breath. He mopped his forehead with the towel. He glared at Prather. All he'd wanted to do was work out in peace, maybe mend a few fences, and what he had to do instead was, he had to listen to this crap.

He shook his head in disgust.

The thing was, he was right. And both of them knew it. "My point is," he said, "when you get right down to it, you're as white as any of the rest of us. Hell, the fact is, you're maybe even whiter."

And then he turned on his heel and stalked out.

3

The hallway was deserted.

Keel stood there, letting the anger dwindle to an ember inside him, and then he turned toward his suite, the enormous span of the day stretching before him: hours of time and nothing to fill them. He could always come back to the gym when Prather wasn't around, but in the meantime . . .

A shower, he supposed. Maybe some pool.

Halfway to his room, a noise—what?—halted him in his tracks. His first thought was that it must have been the furnace clearing its throat: it had that same subaudible quality—the susurration of air in hidden ductwork or a murmur of faraway traffic, heard but unheard, the constant backdrop of your thoughts.

His second thought was that someone had called his

name: his real name, the one he'd been born with. It
seemed to hang in the air—

—*John*—

—a sound that was not a sound but only its echo in the
memory, musical and silvery: a woman's voice.

The hair along his arms prickled. He felt a stirring in
his groin.

Keel turned, gazing the length of the corridor—past the
elevator bay and the cluster of common rooms to the far
end, the suites belonging to Lomax and Abel Williams, the
door into the unrenovated wing, the south stairwell with its
glimmering red EXIT beacon. Memory beckoned: the moment in the lobby, that sense of presence stirring. And
something else, something further back that he didn't want
to think about, that he *wouldn't* think about—

Instead, he listened, listened with every fiber of his body,
listened as few people even knew a man *could* listen. He
listened as he had been trained to listen, with the taut sus-
pension of being that comes when your life hangs on de-
tecting an enemy in the next room: a stealthy scrape of
boot leather, a hiss of indrawn breath. He *listened*.

And he heard nothing.

Not a footfall on the plushly carpeted floor, not a grunt
of exertion from the weight room. Not even the timpani of
his own restless heart. It was his mind playing tricks on him,
that's all, a product of Lomax's relentless litany of horrors.

Screw it.

Keel turned back toward his room—and once again a
noise stopped him in his tracks. This time there was no
mistaking it: It *was* a woman's voice—

—*Lisa it sounded like Lisa*—

—soft, alluring, beckoning him the length of the corridor.
John, it whispered, *John,* and almost against his will, Keel
found himself responding, flesh stirring, blood throbbing at
his temples. He lifted his hand. He took a hesitant step
back down the hallway, toward the south stairwell, and
then another, and then he forced himself to stop. He stood
rigidly, listening, a muscle leaping in his jaw—

"Fletcher?"

He came to himself with a start. The hallway stretched
before him, shorter now. The south stairwell loomed closer.
Had he come so far?

Turning, he saw the doctor, Lara, standing hipshot in the doorway of the infirmary, her arms crossed over her breasts, her head cocked quizzically. Her eyes narrowed, and he became suddenly—embarrassingly—conscious of his enormous arousal, his penis straining against the clinging fleece of his sweats.

"You okay?" she said, and suddenly the night's dreams flooded back to him, the long smooth lines of her thighs, the taste of her flesh, her nipples ripening under his tongue.

He licked his lips, dredging words from the dry lakebed of his belly. "Yeah," he said. "I'm—I'm fine."

Then with as much dignity as he could muster, he started past her, down the endless corridor to his suite. Inside, with the door locked behind him, he masturbated furiously.

4

In the long gray light of the afternoon, Ben and Abel sat in the lounge. Keel, on the far side of the room, stalked around the pool table, cue in hand. In the intervals between the crack of billiard balls came the constant electrical whir of the treadmill.

"So what do you know about automatic writing?" Ben said.

Abel looked up from his book.

"What?"

"Automatic writing. What do you know about it?"

"Why do you want to know?"

"Curious, that's all."

Abel thought about that.

"The thing is," he said finally, "whenever a writer gets curious, I tend to wind up getting slammed in print."

With an air of cool deliberation, he turned back to his book.

"I'm not even doing an article," Ben said. "I'm just talking."

"You're big on puns, you guys." Abel turned a page with a snap. " 'Collect Calls from the Dead.' 'Grave Matters.'

'Dead Wrong'—that one's my favorite. 'Abel Williams and the Big Business of Psychic Fraud,' that was the subtitle. It was in *The Atlantic*, a guy named Martin Falco wrote it. Maybe he's a friend of yours." He glanced up. "So no offense, okay? But if it's all right with you, I'd just as soon sit this one out."

After a moment of pointed silence, Ben turned away. He gazed out the window, where an ashen line of distant buildings sketched itself against the gunmetal sky. Across the room Keel rattled a ball around the perimeter of a hole—Ben heard it drop at last, barreling down through the guts of the table— and as the hum of the treadmill went on and on, he recalled a gerbil he'd had when he was a kid, running the endless circuit of his exercise wheel, and he thought of the arc of his own life, drawing him inevitably back to this place, to this building, to Dreamland, scaling the heavens above his head, eighteen stories coring the leaden January sky. He thought of apartment 1824 and he thought of his own suite down the hall. He thought of his laptop waiting on the desk, its screen glimmering watchfully among the shadows, and he said, "The thing is, it's really *not* okay with me."

Something in his voice seemed to give Abel Williams pause. He folded the corner of his page and looked up, studying Ben. "You're persistent, I'll give you that much."

"You don't know the half of it," Ben said.

"Why is that, I wonder?"

Ben said nothing.

"There's something to this, isn't there? Something personal."

Across the room, Keel broke a freshly racked triangle of balls.

And still, Ben said nothing.

"Funny, how you guys act when the shoe's on the other foot, isn't it?" Abel tilted his head to the ceiling, musing. "Automatic writing. Bogus. I think that's the conventional wisdom."

"I'm not asking for the conventional wisdom."

"When it comes to automatic writing, even true believers aren't true believers anymore."

"Why not?"

"All that nineteenth-century crap has been pretty convincingly disproved. Cheesecloth apparitions, ectoplasm, physical mediums. It's actually a little embarrassing, isn't it?"

"You don't sound much like a believer yourself," Ben said.

"I know what I can do, that's all. I believe in that."

"What *do* you do, Abel?"

"How can I explain it? It's like describing color to someone who's been blind from birth. You don't have the sensory experience you'd need to understand." He shrugged. "It's like I told you in the lobby the other day. I sense . . . energies. They have the weight of personality, they have a weight of knowing. Sometimes I he—" he said, and then he broke off abruptly.

In the moment of hesitation, as he watched a shadow flit across the other man's face, a flicker of intuition ignited in Ben's mind. Nothing to fire his thoughts—not yet—but it was something, anyway: a halting glow that might yet flare into the warmth of knowledge. "Sometimes you what?" he said, cautioning himself not to push too hard.

Abel Williams smiled. "See how clever you are? This isn't about me, remember? You wanted background, that's all. Automatic writing."

"You already said it was bunk."

"As proof of survival beyond death, yes."

"But?"

"Let me give you an example: there was a nineteenth-century medium, I forget her name. But in her trance state, her spirit guide used a lot of automatic writing."

"Her spirit guide?"

"Her 'control' in the afterlife." Abel waved his hand. "Victor Hugo, at one point. A little while later, a guy named Cagliostro, a courtier at the court of Louis XVI. A little while after that Marie Antoinette herself."

"Dead peasants just aren't that talkative, are they?" Ben said. "Too hard to dig up the necessary facts."

"Dead peasants would be that much harder to disprove, too, wouldn't they?"

"Are you speaking from professional experience?"

"See, there you go again," Abel said, but he didn't seem to take offense. He leaned forward, setting aside his book. "This isn't about me, remember? The point of the story is that each of the control personalities wrote a markedly dif-

ferent script than the medium herself did. Or each other for
that matter. Spiritualists took that as evidence for survival."

"So what happened?"

"Like I said, a medium who channels the rich and famous
is easy to check up on. Turns out her spirit controls made
claims that violated established historical record. Plus, their
handwriting didn't match the surviving letters of the historical figures she claimed to be channeling."

"So she was a fraud."

"*That's* where it gets complicated."

Abel sat back, crossing his arms. In the silence, with the
gloom beyond the windows deepening, Ben realized that
Keel had drifted out of the room. There was no sound but
the whir of the treadmill, on and on and on.

"She's like the Energizer bunny or something," Abel
said.

"What do you mean?" Ben said.

"You know those old TV com—"

"No. The medium. 'That's where it gets complicated.' What
do you mean? She's either a fraud or she's not a fraud."

"It's not that simple," Abel said. "Most mediums fall
into a kind of self-induced trance, right? A disassociative
state independent of memory, volition. The point is she
probably believed she *was* in touch with the dead. The scientist who studied her on the other hand—his name was
Forney or Florney, something like that—concluded that her
writings were produced subconsciously."

"Like dreams."

"If you follow Freud's thinking." Abel shrugged. "Some
therapists use the technique, so there's at least some credi-
bility to the theory."

Ben sat back, thinking of Paul Cook.

Years after that visit to the Santa Monica library, Paul
had told Ben that he had suffered a form of post-traumatic
stress, that the obsessive writing was akin to the flashbacks
combat veterans sometimes experienced. The horrific imagery had been a measure not of his own latent potential for
violence—as Ben's parents had feared—but of the violence
that had been done him. Deal with the root trauma, the
symptom would evaporate—that had been Paul's therapeu-
tic strategy.

It had worked, too—or so Ben had believed.

But what if there was more to it?

The writing had returned, after all—and this time its character had changed. It read less like flashbacks than warnings, harbingers of the perils that awaited him here in the place where it had all begun, here in Dreamland.

Do you believe in ghosts?

He knew what Paul Cook would say: the only ghosts are the ones inside your head. And the only way to exorcise them is to face them.

Ben looked up.

Night curtained the windows. The lights of the distant city beckoned him, he could feel their lure.

"Ben?"

He turned to Abel Williams.

"I'm right, aren't I?" Abel said. "This isn't just random curiosity. This is personal." Something in his tone reminded Ben of Paul—a solicitude that could hardly be resisted, an eagerness to listen that Abel's clientele must have heard there all along.

They stared at one another in silence, a silence as deep and unplumbed as the sea. Even the sound of the treadmill had stopped.

Ben felt the pressure to unburden himself, a hard knot in his throat.

He swallowed, forcing a smile.

"What do you know?" he said. "Lara's decided to take a rest."

Abel smiled back coldly, and the moment slipped past. "Maybe her batteries ran down," he said, reaching for his book.

5

Voices. Sometimes I hear voices.

That's what Abel had been about to say to Ben. *What do you do, Abel?* he'd asked—a simple enough question, one Abel had heard a thousand times before, and out it

came, the standard answer, fuzzy and pleasantly ecumeni-
cal, with just the slightest sheen of scientific plausibility. He
could have expanded—in the past, on *Larry King*, on
Oprah, he'd done exactly that.

Start with first principles, he might have said: the First
Law of Thermodynamics, basic Newtonian physics. Energy
can never be lost, it can only be transformed. What is life
but energy, death but transformation?

He could have said that, he'd said it a thousand times in
the past, but he hadn't. Instead he'd almost let it slip, a
truth that had never been a truth before, not until he came
to this place, not until he came to Dreamland, not until he
had fished that photograph from the debris in Apartment
1824 and the voice of the little girl—

—*I'm here, Abel*—

—had spoken in his head, so clear she might have been
standing at his shoulder.

He had almost said as much to Ben Prather.

Why?

Because the voices were on his mind. They were constantly on his mind.

Because he could hear them, even now he could hear
them—congeries of whispers in the faraway corners of the
room, like wind sighing through tall grass, whispering, whispering, whispering. And what if, once sensitized, he could
never quite tune them out again?

A thought came to him out of the air, unbidden:

There was a world and there was a fence and there was
a world beyond the fence.

Memory battered at the threshold of his consciousness.
Abel clutched his book with whitened knuckles and shouldered closed the door against it, skimming the words before
him without any real comprehension.

He could feel the weight of Ben's scrutiny against his
skin.

What if he was going mad?

Carefully, without looking up, Abel reached up and
turned the page.

6

About one thing, anyway, Abel had been wrong.

There was a battery in Lara McGovern's heart that would never run down, no matter how often she tapped it.

She ran.

In the stillness and shadows of the declining day, in the empty gym which already smelled of sweat and iron and the thick black grease that had been used to lubricate the Nautilus machine, she ran. She ran until her tee shirt hung damp against her body and the locket dangling between her diminished breasts clung there in a viscid film of perspiration. She ran until she could smell the sharp tang of her own odor, until her body rebelled—until her aching feet recoiled from each collision with the flying belt of the treadmill and the long muscles in her thighs screamed and each breath lacerated her lungs. She ran through the pain into an all-too-momentary blur of endorphin joy and she ran through that, too, and even then the battery in her heart never gave out.

It couldn't. From the day Katie Wright had slipped between her sleep-fumbled fingers—

—but she didn't slip, did she, she—

—every breath, every thought, every waking instant of Lara's life and most of the other ones, too, had been devoted to recharging it. She ran to deplete it, ran until exhaustion overtook her at last, only to wake too soon from fraught and terrifying dreams to find that battery full and pulsing in her breast.

"You're too thin," Dan Sutherland had told her the day he called her back to Mercy General—the day this had all begun. Escorting her through antiseptic-smelling hallways abustle with doctors and nurses who wouldn't quite meet her eyes, through Admissions, past the ER, and into the thick August heat that clogged the streets beyond, he pressed her on the issue. "Are you eating right?" he said. "Are you getting enough sleep?"

He said, "Are you taking care of yourself?"

Lara had turned to face him, brushing a strand of limp hair out of her eyes. She stared into his lean, freckled visage as a train thundered overhead. In the percussive aftermath of its passage, she said, "Shit, Dan, would you be?"

They both knew the answer to that one.

Sutherland looked away. He rubbed his long jaw with one hand. "Well, try," he said. "You're a good doctor. We need you around here."

"Obviously."

The bitterness stung him: she could see it in the tiny muscles that tightened around his mouth.

"This thing with Ramsey Lomax. Give it some thought. You can do some good that way. If she had to die—"

—she didn't she didn't have to die—

"—make sure it didn't happen for nothing."

"Right. Thanks, that helps."

She started to turn away, but he reached out and took her arm. "I'm serious, Lara. These things happen. They're terrible, but they can be forgiven."

"You mean I can buy my way back into the hospital's graces."

"If that's the way you want to look at it. All I'm saying is, give it some thought." He squeezed her arm gently. "You're a good doctor. You've worked too hard to throw it all away. So give it your serious consideration. And in the meantime, take care of yourself. You're too damn skinny."

"Well," she said. "Okay, then. Thanks."

Turning, she struck off toward the El, and though she ignored the frustrated syllables he threw at her retreating back—

"Lara!"

—over the days and weeks that followed she found herself doing everything he'd asked: thinking over Lomax's offer and trying—that was the key word, *trying*—to take better care of herself. She'd had better luck on the first count than on the second. Even as she climbed the stairs to the train platform that afternoon, she'd known that in the end she would take what Lomax had to offer. Any other course was madness: buying her way back into her profession was better than giving it up forever. Better to surrender her sense of what was right and appropriate than surrender her role as a doctor—her sense of purpose and identity, her very self.

But as for taking care of herself, that was harder. Oh, she would try: not for her any of the old predictable pathways to self-immolation—drugs, booze, promiscuity. She'd seen too much of all three in the ER. She had too much self-respect to destroy herself that way.

But one could run.

There was nothing wrong with that. How many times had she said so herself, to some poor benighted soul in the ER? "You ought to consider getting some exercise, it would do you some good."

And so she ran. She ran day after day, in the mornings through a lakeside shimmer of light, in the afternoons along the cindered track of a nearby high school. She ran for hours, she ran for miles, she ran until the flesh melted off her bones, until she could count the ribs beneath her skin, until her cheeks grew hollow and the corded muscles in her thighs stood out in sharp relief. She ran until Katie Wright's face disappeared in a white haze of exhaustion. But no matter how hard she ran, no matter how fast, when the haze cleared, Katie Wright loomed up before her.

Some things you just couldn't run from. Some things you had to face.

That was what Lana said inside her head.

What do you know? Lara thought. *You're dead.*

Not by a long shot, girl, Lana said. *Not as long as you draw breath.*

And what was there to say to that? Some truths were inarguable.

So there in the gloom of the little exercise room, Lara lowered her head and ran. She ran and she ran and she ran, and each step she took, each thumping concussion of foot and speeding belt, pumped an acid wash of energy, raw, corrosive, to the battery inside her heart. She ran, there in Dreamland, jutting sole and impregnable from the broken pavement of the dead lands, with the night leaning like black glass against the windows and the faintest glimmering of light from the corridor at her back frosting her bobbing shoulders. And when, breath heaving in her lungs, she lifted her face at last, it was that juxtaposition of elements—the light from the corridor and the obsidian well of night outside the window and maybe even Dreamland itself, though even then she could not bring herself to believe—which drew her up short and breathless, terror hammering inside her breast.

She had seen something.

There, through the shadowy cage of braided cords that was the Nautilus machine, she had *seen* something, she had glimpsed it in the window opposite, a palish oval blur, a face, peering in at her from the icy air five stories above the frost-heavied hardpan below—and in that flying moment with the sweat burning in her eyes it looked like the face of every person she had ever lost.

It looked like Lana's face.

She touched a button and the treadmill ground obediently to a halt. Lifting the tail of her tee shirt, she wiped the perspiration from her eyes, and in that interval of stinging blindness—a second, maybe two—she knew that when she let her hand fall away once again, the face would be gone.

It was not.

It was still there, looking in at her. It was Fletcher Keel's face, a hollowed-out reflection in a yellow doorway, floating there atop the blackened glass.

"What are you doing?" she gasped, turning, all too suddenly aware of how she had lifted the tee shirt to wipe her face, of the panic in her eyes and the anxious little knots of her nipples, visible through the sheer fabric.

Keel stood in the doorway, backlit from the hall. He seemed to fill up the narrow aperture, his big hands hanging at his side, and how had it happened that she had not felt his shadow fall across her?

"What are you doing?" she said again, and Fletcher Keel smiled.

"Looking at you," he said.

Abel Williams
Takes a Fall

1

"What do you miss most?" That was the question Lara posed to Abel and Ben over breakfast the next morning.

"Miss?" Abel asked. "About what?"

"The world," she said, waving her spoon vaguely at the window. "You know, what do you miss?"

But Ben didn't need the elaboration. He'd known what she meant from the first: he felt it, too, a sense of isolation that transcended mere seclusion, a sense not so much that they had retreated momentarily from the world but that everything beyond these walls had simply disappeared—streetcars and subways, taxes and television, the whole ball of wax, *poof,* just gone.

They'd hardly gotten started—they were, what, three days into this? four?—and they were having the kind of conversations you'd expect in the rec room of an Antarctic research station along about the middle of winter. How long before genuine cabin fever set in? he wondered, with an uneasy stirring in his guts. It was something to think about, anyway. He poured a cup of coffee, snagged a carton of cream from the steel monolith of the refrigerator, and joined them at the table.

"Well?" Lara said.

Abel wrinkled his nose. "I'm thinking," he said. And then: "White noise."

"White noise?" Ben said.

"You know, TV, radio—traffic even. I'm the kind of person, I like to have something on in the room, even if I'm not listening to it."

"Why's that?" Ben said, thinking about last night, that odd moment of hesitation—

—sometimes I he—

—when Abel had seemed to hover at the verge of some deeper self-revelation.

Abel shrugged. "I don't know. I never thought about it, I guess."

"Ben brought a CD player," Lara said.

"You could have brought one of those white noise machines."

Abel struck his forehead with the flat of his palm. "See, why didn't I think of that?" He poked at his Cheerios with his spoon. He looked up at Lara. "What about you? What do you miss?"

"Starbucks."

"Starbucks?"

"We have coffee," Ben said.

"I don't want coffee. I want a triple latte with whipped cream and those little flakes of chocolate on top."

"You don't look like the type," Abel said.

"Sure I do," she said. "One exercises, one can indulge, right?"

Ben glanced up, half expecting Abel to make another crack about the incessant whir of the treadmill. "You should have mentioned it to Lomax," he said. "I'm sure he could have accommodated you. He seems to have spared no expense."

"Speaking of our mysterious host, where's he been keeping himself?" Abel asked.

"Beats me," Ben replied.

"Well," Abel said, pointing at him with his spoon, "I'll tell you one thing, anyway."

"What's that?"

"There's something weird about it, his whole obsession with this place. I bet you looked into it, didn't you?"

"I imagine you did a little investigation of your own."

Abel laughed. "You're just not going to cut me any slack, are you?"

"It's nothing personal. Besides, we've already established that being a fake doesn't necessarily mean *knowing* that you're a fake, right?"

"Yes, we did have that conversation, didn't we?"

Lara groaned.

"What?" Abel said.

"Just cut it out. Things are tense enough without you guys going at it, too."

"Who's tense?" Ben inquired.

"I am for one."

"Yeah? Why's that?"

"You mean other than Lomax's little stories?"

"Yeah. Other than that."

"Nothing. Forget it. I should never have brought it up." Ben and Abel exchanged glances.

"Seriously," Abel said.

She muttered something into her cereal bowl.

"What?" Ben said.

She looked up at them, then, and Ben felt the emotional tenor of the room darken. "Keel," she repeated. "Keel bothers me."

"He do something?" Abel asked.

"No, he didn't do anything." Lara took a breath. "Look, I don't want you to say anything, okay? But he looks at me sometimes, you know?"

"He looks at you?"

"It's the way he looks at me. If you were a woman you'd know."

"He threaten you?" Abel asked.

"No. Nothing like that. It's just—last night I was on the treadmill, I suddenly realized he was standing in the doorway. I don't know how long he'd been there, but when I asked him what he was doing, he was very . . . weird. 'Looking at you,' that's what he said." She looked up. "It's just me, I guess. I keep thinking about that girl, that's all. Theresa Matheson."

She stirred her cereal for a moment and then let the spoon drop with a clatter. She pushed the bowl away.

"I really don't want you to say anything," she said.

"We won't," Ben replied.

"Don't worry about it."

In the silence that followed, Ben opened the carton of cream and poured some into his coffee. He stirred it slowly, watching it fade from black to a milky shade of caramel. Reaching out with one hand, he adjusted the box of Cheerios so he could read the copy on the back panel.

"You know what I miss?" he said. "I miss the morning paper."

Abel Williams had not lied.

In his suite, during the long hours after breakfast on the fourth day of fourteen days that already felt as though they would never end—on the fourth day of fourteen days that were hurtling past so quickly he could already feel his opportunity slipping between his fingers—Abel brooded on this fact. He stared down at the snapshot of the little girl on the coffee table—or, more accurately, at the back of the snapshot, for he had turned it facedown. He didn't want to look into her eyes, didn't want to hear her voice—

—I'm here, Abel—

—didn't even want to *think* about her voice. So he sat there staring at the antediluvian date—1979—printed on the back instead, his guts churning, and he thought about Lara McGovern's question over breakfast: What do you miss most?

White noise, he had said, and he had not lied.

What he missed most, what he wanted, what he *needed* more than anything else in the world, was white noise—the hum of the exhaust fan in the half-bath of his Gold Coast condo, the blare of Muzak in a department store elevator, the bellow of a distant jackhammer. Anything. Anything, so long as it would drown out that incessant choir of whispers.

Which, come to think of it, was a little like white noise itself.

Ha, ha.

The problem was, Abel couldn't focus on the issue at hand: the issue of Ramsey Lomax. As long as he could hear the voices—and he was hearing them all too frequently now, a spate of whispers from the bedroom, a trill of hisses in the bath, all of it pitched so low, so nearly subaudible, so almost entirely *not* there that he could detect no words, only a ceaseless sighing cadence, like waves washing on a faraway beach—Abel couldn't focus on *anything* else. His mind plucked at the voices instead, worrying them for the faintest hint of meaning—

—*was that a word, a phrase*—

—like an obsessive spinster worrying a loose thread in her skirt.

Intellectually, he understood that there were no voices. He was hearing water in the pipes, he had fallen prey to some unpleasant physical condition that produced aural hallucinations, he was perhaps going mad—whatever. *There were no voices.* But this sane, logical fragment of his mind hovered disembodied over the heaving sea of his irrational self, tethered by the merest filaments of reason, while that other self, storm-tossed, turbulent, and supremely *un*reasonable, insisted that he was not only hearing voices but that the voices were *real,* that they emanated from a real place, and he *knew* that place, he had known it all along in some black and secret recess of his heart. As a child, he'd had a name for it: the world beyond the fence.

The phrase alone set cold fingers climbing the knuckles of Abel's spine.

And overlying all this was the pressure of time. Three days gone already—

—*was it three days?*—

—the fourth one on the fly, and how much progress had he made? How close had he come to unlocking the secret that had brought Ramsey Lomax to Dreamland? The goal had been to make himself indispensable, and it should not have been that difficult. He'd done it a thousand times with other clients. All you had to do was listen.

That was it, the secret of his art: listening.

Listen close enough, and there was not a person on the planet who wouldn't tell you exactly what they wanted to hear. What they wanted was to see themselves reflected, like Narcissus in his fatal pool. Once you understood that, you could have anything you wanted.

Anything.

Abel knew what he wanted, and he knew that Ramsey Lomax could give it to him. But time was on the fly: Abel could almost feel it, the seconds peeling away into eternity as he whittled down the hours here in his suite, staring at the rust-stained back of a snapshot he did not have the courage to look in the face.

Abel reached out a single finger and nudged the photograph toward the center of the table. He looked up. The light in the room had changed. The day was slipping past. How long had he been sitting here?

How much more time did he intend to waste?

That was the question that compelled him out of his room and into the hallway beyond, the photograph abandoned—but not forgotten—on the coffee table in his suite. There was an excited little surge of whispers—

—*Abel, Abel*—

—as he closed the door behind him, and then they died away.

See? Nothing there, that logical fragment of his brain announced with satisfaction from atop its aerie high above him, and down below, down here where he *really* lived, the tempestuous sea of Abel's greater self fell still. An enormous calm descended upon him.

He proceeded down the corridor through a dizzying abyss of silence.

The others—all four of them—were in the lounge. They were playing cards, gin, careful suits of hearts and clubs, diamonds and spades, laid out across the table before them. Abel stood in the doorway, looking on. Their mouths were moving, but he could barely hear *their* voices. He was hardly there at all. He seemed to be floating high above everything, looking down upon them, their voices swirling up to him on half-comprehended vagaries of wind.

And then Lara was looking back at him, her wry mouth smiling.

Too late, he realized that she was talking to him.

"What?" he said, his voice muffled in his own ears. "What did you say?"

"I said, where've you been?" She laughed. "You too good to hang out with the rest of us?"

"No," he said, and on that word, the volume suddenly jumped back to normal. He reached out a hand to steady himself as the world rushed up to envelop him, color and light and the thump of blood at his temples. "I've just been thinking," he said, and his gaze fell upon Ramsey Lomax, watching him over a fan of cards, his eyebrows lifted in expectation.

"A laudable enterprise, Mr. Williams," he said dryly, but Abel hardly heard him so eager was he to purge himself of the words tumbling helter-skelter out of his mouth.

"I thought it might be interesting to do a reading," Abel said, staring directly into Lomax's eyes. He shrugged, *faux* casual. "I've been . . . sensing . . . some things, I thought it might be interesting to explore them," he said, the words coming so fast he hardly knew where they were coming from, only that they were coming, and how good it felt to unburden himself at last, how good to feel that leaden shroud of pressure lifting, how good, finally, to begin. He addressed the group as a whole, but his gaze never deviated from Ramsey Lomax's face, the curving prow of the nose, the eyes intent upon his own. "I thought I'd see if you guys were interested."

He paused to draw a breath. The succeeding silence was voiceless, pristine.

Smiling, Ramsey Lomax folded his hand. "Why not?"

"Great." Abel stepped through the doorway, into the room. "We can do it here," he said, but Lomax was standing, smoothing his slacks—

"Why not try it where the spoor is freshest?" he said. "Why not try it in the lobby?"

And, just like that, the relief Abel Williams had been feeling translated itself into an uneasiness so stark and numbing that it took the significance of this statement two or three full heartbeats to climb that wind-blown tether to his brain.

The lobby. Of all the places in the building, Lomax had chosen the lobby.

Yes. And why not? he thought.

It was a place to start, anyway, and in spite of the uneasiness welling up within him, Abel felt an answering smile spread itself across his face.

"Whatever you say," he said.

That was how it began.

3

For Fletcher Keel, the moment when he looked up and saw Abel bobbing in the doorway had a distilled and glaring clarity.

He'd been staring in frustration at his hand, a random jumble of hearts, diamonds, and clubs, with a lone dissenting spade standing bravely front and center, when he'd sensed the other man approaching down the hall. There was nothing supernatural about this. Old reflexes died hard, that's all: even now, more than two decades since the day he had turned in his badge—

—except you didn't turn it in they took it from you—

—years after disuse alone (and never mind the oceans of booze, the raw tonnage of pills) should have eroded his skills, Fletcher Keel remained preternaturally vigilant. He retained the habit of parsing the world into quadrants and monitoring them, one by one, in their unceasing round. Even here, studying the disastrous fan of cards in his hand, he sensed at some nearly unconscious level the steady pull of Ben's respiration, the peripheral glow of Ramsey Lomax's shaven skull, the faint lilac scent of Lara McGovern's body spray (which inspired a not-unpleasant tingling heaviness in his groin)—and, yes, the faint rustle in the hall that announced Abel's arrival.

He never doubted it was Abel. Who else would it be, after all? There was no one else *in* the building—and if he had any doubts on that score he was nowhere near ready to voice them, not even to himself. No, he knew it had to be Abel, and so he didn't bother looking up. He just continued to gaze in mute resentment at his hand, until Lara spoke—

"Hey, Abel, where you been? You too cool to hang out with us?"

—and something in her tone of voice, a certain playful lilt, caused Keel to lift his head.

What he saw shook him a little.

What he saw was Abel Williams, his hip cocked against the doorway, apparently at ease. Any other observer might not have noticed the tell-tale signs that suggested otherwise—the subtle quaver in Abel's voice, the grinning white crescents of his knuckles as he clutched the door frame, most of all the glittering sheen in his eyes. But Keel had seen that glitter before—in the eyes of a drunken GI who'd made the near fatal miscalculation of taking a swing at him in a Munich beer garden, in the slit-swollen gaze of a coke-addled hooker and, most recently, during a stint as the doorman at a Nacogdoches dive, in the face of a wetback with a skinful of crystal meth who had come after him with a knife. What it meant, that glitter, was that a vital line had fallen somewhere in the tangled region of inhibition that lay on the border between impulse and action; reason had taken a flyer and something else—drug or drink or plain old-fashioned perversity—was in command.

What it meant, that glitter, was trouble.

Keel felt a tug of memory—a subterranean ripple that fell a hair short of genuine recollection—but he shunted it aside, and watched the whole thing play out. A reading? Sure, and in the lobby, too—despite the shadow he'd imagined stirring in the empty stairwell.

Why not?

Trouble didn't scare him, it never had. Besides, he thought, staring down at his cards, he was already a hundred points in the hole.

What else did he have to lose?

4

No one spoke in the elevator.

They stood there, huddled like children as the lurching, paint-scarred car descended, busy with their own thoughts: shadows in stairwells and the falsetto laughter of a child. The unblinking gaze of a dead and sodden rat.

Lara felt a gout of hysterical laughter lodge in her throat. It might have been a scream.

Then the doors slid open before them.

5

It was a lobby, that's all, Abel told himself.

A lobby: two elevator slots, a wall of mailboxes with apartment numbers stenciled on their windows, and a curving counter where a doorman might have whiled away the hours. Just a lobby, and never mind that the retracting metal doors of one of the elevators had been cannibalized for God knows what purpose and the empty shaft beyond plummeted unimpeded into the black depths of the basements and subbasements below. Never mind that the rows of mailboxes had long since been defaced, locks broken, glass spiderwebbed with cracks, doors ripped utterly away to reveal naked slots in which no letter had fallen for years. Never mind that no doorman had ever stood behind that curving counter, or that sometime in the long decades before the Housing Authority threw up its hands in frustration and walked away it had been crudely boxed in by a scarred shield of bulletproof glass, complete with a pass-through tray, like the counter of a late night Gas and Go. Never mind any of that.

It was a lobby—a chilly, unheated lobby, true—but a lobby all the same. And every apartment building on earth had a lobby.

Never mind that a lobby, by definition, was a point of transition, a threshold between the building and the world beyond, and that there was nothing to prevent him from turning on his heels and walking out those doors into the declining January day beyond. Never mind that he could walk out of Dreamland forever.

He'd come here for a reason. He wasn't going anywhere. He wasn't giving up. It was a lobby, that's all. He could handle a lobby.

And besides, there were no whispers. The voices had fallen still. There had never been any voices, just tension, just tension and anticipation and an overactive imagination, and all it took was work—

Abel glanced at Ramsey Lomax.

—to silence them. Purpose. Something to do.

Keep busy—that's the secret of being happy, his father had told him once—and why should it disturb him, here in this place, at this moment, to think of his father?

Unbidden Abel's fingers sought the watch, like a shackle at his wrist.

The elevator doors rumbled closed.

No voices. Nothing to fear.

Abel turned to the others.

"So," he said. "Let's get started."

6

Everything depended on the pitch.

Ideally, someone else delivered it—on *Messages*, Abel had employed a veritable strike force of pitchers, assistant producers mostly, polished and comfortably bland, who worked the studio audience for an hour or more, moving through the rows and chatting people up, before Abel so much as stepped on stage. To the unschooled eye, they might have been undertakers, sincere, attentive, above all concerned: *You okay, ma'am? You comfortable? Can we get you something—some water, a tissue maybe? We understand how hard this is.*

In actuality, however, something else was going on—and nothing so insidious as the deliberate intelligence-gathering Abel's skeptics sometimes accused him of (not that anyone was averse to picking up the useful tidbit here and there). No, the real purposes of the pitch were more subtle: to put the audience at ease, to sharpen their nervous anticipation and their already hair-trigger emotions. And most of all, to lower expectations. Because the less they expected, the more they would grasp to find some connection, *any* connection, to the words coming out of Abel's mouth.

That was the closer's job.

The best closer Abel had ever known was Gale Parker, the woman who'd sold him on *Messages* to start with. By the time she stepped on stage and introduced herself, the audience was primed. And by the time she wrapped it up—by the time Abel bounded out from the wings and the cameras started rolling—the audience was practically humming with anxiety. It was primal, palpable. You could actually feel it, like the charged air that augurs a storm: a needling sense of static expectation, of pent-up energies about to be released.

Ideally, anyway.

Unfortunately, this was in no way an ideal situation: unlike Abel's usual audience of fifty or sixty people, self-selected and inclined to credulity, this was a group of four, at least two of them actively skeptical. And this time he had to play all the roles—he had to make the pitch, he had to close the deal, he had to do the reading. Just like the old days. Yet it was Gale's speech—or an appropriately modified version of it—that he fell back on, and these were the first words: "No promises."

Abel let them hang there, just as Gale always had, while he took stock of the others, arrayed in a ragged crescent on a clutch of rust-eaten folding chairs they'd found stacked against the security counter. Then, leaning forward in his own chair—it creaked ominously, exuding a faintly ferric odor—he clasped his hands between his knees, and repeated the phrase: "No promises. You have to understand the way this works. Imagine the worst cell phone conversation you ever had—random static, the signal cutting out, all those weird beeps or clangs. Then imagine that the person you're talking to is speaking a language you don't know, so you can't rely on anything but tone to deduce his meaning. Now multiply those difficulties by a factor of ten or twenty. That's what I'm trying to do." He looked up. "It's a false analogy, of course. In reality, it's not a conversation. There are no words—"

—no voices—

"—only . . ." He shrugged. ". . . vague impressions. You with me so far?"

Lara and Ben exchanged glances.

Keel nodded skeptically.

Lomax was impassive, his arms crossed over his chest.

"So it's a bad analogy, but let's carry it a step further: you're on the phone, but you don't have the faintest clue who's on the other end of the line."

He sat there, contemplating them, trying to find that zone of concentration, that inner intuitive space that he usually summoned in the comfort of his dressing room. There was little comfort here. It was cold, and outside the wind gusted intermittently, rattling the plywood panels affixed over the doors. Yet he sat there all the same, trying to relinquish the pressure, the sense that this was the most important reading he'd ever done, that he'd acted hastily in running out of his room like that—

—why had he run out of his room like that—

*—*that he should have thought things through. Trying to live in the moment, deep in his nerve ends.

"It could be anyone," he said. "Sometimes—usually—there's a connection with someone in the room, someone at the sitting. But the only way we can figure that out is if we work together, okay?"

Ben's eyes flickered with something that might have been cynicism. Abel let it pass. He didn't have to convince Ben. Not Ben, not Lara, not Fletcher Keel. The only person in the room he had to convince was Ramsey Lomax.

"So that's all I have: tone, the color of an emotion, an intimation. That's what's going to happen here. I'm going to be tossing out impressions—whatever comes to me, whatever I sense in the room's"—he hesitated, making air quotes with his fingers—"'energy.' I'm just going to throw it out there. Your job is to let me know if anything rings a bell. Okay?"

Lomax, his arms still crossed over his chest, cleared his throat. "Never fear, Mr. Williams, we'll all be suitably co-operative. Now—assuming you're done with the disclaimers—perhaps we can get the show on the road."

And that was the thing: Abel didn't *want* to get the show on the road.

Something in him resisted, some deep component self.

And yet, maybe, just *maybe*, that core reluctance was a gift. The thought triggered an intuitive humming in his bones, something akin to the one he'd felt fourteen years ago, hunched drunkenly over a Ouija board as he plotted his assault on Susie Whatshername's virtue. Yes. He could *use* his discomfort. He could exploit his reluctance.

The reluctance authenticated him: Fakers had nothing to fear.

Leveling his gaze at Lomax—*no one else mattered*, how liberating a thought that was turning out to be—Abel said, "No. As a matter of fact I'm not done. There's something else. I did a reading here once before. In Dreamland. In this room. *Hard Copy* hired me, back when the story of that girl—Matheson—was hot. We came down here, we did it right here." He paused. He took a deep breath, uncertain suddenly how much of this *was* a put-up job. He said, "I didn't want to come back. I wouldn't have, if my show hadn't tanked."

Silence greeted this confession.

"Why is that?" Lomax lifted his chin.

"Something happened."

Abel licked his lips. He didn't want to say what had really happened—didn't want to mention the whispers stirring in the dry mouth of the empty elevator shaft, didn't even want to *think* about that searing glimpse of Theresa Matheson's final agonizing moments on earth—but he had to say something. Here, as in all things, vagueness was his watchword: what went unsaid possessed infinitely more power than any words.

"I don't know what it was, I don't understand it exactly, but there was something here. Something I've never felt before."

"What was that?" Lomax said softly, leaning forward almost imperceptibly, and Abel felt something open up inside him: a renewed confidence, a certainty. He'd set the hook; now all he had to do was reel it in.

He swallowed. "There was a single moment there—just a few seconds—when—when—" And if his voice caught for an instant, if for a single pulse of his heart his brain resurrected that image of Theresa Matheson, and his core reluctance—

—terror it was terror—

—reasserted itself, no one else seemed to notice. Taking a breath, he pushed on: "—when I had a connection that was deeper than anything I've ever felt, so deep it . . . frightened me, actually." He forced a laugh. "Other than that, the reading went badly. Very badly, to be honest. *Hard Copy* never used it."

"What was so bad about it?" Ben asked.

"Except for that one moment, I couldn't *get* anything. The room was full of Theresa Matheson's friends. She *died* here. There should have been some connections, and now, the weird thing is . . ."

Abel let his voice trail off. He stood, scraping his chair across the chill concrete, utterly in command of their attention. The lobby, silent—

—voiceless—

—suddenly belonged to him in a way that no other place on the planet had ever belonged to him, no place but the stage. He owned it now. He owned *them*. He paced, letting his face relax into a semblance of empty concentration, the expression of a man trying to hear the voice on the far end of a static-ridden line—

—a party line, something whispered deep inside him—

—the expression of a man distracted beyond mere distraction, a man barely present at all except in the most prosaic and physical of ways. It was all practiced illusion. In reality, Abel was never *more* present, never *more* aware, than when on stage. He paced before them, vigilant for the slightest stir of interest: a rustle of clothing, an involuntary sigh.

He turned, watching them without seeming to watch them. He spoke slowly, his voice a monotone. "What's weird is, I'm sensing more connections *now* than I did then. I'm sensing connections with people in this room . . ."

He drifted into silence once again. How powerful silence was. How discomfiting. People couldn't help wanting to fill it.

Lara took the bait, her voice puzzled. "With *us?*"

"More than one of you," he said. "Loss. An incredible sense of loss."

He cautioned himself to avoid the temptation, to avoid the obvious. Avoid Theresa Matheson.

Slowly, then, his voice soothing, coaxing: "Someone here, among us. I'm getting a sense of . . . kinship?"

"Here?" Lara said, puzzled.

Abel gestured vaguely, as if groping for words. "Everywhere. They're drawn to us, the ones they've left behind. They're always with us."

He paced, his face blank, inwardly exultant. He had forgotten—off stage, he always forgot—just how easy it was, how simple to summon it up, how close to the surface it ran, this river of grief flowing just under every human skin. Name it, and it was there. How naked their faces were, how clear the ripple of emotion.

Abel could see it in Keel's face, in Ben's—he could see them fighting it. The obdurate set of Keel's mouth, the furrowed ridges of Ben's brow. Lomax sat straight, his arms uncrossed, receptive, his fingers curled loosely at the edges of his seat. Lara leaned forward, her lips moist, slightly parted. Her hands balled in fists in the narrow valley of her lap.

He had her. Fixed and fascinated. More than any of them, she belonged to him.

In silence, pacing, Abel followed his intuition. Go with her, it said. She's ripe for it. Snare her, you snare them all, sooner or later. And why had he ever worried? After all, there was time yet. There was plenty of time.

Abel dropped his voice an octave. "Kinship," he said thoughtfully. "A close friend . . ." He scrutinized her, dragging the word out while he waited for a light of recognition to come into her face, but there was nothing there, no spark. Projecting a note of certainty into his voice, a note of revelation, he said, "No. A family member, a loss that wounded you deeply . . ."

Yes. There it was, the light in her eyes: he'd touched something, a tender spot. A wound.

He moved away from her. He didn't want to crowd her.

But for the damp echo of his feet upon the concrete, the lobby was utterly silent: a blessing, a benediction of silence. All it took was work—

—*keep busy that's the secret of silencing the voices,* he thought giddily—

—and now, with his back to her, Abel said, "I'm sensing . . . there was a heaviness . . ." Turning, watching her slant-wise, he laid his hand against his breast. "There was something in the chest area."

"Pneumonia . . ."

The old folks' friend. "Your mother."

A shot in the dark. Abel saw it go wide. He saw the light flicker in her eyes, and quickly, even as her lips shaped the denial, he shook his head, hastening to fill the silence: "No, that's wrong, it's something else. I'm sensing that she was younger. Your sister. It was your sister, wasn't it?"

Lara's face lit up. It was like pulling the lever on a one-armed bandit, and watching black bars, one two three, spin to a stop the length of the dial: jackpot, a rain of coins overflowing the tray. He turned, fixing her with his eye. Sister, she had a sister . . .

Young people didn't die of pneumonia. Young people beat pneumonia. The respiratory stuff was a red herring, symptomatic of some larger affliction, AIDS or cancer, which one was it? And he looked at her, at Lara, thin to the point of gauntness, eaten up with something, punishing herself like some medieval flagellant. He looked at her—thin, white, highly educated—the whole profile wrong for AIDS, dead wrong, ha ha, no pun intended, it was cancer, it had to be. He felt the certainty in his bones.

"It was the chemo, wasn't it? It weakened her immune system, she got pneumonia, but it was the cancer that killed her."

A single tear trembled at the lip of Lara McGovern's left eye. Then it spilled over, drawing a glistening line down the hollow of her cheek.

The money shot.

It was all Abel could do not to pump his fist. Triumph flooded through him, an intoxicating rush. He turned away lest someone see it in his eyes, and just then—just for an instant—his concentration faltered. Just for an instant, he let himself slip into that sunlit July day almost two years gone, Dreamland stark against the pristine sky—yet shrouded in a darkness that fell just short of visible, a darkness he could feel inside his bones. He sensed Theresa Matheson's friends encamped around him, silent and resentful, the *Hard Copy* producer fretting just out of camera range.

Now it came back to him: that sense of anxiety as the

reading went bad. He turned as he remembered turning and there it was again, in the eye of memory, the *Hard Copy* producer's absurd shrine of candles and roses and photo enlargements, Theresa Matheson staring back at him from half a dozen burnished frames.

The temperature seemed to drop ten degrees, his breath vapor in the air.

No, he thought, wrenching himself back into the moment. *No—*

Too late.

Came the whirlwind, came the thunder, the clamor stirring to crescendo in the dry throat of the abandoned elevator shaft—

—voices my god so many voices—

—and gushing out at him, an invisible wave. Abel staggered like a man leaning into raging wind or water, and still it came on, a sound that was not sound, that he heard not with his ears but in his bones, in his sinews and in his cells, vibrating like the struck surface of an enormous bell, a gale of voices, a geyser spewing up from some black and unimagined depth a few half-familiar phrases—

—I'm here Abel I'm—

—here we're all—

—here don't leave me please don't leave me—

—here—

—fragmentary, fraught, and gone again, submerged in that onrolling tidal swell.

Stunned, Abel lifted his hands as if to ward it off, that insane babble welling up the empty throat of the elevator shaft, and then, as if an invisible curtain had parted—as if time itself had split asunder—

—there is no time not here not in this place—

—plummeting him into a past twice removed—once again he was there. There: in the lobby, Theresa Matheson spread-eagled on her back, her heels drumming the table as a black kid, jeans bagging around his knees, drove himself savagely into her, over and over again.

Here, too, cacophony assaulted Abel. Music hammered out of a boom box—frantic, discordant, a thunderous backbeat overlain by the menacing taunt of gangster rap. Theresa Matheson screamed—over and over again, with a dull, relentless monotony—as she fought the hands holding her down, the hands clutching at her, the hands mauling her. Her attackers answered in kind. The room rang with their jeers, with their laughter and their mockery, their hatred, their rage. How many of them were there? Ten? Twelve? More? They seemed to multiply by the dozen, by the hundred, there in the moted furnace of a July day two years gone: a host of shadowy presences encircling the ring of men closest to the table, a throng, a legion—

—my name is—

—of avid faces, men, women, children, their teeth bared and white in eager grimaces, their muscles taut under dark skin. There and not-quite-there, in a thousand whispering and resentful voices, they urged it on, the horror at the center of the room.

Worse: they sensed Abel's presence and they hated him. Abel did not know how he knew this, but he knew it. He knew it with an iron-clad certainty that brooked no denial.

Maybe he screamed. He thought he did, anyway, a scream even he could hear above the phantom dissonance.

No, he thought, *no—*

And then the darkness took him.

7

In a silence pristine and pure—in a blue-black cold they hardly noticed, they were so transfixed—they watched it happen.

It was nothing much to see.

One minute Abel was walking away from them, perfectly in command of his faculties. The next, he moaned, a sound a fevered child might have made.

Keel stirred, and something changed in Ben's face.

Lomax leaned forward, his rusty folding chair creaking with his weight.

Lara, still wiping at her eyes, looked up in time to see Abel fold in upon himself and collapse.

8

She was at her best in a crisis.

Her personal life was a disaster, she'd managed to lose the only job she had ever aspired to, she'd failed miserably in keeping that long-ago promise over Lana's casket—but from the wreckage of her sister's funeral, Lara had salvaged at least one vow she could cling to: never again would she lose her head in a moment when someone needed her.

Your personal problems came second to saving a life, it was that simple.

So when Abel Williams crumpled to the floor, Lara was the first one to her feet. By the time the others had gathered around her, she had already started her assessment, moving down a mental checklist point by point, the ghost of Lana which Abel Williams had somehow—

—*how?*—

—summoned up temporarily forgotten. For the moment anyway, she was focused entirely on Abel himself: his breathing and the pallor in his face, his pulse, racing beneath her fingers.

"What ha—" Lomax said, but Lara shushed him.

Staring down at her watch, she counted. By the time the second hand completed its initial sweep and started around again, Abel's heart rate had slowed. By the time it swung into its third circuit, his pulse was back to normal: strong and full, seventy-four beats a minute. Lara released his wrist and glanced up into a circle of anxious faces.

"He okay?" Ben said.

"I think so."

"What the hell happened?" Keel asked.

"I'm not sure."

Sitting back on her heels, Lara looked Abel over. Color was already coming back into his face. She saw no evidence of broken bones. No bleeding.

"Here," she said, gesturing. "Help me roll him on his side."

"Are you su—" Keel said.

"Of course I'm sure."

The words came out more sharply than she'd intended. Shaking his head, his palms lifted in mock surrender, Keel knelt across from her. Together, he and Ben wedged their hands under Abel and shifted him, dead weight. Abel's mouth gaped open. He shuddered, and Lara thought he was going to throw up, but no—it was his respiration settling into a deeper rhythm, steady and slow, like a man sleeping.

"Did he hit his head when he fell?" she asked. "Did anybody see?"

"He hit everything," Keel said coolly.

"But not his head," Lomax told her. "Not badly, anyway."

Abel moaned. His eyelids fluttered.

"Abel?" Lara said. "How you feeling, Abel?"

He muttered something, she wasn't sure what it was.

Lomax knelt at Lara's shoulder, crowding her, and when she glanced back at him the intensity in his face startled her. There was something frightening about it, something hungry and utterly without mercy, like the glint in a raptor's eye when it spotted movement in the moonlit grass below. Looking at him, Lara felt her confidence weaken. Renewed doubt assailed her—doubts about Lomax and his reasons for coming to this place, doubts about her own mixed motivations for accompanying him. Doubts about her competence.

"What did he say?" Lomax asked.

"I don't—"

Abel spoke again, interrupting her. "So . . . many," he said distantly. He shook his head. Swallowed.

"So many *what?*" Lomax asked.

And then Abel snatched Lara's hand, clutching it painfully, like a drowning man. His eyes snapped open, and she found herself gazing into an abyss of paralyzed bewilderment. He reminded her of a patient she'd seen during her psych rotation, a paranoid schizophrenic so pathologically disconnected that he had retreated to a corner the first time she had walked into the room, his shoulders hunched in expectation of some cosmic blow. He'd been a mutterer, too, shifty-eyed and raving, constantly glaring at her from under lowered brows. *Spare parts,* he'd muttered repeatedly, his eyes glittering with emptiness, *spare parts spare parts-spareparts,* until finally he'd exploded, *get away from me getawayGETAWAYFROMMEYOUBITCH,* and Lara had retreated near tears. Later, she had learned that her lab coat had set him off, that in the peculiar architecture of his delusions, doctors were homicidal maniacs, forever in search of donor organs fresh for harvest. The whole unnerving scene had been engineered for her benefit, a tradition of sorts. Welcome to the ward: a little initiation ritual-cum-learning opportunity for new doctors on the floor. The lesson?

Madness is utterly impersonal. Madness doesn't care.

Those were the words that came to Lara now, gazing down at Abel. The resemblance was so profound that she half expected him to lurch erect and seize her by the shoulders, to scream those words into her face—

Spare parts spare parts SPARE PARTS—

Instead, the pressure on her hand relented, the void filled up with personality, and the cold—

—when had it gotten so cold?—

—retreated. Instead, he was only Abel: a little dazed, but Abel all the same. "What happened?" he said, but before Lara could answer—before *any* of them could answer—Lomax repeated his question:

"So many what, Abel?"

Lara glanced sharply at him, wondering if anyone else had noticed the sudden shift into the familiar.

Abel pushed himself into a sitting position. "What?" he said.

" 'So many,' you said, but you never said what."

Abel hesitated, repeating the words, drifting.

Lara, watching, saw him stiffen with memory. He looked up, wide-eyed, and she found herself staring once again into that dizzying vacuum. Then a steely glint of self-awareness obscured it. It was like watching a privacy gate slam shut inside his eyes. And then he really *was* Abel again—not the true Abel she had momentarily glimpsed, frightened and confused, naked all his veils of self—but the old Abel from that first night in the kitchen, always on stage, less a person than a performance, self-assured and owner of a certain facile charm.

"It was something you said," Lomax said.

Abel shook his head again. His face clouded, and now Lara found herself wondering if this too was feigned and, if so, how expertly. "I don't know. I can't remember. What happened?"

"You fainted," Ben said.

"Try to remember," Lomax said. "*Try.*"

"Later," Lara said, and when Lomax started to protest, she let the slightest edge creep into her voice. "I *said* later."

Lomax stood with an unrepentant glare.

"You know where you are?" Lara asked Abel.

"Harold P. Taylor Homes. Tower Number Three . . . Dreamland." He gave her a faint, rueful smile, but if he'd been aiming for humor the effort fell short. The name hung in the emptiness like an accusation. "So what happened, Doc?"

"I don't know. We'll have to look into that, won't we? You think you can walk?"

"Sure," he said, but his optimism proved unfounded. He made it to his feet all right, but they were unsteady feet indeed. Weaving slightly, with Ben on one side and Lara on the other, their hands cupped and ready at his elbows, he made his way to the elevator.

None of them spoke on the way up.

9

Upstairs in the infirmary, Abel reluctantly submitted to a more formal examination. Lara listened to his heart, checked his blood pressure, and took his temp (all normal), quizzing him as she worked: Had this sort of thing happened before? Had he felt anything unusual prior to passing out? Weakness? Dizziness? Light-headedness?

No, no, no, and no.

"What about smells?" she said, watching him button his shirt.

"Smells?"

"Oranges, maybe? Cinnamon?"

He shook his head.

"Flashes of light?"

"Afraid not."

"Voices?"

His fingers fumbled. "I hear voices for a living, Doc."

"I thought you sensed energies."

He looked up, flashing her a faintly self-mocking smile. "Touché."

"I'm serious, Abel. I'm just trying to do my job."

He crossed his arms and propped himself against the examination table. "You're right. I'm sorry. No, I didn't hear voices. What's with the inquisition?"

"Hallucinations sometimes mark the onset of grand mal seizures. Olfactory hallucinations are especially common."

"Did I *have* a seizure?"

"I'm not sure what happened to you, Abel."

"Probably, nothing," he said. "Something I ate. Right?"

"*Did* you eat today?"

"Actually, no," he said. "Not since breakfast. So you think that's it?"

Lara sensed she was being offered an out. She hesitated, and then—she couldn't help herself—she relented. "Could be."

"Good. So"—he lifted his eyebrows—"if we're done . . . ?"

"Well there's a dozen other things I'd like to do."

"Yeah?"

"Yeah. An EEG for one thing. Maybe a heart monitor."

"Please tell me our benefactor's budget didn't stretch so far."

"Alas, no."

Abel snapped his fingers. "Darn. Well—maybe, next time, right?"

"I guess."

"So I'm going to get something to eat now. Feel like tagging along? You can make sure I eat all my veggies."

But now that the crisis was past, she wanted a few minutes to think, a little time to work through what exactly had happened downstairs—and not just the fainting episode, either. She wanted to think about Lana.

"Another time, okay?" she said. "I'm tired."

"Okay, then," he said. "See you around, then."

"I'll be here." Smiling to take the sting out of it, she turned away, gathering up her tools.

"Listen," Abel said. "If it's about what happened down-stairs—"

"It was nothing, Abel. You're right: you probably just needed something to eat."

"You know what I'm talking about."

Lara stood silently by the computer workstation, unwill-ing to answer him, her fingers resting lightly atop the shelf of CDs, a neat little row of medical databases containing all that was known or could be known about human frailty—more certainly than any single practitioner could ever hope to master—and yet in all those dense columns of text not a single word that explained this sudden clutching at her heart. All that knowledge about serotonin and neurotransmitters and the emotion centers in the brain, and none of it—*none* of it—was sufficient on the subject of grief.

None of it.

For a bright segment—a brief half hour or so in the bus-tle and pressure following Abel Williams' collapse—it had flowed uninterrupted in its subterranean course, unseen even by her, this hateful current of misery and loss which Abel had tapped inside her heart. Now it bubbled to the surface again. Lara's fingers twitched—anxious to busy themselves smoothing the fabric of her slacks or wiping away the line of dust along the lip of the monitor, anxious to do anything other than rest in stillness atop this utterly inadequate, this absurd compendium of all the things that could go so disastrously wrong with the human species. She commanded them to be still. She stood there, outwardly calm, a bland smile pasted on her face.

Abel outwaited her. His silence compelled her to speak. "It's nothing," she said.

He moved toward her—a half step, that's all. He looked her in the eye for half a second, and then his gaze slid down and away, toward the computer workstation. Toward the photo of Lana she'd propped beside the keyboard.

He blanched and seemed to rock a little, suddenly uncer-tain on his feet. He reached out a hand to brace himself against the wall.

"Abel?" she said, but he interrupted, his voice a dis-tant monotone.

"That's her, isn't it?" he said, except it wasn't a question, not really. It was a statement of fact, flat and declarative.

"Abel—"

"Your sister. You were twins. Identical."

"Abel—"

"It was a long time ago—"

"I don't want to talk about this, Abel."

He fell silent, and in the silence Lara reined in her own galloping emotions. She focused on Abel, on her patient, on her duty here and now, in this fleeting present. Abel: clutching at the wall like a drowning sailor clutching at a drifting spar. His pallor hadn't retreated, but he seemed steadier somehow, resigned, less like a man in the fresh aftermath of some catastrophe than a terminal patient who'd lived too long in the shadow of eternity.

She pitied him suddenly. She pitied him and feared him, too, and maybe it was this combination that motivated her to say what she said next. She didn't know why she said it, or what she meant by it, or even what she intended to say until she had already said it, the words dying away into the air-conditioned hush. All she knew was that she believed it. Fervently.

"I don't think you should stay in this place," she told him, and Abel, looking up, gave her a faraway smile. "I think you should go home."

"I'll keep that in mind," he said, and then he stepped into the hallway and closed the door gently behind him.

10

Finally alone, Lara let herself go to hell.

Only when the sobs retreated—fifteen minutes, maybe twenty, and even then she felt torn and bloodied inside, like she'd just glutted herself at a banquet of broken glass— did she manage to get past *what* Abel had told her to the more important question: *how* he had known it. It was a soul-shattering moment, a moment in which she felt all the cool scientific dams she'd spent a life constructing tremble in their foundations. A cold wind reached her from the turbulent waters on the other side.

Shivering, she stood and walked to the window: night coming on, the ruins of Dreamland brooding under a murky shield of clouds. This place. My god, this place.

Turning, Lara surveyed the infirmary, this little exam room so like the other rooms where she'd spent her days these last eight years: the vinyl exam table with its pristine roll of paper, the tongue depressors and cotton swabs in their rows of jars atop the counter, the ranks of stainless-steel instruments, the square box of the autoclave, all of it shining and sterile in the flat, even radiance of the bulbs set overhead, all of it bright and safe and unutterably false—all these careful hedges against the night. She saw it as if for the first time. She saw how hollow it was, how little power it possessed, this little bubble of rationality at the heart of nightmare. She perceived the weight of mystery and terror that weighed always upon it, like the pressure of ocean ten thousand fathoms down, all that black, black water.

How had he known? And if he *had* known, what did it all mean and how was she supposed to deal with it?

That's when her gaze lit upon the telephone. She lifted it. She turned her face to the wall, she brought the receiver to her ear. Her fingers entwined themselves in intricate coils of cord. She didn't know what she had expected—ringing? A dial tone? Whatever, she didn't get it. What she got was silence, the empty hush of an open line. And then there was a voice, distant, calm, like the voice of a NASA flight engineer calmly noting telemetry even as the booster rockets erupted into flames on the launch pad.

"Mercy General," it said, and something twisted inside her at the words. Mercy General, everything she'd left behind: so close she could summon it all to life simply by picking up a phone, and yet, somehow, impossibly remote.

"Hello?" the voice said.

Lara sought to match it with a face. But no, it was a stranger, faceless: a voice, nothing more.

"Anyone there?" it said.

"Hi," she said. "This is Dr. McGovern."

"Evening, Doctor. You folks have a problem there?"

"No." She tilted her forehead against the wall and closed

her eyes. How could she explain? How could anyone explain? "Everything's fine. Just checking in."

"Okay. Well. We're swamped here, so unless you have—"

"No," she said. "We're fine."

"Have a good night, then."

"You, too," she said. "You have a good night."

Lara reached up without opening her eyes and cradled the phone. Then she just stood there, her forehead drawing from the wall its cool comfort. After a time—she couldn't say how long—she sighed. She straightened and turned, opening her eyes.

Ramsey Lomax stood in the doorway, his bald pate gleaming.

"You're free to leave, Doctor," he said. "All you have to do is say the word."

But she thought of Dan Sutherland and Mercy General— she thought of all she'd left behind—and when she spoke, her voice echoed strangely in her ears. It was like she wasn't even talking at all. It was like someone else's voice.

"No, no," the voice said brightly. "I'm staying."

11

No.

She would stay, they would all stay, for—let us be honest here—what else could they do? So exquisitely constructed were the traps that contained them, so finely and so carefully wrought—the work of a lifetime—that most of them hardly knew they existed, and even those that did, that sensed (as Lara did, and Ben) in some dim benighted way the steps and missteps that had brought them to this end, were powerless to free themselves.

So they stayed, and Dreamland, outward emblem and internal arbiter, contained them. Patient, cold, and infinitely removed, as from some lofty precipice, Dreamland observed them. Dreamland saw everything—saw them share a joyless meal of cold cuts in the kitchen (Abel, contrary to his promise, did not show), saw them snatch a few desultory moments of conversation in the lounge (they talked around everything; none of them mentioned the events in the lobby or inquired into the genesis of Lara McGovern's tears), saw them retreat at last to the privacy of their own quarters, like mollusks deep chambered in the solitary nautilus of self.

Dreamland—and Dreamland alone—knew them.

And if it acted at all—if it spurred Ramsey Lomax to retrieve a videotape from a bottom drawer, slide it with nervous fingers into the mouth of a contraband VCR and television unit, and stare with bated breath at an image of Abel Williams flickering upon the screen; if it visited upon Fletcher Keel dreams of whiskey and of women or afflicted Abel with a prattle of disembodied whispers as he stared sleepless at the cage of shadows printed on his ceiling; if it mocked Ben through the dead screen of the laptop he dared not switch on—none of them could say for sure.

Night Wanderings

1

Sometime in the midnight reaches before dawn of the fifth day—or was it the sixth?—Fletcher Keel opened his eyes. Sleep-fogged, only half-awake, he gazed into the darkness and pondered this question, filing through the events of the past week. It should have been easy enough, this reconstruction, yet somehow it defied him. He could call up specific moments—that sense of something staring back at him from the south stairwell or the prickly conversation with Ben in the weight room—but when he tried to piece them together, to line them up like so many beads upon a string, everything seemed to blur together, an incoherent haze of panics and renewals, all of it impossibly insulated from the world outside Dreamland's walls.

So how many days was it? Five? Or six?

Sighing, he kicked at a tangle of sheets and started through it again, working methodically forward from that bad moment on the flight. *That* was clear enough, anyway—clearer than he would have liked, actually. So was the round of introductions, those initial disconcerting moments in the lobby, and, yes, the first night, too, waking suddenly from unquiet dreams—

The thought derailed him, stranding him in the present.

He'd been dreaming just now as well, hadn't he? And something in the dream had awakened him. What was it?

Keel rolled over to glance at the alarm clock on the nightstand, and just then something spoke out of the darkness: a voice, a woman's voice, thick with dreamy urgency.

John—

"Who are you?" he whispered. "How do you know my name?"

Nothing.

Keel sat up, his bare flesh prickling. A gust of wind shouldered the building, rattling the window in its frame; the sound sparked an image in his mind: Lomax's glazier running a jagged shard of glass the length of his forearm. The whole thing was strangely vivid. He could see everything: the strained intensity in the man's long face, his knuckles white and trembling as he drove the glittering blade deeper and still deeper, the bright arterial blood welling from the wound. Wincing, Keel reached out to switch on the lamp.

The darkness swelled—

—*John,* it whispered, *come to me*—

—and his fingers closed themselves into a fist. Lisa, he thought. In darkness, he pulled his hand back and reached for the battered tee shirt and frayed jeans he'd left at the foot of the bed. In darkness, he pulled them on. Barefoot, he moved into the outer room of the suite. He stood there, gazing at the line of light under the door.

Now what?

As if in answer, the summons came again, echoing inside his head: *John, come to me, come*—

Opening the door, Keel stepped into the desolate hallway. The light burned away the final webs of sleep. It *had* been a dream, he thought. Some kind of freaking dream. And his name was Fletcher. His name had *always* been Fletcher. He glanced up and down the corridor, all plush carpet and indirect illumination, like some kind of luxury hotel, and he had to resist a sudden, almost overpowering urge to hack up a big yellow loogy and blow it all over the scalloped, eggshell finish of the walls.

Lisa, my ass, he thought. It was a dream, that's all. Lisa was gone, Lisa had been gone for years. That was another life, another man.

My name is Fletcher.

He turned back to his room, disgust clogging his throat.

Yet just as his hand closed over the doorknob, he heard it once again: that rush of expectancy in the air, the whole building drawing breath. Something brushed invisibly past him, shivering erect the blond down at the nape of his neck, and there it was again, that voice, Lisa's voice, urgent, crooning in his ear:

Come to me, John.

Images flickered on the sleep-dazed screen of his mind: a curve of hip and breast, a woman's breath hot against his throat, the taste of whiskey on his tongue. His cock twitched, stiffening. *No,* he thought, *no, it's a dream—*

But it wasn't a dream.

It was real and it lured him, that voice. It lured him all unwilling down the long hallway, past the infirmary and the elevator bay, past the lounge, past the kitchen. Abel's suite slipped by unnoticed on his left, Lomax's on his right. And then he was there, hard against the fire door into the stairwell, the south stairwell, his hand curled loosely around the door handle.

John, the voice whispered. *Come to me . . .*

Keel swallowed.

Memory tugged at him: that stir of presence in the darkness, and something else, deeply buried, long forgotten. Something he didn't want to remember. Blood thundered at his temples. In some hidden antechamber of his heart, his father stepped out of the shadows.

Don't do it, John, he said. *You're not strong enough. Don't step inside that door.*

And her voice—

—whose voice?—

—Lisa's voice—

—answering, drawing him close against the door, cheek to metal, cool as porcelain against his skin. His penis throbbed, rigid against the seam. *John, come to me. Come, John, come.*

Fletcher Keel whimpered, unaware that he had even made a sound.

Don't, his father said. *Don't do it.*

Keel sobbed, a single hoarse gasp of longing and of dread.

"Fuck you, Dad," he said.

He flung open the door and stepped into the darkness on the other side.

2

It boomed, that door. It clamped into the frame at his back with a metallic crash loud enough to rouse whatever powers or principalities of air that might have slept inside the walls of Dreamland.

But Dreamland *wasn't* sleeping, Keel did not quite allow himself to think as he stood in darkness on the other side; oh no, it was awake, or if it did sleep still, it had long since started stirring: in the hour when they had first set foot inside the crumbling lobby—four days gone, or five, or six—or before that even, months ago, when the first of Ramsey Lomax's contractors had braked his rattling pickup in the crumbling courtyard outside; stirred then, and had been stirring during all the long hours since toward some full and watchful awareness as yet unachieved. And that part of him—that not-quite-conscious self—shuddered to hear the sound of that door as it echoed unmuffled the length of the corridor, shattering for the space of a single startled heartbeat the predawn stillness.

In the neighboring room, Ramsey Lomax opened his eyes. Ben, at the far end of the corridor, sat up abruptly, reaching for his bedside lamp. In the suite opposite, Lara, too, was stirring.

Of them all, Abel alone slept on.

And even he moaned aloud at some whispered portent in a dream—moaned and thrashed his sweat-stained sheets and fumbled with blind fingers at the broken watch cinched tight around his wrist.

3

Ben stood, rubbing his eyes.

It was just after three o'clock and he could not say what had awakened him. Sleep had eluded him for hours—there had been Abel's trouble, and Lara's too, and, more pressing still, his own worries. His fingers ached with unreleased tension, the habit of a lifetime abruptly forsaken. How long since he had passed a day without writing? How long since first he had taken a pen in hand—a pencil, actually, one of those big, fat orange-yellow pencils especially engineered for clumsy first-grade fingers—and tapped the reservoir of poison in his heart? How long since he had begun to drain it, drop by drop, day by day, word by solitary word? Two decades and more, at least.

He practically twitched with the need to unburden himself of words.

He flipped on the light in the living room, sat down at his desk, and booted up the computer. It clicked and whirred, and then the welcome screen came up. Ben dragged the cursor over the word-processing icon, and paused there, his finger hovering.

Do you believe in ghosts?

You should.

"Shit," he said, and shut down the computer.

He stood, pacing, all too aware of the blank screen at his back: like an eye, coldly observant. He turned and snapped the screen shut.

"Now what?" he said aloud, and though he wasn't expecting an answer, an answer came.

Apartment 1824, Paul Cook said inside his head. *Nothing can change, not until you face Apartment 1824.*

4

On the landing, Keel swallowed.

"Who are you?" he whispered, but no answer came.

Shifting on his feet, he peered into the dark. He could see nothing, not the faintest glimmer of light, but the blindness seemed to have sharpened his other senses. Sound was magnified—his breath labored hoarsely in his lungs, and even the tiniest movement unleashed a symphony of rustling echoes. The concrete floor beneath his feet felt particulate and cold. And the smell—damp and cool as a root cellar—the smell had not changed. In all these years the smell had not changed, a dank sandy stench compounded of wet concrete and mold and stale urine that had seeped into the stone, of the menthol bite of discarded cigarette butts, and the ashen ghosts of expended gunshots. He drew it in with his breath, that smell, and for a moment memory threatened to crush him. For a moment it was all too close, so close he could almost touch it: the ring of boot heels on the stairs, the walls of pitted, paint-strewn block jumping in the uric intersection of the flashlight beams, the killing weight of the weapon in his hand. It had ended here, his father's legacy of honor, and a diminished life had begun. All these wasted years . . .

Keel drew in a long breath.

Anxiety welled through him, dampening the heat of his arousal, and then that voice renewed itself, rising up the well of stairs to peal inside his head like a bell, so clear and cold:

Come to me, John—

Like a beckoning finger in the dark, that voice. Like ice on blistered skin. It soothed and calmed him.

Come, it said.

And why not? What else did he have to lose?

Keel's hand closed around the iron rail.

In darkness, he descended.

5

Lara had already been awake for fifteen minutes when she heard the door snick closed across the hall.

Sleep had been a long time coming, and when it finally *had* arrived, it had been a restless tossing kind of sleep. She had dreamed a long, confused dream about Mercy General. Abel had been there, and Ben, too, still and cold on gurneys in the glare of the abandoned ER, their dead eyes accusing. And then she'd found herself walking down an endless corridor in a place that was somehow, simultaneously, Dreamland and Mercy General and the house she'd grown up in back in Wilmington, the house which had seemed so huge when she was a girl and which now, when she returned for a visit (*why don't you visit more often?* her parents always said), seemed cramped and airless and damp, as if mushrooms might any moment sprout from the humid weave of the carpet in the hallway. Only, in the dream, there was no carpet. In the dream, the hallway was tiled and sterile, cavernous. She stood in the doorway of her childhood bedroom, watching children at play: her sister and her younger self, so alike that even she couldn't say for sure who was who. She smiled, she lifted her hand as if to summon them—and then, from behind her, came a telltale rustle of fabric. She turned, knowing that she should not turn, but powerless, in the way of dreams, to stop herself. A man who was Fletcher Keel and not Fletcher Keel, a man who was an altogether different man, stood at the nurse's station. Blood spattered his clothes and he held a knife, one of the gleaming steel blades from Dreamland's kitchen—but that wasn't what frightened her. What frightened her, what sent a nauseating flood of terror through her veins, was the figure that stood beside him, frail and wizened in a gore-stained hospital gown, limpid eyes huge and staring. *It should have been you,* the figure said, and Lara came awake with a start.

She lay frozen in the dim red glow of the alarm clock, waiting for the dream to recede, and then she switched on the light. Lana stared back at her from the nightstand, still seven years old after all this time.

You were twins, Abel Williams said inside her head. *Identical twins.*

Not anymore, she thought, and reaching out, she turned the picture facedown.

It didn't help any. There was no escaping Lana, was there? No escaping the locket that dangled like a stone between her breasts, or the nightmare images that even now flickered at the perimeter of her thoughts.

There was no escaping what had happened in the lobby.

He had known, she thought as she pulled on a pair of jeans. Somehow Abel Williams had known. He had known about Lana's cancer, he had known about her scary-bad bout with pneumonia—

—but not how you wanted me to die, he didn't know that, did he, Lara—

—he had known the whole sordid story. He had known they were twins.

How? And what scared her more—this public exposure of vulnerability, her tearful humiliation in the lobby, or the way the whole episode undermined everything she'd forced herself to believe? For if it *had* happened—if Abel hadn't conned her, somehow, if he really *had* known—then a lifetime of hard-won skepticism went right out the window.

Dressed, Lara drifted into the outer room of the suite. On the love seat, with her legs tucked underneath her, she chewed at her thumbnail, all too suddenly aware of how silent the building was, how isolated: a vast wind-buffeted monolith jutting above the ruined moonscape of the projects.

"I'm sorry," she whispered. "I'm sorry, Lana."

But there was no answer. Even the voices in her head had fallen silent.

She felt tears start up in the corners of her eyes. She swiped angrily at them and tapped one fist against her thigh.

"Dammit," she said. "Dammit."

And just then, from across the hall, came the sound of a door quietly closing. She felt so desolate in that moment, so fathomlessly cold and alone, that had it not been for the memory of Fletcher Keel—

—*his clothes his blood-spattered clothes*—

—watching her on the treadmill, she might have yanked open her own door without a second thought. Anything for a little company, right? As it was, though, she pressed a cautious eye to the peephole instead. The hallway was empty. The doors to the suites opposite—Keel's to the left, Ben's to the right—stood shut.

Cracking her own door, Lara peeked out. Ben was just turning into the elevator bay.

Without even thinking about it, she stepped into the hallway after him.

6

Ramsey Lomax turned on the desk lamp and sat in the sleek art deco chair. It calmed him, the glossy luxury of that chair, its understated elegance and comfort. He liked fine things and for more than four decades now, from the moment he could afford to buy them, he had surrounded himself with them—paintings and sculptures he had no feelings for, first editions he would never read, cars that purred so silently and smoothly you hardly knew you were moving at all. Deferential servants. The best wine. Women most of all.

Before his marriage, during it, and afterward, too, during the decade since Sara had died, he'd enjoyed plenty of women—handsome, clean-limbed, enthusiastic—and none of them in all those years had meant any more to him than the cars or the wine or the Gold Coast apartment. Which is to say none of it, the women or the wealth, had any intrinsic importance. It signified, that's all—his success, his power, most of all his need never again to feel beholden. It signified and soothed him, and so he indulged it. Why not?

He had no patience for self-deception. Besides, he could afford it.

Yet none of it calmed him now.

Not the chair and not the marble credenza; not the framed Haring sketch over the desk, in which he could see his own reflection, ghostly and gaunt, his strong-boned face half in shadow. He stared at himself, the sound of that stairwell door echoing in his thoughts.

So it had begun.

Five days in—or was it six? (this imprecision, which wasn't like him, momentarily nagged at him)—and finally it had begun. That afternoon in the lobby, when Abel Williams had collapsed during his absurd manipulation of the doctor, Lomax had felt a seed of hope lodge inside his breast. Now that someone—

—*who?*—

—had ventured out into the night corridors of Dreamland, he felt that seed swell and burst, sinking the first questing roots into the aching loam of his heart.

"Please," he said aloud, his voice husky. It was as close as he could come to a prayer.

As the word died on his lips, he drew open the desk's central drawer.

Inside, on a bed of green velvet, lay an envelope.

7

Hesitantly at first, and then with growing confidence, Keel descended into a well of night. The dark was like syrup, pouring in at his nostrils and mouth, in his ears, through the pupils of his eyes. It filled his lungs, spun tenuous threads though his arteries, rooted itself deep in the fabric of muscle and bone. Finally it blurred even the edges of his awareness, the impermeable envelope of self. He sensed the topography of the stairwell as he might have sensed his own body: with the same certainty, the same careless grace. His feet fell naturally at the edge of every riser, he lengthened his stride for every landing, he compensated without thought for every turning of the way.

Downward, he went. Downward, his hand loose upon the iron rail.

Ten steps, twenty, a hundred and twenty. Two landings, then four, then six and eight, until finally he lost count, until finally he had descended farther than he had ever intended, beyond the lobby, beyond all logic or reason, into the subterranean guts of the building, an alarm trilling like a telephone inside his brain.

Keel ignored it. He knew the voice he would hear at the other end of the line. It was his father's voice. He knew what it would say.

Go back, John. Go back. It's not too late.

Part of him longed to do just that, to turn and begin the long ascent into the light. But another, stronger self had ears only for that other voice, the woman's voice, Lisa's voice—

—come to me—

—as it boomed like a siren's song through all the chambers of his brain.

Downward, it sang, and downward he went, his prick rigid in his trousers. And by the time he reached absolute bottom and paused in blindness before another metal door, the entire weight of the building balanced above him, that alarm bell of anxiety had faded. Only the crooning summons remained, cutting through his thoughts with an edge honed by more than a decade of pent-up need.

Come to me, it whispered.

Moving with absolute certainty in the dark, Fletcher Keel put out his hand and opened the door.

8

On the eighteenth floor, the elevator doors retracted in silence.

Lara hesitated at the threshold, studying the elevator bay

as if she might be asked to recall it for an exam—the heap of molding carpet remnants, the malodorous garbage bag of bulging black plastic, the ancient scuffs on the dull concrete floor where somebody must have dragged a piece of furniture back when Dreamland was still habitable and there were people willing to inhabit it. What she was really doing was delaying the inevitable, of course. She supposed Ben must have done the same thing.

In fact, she was a little surprised she hadn't run into him right here, still dithering.

She knew where he was heading. She had known it from the moment she'd seen him turn into the elevator bay thirteen floors below. And she should have known it before that. But for her own self-involvement, Ben's behavior during their little tour the other day would have alerted her. *Then again, Lars,* Lana put in, *but for your own self-involvement, Katie Wright might be alive even now.*

Right.

Which really didn't bear thinking about, did it?

As if in answer, a silvery tremolo, like the mocking titter of a child, chimed in the hallway around her, and Lomax's warning—

—it's unwise to wander here alone—

—ghosted through her mind. But it was nothing, she told herself—the glassy harmonic of wind in a shattered window, that's all. Instead of punching the elevator button and riding the car back down to the warmth and comfort of the fifth floor, Lara steeled herself and turned down the corridor toward the south wing. Her imagination had gotten the best of her in the lobby yesterday. She wasn't about to let it happen again. Besides, once she caught up with Ben she wouldn't be alone anymore, would she?

But the corridor, narrowing before her in diminished perspective, had a surreal, dreamlike quality. One or two lingering bulbs flickered dimly overhead, casting down sickly pools of radiance. Elsewhere, a wan blue light held sway, brightening to ghostly incandescence in the moonlit doorways and deepening to black in the intervals between, where graffiti-scrolled planes of icy block scaled the dark like the walls of some gargantuan labyrinth. The wind kicked up, rattling a door against its frame. In the distance, she heard that tingling falsetto laughter once again.

Almost against her will, Lara quickened her pace.

Doorways whisked by, whispering with malign intent. The corridor lengthened inexorably before her, like a corridor in a dream. It reminded her suddenly of *her* dream, the one which had awakened her, and she found herself wondering if maybe she was *still* dreaming—if somehow she had dreamed herself awake and, waking, plunged deeper yet into a maze of sleep, where the tiled and sterile corridors of Mercy General might metamorphose as if by magic into the walls of her childhood home or the ruined passageways before her, where she might at any moment come face-to-face with the blood-stained specter of a man who was and was not Fletcher Keel, or, worse yet, the waiflike and accusing eyes of the child who was and was not Lana but some other child—

—Katie was it Katie—

—the lost and lingering apparition of all lost sisters in all the passages of years. Her heart pounded. Her breath grew short.

Then, abruptly, she was there, at the dogleg turn of passage into the south wing, and as when waking from a dream, the world reverted to its old, familiar self. The corridor was just a corridor, nothing more. The wind was just the wind. And Ben—Ben was only Ben. He stood at the distant terminus of the corridor, in a nimbus of moonlit blue from the yawning doorway at his back, and gazed in silence at the shuttered face of apartment 1824.

Ben, she thought, and she must have spoken it aloud, for as she started down the corridor, he turned to face her, his hands restless at his sides, his dark features clenched blindly, fistlike, in some cloistered agony of grief. It shamed her, that expression, as though she had intruded upon some intensely private ritual, yet she never hesitated. When it came to hurt, Lara did not, would not, hesitate, ever again; she *was* the maternal one—Lana had been right about that much anyway—it was her cross to bear. And so she moved toward him, repeating his name softly, like a talisman, summoning him back from that reverie of guilt and sorrow as she would have coaxed a man from the edge of a precipice. "Ben," she said, "Ben," and after a moment's hesitation, he took a halting step or two to meet her. In that fraught, clockwork stumbling, she intuited all at once what she must

have been piecing together at some unconscious level from
the moment he had first turned in flight from apartment
1824: the shape and dimension of his sorrow, its latitude
and weather.

How could she have missed it?

Face-to-face they paused, two feet apart.

"It was you, wasn't it?" she said. "The little boy in that
apartment, it was you."

His lips worked soundlessly. He exhaled, and dragged in
a choking breath. He turned away.

In the silence Lara was conscious of the water dripping
from the burst pipe overhead. She looked up at it, an intricate stalactite of sculpted ice suspended from the lip of the
shattered pipe. A single moonstruck droplet clung precariously to its sharpened end, and then it plunged away, to
shatter with a *plink* against the ice-skimmed puddle below.
When she lowered her gaze, he was there, fully present
once again, staring into her eyes.

"I can't," he whispered. He drew a breath. "I can't go
in that place."

"You don't have to. Listen. You don't have to do that."

"I stand there, I look at the door, my heart, it's like I
seize up inside—"

He clutched at his chest, and she saw how washed-out
he was, how drawn and pale. Beads of perspiration jeweled
his forehead. His breath came in shallow heaves. She did
not have to touch him to know that his pulse was galloping,
his heart fluttering like a trapped sparrow in its bowl of
ribs. He bent double, as if he might throw up.

"I can't," he whispered. "I don't . . . understand . . .
what's happening . . ."

And then she did touch him.

She took his arm. She steadied him, and when he spoke
again—when he said, "I need . . . some air," she turned
him back toward the apartment, toward the glimmering
EXIT sign, the metal fire door, and the stairwell on the
other side.

"No," he said. "*No!*" In a panic, he resisted. Then, all
at once, he surrendered. Arm in arm, they lurched past the
mute entryway of apartment 1824 and banged through the
fire door beyond. In the darkness of the landing, a column
of steep iron rungs circled invisibly toward the roof. She

might have missed them altogether but for the guide of memory and the intermittent complaint of the door above, groaning in its frame with every knife-edge gust of wind.

And in the tumult of the moment she *did* miss something else.

They both missed it, though her foot had grazed it in the corridor as they passed and sent it spinning across that thin-skinned pool of ice. It fetched up against the far block wall and shattered with a sound like brittle twigs cracking underfoot: the corpse of the rat which only days ago had lain sodden there and freshly dead. How utterly skeletonized it was, and how soon: stripped of flesh to its white and grinning bones.

9

In darkness, disoriented, Keel thought: Imagine.

Imagine eight stone slabs, Dreamland, Tower Three and her seven sisters, featureless and vertical, erect against a sky of humid August steel. Imagine a battalion, mazelike, of squad cars, ambulances, and fire trucks idling their poison into the choking air. Imagine the buzz and chatter of the dashboard radios, the grunted oaths, the barked commands, the distant *whup-whup* of a chopper circling overhead. And in the midst of all this chaos, imagine a man. He has a way of moving purposefully and quickly, this man, with a kind of unconsidered grace; he is quick-tempered, and capable of charm. He is, in other words, a man not unlike yourself.

But—pay attention now, this is all-important—this man: he is not you.

Imagine him—

Peripherally aware of all this and more: of the fire team crowded at his shoulders and the sun pulsing like a white-hot coal in the sky, of the trickle of sweat oozing down the channel of his spine. He knows the weight of the weapon in his gloved hands. He senses the eyes of the civilian evacuees upon him, women and children mostly, these citizens of a darker nation pressing resentfully against the line of uniforms at his back. He's unlearned but intelligent, this man. He has a kind of animal cunning. He knows how he and his companions must appear: more like gigantic insects than human beings, their strange white faces suspended inside exoskeletons of matte black body armor, each of them sporting the kind of semiautomatic firepower most people never see outside of action movies. More like storm troopers than saviors, the invading SS in the Warsaw ghetto.

He knows all this, intuitively, but he does not care.

In that moment, with the sun beating on his armored shoulders, he cares about nothing but the sheaf of age-yellowed blueprints spread across the hood of the squad car before him, anchored there by gloved hands like his own. Those blueprints may well hold the key to his survival. In fifteen minutes, twenty at the most, he'll be inside that building. He'll be ascending the blind well of the darkened stairs—

—*the south stairs, John*—

—*that's not my name my name is*—

—toward a confrontation with whatever awaits him in the stultifying heat of the upper stories, in that rathole warren of crack dens and cinder block corridors. A confrontation with something that can kill him. He's confirmed that with his own eyes, the man in the matte black Kevlar—saw through the sweep of the binoculars clipped to his belt the body of a man writhing in a pool of his own blood there on the heat-softened blacktop of the central plaza. Three times in the last twenty minutes, an ambulance crew from Mercy General has tried to retrieve him. Each time, gunfire from the tower drove them back. The imaginary man in the black armor saw it with his own eyes, so he studies those blueprints like he's never studied anything in his life up to now—not the weapon in his own hands (which he can field strip and reassemble blindfolded in three minutes flat), not the lessons of his father more than ten years gone, not the faces of his sisters or his mother or the almost-woman that he thinks he loves. He studies those blueprints because the truth of the matter is that for all his training, for his four years in the service, his months at the academy and on the street, for all his endless hours of rehearsal on

the range, he's never once come under live fire; the truth
of the matter is, he wants to know exactly where he is and
where to go—

—*to hide*—

—when the shit starts raining down. The truth is he's
scared. So he imprints the layout of that building in the
gray matter of his brain.

Imagine it, Keel thought. It is not memory. It's imagination only. So *imagine* it.

And he imagined it. Standing there in the dark with
that summons—

—*come to me John come*—

—still beating in his ears, he saw as if projected on a
screen those disintegrating blueprints fished somewhere out
of a file in the bowels of the special gangs unit. Saw the
squarish block of the tower cored through with the twin
elevator shafts, saw the metered heights of the four stairwells, one each at the corners of the lobby and the extremi-
ties of the building's outflung wings. Saw in particular the
stairwell that had been assigned to the fire team of that
other and imaginary man. With a mental flip of age-ivoried
pages he could almost see himself at the base of that stairwell, deep in the labyrinthine substructure of the tower
above.

What lay before him?

Storage, that's what the blueprints said. An enormous
storage room, twenty feet high or more, girded at intervals
with titanic archways of formed and rebar-reinforced concrete, marching in colonnade away from him: the building's
lowest level, its dank and secret heart. Keel had a sense of
spacious emptiness in the darkness, cool currents in the air,
a scent of damp stone emanating from the glossy upturned
eyes of subterranean pools. He could see it all so clearly
in the blueprints. A row of doorways sketched themselves
in blue ink along the far wall: tool rooms and workshops;
the lair of an ancient and enormous furnace like a dragon
rusting, rendered obsolete by Lomax's renovations, its ferric odor faintly seasoning the air; a lounge and office area
for the maintenance staff. He could sense it somehow—

—*how?*—

—he could see it in the imaginary blueprints in his head,
but he could not *really* see it. He could not see it with his

eyes, so to confirm it he called aloud into the darkness, "Who are you?"

The echo came rolling back to him in waves, out of the cavernous grottoes overhead, off water and from the mouths of damp stone, down the whispering gallery of arches.

. . . who are you who are you who are you who . . .

Fletcher Keel grimaced. The hairs along his arms shivered themselves to attention, his scrotum shrank into the shelter of his body, the heat of his arousal retreated. For the space of an instant the house of lies he'd spent the last two decades erecting trembled in its bones. The weight of memory lipped the surface of some internal dam, and the man he had imagined or remembered—

—it wasn't memory it wasn't—

—almost merged into the man he had become. Then, just as the last echo died, the summons renewed itself.

I'm yours, it said. It said, *I'm yours for the taking.*

It might have *been* an echo, except that it was a woman's voice. It was Lisa's voice, it was Susan Avery's voice, it was the smoky whiskey-timbred voice of every woman he had ever known, in every bed, in every bar and brothel, in every backseat where he had bought or stolen the sweet oblivion of a momentary spasm.

And it was coming from the building super's office—an office with a rump-sprung sofa to accept the weight of their coupled bodies. He did not pause to question this, to wonder how he knew it or how it was he found his way surefooted through all that void of dark. Images cascaded through his mind—the rounded promise of the flight attendant's breast at his cheek or the perfect inverted heart of her ass as she leaned toward the passenger before him, the fleeting taste of Susan Avery's lips against his own—and in the haste of his tumescence he did not pause to wonder what it was that crackled like kindling underfoot as he hurried down that avenue of arches.

He didn't think of it at all on any conscious level. He hardly heard it. But even in that frenzied moment of desire a fragment of his ever-watchful being, frightened and deeply buried, registered the sensation of something brittle snapping underneath his unshod feet. At some level, even then, he knew.

Whatever it was, it wasn't kindling.

10

"Breathe," Lara said. "Just breathe."

But a vise had clamped down on his chest, and he could not breathe. He clutched at her with one hand and bent at the waist, heaving.

"Feels . . . like . . . dying," he managed to choke between gasps.

"Just breathe. It'll pass."

It felt like it would never pass. The tar-pebbled deck of the roof pitched like a ship in a storm. Nausea flooded his mouth, hollow and metallic. His heart raced. And he was hot, a prickly suffocating heat, like being smothered in asbestos or air-blown insulation, truckloads of the stuff.

"Breathe," Lara said. She touched his chin, lifting his face. She held his gaze. "Breathe with me," she said, and he caught the rhythm of her respiration, this breathing: the long, slow intake of air, the tremulous pause that followed at its peak, and then the exhalation, emptying through pursed lips every last chamber of the lungs, until finally—

"Breathe."

—you hungered once again for air, and you caught at the black wind sweeping across the rooftop, and you drew it in. *Breathe,* she said, and he breathed. Like a lifeline flung to him, this imperative, reeling him back in to the world: eye to eye, breath to breath, even their heartbeats falling into step at last, until finally the intimacy was too much for him—

Ben turned away.

He stood at roof's edge, calmer, his hands flat atop the chest-high parapet, and thought of Dante Morris. He thought of the long fall from that cold height, eighteen stories, the skyline stretched like a painted scrim on the horizon, the earth spread out below you depthless as a plate, acquiring form and dimension as the pavement hurtled up to meet you. If it had happened tonight, that fall, it would have been a fall into darkness. A black and solitary pillar, Dreamland stood in the center of a charred pit of wreckage and debris: the dead lands were dark, ringed round by the lights of a still-living city.

Lara leaned beside him, elbows on the wall.

"You okay?"

"I'm okay," he said, without looking over at her. Then: "Thanks."

"Just doing my job."

They were silent, the sky an opalescent shield of cloud and reflected light, and the city silent too, silent as a city in a dream, miragelike and distant beyond the ashen mounds of waste below.

"So what's that mean," he said. "A panic attack?"

"Nobody really knows, actually. Symptomatically, anyway, it seems to be a distortion of the fight-or-flight reflex, the body getting its wires crossed—the accelerated heartbeat, the adrenaline rush, the whole thing. You're probably one of the lucky ones."

"Sure feels lucky."

"Some people have them all the time," she said. "Yours, on the other hand, seems to have been situationally triggered."

Ben said nothing.

"It *was* you, wasn't it? The little boy in that room?"

He turned to look at her. The wind kicked up just then, veiling her face in streamers of dirty blond hair. When she brushed it back, hooking it with an economical little gesture over her ear, what struck him was not the squared-off line of her jaw or the prominently boned ridges of her cheeks. What struck him was how freckled and pale she was. How white.

"What if it was me?" he said. "Whoever it was, he died in that apartment, too. Whoever it was, he doesn't have anything to do with me."

"Why are you here then?"

"What's it matter?"

"Like I said: I'm just trying to help."

"What were you doing, anyway? Following me?"

Lara made a sound that wasn't quite a laugh: a plosive little *huh* of disgust or disbelief. She gazed out toward the skyline. "You've got a real chip on your shoulder, you know that?"

"Well, were you?"

"What if I was?"

"Lomax put you up to it?"

The accusation seemed to shock her. She wheeled toward him, her eyes widening. "No," she said. "No! It's—" She hesitated, biting her lip.

"It's what?"

She turned away, crossing her arms over her chest. "I was having some trouble sleeping, that's all."

"Oh," he said, as if that explained everything, and then neither of them spoke for a time. The cold was crystalline, the wind edged with ice, and neither of them was dressed for this parley beneath an unstarred January sky that gave no hint of any dawn that might be coming. But they stood there all the same, staring out across a sea of darkness toward the distant shoreline of the city. To Ben, it did not look much like a city, after all. It did not look like any real place he had ever seen. It looked like a child's toy or a painted stage flat. It looked like an image in a telescope, impossibly remote. Four days—or was it five now?—and already the comfortable, daylit world he'd left behind seemed so distant, so impossible to imagine, that he might have been here all his life. He might never have left Dreamland at all.

You've got a real chip on your shoulder—you know that?

He exhaled slowly. He swallowed.

"So this trouble sleeping," he said. "It have anything to do with the thing in the lobby?"

11

The woman was waiting for him in the super's office.

The minute the door closed behind him, shutting him inside a vault of darkness, Keel could smell her. A part of him—that rational and uneasy fragment at his core—lodged a weak protest, but he ignored it. He could smell her, after all. He could *smell* her—the faint floral hint of her perfume and underneath that, fainter still, and sweeter, the bouquet of her flesh itself. Most of all he could smell the ripe, piquant musk of her sex. It prickled in his nostrils like the smoky heat of whiskey, too palpable and earthy, too undeniably *physical*, to brook even a whisper of doubt.

She was there.

His cock stood upright against his belly. Rigid. Aching.

She was there.

"Who are you?" he whispered, and the answer, when it came, came not in words but in the lightest brush of lips against his lips, like the wings of a moth as it alights for a moment and is gone.

Fletcher Keel moaned and in the darkness he reached for her.

With his hands, he saw her: the sweep and fall of hair at her shoulder, the weighted pressure of her breasts, the smooth plane of her belly, the lean curve of her hips. Slipping lower then, to the moist heat at her core, he drew her body against his own, his mouth to hers, her breath warming in his lungs, their hearts falling into lockstep rhythm. Through the sheer fabric of his tee shirt, he felt her nipples bud, and he was aware suddenly of how constricting his clothes were, how warm he was, how welcome those hands, knowing, at his trousers.

Gasping, he stepped away, skinning his tee shirt over his head.

The darkness seemed to wheel around him, vertiginously.

"Who are you?" he whispered.

But her hands—

—*whose, whose hands*—

—were busy down below, and her heat was all around him in the air. Like a snake shucking its outworn husk and sliding newborn into the sun, he stepped out of his jeans, and stood naked in the warm and velvet dark. "Who—" he said, and with her lips she answered him. With her weight she bore him back, and, yes—it happened just as he had known it would—an ancient rump-sprung sofa spread its arms to receive him. She straddled him, her mouth dipping to meet his kiss, her hair grazing his shoulders like a teasing veil flung forward to enclose them. His breath was wild and panicked in his lungs, terrified and hungry.

"Lisa?" he said tentatively. "Susan?"

With his hands he saw her. With his hands he traced the delicate stem of her spine, like a flower bowing to the wind. With his hands he cupped her flanks, drew her up and lifted, imbedding a single finger to the knuckle in her heat. He suckled at the knubbed pearl of her breast, and then she drew away, lowering her face to feed hungrily at the hollow of his neck, her breath hot against his skin. Lower then, and still lower, her hands busy in his lap, she took between her lips each nipple one by one, her tongue swirling darting teasing, drawing always down behind it a line of cooling moisture, until at last she knelt before him, there on her knees on a floor which he knew even in the darkness—

—*how?*—

—to be a checkerboard of cheap black and white tile, dusty now, and broken by the abuse of years.

Keel hung in perfect equipoise, suspended between terror and desire.

"What's happening?" he whispered, leaning forward. "Who are you?"

With his hands he saw her, the squared angle of her jaw and the sharp planes of her cheekbones: not Lisa, who had passed out of his life like a dream all those years ago and—who knows?—might not anymore exist at all except as a shadow in his mind of the past he had worked so hard to forget; not Lisa and not Susan Avery either, who had hardly stepped *into* his life, who had but pressed her lips to his for the first time, and then not entirely willingly, just as that same past reached out to reclaim him. No. Not the past that was gone or the future that might have come to pass had he stayed in San Antonio. She was entirely of the moment, this woman, entirely of the here and now.

He felt his lips shape her name.

"Lara," he said.

And then she took him in her mouth.

12

Ah, yes, Lana said inside her head. *The thing in the lobby. What about that, sis? What* about *the thing in the lobby?*

Brushing hair out of her eyes, Lara studied Ben, slim and dark and not unhandsome. He gazed back at her unflinching, his eyes shadowed, deeply recessed and knowing. There was a tenacity there, a brusque disregard for social pieties, that was maybe crucial for someone in his line of work. *What brings you here, anyway?* he'd asked her once, and now, whether he knew it or not, he'd found another way of asking the same question and she had an idea that he would keep on asking it until he got an answer that satisfied him.

Crossing her arms, she said, "My sister."

"Your sister. Theresa Matheson was your *si*—"

"No," she said, lifting her hands. "No! My sister— A long time ago, my sister . . ."

"She died?"

"In Wilmington. A long, long time ago."

"How long?"

"I was nine."

He sighed. "It's not long enough, though, is it?" he said. "It's never long enough."

And why shouldn't he sympathize? Who would know better, after all? Some wounds never healed, that's all. Or if they did, something always came along to tear them open once again. She felt her hand rise to touch the locket at her breast, the face of Katie Wright blooming like a terrible flower in her mind.

"She's been on my mind lately, I guess."

"That what brings you here?"

She shrugged. "Like I said before, it's boring."

He gave her an appraising glance, and then shrugged. "Okay, then," he said. "Abel though—" He shook his head. "You understand that Abel's little show in the lobby, that was nothing. You know that, right?"

"It *felt* like something."

"Sure it did. That's the business our friend Abel is in: making nothing *feel* like something. And he's good at it, I'll give him that."

An instant passed in silence, two or three heartbeats. She looked out across a gulf of darkness at the glittering facade of the skyline. It reminded her of an enormous ocean liner slipping by in the night, the *Titanic* maybe, or, better, the distant lights of the *Californian* on the horizon: so close she could almost touch it, yet no help to be had there, the dark waters already lapping at her feet. She shivered.

"Cold," he said.

She glanced up at the clouds, heavy with weather. "A storm's coming. You can smell it."

Still, they only stood there, neither one of them anxious to descend back into the wrecked building below. She supposed he dreaded facing 1824 once again and she couldn't much blame him: it was an emotional Waterloo, a panic attack: a sense of dread and terror, of premonitory doom so deep and paralyzing that the uninitiated could hardly fathom it. Better the icy rooftop than risk another such episode. Yet she couldn't help feeling it was more than that, too, that something yet unspoken lay between them, some unfinished business.

"You don't believe in him, do you?"

"No," she said, too abruptly. "No. I don't. I don't believe him."

" 'Cause it's cold reading he's doing. That's all it is."

She blew her breath out in a cloud. "What's that?"

"It's a technique they use, people like Abel." His tone of voice told her what he thought about people like Abel. He turned to face her. "He didn't tell you a thing. You told him and he just tricked you into thinking it was the other way around, that's all."

"What do you mean?"

"He asked you a bunch of questions, that's all. You provided all the answers."

"No." She shook her head. "He knew things, he—"

"He knew nothing," Ben said. "It's guesswork, that's all. He starts out vague as he can be. He's got a sense of 'con

nection' with someone in the room. What's that supposed
to mean? A friend, he said, and no one bites on that so he
revises it. Says it's a family member, and that's a pretty
safe bet, don't you think. Is there anybody on earth who
hasn't lost somebody? And maybe he sees you react a
little—he's observant, he has to be—so he focuses on you.
Says he senses this person had a heaviness in the chest, and
that could be anything, too, couldn't it? Heart attack, cancer, you name it, and you come out with pneumonia, *you*
did. You just handed it to him."

"I didn't," Lara said.

But she had, hadn't she? She remembered it now.

"Then he says it's your mom," Ben was saying, "and
when you don't respond he corrects himself, says it's your
sister. And the thing is, people our age, they don't *die* of
pneumonia, they get better, so he knows it's got to be
something else, and he goes for cancer. I mean, what else
is he going to go for, right? See how he played you?"

And she did. She laughed suddenly, surprised, though
she didn't quite know why.

"Like slot machines," he was saying. "People plug quarters into slots all night, maybe win two or three times, but
that's what they remember: the hits. They *want* to believe.
People want to believe."

"Not me," she said, shaking her head.

He lifted his eyebrows.

"No," she said, and it was true: where she might have
expected a spark of resentment at Abel, she felt instead
only a bottomless sense of relief. The fear and doubt which
had stricken her when he'd departed with that stupid joke
about eating his veggies, the fear and doubt which had inspired that dream of Fletcher Keel—

—his clothes his blood-spattered clothes—

—which had momentarily threatened to undermine everything she had worked her whole life to believe—the
whole oppressive weight of it had abruptly lifted. She
looked up at Benjamin Prather. She could have hugged
him. "Really," she said. "I'm glad. If it had been true . . .
I mean what would I believe then? I'm a doctor, I'm supposed to be a scientist, right?"

She laughed again, and this time he joined her, but when
the sound of it dissipated into air, incongruous as a covey

of doves lifting itself in flight against the darkling sky, Ben
still looked troubled.

He probed the pebbled roof with the toe of his shoe.
"Still—and no offense—but it's hard to imagine Lomax
buying that line. He's a canny old guy. There's something
else going on here, something we haven't seen yet."

And as suddenly as he had evoked her relief, he dismissed it. Because what came suddenly into her mind was
a picture of Abel reaching out to steady himself against
the door frame, his face blanching as he stared at Lana's
photograph, like he'd surprised himself. Like he'd *scared*
himself. *That's her*, he'd said, and it hadn't been a question
either. *That's her. You were twins, you were identical twins*,
and how could he have known that, how could he have
guessed that, because they had stopped being twins a long
time ago, they had stopped being twins more than twenty
years ago, she was thirty years old and Lana—Lana hadn't
aged a day, Lana would be nine forev—

"Lara?"

Ben's hand at her elbow—gentle, so gentle, barely there
at all—summoned her back. She looked up. *There* is, she
wanted to say. *There* is *more to it than that. What happened
in the lobby? Why did he faint? And how did he know
about Lana? How? Tell me that*, she wanted to say. *How?*

But gazing up into the puzzled skepticism of Ben's face,
she found herself biting off the words instead, swallowing
them like stones. And still it hung there between them: that
unsaid something, unfinished business. She didn't know how
long they stood there like that, staring into each other's eyes,
maybe ten inches apart, only that it was a long time, and the
wind started up again and cut across the roof like a blade,
quartering the night. He drew his hand away, then, and she
wanted it back: that touch, that human connection.

"You okay?"

"I'm fine." She forced a smile and shivered once again.
"It's cold," she said. "Come on."

Together, not touching, they turned away. At the door,
deferential and courtly in his way, Ben stood back to let
her precede him. And then the door closed behind them,
shutting out the lights of the city, bright twin of this, its
darker sister. Shutting out the night. Or shutting them inside it.

13

In the same moment, thirteen floors below, Abel Williams thrashed his sheets, crying aloud in sorrow or in terror. And deeper still, deep in the bowels of Dreamland, in the fleeting moment just before he came, Fletcher Keel's eyes suddenly snapped open. For an instant—the space of a single heartbeat, and maybe less—he felt as though his prick had been imbedded in a block of ice. An image of Lomax's glazier gripped him: the wounds gaping at his wrists, the bloody shard of glass he'd used to make them, the dawning horror in his eyes: *What have I done? My God, what have I done?* Then his climax seized him, roiling, tidal, lifting everything before it, and that numbing sensation of ice, if it had even existed at all, was swept away.

Seven floors above him, Ramsey Lomax sat in his art deco chair and stared down at the envelope in the drawer, stark white and tidy on its mat of velvet green.

When he reached for it, his hand was trembling.

The Next Day

1

Waking was like coming out of a fog.

He had been dreaming—he was *still* dreaming, he knew that—but most of the dream was lost back there in the mist, blurred shadows, more sensed than seen: an out-stretched hand, the echo of a voice—

—*we're here, Abel, we've* always *been here*—

—the shape of a stunted apple tree lifting winter-barren arms against the sky.

The tree gave him pause.

He knew that tree, he could taste its apples sour on his tongue, strong enough to clear out the mists, to root him if only for a breath in space and time: here, in the house in Copperhead, in his boyhood bedroom high up under the eaves, the window frosted with his breath.

It was like he had never left, like he had not so much dreamed it as summoned it back out of time: the room dimly aglow, lit only by the bedside lamp over his shoulder; the uncarpeted hardwood chill beneath his feet; the window itself, mullioned in dark wood, a crack bisecting his reflection where an errant ball had struck the pane. *His* room, intact, unchanged. Out there, the streetlight; in here, the cage of shadows on the ceiling. Downstairs in the cozy oven-smelling kitchen, a late dinner warming on the stove as the second-shift whistle flared and died away into the darkness, the whole house hushed in expectation of his father's boot upon the stair.

Abel only stood there, looking out, letting the shadowy figures in the fog recede. Maybe this was the place where dreaming left off and reality began. Maybe his whole life up to now—Susie Whatshername and *Messages from Beyond* and Dreamland itself—had been a dream.

Maybe his father had never died.

He leaned his head against the glass and sighed. His breath fogged the glass, and when he lifted his boy's hand to clear it, there lay upon the glossy surface underneath a single flickering blur of color, an impressionist dab of white, like a lily, or a rose.

A foreboding stone plummeted through his breast as he looked at it.

He did not want to turn and face it, that mysterious white blur. More than anything else in the world, he did not want to turn and face it—yet with a kind of dread inevitability he found himself doing exactly that, pivoting on his heels, helpless in the way of dreams to stop himself, the room suddenly brimming with strangeness, like an overfull cup. His bed was gone—his bed, the nightstand, the WVU pennant on the far wall, all the familiar landmarks of his childhood, gone, gone, gone.

In their place, refulgent in the gleam of a hidden ceiling spot, stood a casket, its lid closed. Ornate candelabra burned at either end—that was what he'd seen in the glass, the guttering reflection of a candle flame, neither a lily nor a rose—flanking the bizarre centerpiece on the glossy lid of the casket: a framed snapshot of his father and an old-fashioned rotary telephone, squat and venomous as a toad.

Abel swallowed.

His father gazed back at him, mute and frozen, his face under the mining cap gaunt and smudged with glittering streaks of coal. He stood in the cage of the mine elevator, the earth laid open like a wound at his back. Abel stepped closer, lifting one tentative hand, his eyes fixed on the photograph.

"Dad," Abel said. "Oh, Dad . . ."

And then the telephone started to ring.

2

Keel opened his eyes. He did not immediately know where he was, and he did not much care. He had slept as small children sleep, trusting and deep, without stirring, and for a moment he was content simply to lie still, suffused with a drowsy sense of well-being. He had the fleeting thought that if he lay very still he might find that he hadn't woken up after all, that he had only dreamed of waking and might at any moment slip once again beneath the surface of consciousness into the forgetful depths underneath.

It was dark enough, anyway.

In other respects, however, his environment seemed disinclined to cooperate. The air was a touch too cold for one thing—he was naked, he realized—and the silence too all-pervasive. A spring was digging into the small of his back. He shifted slightly, hoping to relieve the pressure, and memory flared inside him, strobic flashes punctuated with darkness. The summons in the air and the blind descent of the stairwell. Most of all the woman—

—Lara could it have been Lara—

—kneeling in the darkness before him, to take him in her mouth.

It all seemed fuzzy now. Remote and unthreatening. Like a dream, he thought. Like he'd been sleepwalking or something.

He sat up. A subterranean chill gripped him. The air tasted stale and cool, like the air in a soda bottle after the soda has gone flat, and the taste of it in his mouth brought it all back home to him: the reality of Dreamland. Not Albuquerque or Santa Fe or San Antonio or any of the other sun-blistered cities where he'd momentarily washed up in the last two decades. No, he was waking up in Dreamland, and not in his comfortably anonymous upstairs suite, either, but down here in the building's hidden heart.

Don't go back, Susan Avery had told him.

But he *had* come back, and what harm had come to him? None. Nothing at all had happened. A handful of unpleasant dreams and a few episodes of almost-memory, disturbing on the face of them perhaps, but so distant that you could almost pretend they didn't matter at all. They might have happened to some other man. You might have imagined him. Maybe you did. And now this: the best sleep you could remember having in years.

"See, Suze," he said aloud. "Nothing to worry about."

Bracing one hand against the back of the sofa, Keel stood. He moved with confidence despite the darkness. He could not see exactly, but he had a clear sense of the room's layout—the filing cabinets on the wall to his right, the desk just across from them—and if some fragmentary component of his personality—

—Susan, maybe, or dear old Dad—

—wondered just how that could be, Keel wasn't inclined to indulge them. He felt good. For the first time in years, he'd slept like a baby and he felt just fine, thank you. He wasn't going to let any sniping from the peanut gallery ruin it. As if to prove it, he reached out and switched on the reading lamp—he knew somehow that it was an adjustable gooseneck lamp hinged halfway up the five-foot post; he had a picture of it in his head, and he didn't bother worrying about that either. Yet there was something gratifying all the same—a kind of vindication—in reaching out and finding it just where he expected it to be, and driving home the switch.

The room looked just as he had imagined it: the black-and-white checkerboard tile, his footprints faintly visible in the dust, the spavined sofa, the row of metal filing cabinets. The desk stood just where he thought it would, a standard government-issue desk, dented and gunmetal gray. Everything about the place projected a sense of abandonment—from the avalanche of yellowing memos and coffee-stained invoices on the desk to the freebie wall calendar (ERIC'S AUTO PARTS—WE'RE THERE WHEN YOU NEED US!), nine years out of date—but there was something comfortable about it, too. It was neither as rundown as the apartments upstairs, nor as impersonal as Lomax's renovations. It was just . . . well, homey.

Keel stooped to gather up his clothes and dressed without haste. Warmer then, he lowered himself into the creaking wooden chair before the desk. He surveyed the office as he reclined, studying the wall calendar (girls in bikinis posed against an array of shiny street rods) with some leisure and chuckling at the framed novelty sign hanging over the desk (IF I WANT TO HEAR YOUR SHIT, it announced, I'LL SQUEEZE YOUR HEAD). He picked up the name plate on the desk—DENNIS EAKIN, it read—and then, idly curious, pulled open the desk's middle drawer. It contained the usual office debris—a stack of business cards, a cache of paper clips and ballpoints, a crumpled pack of Winstons. Another drawer held hanging files—old Dennis appeared to have been truant the day they discussed alphabetical order—and still another, a variety of hand tools: a hammer, a couple of box-cutters, a pair of broken pliers.

Yawn, yawn, and yawn again, Keel thought.

He opened the final drawer, bottom right, twice as deep as the others. More memos, a box of pencils, and . . . something else: a bright corner of slick cover stock, just peeking out from underneath a box of letterhead.

Keel snorted. "Dennis, you old horndog," he said, shoving aside the letterhead, and yes, he was right, it was exactly what he thought it was, a magazine—a stack of magazines, actually—much thumbed and swollen with dampness. He gathered them up and fanned them out atop the drift of memos in front of him, a poker hand of convenience-store pornography: *Juggs*, *Hustler*, two issues of *Gallery* ("Home of the Girl Next Door"), and a tattered digest-size copy of *Penthouse Forum*. Gazing down at the garish parade of airbrushed flesh, Keel couldn't help feeling a faint stir of last night's excitement at the base of his belly.

He felt something else, too, a dawning suspicion (though it was really more than a suspicion, wasn't it?) that maybe, just maybe, he hadn't exhausted the contents of Denny's stash. Part of him—the part he associated with Susan Avery, the part he associated with his father—suggested in no uncertain terms that this might be a good time to suspend the search and vacate the premises. The other part of him—the Fletcher Keel part—reached down and pulled the drawer out to its limit.

He knew what he was going to see there before he saw it. He knew it the same way he had known that the lamp was one of those old-fashioned gooseneck lamps. He knew it the way he had sensed even before he opened the office door last night that there would be a sagging, mildew-smelling sofa to receive him. He did not know how he knew it. But he knew it all the same. Dennis, that old horndog, was also a secret tippler, the kind of man who likes a nip in the morning to get his motor running and another one before lunch to prime his appetite and three or four more during the afternoon just to keep things running smoothly. And he knew that bourbon—cheap bourbon, Ten High toward the end of the month, Old Crow if he was feeling flush—was Denny's poison of choice.

There were three bottles at the back of the drawer: two liters of Crow, their plastic seals unbroken, and—surprise, surprise, Denny was busting the budget, he must have scratched off a lottery winner right there on the counter—a pint of Jack, green label, the good stuff, maybe a quarter gone.

Keel grunted, a plosive little *huh* of exclamation. Setting the magazines aside, he cleared the desk, dumping the invoices and memos in disorderly heaps on the floor. Then, without making any conscious decision to do so—

—*no, Fletcher,* Susan Avery said inside his head—

—he reached into the drawer and let his fingers close around the cool neck of a bottle of Old Crow. It might have been made to fit his hand, it felt so natural. He held it up to the light, turning it as a jeweler turns a gem, amber radiance swimming in its depths, and then he set it down on the desk. Its companions soon joined it, the two liters of Crow escorting the squat pint of Jack, one on either side, like a couple of sentries marching a POW off for interrogation: Private Daniels, sir, serial number Old Number 7. He laughed, rocking back in his chair to study them. How easy it would be to reach out, spin loose the cap on a bottle—say the Jack, for starters—and lift it to his mouth. He could almost see himself do it. It was like watching a snippet of film leap its sprockets, a stuttering glimpse of things to come, licorice and wood smoke blooming on his tongue—

He laughed again, a strangled, despairing sound.

The bottles stood at attention before him.

He stared at them for a while. He didn't know how long he stared at them.

3

The phone rang again, like an air raid siren going off inside his head.

Abel reached out and picked it up. "Hello?" he said. "Dad?"

In answer came a flood of voices, snaking their way up the coils of black telephone line to hiss mockingly in the speaker at his ear, a dozen voices, a hundred, a thousand voices from the world beyond the fence, all of them saying his name at once, *Abel, Abel, Abel AbelAbelabelabelabel—*

Then, abruptly, he was awake—really awake, this time, sitting bolt upright in a nest of tangled sheets, his name still riding the air.

"Abel? You in there? Hey—" Knocking, a persistent knocking at precise intervals, like the ringing of a phone. "Come on, Abel, you're starting to scare me."

The doctor. Lara.

He took a breath. It was midmorning, after eleven by the clock on his nightstand. Out the window, the sky was gray and heavy. "I hear you," he called. "I was asleep. Give me a second, okay?"

"Okay." The relief in the voice was palpable.

Sighing, Abel stood. The room was silent, so silent that he might have dreamed the whole thing—the nightmare moments in the lobby and the exam that followed, culminating in that moment of surpassing strangeness when he'd happened to let his gaze fall upon the photograph of Lara's sister and it had all come clear to him, a premonition that bordered on certainty, on knowledge, her little girl's voice ringing in his ears. *That was me. We were twins, identical twins—*

Just recalling it, he felt a wave of strangeness wash over him.

Enough.

No more voices, not now, anyway. Maybe you *did* dream it. And the doctor is waiting.

He splashed water on his face and pulled on a pair of faded cords. The outer room was silent. See, he thought, nothing to worry about. But as he reached out and swung open the door he heard a silvery rill of amusement from the far corner of the room. A child's laugh, bright and delicate as the tingling of struck glass.

"What?" Lara said, when she saw his face.

Abel swallowed. "Nothing," he said. "It's nothing."

4

"So yesterday," Ben said in the kitchen. "The thing with Abel."

Lomax looked at him over the rim of his coffee cup. "What about it?"

"Fainting like that. It was weird, that's all."

Lomax shrugged almost imperceptibly. "It was cold down there. We're all under pressure. The doctor said he hadn't eaten."

"True. But I can't help wondering . . ."

"What?"

Ben took a bite of his sandwich, turkey on rye. He studied Lomax as he chewed, the curving prow of his nose, the cold, cold eyes. Lomax sipped his coffee and returned the scrutiny, unblinking.

"Look," Ben said. "You're no fool. You know what Abel is. You know what he was doing down there."

"Cold reading," Lomax said. "Not even a particularly artful example of the technique, I'm afraid."

"So why did you bring him?"

"I also saw him faint—we both saw that—and I don't think he was faking that."

"What *do* you think, then?"

"I'm not sure. As I told you at the start, Mr. Prather, I'm interested in this place, in what may or may not be here, and I have the time and the money to pursue that interest. Mr. Williams had an experience here—you heard him describe it—so I invited him to join us." He nodded. "As I invited you."

"Keel, too? And Lara? They have some connection to this place?"

"You'd have to ask them."

"Oh, come on—"

"No, Mr. Prather, *you* come on. You have a history here yourself, do you not?"

"So?"

"Yet you've chosen not to share that information with the others, and I've respected—"

"I haven't sought to hide it. Lara knows."

"Does she? And how does she know?"

"She asked me."

Lomax lifted his hands, palms up. "Exactly," he said. "And *you* decided whether or not to tell her. As I was saying, I've respected your autonomy in this matter and I intend—"

"What about the first day, huh? Your little tour? Do you call that respect?"

"I wouldn't call it disrespect. We visited every site of significance in the building that day. We could hardly leave out your family's apartment. I'm sorry if it upset you, but I don't think it has a thing to do with me. Do you?"

Ben pushed his plate away.

What *he* remembered about the incident, what had irritated him about it, was not the tour itself but the subtle consensus of the men in the group—exclusively *white* men, too—that in similar circumstances they would have chosen different lives than the gangbangers and the dealers and the welfare mothers. What bothered him was the assumption—unspoken, but clearly present—that the people of Dreamland, *black* people, had somehow brought the horror of their lives upon themselves. That they were responsible—morally and otherwise—for their own misery.

Yet some dissenting component of himself couldn't help wondering if there wasn't an element of truth in Lomax's words—if maybe, just maybe, he had manufactured a fit of self-righteous indignation in order to avoid facing whatever awaited him in apartment 1824. His meltdown last night— his *panic attack,* to borrow the doctor's terminology—cast things in a different light, didn't it?

Lomax leaned forward, placing his elbows on the table. His eyes bored into Ben's. "Look, Mr. Prather, I haven't lied to you. I don't deny that my choices have been self-serving. I asked you to join us because of your past—but I had other reasons, as well, not least among them because I thought it might be useful to have someone with your particular set of skills, your"—he flapped a hand—"your journalistic habit of mind, I suppose. It's the same with the others. I engaged the doctor because I have no desire to see anyone get hurt. And if someone *does* get hurt, I want to be able to treat them. I asked Mr. Williams along because of his . . . sensitivity, if you choose to believe in that sort of thing, to these phenomena. Mr. Keel joined us because it seemed prudent to have some-one present with his experience—"

"He hasn't been a cop for years."

"Yet he's a formidable man, is he not?"

And that was hard to deny, Ben thought, recalling the physical grace Keel had shown at the pool table, the fierce spatial intelligence. He had seemed to see the whole table in a glance, instinctively calculating the complex range of possibilities radiating from each shot: he'd never hesitated the whole time they played, just called his shots and sank them one by one, without a single wasted gesture.

"Yeah," he conceded. "I guess he is."

Lomax spread his hands. "So there you go. All I'm saying is, if you want personal information on your companions— well, you'll have to ask *them.*"

"What about you, then?" Ben said.

"What about me?"

"What's your stake in this? Your personal stake?"

Lomax smiled. "As I said, Mr. Prather, I intend to respect the autonomy of everyone involved. You're free to ask, of course, but no one is under any obligation to answer."

He stood, took his coffee cup to the sink, rinsed it, and loaded it into the dishwasher. "It's been a pleasure chatting with you, Mr. Prather," he said.

And then he walked out.

5

Fletcher Keel came back to himself with a snap, not out of sleep but out of some deeper and more disturbing state: like surfacing abruptly from a blackout, sweaty, hypervigilant, and bereft of memory, filled with cold dread at what might have passed in the interval between. Ten years ago, in a shabby motel an hour outside of Vegas, he'd woken from the fathomless depths of a blackout to find blood on his clothes—not a lot of blood, true, but a good deal more than he could plausibly account for, especially when a thorough personal inspection revealed not the slightest bruise or abrasion. Enough, in other words. Enough to send him out the door to his car, without sticking around to look into the mystery further. Enough to send him gliding to the shoulder of the highway when the shakes hit half an hour later. Probably a bar fight, he'd told himself, gazing out over the lone and level sands toward the distant line of the Sierra Madres. A bloody nose or a busted mouth, nothing serious, it wouldn't be the first time. But even now, waking sometimes in the graveyard of the night, he wondered.

Blackouts had a way of sneaking up on you and wrecking your life.

Case in point: somehow, he seemed to have come into possession of the pint of Jack. He seemed to be holding *it* in one hand and its plastic cap in the other, and though he didn't think matters had progressed quite to the drinking stage—when he eyeballed the level of whiskey, anyway, it looked pretty much unchanged—he didn't think he'd missed it by much, either.

Keel laughed—a jagged, panicky laugh that he didn't much like the sound of.

Unclenching his fist, he let the cap drop on top of the desk. The beveled edge had dug a bloodless crescent in the fleshy pad of his palm. And judging by the crick in his back and the considerable ache in his ass he'd been sitting here for a while. Hours, maybe—the better part of the day. His stomach churned with acid. His mouth was scaly. His feet felt like paving stones at the bottom of his legs.

You shouldn't have come back, Susan said inside his head. *You need a meeting every day at this stage of your recovery,* she said. *Maybe two.*

Which was all very well and good, except that he was already here, there wasn't a meeting inside a mile's radius, and he faced the not-inconsiderable problem of persuading his hand to put the pint down on top of the desk so he could cap it off and push it away. The hand seemed to have developed a mind of its own, and what *it* wanted to do was lift the bottle to his lips and pour a slug of whiskey down his throat. It couldn't hurt to have just a sip or two, the hand seemed to be saying. Just enough to take the edge off. Because when you thought about it, he had a lot to be edgy about.

Somehow he'd managed *not* to think about these things before. Contrived not to notice that he'd come through last night's little midnight ramble, bare-footed and blind, without so much as a stumble along the way. Chosen not to question his recollection—his *imaginary* recollection, ha, ha—of a set of blueprints he had not seen in more than twenty-six years, and then on the fly, in nowhere near the detail he seemed to recall. Elected not to examine too deeply the footprints on the dusty checkerboard—a single set of footprints, it was worth noting, which raised all sorts of interesting questions about just who—

—or what—

—might have gone down on him in the darkness last night.

That right there was enough to drive a man to drink. And that wasn't all, not by a long shot. There was the matter of the blackout itself, too—though you really couldn't call it that, could you, when you hadn't had a drink in nearly three months? Keel had an inkling that the doctor would have called it a fugue state, and there was something frightening about those words. They suggested not merely a temporary setback, they suggested total systemic dysfunction. They suggested outright lunacy. And that wasn't his only symptom. He'd been hearing voices, too. It was a voice that had summoned him here, summoned him not by his own name, the name he had chosen for himself, but by the name he had repudiated, unable to measure up to its legacy of honor. It had summoned him by the name of the imaginary man in black body armor. He was really a memory, that man, a memory of—

—*John, your name is*—

"Fletcher," he said hoarsely. "My name is Fletcher. It's always been Fletcher."

Rage throbbed in his voice. Resentment.

Blood hammered at his temples. He dragged in a long breath, trying to calm himself. Then, stronger, his voice pitched low with certainty, he said, "My name is Fletcher Keel. And I'm an alcoholic."

The words had a kind of power. Like a talisman, they broke the spell he had fallen under, and he caught a glimpse of himself as someone else might have seen him, pitiful and broken, bent in worship at this paltry altar.

"My name is Fletcher, and I'm an alcoholic," he whispered, his voice breaking, and somehow, out of some reservoir he had not known he possessed, he summoned the strength to do what he knew he had to do, what he *wanted* to do, what Susan Avery and his father both would have wanted him to do. Somehow, if only for an instant, he summoned the strength to be the man they had wanted him to be.

He set the pint down hard on the desktop, slopping a quarter ounce of aromatic whiskey over his hand. Then, jerkily, a titanic battle raging inside him, he drew his hand away. He fumbled blindly for the bottle cap, felt it squirt from underneath his fingers. It flipped into the shadows on the far side of the desk and rattled down to the tile below. Keel was already bending to retrieve it when he stopped himself. It was fine, right? Fuck it, let it sit. Let it evaporate. Just go. Just get out of here.

Stiffly, like a clockwork man, he climbed to his feet, pushing the chair into the filing cabinets behind him with a crash. Something fell with a clap, but he didn't look up. His gaze riveted on the triumvirate of bottles, he backed away like a man who has disturbed something dangerous and possibly deadly: a scorpion or a cobra, hood flared, body weaving.

The office door drew him up straight.

Keel stood there, his eyes still fixed on the desk.

The bottle of Jack glowed with borrowed radiance. The air seemed to ripple around it, like waves of heat rising from baking asphalt, as the projector in his mind treated him to another jerky little snippet of his own hand closing around it and lifting it to his lips.

Without turning around, Keel fumbled for the doorknob, twisted it, and edged through the door into the darkness beyond. There, the door latched behind him, he turned away at last. His legs rubbery, he slid to the floor, his hands resting on his upraised knees. And even then, safe on the other side, he could still feel the pull of the bottles, steady and certain, like the gravity of an extinguished star.

6

"Let's walk," Abel said, closing the door behind him.

Lara didn't bother with preliminaries. "You lied to me."

"Did I?" Abel inquired mildly.

"You didn't eat last night."

"Mea culpa, Doc. Who are you, my mother?"

"I'm your doctor," she said. "For now, anyway."

"You planning to drop me as a patient, or something?"

"You don't take my advice, I might."

"Tell you what," he said, wheeling to face her. "I'm hungry right now. Why don't you join me, you can make sure I eat all my veggies?"

He smiled the same playful smile he'd used on her that first night, cleaning up the kitchen, but it seemed forced now, artificial, the wattage of his charisma dimmed by anxiety. Weary lines framed his mouth, and his eyes were bloodshot, as if he'd slept restlessly, or maybe not at all.

"You already used that joke, Abel. When you lied to me. Remember?"

"Oh."

"You get any sleep?"

"A little."

"Really?"

"Really. Listen, if you're going to give me the third degree, let's at least get something to eat, okay?"

"Okay."

Shrugging past him, she pushed through the door into the kitchen, cavernous and dim, empty, too—or so she thought until she touched the light switch, summoning the overhead fixtures into life. Ben stood at the window, a coffee mug in one hand. He gave her an uncertain smile, a little of the morning-after awkwardness, though there hadn't been any night before, not unless you counted the oddball intimacy of their rooftop parley. And what was it exactly, that unspoken link she had felt close between them—more evidence of the unseen connections and half-hidden agendas she sensed everywhere around her? Or something else, something personal?

"You were right, Lara," he said, lifting his mug to the window. "It looks like a storm's coming."

They crossed the room and stood beside him, wreathed in the aroma of coffee. An armada of lowering clouds, backlit by the distant cinder of the January sun, had seized the sky, and a hazy cast of light filled the air. The dead lands looked jaundiced, a sickly yellow blight expanding outward from the point of infection, from Dreamland, threatening even the remote towers of the yet-inhabited city. The wind gusted audibly, and Lara found herself thinking once again of the *Titanic*, stranded in the icy latitudes of the North Atlantic, dark water on the rise.

Ben finished his coffee.

"You gave us a scare yesterday, Abel," he said from the sink. "You feeling better?"

"I feel okay."

"You guys ever figure out what happened?"

"A nutritional deficit," Abel said. "Nothing a square meal won't take care of. Right, Doc?"

"It's a theory, anyway." She looked at Ben. "Have you eaten?"

"Just finished, actually. A sandwich." He closed the dishwasher. "There's some stuff in the fridge."

"Good," Lara said.

Ben hesitated, as if he wanted to add something, and she

felt it once again, that wordless tug between them. Then
he smiled and it disappeared. "So anyway," he said, "I
think I'll see if I can get some writing done. Enjoy your
meal."

7

Back in his suite, Ben found himself pondering the irony
of his words. *I think I'll see if I can get some writing done.*
What was the joke about old men and sex? By the time
you finally figure out how to do it right, you're not capable
of doing it at all. The spirit's willing but the flesh, the flesh
is weak . . .

Something like that.

He was paralyzed, anyway. Terrified to sit down at the
keyboard. And when he couldn't write, when the poisons
built up inside him, unreleased, things had a way of turning
ugly. Which brought last night's little rooftop scene clamoring back to him—the panic rising like dark wind inside
him, gale force, scattering everything—reason, coherence,
purpose—pell-mell before it. Jesus. Thank God Lara had
been there—though that opened another can of worms,
didn't it, for he'd felt something, too, looking into her eyes
as she coaxed him back from the edge of panic. A link of
some kind, humming and invisible, like a circuit closing in
the icy air between them.

It was all knotted up inside him—not just his own unremembered past, but the scene with Lara, too, and Lomax's
faintly mocking responses to his questions. Most of all the
sense that he was but one or two crucial steps away from
unraveling the whole thing. Lomax was no fool, that was
clear in everything Ben had read about him; nor was he
subject to whim—one did not achieve his level of success,
much less sustain it, without a certain cold discipline. He'd
had his reasons for coming here, and he'd had them for
choosing the companions he had brought along, as well.

What were they?

Pacing—love seat to desk (the laptop waiting) to door, and once again around—Ben tried to untangle it, but every time he grabbed a loose thread and started to pull, the knot seemed to tighten elsewhere—in his solar plexus or high in his chest, making it hard to breathe. He was accustomed to thinking at the keyboard, his fingers wired directly to the logic centers in his brain.

No. Something about the image felt wrong.

Not the brain, with its cool mathematical structures of logic, but what? The answer came to him in a line from some old poem he'd read in college: not the brain, but the heart. The foul rag-and-bone shop of the heart. What had Paul said? Writing—*his* writing, anyway, obsessive—

—*automatic*—

—and virtually independent of intent—offered nothing less than a direct line into the subconscious. Every time he took his pen in hand, he sank a well into the vast reservoir of anxieties, terrors, and half-formed memories buried deep in the geological strata of his own history, like a scientist coring an Antarctic glacier: the world that is and the world that was, perfectly preserved a hundred fathoms down.

Something frightening about that, he remembered saying. *Like being possessed.*

No. No! Paul had wagged a finger in his face, an old man by then, shrunken, his hair patchy and white, nearer to death than either of them had imagined. He had lifted his wineglass and closed his eyes, inhaling the bouquet with visible pleasure, as if it carried him off to a better place than this, a place where Ben could not follow. He laughed ruefully. *Maybe a little,* he conceded. *But—* The finger again. *But also useful if you listen carefully.*

Why is that?

There was something gnomic in the reply. *Your brain,* the old man had said. *It thinks, and so it knows.* He thumped his chest. *But the heart knows, too.*

What do you mean?

Paul had merely shrugged. It wasn't until later that Ben started to understand—until Paul had died and he found himself standing over the casket, realizing for the first time maybe that the man inside it had been his father in some crucial way that defied articulation—some way that his own fathers, biological and adoptive both, black *and* white, never could have been.

Heart knowledge.

The brain parses the world with logic; it divides, it categorizes and classifies, shoving everything into neatly labeled pigeonholes.

The heart intuits. The heart connects.

Ben's circumambulations had brought him back to the desk, the afternoon waning in the windows, the clouds still scowling. The laptop glimmered up at him. A cold fist squeezed his heart.

He had no memory of turning it on.

He sat down before it, resting his fingertips lightly atop the keys.

The truth lives down in the muck, he thought. In the heart's basement, where everything mixes together.

The heart knows that the world is neither black nor white. The world is gray.

8

Fletcher Keel got to his feet.

It was colder here in the airy vastness of the main basement—a clammy unwholesome cold that seemed to emanate from the concrete and settle in his bones—but the allure of the bottles was diminished. Not completely, true— one wouldn't want to say out of sight, out of mind—but it was better, anyway. He could handle it. He found himself repeating the statement aloud—

"You can handle this. Come on, you know you can."

—but it didn't have the reassuring ring he'd hoped for. The words sounded cheerless and hollow, dwarfed by acoustics, so much empty bravado, like whistling by the graveyard. The darkness was cryptlike, impenetrable, unrelieved by the line of light under the doorway at his back.

He could feel its pressure on his skin, an almost physical weight.

And what would it hurt to have a little light?

The switch had to be nearby. He could see it in his mind, a metal switch plate with a whole row of switches, five or six of them, just to the right of the door. But just as his fingers closed over them, unerring, ready to throw them home, a voice—

—*my God that voice*—

—spoke inside his mind.

You don't want to do that, it said. *Not yet.*

It was reedy and thin, that voice, sexless, yet it had an easy mastery, a certain cold command. And he knew it: it was the voice inside the voices, the ones that had drawn him here in the first place, down into the building's secret and unwholesome heart. He might have been listening to it for years. When it spoke it summoned up a memory of something cracking underfoot, a brittle snap like kindling—

—*but it wasn't kindling, was it, it was*—

—as it succumbs to the all-consuming flame.

Keel drew his hand away. He swallowed.

The darkness wheeled around him, impervious to vision. Yet he could see. He could see as he had seen last night, gazing at the imaginary blueprint in his head; could see as he had seen the super's office, with a certainty that brooked no doubt. The basement stretched away before him. He could see it: the colonnade of arches, the high ribbed ceiling with its conduits of electrical cable, thick as his arm, the rusting plumbing and the ancient ductwork, the building's guts exposed, its sclerotic and still-beating heart.

It was all right there before him. It was all inside of him.

He needed no light. Last night, he had not stumbled. He would not stumble now.

He drew in a breath permeated with the damp odor of stone, the ripe earthy stench, faintly organic, of pools where sunlight never falls, and then, like a man diving from a pier to strike off swimming into unguessed ocean depths, he stepped away from the wall and started toward the stairs.

9

"The truth is," Abel said over sandwiches, "I'm not sleeping so well."

Lara watched him over the table. He spoke like a man picking his way across a minefield, choosing each word carefully, fearful that it might blow up in his face.

"Dreamland," he said. He shook his head. "Appropriate name, huh?"

"You having bad dreams, Abel?"

"Yeah. When I sleep at all."

She took a bite, chewed thoughtfully.

Abel swallowed and pushed the plate aside. He'd eaten maybe a third of the sandwich. A glass of seltzer water sat untouched before him. "Any chance you can give me something? To sleep, I mean?"

"I know what you mean."

"So can you?"

"I can. *Will* I, though? That's the question you ought to be asking."

"It's just for a few days, until we get out of this place."

"Why don't you leave now?"

He turned the water glass in its ring of moisture, releasing a trail of pent-up bubbles. She watched them buoy weightlessly to the surface, released from whatever chemical bondage had held them there, imprisoned in the water.

She looked up at Abel. "Really," she said. "Have you given any thought to what I said last night? To leaving?"

"Why don't *you* leave?" he asked. "What's keeping you here?"

She said nothing.

"Well?" he said. "I take it you didn't just voluntarily surrender your residency, right? You must have a reason."

"It's *my* reason," she said.

He gave her a moment of barbed silence, and then he said, "I bet Lomax knows it."

She took a bite of her sandwich, chewing deliberately.

"You don't have to tell me," he said. "It doesn't matter what it is. The point is, it's something. That's the kind of man he is, our benefactor. He's got something on every one of us, some kind of hold. Otherwise we wouldn't be here."

She spoke without quite realizing she was going to: "Only if we let him."

"What?"

"He only has something on us if we let him have it. Look, Abel, you can walk away from this. There's nothing to keep you here. You're young, you've got plenty of money—"

"It's not about money."

"What's it about then?"

"My show was canceled."

"So?"

"Lomax has connections. He—" Abel threw up his hands in frustration. "Nothing. Forget it."

"You think he's going to get you a new show, or something?"

"Maybe."

"*Why?* Why would he?"

He leaned toward her, his voice rising. "You don't understand what I do, do you? You don't understand how much people need it. If I can figure out what he wants, what it is he needs to hear—"

He broke off abruptly, realizing perhaps that he had gone too far.

"Then you're the one who has the power, right?" she said. He smiled weakly, starting to protest, but she cut him off, her voice cold: "You're a fraud, Abel, you're a—"

"Do you really believe that, Lara?"

She bit her lip.

He laughed humorlessly. He propped his elbows on the table and massaged his temples, his cuff slipping back to expose the watch strapped around his wrist, the cracked crystal and the black gunk underneath. It made her think of his water glass for some reason, pent-up bubbles shaking off the weight that pinned them down. It made her think of the locket.

It made her think of Lana.

Abel's thoughts must have been moving in the same direction. "This is about yesterday, isn't it? About your sister?"

And now she felt it, the resentment that had eluded her last night on the roof. Her voice was cool. "I don't appreciate being toyed with, Abel."

"I didn't toy with you."

"Oh, come on. Ben explained the whole thing to me. I'm not stupid."

"No, Lara. I'm telling you, I didn't—" He pounded his fist on the table. "*Listen to me!*" He hesitated, and when he spoke again his voice had a renewed urgency. "Listen, something happened last night, and you know it did. Do you think I faked passing out? Do you?"

She mulled it over, the pallor, his pulse pounding underneath her fingers. And something else: how cold it had gotten, and how quickly. Just thinking about it, she could almost feel it once again, that cold. She studied her plate—a crust of wheat bread, a handful of chips—and pushed it suddenly away. She licked her lips.

"What about . . . you know, upstairs?"

"In the infirmary?"

She nodded.

"It was real, Lara."

"Then you should leave." She looked up; she met his eyes. "Abel, you should leave."

"Maybe we should all leave, Lara. Have you thought of that?"

She looked away.

"See? You can't do it either," he said. "He's got something over you. I don't know what it is—"

"I'm surprised you can't just pluck it out of the air—" she said, trying to derail him, but he went on unperturbed, not even breaking the rhythm of his sentence, his voice strangely gentle, saying, "—but he's got something over all of us. None of us are going anywhere."

"It's not worth it," she said abruptly, ignoring the truth of the insight. "Don't you see? What if you *did* get another show? How long would it last? Three years? Four? It's not worth it."

"It's more than that," he said. "After yesterday, after what happened—I have to know, Lara."

In the pause that followed, the kitchen seemed glaring and overbright, Dreamland too silent. There was something brooding and observant in the stillness, something hateful and aware. For crazy as it all sounded, she hadn't exactly enjoyed a good night's sleep last night either, had she? She, too, had dreamed—of a man with bloody hands who was and was not Fletcher Keel, of a girl who might have been her sister.

She met Abel's appraising eyes. "What do you have in mind?"

"I want to do another reading."

"And if you collapse again?"

"You'll take care of it."

"Look, Abel, you need to understand: I'm not that well equipped here. I don't understand what happened yesterday. If there's a problem—a serious medical problem—"

"I understand the risks."

"Do you? Because I'm not sure you—"

"I just need to get some sleep first, Lara. A good night's sleep."

She hesitated, words dying on her tongue, marveling at how neatly he had closed this little conversational circle, trapping her inside. Almost against her will, he had engaged her in a negotiation. *Almost,* Lana whispered mockingly, and Lara cringed. For when it came right down to it, who was manipulating whom? When it came right down to it, she wanted a second reading just as badly as he did, for a part of her—the part that had registered that abrupt drop in temperature, the part that had felt a surge of hope when Abel Williams had described her sister's illness—wasn't entirely convinced by Ben's easy logic. A part of her wasn't convinced at all.

That was the part of her that spoke now, summoning up a memory of her parents. She must have been eleven then, maybe twelve, Lana gone but not forgotten, just the three of them, ill at ease on the molded plastic chairs in an auto dealer's cubicle back home in Wilmington. The salesman had stepped out to confer with his manager. Her mother, meanwhile, agonized: it was a few hundred dollars, why not just take the price and be done with it? Her father drew himself up in his chair: *When you're negotiating, Penny,* he said, *you negotiate.*

So negotiate, Lana said.

Lara swallowed, lifting her fingers to touch the locket under her shirt. It hung there like a stone. "Tomorrow, is that what you have in mind?"

"In the afternoon. I was thinking—"

"You'll eat something tonight? A full meal?"

"Jeez, La—"

"I'm serious, Abel. If you want to understand this—if there's anything to understand—we have to rule that out."

He lifted his hands. "Sure. Okay."

"And something else."

"What?"

"If anything happens tomorrow during the reading—*anything,* Abel—you're done."

"What do you mean, done?"

"You're out of here. Finis. Kaput. You're off to the hospital for a full round of diagnostics."

"Come on, Lara—"

"Pleasant dreams, Abel." She put her hands flat on the table and started to push herself to her feet.

"Fine," he said. "Whatever. Just sit down, for Christ's sake."

"I'm serious."

"Okay. All right. I'm serious, too."

"Really?"

He took a breath. "Really."

She lowered herself back into her seat. Wind rattled the windows. Abel reached out to reclaim his plate, picked up his sandwich, and started to eat.

10

He was there before Lara knew he was there, a reflection in the screen before her, a featureless shadow under lines of scrolling text. She jumped, turning in her seat to face him. He hovered in the doorway of the infirmary, reminding her of—

—*his clothes his blood-spattered clothes*—

—that evening in the gym, how creeped-out she'd been when she looked up to see his face floating in the glossy mirror of the window, five stories up, his gaze fixed upon her as she ran.

"Jesus, Fletcher, you've got to stop sneaking up on me like that!" she said, the words out before she could stop them, registering in a fleeting instant the look on his face, how remote it was, how inward-turned and private, like the face of an autistic child or a catatonic, someone only half-way in the world.

"Doc," he said, and it was gone, that expression; it might never have been there at all. He grinned sheepishly. "Oh, hey, sorry, Doc. I didn't mean to scare you."

Barefoot and disheveled, he paused just inside the door to look her over. She had to suppress the impulse to fold her arms across her breasts.

"No, it's fine," she said. "You okay?"

"Yeah, I was just, you know—" He waved a hand vaguely. "—passing by. I saw you in here. Thought I'd say hello."

"Hi."

"Hey."

He laughed too loudly. He looked weary, his face drawn and pale, his eyes bloodshot. Everything about him seemed slightly rumpled, his hair matted, his clothes wrinkled, his feet—

She drew a breath.

His feet were more than dirty; they were filthy: dark crescents rimming the nails, streaks of grime thickening to crud in the crevices between his toes, a single bright patch of flesh, unsoiled, high on the inner arch of his left foot, startling by contrast. There was something disturbing about it—not the feet themselves, she had seen dirty feet before, but his blithe unawareness of them. What was he doing wandering the hall like that? Why hadn't he cleaned himself up? And—perhaps the most interesting question of all—how had they gotten that way in the first place?

Try not to be dense, Lars, Lana said. *You know how they got that way.*

And she did, didn't she? He'd been roaming the corridors of Dreamland, barefoot and alone—this despite the debris they'd seen everywhere on their little tour the other day, despite the broken glass, the crumbling shards of masonry, the occasional discarded needle (one thing you learned in the ER, you learned to watch out for sharps); despite, most of all, Lomax's oft-repeated warning about wandering off alone.

He was saying something, she'd missed it.

She looked up. "What?"

"I asked what you were doing."

"Oh." She glanced back at the computer. "Oh, that. I'm reading up on something."

He stood there, an expectant look on his face.

"For Abel," she said, flustered. "You know, yesterday in the lobby. I just wanted to make sure I'm not missing something."

"Right. That makes sense."

In the breathless moment that followed, both of them at a loss for words, she had to resist the urge to stare at his feet. Outside, the wind suddenly picked up, swirling noisily between the outstretched wings of the building.

Keel smiled. "Well," he said. "I'm off. See you around, I guess."

He was gone before she could answer, moving off in the direction of his suite. She turned back to the screen, reached for the mouse—and then, before she had quite figured out she was going to do it, she stood and followed him into the hall. He was halfway to his door, striding purposefully down the corridor, his bare feet hushed against the deep-piled carpet, before she caught up with him.

"Fletcher."

He turned, waiting.

"Are you sure you're all right?"

He hesitated—the briefest moment of indecision, she could see it in his eyes—and then he said, "Yeah. I'm fine. Really. Why?"

Because you look like hell, she wanted to say. *Because everything seems crazy and out of control and something about the look on your face when you came into the infirmary took me by surprise and because your feet, for Christ's sake look at your feet. Yes, and one other reason. Because I'm afraid.*

She stood very still, listening to this simple truth resonate within her.

"Doc?"

"I just wondered. You look a little tired, that's all. Are you sleeping okay?"

"Yeah. Yeah, I'm okay. I slept good last night."

"Good." She held his gaze. "If you have any problem . . ."

"Right. You bet."

"Okay, then." She nodded, and started back toward the infirmary. She had only gone two or three steps when he spoke again, his voice tentative.

"Hey. Lara?"

Her name in his mouth—her given name, not the faintly mocking title he had always previously employed—stopped her cold. She turned back to look at him—his face riven, his shoulders hunched, his big hands flexing at his sides—and she saw suddenly what she should have seen from the first, back there in the infirmary: he too was afraid. Something had happened to him out there in the desolate corridors of Dreamland and it had frightened him. Badly.

"What is it?" she said.

He cleared his throat. "Last night," he said. "Last night, were—did you—"

"What? What is it?"

He looked stricken, his eyes wide.

"Nothing. Never mind, it's nothing," he said.

She reached out to him, but he lifted his hands as if to hold her at bay. He backed up a step or two, his mouth working soundlessly, and then he turned away.

"Fletcher—" she called after him.

But he didn't look back.

11

His portentous second self—if that's what it was—had vanished.

Exhausted, empty anyway of words, Ben sat back, only half aware of the music issuing from the CD player—a muted piano melody, interlaced with a deceptively simple acoustic guitar line—and scrolled slowly through the afternoon's work: a rough account of Abel's reading in the lobby, the chaos afterward. He'd tried to get it all down—sights, sounds, scents, the rhythms of the conversation itself—as accurately as he could, from the abandoned hand of gin to the tense moments in the elevator, Abel still dazed, leaning wearily against the rear wall as they made their slow ascent. There were no interruptions, no subliminal forebodings imbedded in the rhythms of his prose.

Yet something there nagged at him, some connection he couldn't quite put his finger on, something someone had said. He had a good memory for that kind of thing—the importance of accurate quotes had been drummed into his head in graduate school, and he'd made a discipline of it in his working life. He'd never used a tape recorder, both because he didn't want to hassle with the technology—carrying spare batteries and cassettes, fussing with the mike, making transcripts—and because he didn't want to rely on it. Tapes failed, recorders had things spilled on them, but the story kept happening. The story didn't care. So he had cultivated the habits of listening and observing, of recollecting events with accuracy.

He had it right, he was almost sure of that. But why did it matter?

Ben stood, stretching, and moved to the window. Daylight had faded, a smoky twilight under a lid of oppressive cloud. Lights winked in the distance, faint and faraway, like candles ringing the black desolation of wasted blocks surrounding Tower Three.

He'd been at it for hours, and he felt the weariness as a tension in his shoulders and lower back. He was hungry, too. He could knock on Lara's door, see if she wanted to tag along . . .

He closed the curtains and turned away, the idea evaporating half-formed.

He switched out CDs, putting on Mingus, something to get the blood moving, wake up his brain. Then he sat down in front of the computer, and started scrolling through the day's work again, line by line. It was here somewhere, he knew it was. But where?

12

Keel closed his eyes and lifted his face to the relentless pulse of the shower, welcoming the sting against his skin, and still he felt it, the tidal pull of memory.

That sense of presence stirring in the south stairwell.

That reed-thin voice inside his head. The sexless voice. The voice of many voices that could always, if only for a time, be anything, anything at all. Anything you wanted it to be.

"No," he whispered into the thrumming cascade. "No—"

And then he was there, God help him he was there, he was—

—there, staring slack-jawed as a helicopter wheels overhead through a vault of steel-wool sky, shedding down upon his upturned face a doppler-shifted rain of spinning rotors. There's a hand on his shoulder, shaking him, and he sees that they're folding up the blueprints, the whole team jittering with eagerness, like thoroughbreds being hustled into the gates. Mitchell's face looms before his startled eyes, leaning close, strained shouting in his ear, *let's go, let's go, baby, it's show time,* and they're on the move, no time to think, weaving through the labyrinth of squad cars and ambulances at a not-quite run, sweat grooving in the channel of his spine, the black Kevlar chafing with each thudding impact of his booted feet. Up ahead, Mitchell pauses for a few final words with the chief, but he hardly has the time to catch a breath before they're moving again, his weapon swinging in his gauntleted hands, and he can't think, he can hardly hear over the crackling chaos of police radios and shouting and sirens, the wheeling roof lights touching everything with blood, his heart pounding, each and every nervous face that turns to track his progress twisted and hateful as the faces in a dream. A couple of uniforms pull back the doors to admit them, like a wide mouth waiting, and just before it swallows him up, he snatches one last glance at the world he's about to leave behind, but all he sees is Dreamland, steadfast and implacable against the sky.

Then, boom, they're inside, the doors slamming shut behind them, and quiet comes down like a curtain. Half the fluorescent bulbs overhead have burned out, and the other half have the dim, shuddery look that means they're about to go, so the whole place has a greenish flickering cast; the air is stale, the heat so thick he can feel the sweat greasing his face. Mitchell's directing traffic, splitting them into teams, one for each stairwell. The uniforms have shut down the elevators and sealed every stairwell on ten; no one's going in and no one's coming out, not until they take the shooter down. He thinks suddenly that he's going to be sick. The room ripples and jumps around him, his gorge pushing like a hand at the back of his throat. He can't seem to catch his breath. All he can think of is Lisa, Lisa, Lisa. It's like a clock booming in his brain, counting down the seconds of his life—

You okay? The voice hoarse, Mitchell's face in his face, he can smell the coffee on his breath. *You okay, man, you need to step out, I need to know now—*

Something in him leaps at the idea, and it's like a revelation: what he's feeling is fear, not thoroughbred nerves but stark lunatic fear, it's like a black wind crying out inside him, it's all he can do not to collapse whimpering right there on the floor—

Keel turned his shoulders to the needling spray. He smacked his open hand against the wall, not wanting to recall any more, but there was nothing he could do, the tidal pull of memory took him out once again into the black, black water, Patrick Mitchell's voice in his ear, saying—

—you look fucking green, Martin, and I got no time for this, you need to step out, yes or no, I need to know, the words hissing low in his ear, and the only thing worse than the fear is the humiliation. He can feel the fire team's eyes upon him, he can feel his father's eyes, his fucking war-

hero father nearly ten years dead. Every day he can feel his father's weighing eyes upon him, and it's not hard to imagine what he would make of this little exercise in cowardice, is it—

He speaks before he knows he's going to. *Fuck no,* he says. *Let's get it on.*

Mitchell studies him, nods almost imperceptibly, and waves them forward. They're on the move, then, through the flickering gloom and into the stairwell, the long climb before them, two turns at the landings, the light of the lobby falling away behind them, going going gone. Darkness envelops them, utter and complete. Gangbangers don't like the light. They bust out the bulbs in the wall cages so often nobody bothers to replace them anymore, and so the fire team switches on the flashlights mounted over their weapons and climbs on in silence, climb baby climb in a tangle of intersecting beams, up the south stairwell where twenty-seven years from now a man named Fletcher Keel, a man he cannot yet imagine, will sense a presence stirring, and feel the weight of memory shifting, something dark and unwholesome surfacing through all the lies that are his life. What he will remember is what happens to this man in the south stairwell, this man who will one day seem so distant in time and space that Fletcher Keel can hardly recall him at all, can hardly imagine him and will one day let himself believe that that's all he ever was: imagination.

But that's not true.

He's real and what Fletcher Keel will someday remember about the stairwell is a stunning little epiphany—

Fear is a doorway.

Open it up and anything might come in, anything at all—

Keel hammered the wall, remembering. The reed-thin voice with the sneer of cold command sounded once again in his mind, and he thought about fear and the south stairwell.

Fear was a doorway.

Open it up, anything might walk in.

* * *

He remembered what it felt like even now, there in the darkness, the fire team climbing, when it came to him.

It felt cold and hating.

It felt like power.

It felt like nothing at all. Not shame and not fear. Not love and not remorse. Just nothing. Nothing at all.

It felt like the void.

It was the best feeling he'd ever had.

"No," he whispered into the thump and drizzle of the shower, thinking of the reed-thin voice that had seized him in the basement, thinking of the long trek in darkness, Dreamland opening before him its manifold and secret ways. "No."

He leaned his forehead against the moisture-beaded plastic of the shower wall and let the water pour across his shoulders, trying to summon back the strength he'd felt in the program. The twelve steps. Susan. Against negation, affirmation. Against the lying voice that had lured him to the basement, the voice of truth. And against the reedy voice inside the lying one, the voice of honor.

Twelve steps.

Susan's voice, his father's voice, please God his own true voice.

Step nine: *Make amends.*

He adjusted the water to scalding and stared down at his feet, watching his own filth swirling into the drain.

God he wanted to be clean.

13

They ate together that night, the first time they'd done that in days. Lomax's notion that they would divide the cooking and set a rotation had fallen by the wayside somewhere along the way, Lara wasn't sure when. She wasn't sure about a lot of things suddenly—Abel's collapse and Keel's increasingly erratic behavior, the wordless tug of emotion she felt with Benjamin Prather, all mysteries. Of one thing she was certain, though: they were all on their own here, random particles accelerating in their own eccentric orbits, alone but for chance collisions in the kitchen, the corridor, or the lounge, and God save them any explosions.

It seemed unwise, such isolation.

But that night, if only for a span of hours, they were together. She made it happen: she cooked the meal, she walked the corridor and banged on every door, she drew them together at the trestle in the kitchen—conversation halting, the air clamoring with unspoken tensions, but a *meal,* and in the best sense of the word: food as more than sustenance, as communal experience. Supper, her mother would have called it. The last supper, Lara would later come to think of it, but of course she didn't know that then.

She told them about Abel's reading over stir-fried chicken, and outlined their agreement over dessert, enlisting the others by way of holding him to terms. "Anything happens to him," she said, "anything we don't understand, he's out of here, agreed?"

A circle of solemn nods, Lomax grunting his reluctant assent.

"Abel?" she said.

He shook his head, bemused. "Agreed."

So it was decided. After dinner, they played cards in the lounge for an hour or so, and then, one by one, they drifted off to their suites, Keel first, strangely subdued, his long face scored by weariness, Lomax and Ben soon after that. In the infirmary, Lara took a bottle from a locked cabinet, shook out a single white pill, and handed it to Abel.

"Ambien," she said. "Ten milligrams. You'll sleep like a baby."

Like a baby, he thought.

He did, too. He swallowed it not half an hour later, and sat on the edge of his bed gazing at his own bifurcated reflection in the crystal of his father's watch, time forever stopped thirteen minutes short of noon, while he waited for it to take effect. He pictured it happening, the pill dissolving in his belly, surrendering itself to its constituent elements, dispatching them by the thousand, tiny ambassadors of sleep, into the stream of his own unquiet blood. The last thing he remembered was reaching out to shut off the lamp and lying back in the cool sheets, an assembly of whispers following him down into the dark.

The others weren't so lucky.

Alone in their suites, they hovered at the near frontier of sleep, Lomax restless in his old man's bed, and Lara thrashing in her sheets, dreaming of Mercy General. Keel was awake long into the night, honing the edge of needs he dared not name. In the suite next door, Ben sat gazing into the ghostly well of his monitor, rocking gently, his fingers flying, chasing down connections yet unseen.

It was after midnight when he shut off his light.

The wind quickened, driving the temperature down through the single digits and into the subzero, mercury contracting, five below, then ten, and colder still by any human reckoning, a killing cold. Dreamland stood, impervious to weather, holding fast its silences inside walls of block and stone, its darknesses, too, and a cold still deeper and more cold.

At just after one o'clock it started to snow.

The Reading

1

The words were waiting for Ben when he woke up, centered on a glimmering screen of white. Six of them. Six simple words, and they undermined everything he had managed to fool himself into believing yesterday afternoon—that he could work at Dreamland without slipping once again into the obsessive patterns of his youth, that he stood on the verge of unraveling the mystery of Ramsey Lomax, that Paul Cook had been right and the foreboding little interjections in his prose were nothing more than subliminal communiqués from a second self, long traumatized and deeply repressed.

Six simple words, and they did more than challenge that conclusion. They mocked it. They mocked Paul and his belief in Paul. Now, at just after nine o'clock in the morning, Ben stood in front of the computer and read them over once again:

> *Too many Cooks spoil the broth.*

He'd left the lounge early last night, eager to reread the afternoon's work, to track down the connection he'd sensed in his narrative of Abel's collapse. He remembered sitting down in front of the computer, skimming through the day's prose as he had planned, and then, still frustrated, opening a new document instead. He'd intended to make some notes on his rooftop conversation with Lara. Instead—

Instead, what?

Instead, he woke hours later to the image of a small boy hunched and rocking over a tattered spiral notebook, squat pen snug as a gun in the crook of his finger and thumb, digging. Instead, he woke to a familiar line of tension in his shoulders, a dreamy sense of rocking like a dervish at the altar of his keyboard: body memory, in his blood and bones, the fetal roll and hunker of a man in pain or need. He woke without memory of turning out the light, without knowledge of what he had written, or how long. He woke to find that he'd slept in his clothes, like a man too drunk or too exhausted to bother folding back the counterpane.

Like a man possessed.

The thought had shivered Ben to the bone. He stood rumpled and grainy-eyed and gazed out the window, winter in the streets and winter in his heart. Snow spiraled endlessly from a sky of tarnished pewter, softening the wasteland of shattered concrete and twisted steel below: deep already, and deepening. Inches from the window, Ben could feel the cold against his cheeks, his glasses steaming.

He had turned away.

In the adjoining room, the laptop stood atop the desk. Its screen crackled to light, resurrected by the touch of a key, a line of black text—

> *too many*
> *too many*
> *too many*

—marching by like a column of ants, endless pages of them, then nothing at all, just blank screen after blank screen after blank screen, tabula rasa, and what came to him was a vision of himself, that hunched atavistic rocking, spectacles sliding down his nose, hammering out the same two words over and over again, like some kind of machine, tap tap tapping until even recollecting it he could feel the ache in the delicate web of muscles that strung his fingers to the bone. And somehow in all that time he had *never noticed*. Somehow he had managed to turn off his brain, to negate himself, consciousness sieving through his pores like water while something else filled him up. The question was: What? God help him, what?

As if in answer, a single word came once again into his head, a cold whisper, reedy and thin—

Possessed.

He didn't believe in such things, yet it had a curious

power, that word. It *felt* right. Last night at his keyboard
Benjamin Prather had checked out, and something else,
something cold and hateful, had checked in. Something else
had possessed him, he thought, his finger still working the
track ball, empty screens flitting by until at last that phrase
floated up before him, the one that made him go cold inside: six words, like some loathsome bottom-dweller surfacing in an Arctic sea, the week-old body of a whale, shark-
ravaged, turning its bloated belly to the sky:

> *Too many Cooks spoil the broth.*

His guts tightened.
With one hand Ben steadied himself against the back of
the chair. With the other he worked the track ball.
Another blank page blinked by. Then another.
And then, neatly centered, another of those oracular lit-
tle phrases—

> *There are many of us here, Ben.*

—this one triggering a memory of Abel in the lobby, his
eyes flying open like the eyes of a man—
—*possessed*—
—startled suddenly awake.
So many, he'd said. So many.
Ben thought he might be sick. He wanted to turn away,
to run, to lift his face to the sky and taste the snow upon
his tongue, cleansing, a benediction. Still his fingers moved
at the keyboard. Half a dozen empty screens flew by, and
then another column of text scrolled up before him—

> *too many Cooks*
> *too many Cooks*
> *too many Cooks*
> *He's wrong, Ben.*
> *And he has no peace.*
> *He's here.*
> *There are many of us here.*
> *We hate you.*
> *We hate you.*
> *We*

> *hate*
> *hate*
> *hate*
> *hate*
> *hate*

—that single word running on for pages, a dozen of them, two dozen, three, culminating at last in a sequence of repetitions—

> *we hate you*
> *we hate you*
> *we hate*
> *the Cook is here*
> *the broth is spoiled*

—followed by a final spate of white screens, like an iris flickering on a field of light, his finger skating so quickly over the track ball that his eye barely had time to register them, until, abruptly, the end of the file yanked him up short, breathless as a runner at the end of a marathon, three phrases strung like tape across the finish line, or the blade of a guillotine, grinning and cold:

> *the broth is spoiled*
> *the Cook is here*
> *soon enough you'll join him*

2

In the same moment, at nine, with storm light in the window, Keel woke. He had slept badly, like a skipped stone dipping bare millimeters into a choking haze of dreams, only to rebound into the outer air of full wakefulness, hurled back by the physics of his own drowsy trajectory— a restless and uneasy business, worse somehow than not sleeping at all. Jittery and raw, he lay for a long time in a nest of sleep-thrashed sheets, watching the snow come down, pondering the super's office in the basement, and the price a man would pay for sleep.

3

"Ambien," Abel said in the lounge, and Lara looked up from the book she had not been reading. He dropped into the chair opposite, wearing faded Levi's, sneakers, and a tee shirt that must have been red once, washed now to a burgundy that was almost pink. He laced his fingers behind his head and heaved an exaggerated sigh. "Ah, Ambien. If I'd have known the power of the prescribing pen, I might have gone to med school."

"The glamour wears off the first time someone pukes down your top," she said.

Abel slung his legs over one arm of the chair and laughed. He regarded her wryly across the coffee table. "I don't know," he said. "My sainted mother always wanted me to do something respectable."

"Trust me, it's not worth the hassle."

"Hassle? Healing the sick? Saving lives?"

"Fighting with HMOs."

"And there's the money."

"Stick to television. Lots more money there."

Too late, she realized it wasn't the best thing she could have said.

"If you can get the work," he said ruefully.

"Abel, I didn't mean—"

"I know."

Smiling to take the sting out of it, he stood. He surveyed the bookshelves, and then he turned away, pacing, suddenly full of nervous energy. He washed up against the window, fingers drumming on the frame. After a moment's vacillation, Lara set aside her book and joined him.

The snow was still coming down, and not in the lazy

corkscrews she'd woken up to, either. It whipped by in gusts, buffeting the glass, and then whirled once again into the void, thousands of tiny flakes, the distant skyline invisible beyond the billowing sheets of white. And it was silent, too, a deep pervasive silence that seemed to well up from the ruined streets below, seeping into the lobby, the stairwells, the airless corridors overhead. She drew it in with every breath and there was something watchful in it, and she hesitated to speak, to profane its stark perfection, or call upon herself the weight of its regard.

Abel too seemed to feel it. He didn't speak for a long time—and when he did, she had to strain to hear him. "Maybe you didn't make the wisest deal, Doc," he said softly.

"What do you mean?"

He nodded at the window. "It keeps up like this, none of us are going anywhere, no matter what happens."

"You don't have to go through with this, Abel."

He laughed softly. "Oh, but I do."

"What do you mean?"

"I really did come down here to thank you," he said without looking at her.

"For what?"

"The gift of clarity. Getting some sleep cleared my head."

"Did it?"

"There's a funny thing about life, but you never realize it until it's too late."

"What's that?"

"The way it has of disappearing on you."

He glanced over as if to gauge her reaction to this. She held herself very still, gazing out at the snow, waiting to see where he was heading.

"You don't realize it while it's happening," he said after a while, "but every day you're making choices, and every choice you make, the range of possibilities before you narrows a little bit. And somehow, before you know it, you wind up someplace you never intended to go."

"Where'd you wind up, Abel?"

"You said it yourself, Doc. I should stick to television."

"I was joking."

He waved a hand dismissively. "But it's true." He

laughed. "The thing is, I never intended to do what I do. It was a trick I had, a knack. It was something I could do, that's all. I didn't have a job, or any immediate prospects, I was short on cash, so I thought, well, I'll use this trick of mine for a little while, just long enough to get me out of the place I'm in, and then, once I have some money, I'll go off and figure out what it is I'm supposed to do with my life."

"What do you mean, a trick?" Lara asked, thinking of her humiliation in the lobby, feeling now the laceration that she had not felt then, or afterward, on the roof, when Ben explained to her how Abel had managed it.

"A trick," he said, staring straight ahead. "Like a magician's trick. An illusion." He looked right at her then. "Like you said yesterday, I'm a fraud."

Self-loathing radiated from him in waves, dampening Lara's resentment. She said nothing, though, and Abel, too, was still. His nervous energy seemed to have evaporated.

Outside, the wind shifted, veiling the window in snow.

"That's what I figured out this morning," he said, "with the clarity of a night's sleep. I mean, I knew it before, but I never really admitted it to myself. But this morning, thinking things through, I couldn't deny it. What I do—and it doesn't matter how you rationalize it—that's what I *am*. The only choice left is where I'm going to do it—on television for car-loads of cash, or in a store front somewhere at a hundred dollars a pop." He smiled grimly. "I chose door number one, and so I came to Dreamland. As for the rest of it"—he shrugged—"it's too late to change."

"I don't believe that, Abel," she said, turning to look at him. "I believe people can change. We don't have to be prisoners of the past."

"Oh, I think we do," he said. "If we didn't, I wouldn't be so successful, would I?"

It was a difficult point to refute.

Frustrated, Lara turned back to the window. She stared out into the pelting snow, past the hollow ghost of her own reflection—her twin, she thought suddenly. Her double, her other self. She wondered suddenly if Abel was right, if she was a prisoner of *her* past. She wondered what she might have become if Lana hadn't died—what both of them might have become. Tears stung her eyes. She rolled her lower lip under her teeth, biting down until the pain drove them back unshed.

"So you got all this from Ambien," she said. "Maybe I should pop a couple myself."

Abel laughed. "That's only half the story," he said. "You haven't heard the other half yet."

"Yeah?"

"Yeah."

Lara turned away, strolling back to her seat, annoyed by this vulnerability to tears he seemed to summon out of her. She'd spent her life on the other side of this equation—searching out the weaknesses in others and applying a healing salve. You're the one who likes to take care of everyone, Lana had told her, and Lana, as always, was right. Lara wasn't entirely comfortable with the reversal in roles: in fact, she resented it.

She sat back, crossing her arms. "So what's the other half?"

"Ambien gave me the clarity to think everything through. The impetus"—he hesitated—"the impetus came from elsewhere."

He studied her, his back to the window, and when she said nothing, he crossed the room and sat across from her. He leaned forward, he clasped his hands.

"I didn't lie to you yesterday," he said. "Since I've been here I've been . . . hearing things." He swallowed, looked at his sneakers. "Voices." He looked up; he held her gaze. "Since I've been here, I seem to be able to do what I've pretended to do for years."

A giddy cocktail of memories and half-formed thoughts stirred through Lara's mind at this admission—the echoing laughter of a child and the clatter of a wind-blown shade, Abel's words in the infirmary—

—twins you were identical—

—and a wild thump of elation in her chest. What if it were true? My God, did she *want* it to be true? Was that really what she wanted?

Even as she swallowed it down, that cocktail, another thought came chasing hard upon it: that there were levels visible and levels yet unseen, that this was Abel at the top of his game, not confessing—not really—but deepening the con, laying the foundation for whatever effect he hoped to wring out of her at this afternoon's reading. She sensed once again the dizzyingly complex dynamics in play around her, the labyrinth of contending agendas and secrets yet unspoken.

You shouldn't have come here, Lana said inside her head, and she wanted to cry out in response, *But I had to, don't you see? I had to!* And wasn't that also an admission of some kind—that Abel was right, that she too was a prisoner of the past, that everyone was?

"Lara—" he said.

You expect me to believe you, she wanted to say. *You tell me you're a fraud and then you expect me to believe you're not?* And she opened her mouth to say it, but what came out instead was a question: "What happened in the lobby, what you told me—"

"Trickery," he said. "It was my standard act, until"—he stood, and turned away—"the voices, my God the voices, they overwhelmed me—"

She didn't care about that, not now.

"And in the infirmary?" she demanded. "Afterward."

"That was real." He turned to face her, his eyes wide. "Something happened, Lara. I looked at her picture, I looked at Lana's picture, and I could hear her voice inside—"

Had he really said that? Had he said her name?

"—my head, so clear we might have been talking on the telephone—"

"Shut up," she said. *"Shut up!"*

"Shut up," she whispered. "I have to think."

But no thoughts came, only a fuzz of static and that name—

—*Lana Lana Lana*—

—like a siren hurtling down upon her over a foggy highway. Had she told him Lana's name?

She hadn't, she was almost certain of it.

"My sister," she said. "Abel, what's her name?"

"What?"

"What's my sister's name, Abel?"

He came toward her, his face puzzled. "I don't understand—"

"If I find out that you're lying to me," she said, "if I find out that you tracked me down beforehand, that you knew all about me before we ever came here, Abel—if I find that out—"

"What?"

She shook her head, unable to meet his eyes. "I don't know," she said. She laughed. "What's my sister's name, Abel?"

He sat before her on the coffee table. He took her hands. "I have no clue, Lara. Why?"

And then she did it: she looked up, she looked square into his face, his open everyday face, his brow wrinkled in confusion, his eyes green and depthless as a forest pool. If there was a lie there, she could not see it. Vertigo swept over her in a nauseating wave. She teetered on a wire strung over twin abysses, on the left hand terror, on the right desire, and for a long moment she did not know which way she was going to fall. Then the vertigo passed, leaving her stranded there, suspended high above the void, still staring into Abel Williams' guileless face.

"Her name," Lara said. "You said my sister's name."

4

"During the opening credits of my show they used to play this montage of photos," Abel said after lunch, toying under the table with a photo of his own. "The studio audience would bring them in, snapshots, studio portraits, school pictures, whatever—people who had died, the ones they wanted to contact. The production team would cobble it together, a fresh montage for every episode."

"So you saw these before you went on?" Ben said.

A wave of interest circled the table. Keel looked up from the ring of condensation he'd been spreading with one blunt finger. Lomax narrowed his eyes. Even Lara, who knew, seemed to sit up straighter.

Abel didn't rise to the bait. He regarded the other man mildly over the dregs of the meal—soiled dishes, a half-empty bag of chips, a cutting board bearing a quarter wheel of cheese and the knife that had been used to slice it. Half unconsciously, he turned the photo on his thigh, chipping at its grimy patina with the end of a nail. If you listened closely, you could hear it: the rasp of nail against a thick square of old-fashioned photo stock, like a distant whisper.

No one else seemed to notice, however.

A lassitude seemed to have seized them all, the meal done, the hour appointed for Abel's little experiment at hand—a reluctance that was just edging into fear. That's how Abel figured it, anyway.

Was *he* afraid?

He pondered the question, his fingers smoothing the photo against his thigh, flattening the peeling ridges where in some distant past it had been folded and folded again. Apprehensive, sure; reluctant, absolutely. Fear, though? He didn't think so. He'd gotten past that.

No, he thought. I am not afraid.

He had to know, that's all—had to know if he was losing his mind or if something else was happening, something stranger. Had to know if he could learn to control it, to turn it on and off at will. If he could *use* it. Either way, he was not afraid.

He repeated the words to himself, a private mantra.

I am not afraid. I am not afraid.

Whispers stirred in a corner of the kitchen, gathered to a crescendo and fell away undeciphered, water swirling in the mouth of a distant drain.

Abel turned the photo on his thigh.

I am not afraid.

Outside, wind soughed down Dreamland's blank facade. Snow continued to fall. It was close to three, the windows storm-darkened, an early twilight looming in the sky.

Ben stared at him. Waiting.

Abel smiled. "No," he said. "I didn't look at them. They frightened me, actually. I don't know why—or I didn't then, anyway—but they did. They scared the hell out of me."

"Why?" Ben asked.

I was afraid, Abel thought. Afraid they might suck me down into—

—*the world beyond the fence*—

—*like my father oh god like my*—

—a cold dark place I wouldn't be able to escape.

A telephone began to ring inside his head.

I am not afraid, he thought. I am not afraid.

He said it aloud, his fingers nervous on the photograph, tracing the water-stained image of the girl, her dark hair knotted in an intricate pattern of braids, her small face smiling. "They don't scare me anymore."

He added, "I think I'm beginning to understand it."

"Why?" Keel asked, but when Abel answered he kept his eyes fixed on Ben, gazing back at him from across the table.

"Because of this."

Abel leaned forward, lofting the photo he'd been toying with toward the bare center of the table. The heat came on with a *whump*, and an updraft from one of the floor vents must have caught it, for it hung there momentarily, riding a column of air, a battered black-and-white snapshot with a scalloped border aged to the color of an unclean tooth. And then gravity snatched it home and it eddied silently down to the table before them.

5

Fletcher Keel saw it first—recognized it for what it was, a photo, as it drifted gently to the table, glimpsed within it the curving jawline of a child, and watched Benjamin Prather blanch and stiffen. And even before Ben spoke, his voice a hoarse whisper—

"Where'd you get that?"

—Keel understood what had just transpired with an absolute and unerring certainty.

A veneer of perspiration oiled his forehead. His guts spasmed. His fingers clenched the edges of the table. Lifting his eyes the length of the littered trestle—Ben and Lara on one side, Abel on the other—he met Ramsey Lomax's unyielding gaze.

Make amends, a voice cried out within him.

He clamped down on it, returning his attention to the

photo. A little girl peered back at him through a stain of reddish-brown—

—blood it was blood—

—rust. Looking at her, Keel felt time slip its chain, the years unreel. The kitchen shimmered, as through a sheen of water blown back across the windshield of a speeding car. Threads of black mist unspooled at the periphery of his vision, stitching themselves together before his face, weaving a tapestry of night. In the succeeding darkness he was there, in the south stairwell, dank water dripping, breath laboring in his lungs. The fire team ascended in a controlled panic of soft-soled boots and muttered curses. Muffled echoes scaled the risers. The yellow eye of the flashlight mounted on his weapon bobbed like a target on Patrick Mitchell's back.

Just looking at the man sent a flood of shame tumbling through his veins—

—you need to step out, Martin, you look fucking green—

—shame and anger, too; most of all the humiliation of the confrontation in the lobby, mere tributaries to the black and depthless river of fear—

—fear is a doorway, open it up anything might walk in—

—carving its channel through the bedrock of his soul.

There in the south stairwell, it took him.

He felt it seize him and slide inside him, a cold intelligence, utterly remote, swollen with its own sure mastery: strong where he was weak, fearless in the deep places where wellsprings of terror fed the river in his heart, and knowing—God, so knowing. It plumbed him through and through and it knew him, every cell and every muscle, bone and ligament and brain.

Keel swallowed.

Calming himself by sheer dint of will, he stared down into the bloody face of a child—

—LaKeesha, LaKeesha Turner, you stand accused—

—do you understand the charges against—

—the conversation running on without him, Abel saying, "I found it upstairs, in apartment 1824," and Ben responding, softly, so softly, and aggrieved, "My sister, she was my sister," confirming as from a great distance what Keel had known from the minute the photo settled to the table and he saw Benjamin Prather stiffen in his seat and

draw in a single hissing breath, like a man in pain or
sorrow.

Keel sat upright, his face impassive.

Something black and familiar assailed him, dark wings
beating, battering for admission to his soul. Clutching the
table, Keel resisted. He stared at the girl, her face masked
in blood, and he resisted.

The burnt-rope stench of cordite filled the air, a chaos
of gunshots and screaming and the coppery reek of gore
steaming in his nostrils, his finger squeezing, squeezing,
squeezing, three-round bursts, just like Parris Island, just
like the range, his cock rigid as railroad iron—

Not me, he wanted to cry, *not me, the thing inside me—*

His father's voice rose up in response, disdainful and
cold. *Fear is a doorway,* he said. *You opened it, you invited
it in, you welcomed it and bent your knee before it. You
surrendered your honor.*

You. You. You.

And a final voice in answer, Susan's voice, his own true
voice if only he could dredge the strength to sustain it from
the sucking river mud that clogged the bottom of his soul.

Make amends, it said. *Make amends.*

6

After a moment of silence, those words—

—*my sister she was my*—

—still dying in the air, Ben reached out for the photograph, shaking his head in disbelief. "This is unconsciona-
ble even by your standards," he said. "What you did to
Lara was bad enough, but this—this—"

Abel's hand closed over his wrist like a vise.

"Don't," Abel said. "Just don't."

The words faltered on Ben's tongue. For a single frozen
heartbeat they hung suspended like that, in silent tableau,
Abel's hand like a shackle at Ben's wrist, Ben staring down
at it, white on black, startling by contrast, his brain hum-

ming with adrenaline overload. The kitchen screamed with
the lemony tang of dish detergent and light glared back
from every polished surface, the whole place suddenly
sharp-edged and hyper-real as a surgical theater, and Abel
wielding the scalpel, just waiting to carve him up.

Wind clawed the building, flinging a renewed volley of
snow at the window.

"Gentlemen, please—" Lomax began.

Ben cut him off, his voice pitched low. "You're going to
let go of me right now, you son of a bitch—"

"Come on now, guys," Lara said.

"—or I'm going to take your fucking head off."

Still the hand did not relent.

"Ben," Abel was saying. "Ben—you've got to listen, please,
you've got to listen—" And something in the other man's
voice, a hue of desperation or fear, compelled Ben to look
up, to gaze into his face, twisted and desperate and pale, pale
as the hand at his wrist. Hardly a human face at all.

"This is my family," Ben said, his voice rising. "This is
my fucking family, and I will not—*I will not*—" He took a
long, slow breath. Then, his voice taut with suppressed
emotion, he said, "I will *not* let you profane their memory
with your—"

"—she *spoke* to me—"

"—manipulative charlatan's bullsh—"

"Ben, listen—she spoke to me, I heard her voice."

Ben yanked his arm free. Rubbing his wrist as though he
might massage away even the memory of that clinging
hand, he glared at Abel, his eyes unswerving. He shook his
head, uttering a sound halfway between laughter and a sob.

"Fuck you, Abel," he said, and then, turning to Lomax,
"And you, too. Is this what you had in mind? You think
you can just play around in other people's lives? Do you?
Answer me!"

Lomax's lip twitched. Visibly composing himself, he said
nothing.

Ben stood. He scanned the circle of faces before him,
Lara beside him, her eyes obscured by a wing of hair, and
Abel, stricken, with a pleading hand outstretched. Fletcher
Keel flushed and looked away.

"Ben," Abel said. "Please. I'm not—I'm not lying. I hear
her voice. I hear it in my head."

Ben shook his head again.

"You know what," he said. "I feel sorry for you. You're a sick man."

He turned away.

He was almost to the door when Abel spoke again.

"Ben," he said, "she says to tell you—and I don't understand this, I don't know what it means. She says to tell you that the cook is here."

7

The words rolled over him like a wave, one of those enormous breakers that thunder in from the deep cold waters farther out and tumble you down and down before them, the pressure pinning you breathless on a bed of muck and languid weed until your lungs burn and the water turns smoky before your terrified eyes. When at last it passed and he surfaced through all that dark water, Ben felt as such a swimmer feels, brimming with a stark exhilaration that might be terror and might be joy.

He wanted to keep on going, to push through the big double-hung door and into the hallway beyond, to pretend he'd never heard those words in the first place. It was all he could do to turn around and face the others—face Abel—down the length of the kitchen.

"What—" His voice caught, and he paused to clear it, working up a teaspoon of spit to lubricate the words. "What did you say?"

"The cook— The cook is here." Abel hesitated. "Does that mean something to you, Ben?"

"I don't know. Does it?"

Still clutching the picture in one hand, he walked back to the table. He sat down by Lara. Cautiously, he said, "I don't know what it means. It means I'm willing to listen. For a little while, anyway."

Abel blinked. He smiled uncertainly. "Okay. Good."

"So what's going on?"

"That's the thing, I don't really know."

He laughed, a manic edgy laugh with more hysteria than humor, and it came to Ben that he'd gotten the metaphor all wrong: The wave hadn't passed, after all. Or if it had, it hadn't flung him any closer to shore; it had dragged him out instead, into deep, deep water.

"I don't know," Abel said. "I think— I think those photo montages used to scare me because I sensed something stirring inside me. Something stirring in response, you know?" He looked around as if in search of confirmation, but none of them said anything. Abel laughed again. "Something I didn't want to face."

Ben pushed the photo across the table. "It's a picture of a little girl, Abel. She's been dead for twenty-seven years."

Abel averted his gaze. "She's not dead to me."

"So what?" Keel said. "Who is?"

"Indeed, Mr. Williams," Lomax said. "Who is? No one is dead to you, or so you've claimed."

Abel smiled sickly. "This is . . . This is different. This is . . ."

"Real," Lara said quietly.

Abel shrugged, and nodded. "This is real," he said.

8

I am not afraid.

He remembered the cage of shadows on his ceiling and he remembered the telephone on the table in the hallway, an old-fashioned rotary device in gleaming black, so heavy that he had hardly been able to lift the receiver as a child, to bring it to his ear and hear the voices of his neighbors echoing down the party line from the world beyond the high wooden fence that demarked on one side the border of his narrow child's universe. He remembered his father's face and the touch of his work-roughened hands. He remembered his mother's tears. He remembered all this and more. He remembered the stunted apple tree outside his bedroom window, sculpted by the vicious winds barreling endlessly down from the mountain hollows above, and he wondered what black wind had been pouring down through the years of *his* life, and what it might have made of him. Even as a child he'd longed to escape the squalid necessity that had led his father to doom in the deep places of the earth. Now, for the first time, Abel wondered if the life he had chosen, the *work* he had chosen, wasn't some tawdry reflection of a real gift, twisted beyond recognition by that endless stream of grief and fear.

Unbidden, he traced the cracked crystal of the watch on his wrist.

How had he come to wear his father's watch anyway?

Memory beckoned.

A closet door in his mind swung open. The shadow of his father fell across him. He thought: there is a world, and there is a fence, and there is a world beyond the fence.

The photograph—maybe any photo—was a telephone.

He glanced down at it. The girl, Ben's sister, stared up at him from a gulf of years, and he felt something gathering in the room around him, a trickle of whispers that might at any moment become a flood.

I am not afraid, he thought.

Yet he tore his eyes away. Looked up at the others.

"There's a . . . phenomenon, I guess you'd say, called psychometry. You've seen it in movies. Occasionally you read about it: some desperate cop takes an article of a murder victim's clothing, a photo, whatever, to a psychic and the psychic 'reads' the object's . . . resonances. Psychic impressions. Whatever's going on, I think—" He took a breath. "I think it's something like that."

He paused, thinking it through.

"Maybe the photo isn't even necessary. I told you the other day about something that happened in the lobby when I was filming *Hard Copy*. It was very sudden, very brief, but it occurred when I happened to catch a glimpse of Theresa Matheson's photo. The producer had put this huge photo up as set dressing and I—I was doing my thing and I, I . . ."

He shrugged.

He looked at the others, expecting to see disbelief. He

saw none. Lomax had leaned forward, his elbows on the table, his hands clasped, his face rapt. Keel, at the other end of the table, seemed to have disappeared into his own private universe, his face brittle and impassive. Abel glanced at Lara, and then his gaze settled on Ben.

The whispers swirling in the corners of the room surged. A chill gripped him.

I am not afraid, he thought.

He closed his eyes. Took a breath. Opened them.

"The other day, in the lobby, the same thing happened. There was no photo, but I happened to think about that picture of Theresa Matheson, and . . ." He swallowed. "So maybe photos are, I don't know, props or something. Devices that enable me to focus, to access the level of concentration I need to . . . to hear."

"Hear what, exactly?" Ben said.

"The . . . the voices—"

"There's more than one of them?"

"Yeah, there are—there are lots of them. It's not like a direct line. It's like a . . . party line. There are so many of them coming through."

Silence, then.

"So what I propose," said Abel, "is nothing like the reading the other day. What I propose is . . . an experiment, I guess you'd call it."

Lomax put his hands flat on the table. He cleared his throat, and then, crisply, with his customary mien of command, he said, "Well, the lobby seems like the logical—"

Abel and Lara objected simultaneously.

"I'm not ready for that—" Abel started, but Lara overrode him.

"I don't want to risk the lobby. Given what happened to Abel the other day, I think it's best if we stay close to the infirmary. Besides," she added, looking at Lomax, "if you really think the . . . the building's power is weaker here, then maybe it's best—"

"If you're interested in what I *really* think—" Lomax started.

"No," Abel said. "The answer is no."

And then: "If things go okay, maybe . . . maybe later, all right?"

Lomax nodded, spreading his hands in capitulation.

"Okay, then," Abel said. He reached for the photo, and if his fingers trembled, none of them noticed.

I am not afraid, he thought.

That was how it began.

9

Three miles away, an elevated train screamed overhead, showering sparks into fresh drifts of snow. An observer, had anyone been there to observe, might have noted a final handful of hardy commuters fleeing homeward at last, their faces blurred by speed and glass as they gazed numbly into the storm from the heated comfort of their cars.

But there was no one present to observe.

The day—if you could call the muzzy three o'clock twilight day—was unfit for any but the most desperate of pedestrians. At present there were none. Along the streets of the Gold Coast, yellow lights glimmered warmly from the well-insulated houses and condominiums of the city's more fortunate residents; in the ramshackle blocks to the south, citizens of a duskier and more desperate nation hunkered down to weather the storm in pestilent apartments where icy January air gnawed through every chink and crevice. Still farther south, where the shuttered facades of check-cashing counters, liquor stores, and pawnbrokers gave way to block after block of empty storefronts and burned-out row houses, nothing moved but the wind, drifting the streets three and four feet deep in a crusted mantle of pristine white.

The dead lands had never been more lovely, or more lethal. In a cardboard refrigerator box at the back of an alley that the wind had lately breached, a homeless man was engaged in the serious business of freezing to death. He wouldn't outlast the blizzard. When his blood congealed into pink froth—and it wouldn't be long now, already he had succumbed to the fleeting warmth that precedes the fatal plunge—the dead lands truly would be dead, bereft of any human habitation but for the five troubled souls huddled around a table in Dreamland's sole surviving tower, where it stood alone, high above the waste and wreckage, colder yet than any natural cold, and impervious to weather.

The storm deepened.

The snow quickened, drifting knee-deep in the floors of long-abandoned apartments. Wind banged through the mouths of shattered windows, screaming down the black throats of half a dozen deserted corridors. In the kitchen, Abel Williams' fingers closed around the photo of a child twenty-seven years dead, and Dreamland, long drowsing, bestirred itself to full wakefulness at last.

From its cold height it observed him, this paltry man.

It observed them all, arrayed around him like sinners at an altar: the broken creature on his left, gripping the table and grieving honor lost; the sinewy ancient to his right, his hawkish features avid and abject, like a man in need or prayer; and the others, too, both of them halved by guilt, gazing back at him over a table still littered with the detritus of a meal now hours past.

Five souls.

Each of them hungry, each of them riven with sorrows they dared not express and needs they could not name.

Dreamland saw them.

Dreamland knew them.

Abel Williams swallowed, uttered a final avowal of defiance—

—*I am not afraid*—

—and lowered his gaze to the photo in his hand.

10

This time it happened without preliminary.

One moment Abel was gazing down at the photograph, at a girl of maybe six years old, thin and dark as Ben and

with Ben's narrow face, but utterly without his brooding
intensity. The next, the room was wheeling vertiginously
around him. Memory, long repressed, flared at the edge of
his awareness, and he had a fleeting glimpse of his childhood bedroom, his own adult hand overlain with the hand
of a child, clutching a photo not of a stranger twenty-seven
years dead but of his father, his—
    —Dad Dad—
—father emerging unscathed from the mine that had finally swallowed him whole, never to return. The overbright
kitchen sheared away, and he seemed to tumble forward,
downward and in, the photo—
    —the photos—
—scrolling open to receive him, spilling him not into the
rundown apartment where the girl—
    —LaKeesha, her name was LaKeesha Turner—
—had died and not onto the blasted apron of mud and
boot-trodden grass that fronted the mine elevator where
his father was even now stepping down to greet him, but
into another place altogether, a place that was somehow
both places at the same time, and neither of them, a colder
place, and darker still than any place on earth or under it,
where his father and LaKeesha Turner and a jostling
throng of thousands awaited him.
    So many, he thought, so many—unaware that he had
moaned these words aloud, that the temperature in the
room had plummeted, cold, so cold that his breath frosted
the air before his blind and staring eyes, unaware that
Fletcher Keel was suddenly clutching the table with such
ferocity that the muscles in his forearms stood out in ropy
cables or that Lara McGovern's pale hand had crept of its
own accord into Benjamin Prather's dark one, unaware of
all this, and more, of the snow ticking at the window and
Ramsey Lomax's barely suppressed moan of need or fear,
unaware even that he had crumpled the photo in his hand,
aware only of the dark and the cold, and the jostling throng
that pressed whispering upon him, so many, my God, so
many, who knew that death had undone so many—
    It was the girl's voice that came to him first, tentative,
questing—
    —Abel, we're here, Abel, we've always been here—
—through all that dark and cold, a mere trickle of sound,

and for a moment of wild elation, he thought he could control it, could measure it out syllable by syllable, like water through a spigot with a simple turn of hand. Then the floodgate burst, the dike ruptured, the dam crumbled, and a tsunami of voices, whispering, screaming, pleading, and cajoling in a veritable Babel of languages, came spewing out around him—

—*help us you've got to*—

—*with a knife he did it with a knife*—

—*cold I'm cold*—

—*it was a flower that he brought me*—

—*mommy I screamed for my mommy all the way down*—

—too many, my God, too many, and still they came, a thundering deluge of the dead, restless and grasping and all unquiet, and needy, there was so much need, and still they came and came and endlessly came, hungering after his still-living warmth until finally, in a jolting panic—he *was* afraid, oh so very afraid—Abel shrank back, withdrawing deep and deeper into the labyrinth of self, into a warm close cell at the very center of his brain where there were no voices, only silence, an endless gulf of silence where he curled rocking in the dark.

He pitched forward like a felled tree, convulsing.

He did not know it.

He was safe down there in the dark. Nothing could reach him there. Nothing could touch him.

Not even the thing that slid down into the shuddering husk he'd left behind, a cold thing, and dark, with a voice all its own, reed-thin, and hating.

11

In the thrashing instant of confusion that followed, Lara's perceptions dissolved in a montage of stark, disconnected images—of Abel's shoulders hitching in seizure; of the clutching pressure of Ben's startled fingers, there and gone again in the same fleeting instant; of Lomax shoving back from the table. A water glass shattered like a bomb, spraying glittering shards across the tile.

"Jesus," somebody said.

Lara stood, pushing back the bench, everything happening too fast, like an ER trauma with no trained staff to handle it. A hot panic pulsed inside her. She ignored it, no time for it now, letting the hormonal tide sweep her past it, already dreading the adrenaline hangover that would follow, her heart racing, legs shivery and weak.

"What the fuck?" Keel said.

"He's seizing."

"What do we do?" Ben said, his voice calm at her shoulder, and the memory of his touch sprang unbidden into her mind, his fingers squeezing her own.

What the hell did *that* mean?

Abel's feet hammered a frantic tattoo on the tile, and she grimaced, dismissing the thought. He pitched over on his side, rattling crockery, his upturned face a moonscape, airless and uninhabited. Reaching for him, Lara upset a glass, dashing water across the table. She glanced at Keel, and realized that she was talking, snapping out orders like a drill sergeant. "Get him on the floor, try to—"

She ducked a writhing arm.

"Damn it," she said, lunging forward, her fingers closing on his wrist, and, *yes,* she had him: his flesh clammy, his pulse thready under her thumb. "Help me get him down," she said. "Let's get him down, I don't want him to—"

Another shudder tore through Abel, twisting him up and away. The force of it wrenched his arm free and sent Lara reeling backward, unbalanced. Abel landed with a meaty smack, facedown, one flailing arm sweeping the table clean with a spectacular eruption of glassware and tinkling silver, bombs away, the salt cellar shattering, ceramic plates halving themselves along hidden fault lines. The cutting board crashed to the floor with a hollow *whump*. A final cataclysmic convulsion shook Abel, and then, incredibly, unbelievably, he was still.

The room was icy cold, and silent, the snow still pecking at the window. Lara hung her head, winded.

"Damn it," she said. "Damn it."

When she looked up, the others were staring at her with

shell-shocked expressions: earthquake survivors, dazed and mistrustful, awaiting aftershocks.

"Is it over?" Lomax said.

"I don't know. I think so." Lara shook her head and looked at Abel. He was still seated, his torso draped limply across the table, his mouth webbed with glistening strands of spit. His eyes were glazed, unseeing, devoid of personality, and Lara found herself thinking of that night in the kitchen, bantering over the dishes—

—*you wouldn't want dishpan hands*—

Something twisted inside her. "Yeah, it's over," she said. And then, gently: "You hear that, Abel? I'm going to take care of you, now. It's over."

It wasn't, though.

She had just started moving toward him when Abel snapped up like a jack-in-the-box, moving with an awkward, lurching intent, like a wind-up toy or a puppet on a stick. He lunged at her over the table, drawing back in the same jerky motion, his face twisted in a mocking rictus. Startled, Lara uttered a brief, involuntary scream.

"It should have been you, Lars," he hissed in a voice that was nothing like his voice. "It should have been you."

She stumbled back, stunned by the force of those words—

—*you Lars it should have been you*—

—and his knowledge of them, so often whispered in the sanctum of her most secret thoughts. Then the adrenaline hangover caught up to her in a nauseating rush. Her heart hammered, and the kitchen rippled with a glossy unreality, like a mirage seen through the seething haze of heat over a desert highway. She felt Ben's hands on her shoulders, guiding her down to the bench across from Abel—

—*was it Abel,* was *it*—

—and she realized that it wasn't over, after all.

It wasn't even close to over.

12

Abel—or the thing that had been Abel—swiveled its head mechanically, observing them, and tested, under the table, the edge of the blade it had snatched up during that final crashing moment of confusion. A single ruby droplet of blood welled up from the pad of Abel's thumb, plunging unseen to the tile below, and the thing inside him laughed for the pleasure of it—the grating joyless laugh of a creature unaccustomed to laughter. Calmer then, it settled to the business of accustoming itself to this fragile body, readying itself for what was yet to come.

13

In dread silence and in cold they watched it, this thing that was and was not Abel. It rocked stiffly on the fulcrum of its hips, lunging now at one of them and now at another, its movements jerky and imprecise, like a marionette in the hands of a novice puppeteer.

It was Lara who worked up the nerve to speak first, her voice tentative, trembling. "You need to be calm, we're going to help you, we're going to take you down to the infirmary, you're sick and we're going—"

"Shut up, bitch," the thing hissed. It chanted the words like a mantra, weaving the whole time, its eyes darting at each of them in turn, the whole stunned circle of them, drawing them in. Ben sat heavily, his gaze fixed on the thing, then Lomax, and then only Keel was standing, his big hands flexing at his sides, watching. "Shut up," it sang softly, "shut up, shut up, shut up."

"No," Lara said, "please, we just want to help you—"

"Like you helped Katie Wright?" the thing said, jabbing its head toward her, its face intent. "Helped *her* right into the grave, didn't you?"

"No, God—"

The voice shifted into a higher register, the mocking falsetto of a child. "It should have been you, Lars."

"Please, Abel—"

The thing paused. It drew itself erect, pulling in its chin. "Abel?" it said. "Abel stepped out for a bit, I'm afraid."

"Who are you, then?" Lomax said quietly.

"Oh, there are lots of us in here, old man. A legion of us." The thing leaned toward him, smiling, and then it drew away. "I'm afraid we scared Abel off. He left us the run of the place, though. Nice, isn't it?"

It spread its arms, rolling them experimentally and admiring the articulation, like a man checking the fit of a new coat. They saw the knife, all of them, at the same time, shining clean and sharp. There was a hiss of intaken breath, a single crestfallen syllable of dismay—

"Oh."

—the circle tensing. The thing raised its eyebrows in a pantomime of surprise. "What have we here?" it said. It rotated its wrist, catching the light along the flat of the blade. "It's nice, isn't it?" it said. "Pretty." And then it drove the knife straight down into the meat of its thigh— into *Abel's* thigh, Ben thought, and he felt a queasy wave roll through him.

"Jesus," Lara breathed.

"He had that coming, our friend Abel," the thing said. It clutched the hilt of the blade and yanked it out, holding it up where they could see it, a common kitchen knife, maybe eight inches of bright-edged stainless steel, sheathed now in the blood of a man, and transformed into something terrible. "You've all got a little of that coming, I'm afraid." The thing smiled, a rictus stretching of the lips, mirthless and without humanity. A corpse smile.

It resumed its weaving, its movements smoother now, fluid, like a charmed snake. There was something hypnotic in it, and when it started speaking again, a whispering, lilt-

ing kind of speaking, there was something teasing and hypnotic about that, too, as though it was weaving them up
inside a web of words. "We've been watching you," it said.
"We've been listening."

The blade traced languorous patterns in the air.

"What a fine lot you are, each of you hoarding your
little secrets, hmmmmm?" it said, still weaving before them,
lunging now at Keel—

"Had a drink lately, John? Been playing with your cock
any? What would Daddy think of that?"

—and now at Lomax, talking, constantly talking, its voice
reedy and thin and full of malice. "Get you in a lot of
trouble, cocks will, hmmmmm, *Ram*. Written any checks
lately, Ram? Have you? Hmmmmm?"

Lomax flinched, almost imperceptibly.

The thing drew back, carving shapes in the air, and settled its gaze on Ben.

"And you, oh, we know you, don't we?"

"No. You don't know anything about me."

"Oh, but we do."

Ben watched the blade, mesmerized.

"We do, we do. Paul Cook has told us all about you. We
know you better than you know yourself. Ben, poor Ben,
you don't know a thing about yourself. What are you doing
here, Ben? Why did you come back?"

Ben's mouth opened. Closed.

A steady hum had started up deep inside his brain.

The blade flashed, carving the air before him with a faint,
unintelligible whispering. If he listened closely, he could
almost decipher it . . .

"You know what you are, Ben?"

Ben licked his lips. His mouth was dry. His mouth was
so dry. "What? What am I?"

"You're their pet nigger," the thing said.

The word shocked him. All his life it had shocked him.
He'd grown up in a world almost entirely sanitized of that
word, a world scrubbed so ruthlessly free of it that its utter
absence announced its attendance everywhere around him,
hovering unspoken on the lips and in the minds of every
white face that met his dark one, his mother's face, his
father's face.

Paul Cook's face.

"You're not white, Ben, and you're not black, you're nothing at all."

The blade crooned in the air before him, and the blade's voice and the other voice—the one speaking aloud these truths he'd always left unspoken, this secret knowledge of his heart—were one voice, his own true voice, secret and self-hating. *We hate you,* it purred, and he could see the words—

> *—we hate you—*
> *—we hate you—*
> *—we hate you—*

—rolling in a mesmerizing column up a screen inside his mind. A distant hand closed over his hand, summoning him back, but it was too far, too far to come. "Ben, Ben, Ben," the blade sang softly, "What color is your skin?"

And then he jerked awake to see it hurtling toward his chest, bright and glittering through the sheen of Abel Williams' blood.

14

Lara, too, had been mesmerized, less by the weaving dance of the blade or the whispered blandishments of the thing across the table (not Abel, she couldn't bring herself to think of it as Abel) than by the strange effect these things seemed to be having on Ben. A dreamy expression stole over his face as the thing wove its serpentine patterns in the air, and when he spoke in return—

"What? What am I?"

—Ben's voice had a drugged, faraway reluctance, like a man on the edge of sleep, summoned back all unwilling and anxious to be off.

What's happening? she thought. What's happening to him?

A choking sense of foreboding clogged her throat, she

could not swallow it down. His lips moved, shaping soundless words—

—we hate you, we hate you—

—and before she quite knew what she was doing, she found that her hand had crept once again into his hand. How easily it happened, how naturally, and when Lana spoke inside her head—

—what will Daddy say when you bring him *home to old Carolina, hmmmm—*

—Lara dismissed the thought as unworthy.

Benjamin Prather's fingers were dry and cool and not without strength. She squeezed them gently, hoping to recall him from whatever dream he had succumbed to. He didn't respond, didn't stir or squeeze her fingers in return, and she thought suddenly of the knife, plunging in a savage arc into the meat of Abel Williams' thigh. She blew her breath out in a cloud—

—it was cold it was so cold—

—and the air in the room tensed with expectation. The dread in her throat thickened like mortar, sealing her esophagus, making it hard to breathe. Something was going to happen, something terrible was going to happen—

Still clutching Ben's fingers, squeezing with every ounce of strength she possessed, she turned to face the Abel-thing across the table. The knife whipped by more swiftly now, a bloody silver blur, keening as it cut the air, and Abel— the thing that had been Abel—was keening too, singing softly, "Ben, Ben, Ben, what color is your skin," and weaving there before him, its eyes bright and hateful and utterly empty of humanity. An instant before it happened she sensed or saw the gathering intent, the muscles tensing in the thing's arms and shoulders, like a tiger crouching low to launch itself from some hidden bower in the grass, and all the time singing, singing that mocking, hateful little rhyme, "Ben, Ben, Ben, what color is your skin—"

The weaving blade drew back and leaped forward in a single smooth motion, like the arcing strike of a cobra—

Lara hurled herself off the bench, pushing off from feet planted solidly on the floor, tapping the long muscles of her calves and thighs, fortified by all those endless miles along the lake. She used all of it, every bit of strength she had. Her fingers clutched, dragging Ben down with her. For a terrifying, adrenaline-slowed moment, everything seemed to freeze, her lunging body suspended over the tiled floor, the knife descending in its fatal trajectory. She glimpsed something in the air above her, a hurtling shadow, and then a balance shifted.

The floor hurled itself up to meet her. She rolled, tucking her chin to take the blow on her upper arm and her shoulder. Still, it hurt more than she expected, a white-hot nova of pain, centered high in her back and expanding outward. Her body recoiled from the impact only to be slammed back to the floor as Ben came down on top of her, dead weight, driving the breath out of her in a plosive gasp.

Her lungs heaved, clawing at the air for purchase, that awful phrase still screaming through her thoughts:

Dead weight, dead weight, dead weight—

15

For Fletcher Keel, the events just prior to Abel's seizure—and he thought that word might have a dual significance in this context, that Abel was not only seizing but that he'd *been* seized—had a hazy dreamlike cast. It was like being in two worlds at once, here in this kitchen with Abel at the table and there, too, in a moment twenty-seven years gone, still ascending that lightless stairwell toward the fatal encounter that would change so many lives, his life and Lisa's life and, yes, Benjamin Prather's life, change everything, and irrevocably.

And there was worse.

Now, as then, he'd felt that cold presence at his shoulders, beating invisibly about his head like wings, leathery wings that reeked of blood and old resentments, hungry for admission. How he longed to surrender, to relinquish his fear and doubt and give over to its strength. He almost succumbed—would have maybe but for that other voice—

—*Susan's voice*—

—his better angel's voice, crying out within him: *Make amends, make amends.*

He had done some seizing of his own then. He'd seized the edges of the table like a drowning man latching onto a piece of drifting wreckage, and he'd held on, too, he'd held on with every fiber of strength he possessed as the waters rose around him and the black pinions thundered at his shoulders. He held on, and watched the others as through a scrim of frost upon a glass, listened to their voices like the voices in a dream. Then Abel had picked up the photo—

—*LaKeesha's photo, LaKeesha*—

—*you stand accused of*—

—and Keel had a brief vision of the girl pitching over backward as the bullet tore out her throat, her hands fluttering helplessly before her.

And then, abruptly, the waters grew still. That dark attention swerved temporarily into another quarter, the sense of presence at his shoulders retreating. It didn't go away—he didn't think it would ever go away, not so long as he stood inside these walls—but it became more bearable: the wings of a moth—

—*not a dragon*—

—just brushing the edges of his awareness. He'd hardly tasted his relief, like a draught of cool, clean water after a day beneath the August sun, before all hell broke loose—before, not to put too fine a point on it, Abel pitched his fit, not to mention all the weirdness that had followed, the bizarre weaving and the business with the knife and Abel's knowledge of things he could not possibly know—

—*been playing with your cock any*—

—*what would your daddy think of that*—

—things that unleashed a festering resentment inside him. Maybe that was what inspired Keel to do what he did next: his resentment at his father's legacy of honor, his hunger to silence that nagging voice inside his head. Maybe it was that and maybe it was the voice of Susan Avery, urging him to make amends. Maybe it was both.

In any case, he had spent time enough in bars to recognize the symptoms of impending violence—the tightness that seemed to enter Abel Williams' shoulders, the increasing speed and savagery of those slashing gestures with the blade. He'd seen what was going to happen an instant before it *did* happen, and when the blow came, when Abel—or the thing that looked like Abel—drew back its arm and lunged across the table, Keel was already moving, that voice—

—*make amends*—

—crying out within him.

He had a moment's fleeting impression of the scene—of Ramsey Lomax stumbling away from the table, of Lara diving toward the floor, Prather tumbling in her wake, of the blade itself arcing down in a blur of bloody silver, like a smile inverted in the air—and then all that sheared away. His field of vision narrowed to Abel, Abel Williams and the knife, a concentration so fierce, so focused, that he could see the white crescent of each articulated knuckle on the hilt and smell the blood still steaming from the blade. He struck the other man high, wrapping one arm around his torso, battering with the other at the hand that held the knife. The edge parted Benjamin Prather's shirt, laying open the ribbed flesh underneath as Keel's momentum carried them over the table, their feet tangling, clearing whatever crockery remained.

And then they were down, rolling, Abel flailing with the knife. The blade whicked by Keel's cheek, so close he could feel the wind of its passage. It snapped on the tile, and Keel lunged away, scrambling to his feet.

Abel came on undiscouraged. The fear Keel had all this time been holding in abeyance gripped him then, held him fast. He heard his own voice—

"—help me, Jesus, help me—"

—a hoarse plea for deliverance.

He backed away, circling. The room wheeled around him—the wreckage of the table and Ben lurching to his feet, one hand clasped to his ribs—febrile glimpses, Abel Williams always in the foreground.

Lomax loomed up at Abel's back, swinging a chair with both hands. The blow staggered Abel, but it didn't seem to hurt him. He uttered a coarse grating laugh, a rattle of stones in a dry creek bed. He turned, tearing the chair from the old man's grip, momentarily distracted. Keel tensed for the leap, but the impulse froze within him, paralyzed by terror, and the advantage slipped away. The thing—it was not Abel, it could not be Abel—hurled the chair across the room. It faced Keel, brandishing the broken knife, its features twisted with fury.

Half-forgotten skills from training decades past, desperation, his natural grace—these things saved him. Abel—the monster inside Abel—was unschooled, overeager: when it came, it came headlong. Keel feinted to the left and ducked underneath the knife. He grabbed the thing's arm, twisting the blade free, and rode the creature's charge all the way to the tile. He pinned it there, breath screaming in his lungs, and shoved its arm north toward the shoulder blade.

"It's over," he hissed at its ear. "It's over, let him go."

"It's *not* over. We'll have you, too, John, before it's over," the thing seethed. "You're half the man your daddy was—"

Keel drove his knee into the thing's back. "Shut up—"

"—what would he think of you, down there diddling yourself in the basement—"

Keel sank his other hand into the thing's hair—

—it's Abel, Abel's hair—

—and yanked its head back. "Shut up, I'm not listening to you—"

But the thing did not shut up. It laughed. It laughed and glared up at him from one moist, rolling eye, an eye that seemed to penetrate right down to the black river muck at the bottom of his soul, and it kept talking, talking, talking, its neck corded with strain, its jaw clacking, its voice boring through his skull like a bone saw. "What would Daddy think of what you've become, John?" it said, twisting the name into a skewer. "You're a killer, you're a coward, you're a drunk—"

"You shut up," he spat. "You shut up—"

"—you're weak. You're weak, and we'll have you, too, before we're done. You can rest assured of that, John. If you're good, if you do just what we require, we might let you have a crack at the woman—"

"—shut up—"

"—she's good, ask the nigger, he'll tell you, you don't mind a nigger's sloppy seconds, do you, John—"

"Shut up!" he screamed. *"Shut up, shut up, shut up—"*

He smashed the thing's face into the tile, rage lighting him up like a candle, like a constellation, like the sun itself, the whole world burning with incandescence as he wrenched the thing's arm higher up its back and drove its face once again into the tile, and still it was talking, goading him, goading him, and he yanked back its head for yet another blow, he would smash its brains out, he—

"Stop it, stop it. You're going to kill him—"

Keel hesitated, the voice razoring apart that swarm of molten light. He was trembling, all over he was trembling. He took a breath. He looked up into Lara's staring face.

They stood over him in a ragged circle—Ben and Lara, Lomax, too—their expressions blank with horror, and not at Abel, either. No, at him, at what *he'd* done, alone and of his own accord. His fingers spasmed in the Abel-thing's hair. He lifted its head and stared down into the devastated face. "What would your Daddy think of what you've done now?" it rasped, its voice clotted with mucus, breath rattling in its shattered nostrils. It began to laugh, softly at first, the sound growing louder and louder until it seemed to fill the room, echoing back to Keel in wave after derisive wave, and he might have finished the job, might have snatched back the thing's head and slammed its face once again into the tile, might have done it over and over again until he had smashed that laughter into silence, but Lara McGovern reached out and touched his shoulder.

"Enough, Fletcher," she said, and there was something kind in her eyes, something that reminded him of Susan Avery.

A dam broke inside him, he felt it giving way.

He pried open his fingers and lowered Abel's face to the blood-smeared tile. When he spoke, his voice was thick with disdain. "He would have killed you both."

"I know," she said. "Thank you."

"I let him up, he might yet."

"I know. I'm not asking you to let him up. I just— Don't hurt him anymore, okay?"

"Okay."

The thing writhed underneath him, trying to buck him off. "Oh, Daddy would be proud," it whispered, and mocking laughter swirled in the air around him, fanning the ember of rage that still smoldered in his breast.

"Shut up," he hissed. And, then, to Lara, "You do it then. You find a way to shut him up. Or I'll do it myself."

"Okay," she said. "Okay."

She held his gaze for the space of a heartbeat, and then she turned away. A moment later she was gone.

16

Lara came apart in the infirmary.

The pulse in her temple throbbed like a bass line, fragmenting her thoughts, and her endless panicky flight down the corridor had a jaundiced pall, like things seen through the fevered lens of dream. In the examination room, she fumbled her keys jangling to the counter. She realized she was cursing, low and monotonously—

"—damn it, damn it, damn it—"

—on every heave of breath.

She brushed a strand of sweat-darkened hair from her forehead and plucked at the keys. Her hands trembling, she fitted one—she thought it was the right one—to the lock. It skidded off to the side, barking her knuckles.

"Damn it!"

The drug cabinet stood impervious, mocking.

A vision seized her: the pressure boiling in Fletcher Keel's agonized features, his fingers clutching at Abel's hair. And Abel's face. My God, his face.

She dragged in a breath, calming herself. This time she managed to lodge the key at the mouth of the keyhole. She shoved it in, twisting. The lock surrendered with oiled precision.

The cabinet swung open.

She stared into it, overwhelmed by the thronged shelves. Ranks of pills and amber-tinted fluids, cartons of IV bags, sheaves of sample packs, boxes of ampoules and sealed vials, a crazy profusion of drugs. After Lomax's litany of little horror stories, she'd spent a morning organizing and reorganizing them, memorizing everything's location, knowing nothing was going to happen, it was like a vacation, two weeks and she'd be able to reclaim her job, her life, everything she'd lost, but committing herself to the project of organizing the damn drug cabinet anyway, just in case—

and what a bitter taste those words had now, now that all that knowledge seemed to have evaporated right out of her mind. Suddenly, she didn't even know what she was looking for, much less where to find it.

She pounded a fist on the counter.

This wasn't her. This wasn't like her. She was at her best in a crisis, this was her life's work, it was what she *was*, damn it. She had vowed never to lose her head when someone else needed her, she had made a promise to herself, she had made a promise to Lana—

Like opening a floodgate, that name. Suddenly everything came pouring through, Fletcher Keel's twisted physiognomy and the knife, the knife driving straight down into Abel's thigh, the knife laying open the wound in Ben's side, most of all that mocking catalog of her own failures, Abel's—

—but it wasn't Abel. It was something else reading out that—

—taunting register of her sins: Lana and Katie Wright, too, dead, both of them dead. The word tolled in her thoughts. Did she want to fail someone else, did she want to hear those words again—

—it should have been you, Lars—

—did she?

No.

That one syllable stopped her cold, dammed up the frantic cataract of her thoughts.

No.

Not Lana's voice, either. It was her own voice. *Lara's* voice. She wasn't sure she'd ever really heard it before.

No, it said, calming her, and suddenly it was all right there inside her head, her careful inventory of the drug cabinet, what she needed—what Abel needed—Haldol, of course it was Haldol, even its location: on the lowest shelf, far back in the left corner.

She reached for it, fishing in a drawer for a hypodermic with the other hand, that vision of Fletcher Keel's face—

—you shut him up then—or I'll do it myself—

—unreeling in her mind. She shoved aside a row of pill bottles, spilling several of them to the counter below. A handful of sample packs—allergy tablets—followed, then a glass jar that tumbled shattering to the floor.

There it was.

Lara dragged it out, her heart still racing, swept aside
the mess on the counter, prized the box open. Neat rows
of five-milligram vials nested inside. She stripped cello-
phane from the hypodermic, popped the needle through
the taut rubber cap of an ampoule, and drew the drug up
into the reservoir. She hesitated then, debating dosage. Five
milligrams was standard, five milligrams ought to do it. But
images of Abel haunted her thoughts—Abel driving the
knife hilt-deep in his thigh, his crazed strength, the way he
had kept goading Keel through a mouthful of bloody, broken teeth. And that laugh. Dear God, that laugh.

She snatched up another vial and plunged the needle
through the cap, doubling the dosage. Capped the needle
and set it aside. Dug under the counter for a medical kit,
bandages, disinfectant, gloves.

Christ, this was taking forever—

There. Done.

She stole a glance at her watch, saw that she'd been gone
three or four minutes, five tops. Okay, good. She gathered
her supplies and turned away, and that's when her gaze
happened to fall on the telephone.

A fleeting memory seized her. Two nights ago, was it?
Three? She didn't know—didn't even know for sure how
long they'd *been* in this nightmare, and there was something
more than a little disturbing about that, wasn't there?—but
the memory was utterly clear, tactile: the receiver smooth
in her hand, her forehead tilted to the wall, drawing from
it cool comfort to salve her blistered thoughts. And the
voice on the other end of the line, faceless and remote,
radiating the cool competence of an airline pilot saying he'd
turned on the seatbelt signs, things were liable to get a little
bumpy, the tone saying more than the words: nothing to
worry about, folks, you're in good hands.

You folks have a problem, there?

*You bet your ass we do. Problem doesn't really begin to
describe it.*

She imagined herself picking up that phone and saying
exactly that, trying to ignore the selfish dissenting voice that
piped up inside her, the one arguing that if she didn't stick
out the full two-week term, if she dragged somebody else
into this mess, doctors and paramedics and, inevitably, cops,

because, let's face it, what we have here is at least one case of attempted murder and maybe two—if she did all that, well, Ramsey Lomax might just renege on their deal. And where would that leave her? High and dry, that's where.

But somehow all that didn't diminish the lure of the phone. How easy it would be to pick it up. And why not?

It wouldn't take but a minute.

And they'd had a deal, too, she and Abel. They'd *all* agreed to that deal.

She stared at the phone.

Help was close at hand, seventeen minutes away, probably more in this weather—she glanced at the window, all darkness and whirling snow—but that was even more reason not to delay. She rolled her lower lip under her teeth, considering, while precious seconds ticked away.

Finally, she set aside her medical kit and reached for the phone. "Hello?" she said. "Is anybody there?" And she held the receiver to her ear for two full minutes, forcing herself to wait while the second hand on her watch made two complete circuits, round and round and round it goes, but no reply ever came.

No reply at all.

Dreamland

1

"The snow must have knocked it out," Ben said.

Prickly tension reigned in the lounge.

Lara paced. The others watched her—the weight of their scrutiny almost palpable—Lomax from his post by the window, one foot propped against the wall, Keel from the pool table, where he had stationed himself in silence the minute he'd finished helping strap Abel to a gurney in the infirmary. For his part, Ben eyed her mildly from across the room. He had propped himself upright against the back of a sofa, his arms crossed gingerly over his bandaged ribs. She glared at him, annoyed by his insistence on mundane explanations. "So what do you think happened to Abel?" he'd asked her as she cleaned up his side. "Some kind of psychotic break?"

She had bitten back the impulse to tell him what she really thought, unwilling to utter the words aloud—not quite sure *she* was ready to give the idea any credence. Now, despite her exasperation, she settled yet again for dithering uncertainty: "I don't know."

"Well, it's not unreasonable, is it?" Ben said. "Storms like this take the phones out all the time."

"We still have power," Lomax pointed out.

"Maybe we ought to check it again."

"How many times are we going to check it?" Lara snapped.

Ben shrugged, wincing slightly.

"What do *you* think caused it, Doctor?" Lomax asked.

Lara stalked away, unspeaking.

"Well?" Ben prompted.

"You of all people saw what happened to Abel, didn't

you?" she said, wheeling to face him. "You heard the things he was saying."

The tension ratcheted another notch tighter. None of them had yet gathered the resolve to address the issue of the things Abel had said—what they might mean, or how he might have known them.

Secrets, Lara thought. So many secrets.

Ben bit his lower lip.

"Well, didn't you?" she snapped.

Ben looked away. "Yeah, I saw."

"Okay, then," she said, unwilling to push it any further. "Anyway, it doesn't matter what caused it—any of it. The point is, what are we going to do about it?" She paused in her pacing, fixing first Ben and then Lomax with her gaze. "The point is, he can't stay here. *None* of us can stay here. Agreed?"

Lomax dropped his foot to the floor and straightened his shoulders. "I don't think anyone disagrees with you, Doctor. Unfortunately there's at least three feet of snow on the ground and more coming down. It's dark. And the temperature is well below zero. What do you have in mind?"

"There must be . . ." She waved vaguely. "There must be someone close by. With a phone, I mean."

"I trust you remember the drive in?"

Lara said nothing.

"Even if there is someone around, I doubt they would have a phone. I doubt even more they'd be inclined to let a stranger in to use it."

"We could ask them to call the cops. We wouldn't have to go inside."

"People around here are wary of the police, to say the least," Lomax said. "Where would you suggest we go if they *don't* invite us in? And who would stay here with Abel? He's hardly capable of travel."

Lara threw up her hands. "Do you have a better idea?"

Lomax mulled that over quietly. "I propose we put off acting until morning," he said at last. "We'll send someone out at first light. Perhaps the phone will be working by then. If not, the snow may have stopped. At least, no one will be stumbling around in the dark."

"Right," Lara said. "And who's going to go?"

"I'll go," Keel said from the pool table.

The sound of his voice startled her after his prolonged silence. He stood on the far side of the pool table, not looking at them, toying with the eight ball, rotating it slowly on the velvet with long fingers—the same fingers he had used to smash Abel's face into the tile, Lara couldn't help thinking. If they hadn't been there to stop him—

Lara choked off the thought, and the one that came after it, too, Lana's always pragmatic answer. *And if he hadn't been there to stop Abel, what then, Lars? Huh?*

Keel looked up, squaring his shoulders. "It's the least I can do, after . . ." He shrugged. "You know."

Lara had an image of broken teeth and blood-smeared tile.

"Very well, then," Lomax said. "Mr. Keel has volunteered. Do we have a consensus?"

He looked pointedly at Lara.

She turned away, studying the photo affixed to the wall: Dreamland, all eight towers intact, in the bright moment of its inception, drowsing underneath a summer sun. And now? she thought. The answer came unbidden: *Now it's winter. Now it's awake.*

"So we're in agreement, then," Lomax said.

Lara turned to face the others.

"All right," Keel said.

He spun the ball in place, like a top, reminding Lara suddenly of the prophetic novelty she'd had as a child, the magic eight ball her father had fetched home from the toy store one day. How long had it been since she had thought of that, she and Lana hunkered together on the floor of their bedroom back home in Wilmington, posing questions about who their teachers would be in the coming year or what presents they might find under the Christmas tree? An endless stream of optimistic answers had floated up in response—*you may rely on it* and *outlook good* and *signs say yes.*

What would it say now, that magic eight ball? What would it say about their odds of getting out of Dreamland alive? Did they have any chance at all?

And she imagined herself a child again, in her girlhood bedroom, kneeling over the eight ball with bated breath, knowing already what answer would come swimming up through the green murk inside—

Signs say no.

Keel closed his fingers, abruptly checking the ball's rotation. He snapped it toward the nearest pocket with an effortless flick of his wrist, accurate and unthinking. Lara listened to it clatter down through the guts of the table and into the return tray at the other end.

"I guess I'd better get some sleep, then," he said.

2

Prather caught up with him in the hall.

"I just wanted to thank you," he said.

Keel turned back to face the other man, standing stiffly there five feet away. *Tell him,* a voice whispered inside his head, and another one of the AA bromides swirled through his thoughts, the one about admitting to another human being the exact nature of your wrongs. Keel shook his head. "Things got out of hand," he said.

"Well, things would have been far worse if you hadn't intervened, right?"

Would they? He wasn't so sure, suddenly. Wasn't so sure about anything. "I guess."

"Yeah, well, anyway. I wanted to say thanks."

"You're welcome."

Keel turned away and continued down the hall, all too aware that Prather was still watching him. He spoke just as Keel was fitting the key into the lock.

"Keel."

Keel pocketed the key and opened the door. Darkness waited on the other side. "Yeah," he said, without looking up.

"He called you John."

The statement hung in the silence of the corridor like an accusation. Keel stared into his empty suite, the dark swarming with nightmarish images: a blood-smeared swath of tile, the bright circle of the flashlight, like a bull's-eye on Patrick Mitchell's back.

Still he didn't look at Prather. "He was crazy. It was nothing."

"Was it? He knew things. He knew things about me."

This time the voice was raw with chafed feelings. It commanded his attention. Keel's guts cramped. An acidic torch ignited at the base of his throat. Almost against his will, he found himself turning his head.

Prather hadn't moved. He radiated a tense neediness, a stiffness that transcended the soreness of his injured ribs, his eyes invisible behind the reflective shields of his spectacles. *Tell him,* the voice said again, and this time Keel recognized it. It was his father's voice. *He deserves it,* the voice said. Keel swallowed an acidic surge of resentment.

"You were . . . you were the kid in that apartment," he managed.

"Yeah."

But now that he'd made a start of it, Keel found he didn't have the heart to continue. He'd done enough, hadn't he? He'd tried to make amends. What more could anyone ask of him?

"You were a cop once, right?"

That too sounded like an accusation. Keel felt a bright flash of anger—

—*you don't mind a nigger's sloppy seconds, do you*—

—at the question.

"You implying something?"

"Should I be?"

Weariness swept over Keel. He turned back to the darkness of his own suite, quiet now, welcoming. The AA people were full of shit, he thought. The thing to do with the past is let it lie. Let bygones be bygones. He started to speak, hesitated, cleared his throat.

Ben waited.

"That was a long time ago," Keel said at last. "That was so long ago it might as well have been another man."

"And the name? John?"

"Nothing. Really, I have no idea."

"Okay," Ben said. "Okay."

Keel stepped into his suite, into the darkness, and closed the door behind him.

3

Sedated, Abel Williams looked like a wounded child. Lara had done what she could to make him comfortable—swabbed the blood from his face with a soft towel, disinfected his split lip, propped his head on a pillow. In truth, though, there wasn't much more she *could* do for him. He'd need a surgeon to reconstruct his nose and broken teeth. Time would take care of the rest—the swelling, the deep bruises under his eyes.

In the meantime, they'd both just have to wait.

Lara straightened the IV line, loosened the strap a notch where it was biting into his wrists, smoothed the hair off his forehead. "We're going to get you some help," she whispered, the words rising to her lips before she even knew she intended to say them. "Just hang on. All you have to do is make it through the night."

She sighed, embracing herself, cold despite the warm air wafting through the ductwork. The night beyond the windows weltered with wind and snow.

Dear God, would this storm ever pass?

She checked the phone for maybe the fiftieth time—nothing, not even the hiss of dead air. Hung it up again. When she turned, Abel had stirred into bleary wakefulness. He watched her out of drug-addled eyes. Gazing back at him, she fancied that she was looking at Abel, the *real* Abel, not the monster from the kitchen. His tongue appeared, probing at his cracked lips.

Lara moistened them with a damp towel.

He stared up at her from glazed eyes.

"Should . . . have been . . . you," he whispered, the venom in his voice palpable.

"Maybe so," she said. "Maybe you're right."

On the way out of the room, she switched off the light.

4

He knows.

Keel sat in his suite, listening to the storm outside his windows, the voices in his head. An image of Prather came back to him—the tense set of the other man's shoulders, the soulless glare of his glasses.

"He doesn't know shit," he said into the darkness. He said, "It doesn't matter what he knows. We're even now."

But the words sounded false in his ears, full of swaggering bravado. The truth was, you could never be even. Never. He didn't need his father to tell him that.

His guts twisted again.

Keel sat straight, his hands on his knees, enduring the spasms. After his little heart-to-heart with Prather in the corridor, he had reeled into the bathroom, dropped his pants and hunched in agony over the bowl, emptying his bowels in three agonizing gushes. Then he'd just sat there, stewing in his own feculence, replaying the events in the kitchen on an endless loop.

Each recollected impact of face and tile seemed to set off a kaleidoscope of long-repressed memories. Each spray of Abel's blood summoned back still more blood, oceans of the stuff. And not just the blood on his clothes that morning in Nevada, either. Oh no. There was LaKeesha Turner's blood, and her mother's blood, and her sister's blood, too. There was Patrick Mitchell's blood.

You fragged him, his father said inside his head. *Fragged him over that humiliation in the lobby. You're everything he feared you might be. And worse.*

Crouched there over his own stink, Keel uttered his denials to the unhearing air. "I didn't," he whispered. "It was that . . . that . . ."

That thing. The thing that had assailed him in the south stairwell. The thing with the reed-thin voice.

You invited it in, his father said. *Your fear, your anger—those were the doorways. You welcomed it. You own those crimes.*

Now, sitting upright on the armchair in his living room, his guts clenching, Keel accepted it: they *were* his crimes. And even if they weren't—even if the thing with the voice, the black wings beating at his shoulders, *had* been responsible—the others, the one in Nevada, and the other one, too, Tim Underhill, those were all his. There was no way of passing the buck on those, was there?

No, indeed.

And how could you redeem such oceans of blood?

You cannot, his father said inside his head, and a fresh layer of perspiration prickled Keel's brow. He felt empty inside, hollowed-out, his guts twisting. He thought about eating something, maybe that would help, but the idea of facing the shambles of the kitchen—

—the tile, the blood-smeared tile—

—made him cringe. He thought about sleep, but sleep seemed a million miles away.

A memory of the bottles in the basement possessed him, tactile in its intensity: two liters of Old Crow and a pint of Jack, good old Denny Eakin's private stock, all of them standing at attention on the desk. He could almost smell the whiskey, he could taste it on his tongue, wood smoke and licorice and the sweet promise of oblivion, the warmth blooming inside him like a benediction.

He wrestled his thoughts into other channels, the flex of Lara McGovern's ass—

—you don't mind a nigger's sloppy seconds, do you—

—the long hike in deep snow that awaited him, each of them fraught with their own anxieties.

The night stretched before him like a sleepless desert.

Jesus God, if only he could get some rest.

The image of the whiskey bottles floated into his mind.

Fletcher Keel closed his eyes and gripped the arms of his chair until his knuckles turned white.

5

Ben found the file buried in one of the boxes Lomax had shipped for him. What a marvelously devious thing the human brain could be, he mused. The same impulse that had led him to accept Lomax's invitation, that had led him to pack the damn file in the first place, had also enabled him—no, forced him—to consign it unexamined to the closet. You could go through the motions of facing up to the past—but as for actually doing it, that was another matter altogether. That was strictly verboten.

No doubt Paul Cook could have offered some insight on the issue. But the Cook, as it had been lately pointed out, was dead.

He was on his own here.

Ben sat on the floor, and leaned against the bed, the file—a frayed brown accordion folder with an overstressed elastic closure—unopened in his lap. He drew in a breath, wincing as a row of invisible fishhooks embedded themselves in his aching ribs, and let the conversation replay in his mind: the silent corridor, Keel haggard and lean before him.

You used to be a cop once.

That was a long time ago. That was so long ago it might as well have been another man.

But it wasn't another man, was it—much as you might like to pretend otherwise . . . John?

Abel—

—the thing inside of Abel—

—had called him John.

Recalling it, Ben felt certainty blaze afresh inside him. He had known it from the start, hadn't he? He'd seen it that first afternoon in the elevator, something familiar in the set of the man's eyes. If he went back through the notes he'd made that night, he'd see it there, interleaved with those foreboding little warnings—

—*do you believe in ghosts*—

—from—from whatever the hell they came from.

Another goddamn mystery.

Ben opened his eyes and stared down at the file in his lap, bulging with the work of a long-ago summer, everything he'd been able to find about his family's deaths—clippings and dime-a-page off-prints from the microfilm readers in the reference room, police reports, the trial transcript, the whole sordid history, his first experience in tracking down a story from every conceivable angle.

He'd found his calling that summer in the Santa Monica Library, Paul Cook, as always, showing him the way. When you thought about it, every single event in his life unfolded from a few tragic seconds he had been too young to remember. You could trace the line backward from his profession through his matriculation at UCLA and his years with Paul, all the way down to his youth in the safety and affluence of southern California, all of it paid in the coinage of his family's blood—a family he'd never met.

Flinching, Ben snaked a hand into his pocket and retrieved the crumpled photo Abel had discovered among the junk in 1824. He unfolded it carefully, smoothing the seams with his fingertips. LaKeesha Turner stared up at him, a total stranger, familiar only from a few newspaper photos, thirty years out of date.

Ben, Ben, Ben, what color is your skin?

He sighed and opened the file.

6

Ben found Lara in the lounge, staring blankly into the pages of a book.

"I went by your room," he said.

"Yeah, I couldn't stand it in there anymore." She put the book aside, and massaged her temples with her thumbs.

When she looked up, brushing her hair out of her eyes, he was struck by how tired she looked, how pale and tired. "I came out to check on Abel."

"How is he?"

"About as well as can be expected, I guess. He's sleeping, anyway." She smiled wryly. "So what's up? I figured you were holed up in your room, rationalizing things."

"Hey—"

She held up a hand. "No, it's fine. Believe whatever you have to believe."

He dropped to the sofa beside her and put his feet up on the table. He leaned his head back, exhaling through pursed lips.

"How's the side?"

"Hurts like hell."

"I can get you something."

"No, I took a couple Tylenol." He looked at her from the corner of his eye. "Thing is, I kind of want to keep my wits about me."

She laughed. "See, you have come around to my way of thinking."

"Yeah."

"So what changed your mind?"

He didn't answer, just held up the file.

"What is it?"

"Have a look," he said, handing it over to her.

Watching her undo the elastic closure, her fingers graceful and sure, the nails trimmed short, Ben found himself thinking about her hands at his side, how knowing they'd been as she bandaged him up, how confident. He remembered something else, too: how she had clutched at his hand back in the kitchen, how natural it had felt, their fingers winding together like they had been custom-sculpted to fit, like two pieces of a puzzle coming seamlessly together.

"Oh, Ben. When did you put all this stuff together?"

"I was a kid. I must have been eleven or twelve; I just got obsessed with the whole case."

"And your—your parents, how did they feel about it?"

"Hated it. They tolerated it, though. I was in therapy, and the therapist talked them into it, God knows how. I was never able to talk them into anything, not Dad, anyway. So I spent most of a summer in the library, tracking down everything I could lay hands on." He shook his head. "I've been carrying that file for years."

"So how come you to dig it out tonight?"

"Something Abel said. Here—" He reached out, thumbing through the sheaf of shiny microfilm off-prints, still faintly redolent of cheap ink—or maybe he only imagined it, the way he imagined he could still feel the warmth of each slick sheet as it emerged wet and streaky from the cut-rate printers, weighted down with its freight of history. "You don't need to look through the whole thing, just look at the articles from the trial. Here, look at this one."

Lara took the proffered article, skimming the text, her eyes flicking rapidly back and forth across the page. "What am I supposed to be looking for? I don't see—" And then she *did* see it, Ben *saw* her see it, her eyes widening slightly in surprise.

She puffed out her cheeks, exhaling slowly.

"It's him, isn't it?" she said, gazing down at the photo, a shot of a rangy blond man, clean shaven, climbing the courthouse steps, one hand thrown back in a gesture of angry defiance, his face caught over the left shoulder in three-quarters profile. Everything about him, the grace of his posture as he mounted the stairs and the line of his shoulders, most of all the eyes, a hard set that might have been anger and might have been fear, proclaimed his true identity.

"It's him, all right," Ben said.

"I don't understand."

"I tried to track him down once. After he was acquitted—"

"He was acquitted?"

"Oh yeah. There were two snipers, one in each of the bedrooms. When the SWAT team went in, they didn't know that. They found themselves in a cross fire. He claimed the whole thing was accidental—"

"And they acquitted him."

"It gets worse. They not only acquitted him, he stayed in the city for several years after that, trying to get back on the force. Even filed suit once—this was eighty-five or six—seeking reinstatement. Might have won, too."

"What happened?"

Ben sighed. "Kid named Tim Underhill happened," he said. "There's some coverage on that a little further on.

John Martin was working mall security, then, and he picked up this kid, he was fifteen, sixteen, something like that, he lifted a cassette in a Record Bar—remember those places? Anyway, the kid got mouthy, one thing led to another, and John Martin—or Fletcher Keel or whatever the hell you want to call him—ended up beating the hell out of him. Nearly killed him."

Both of them were silent, thinking of the display of temper they'd seen in the kitchen, the way Abel had goaded him way over the edge. Thinking, too, maybe, of the man strapped to the table in the infirmary, his face smashed nearly beyond recognition. Ben was, anyway, and it was hard to see how Lara couldn't be—she'd been the one, after all, who'd had to try putting the pieces back together.

"What happened then?" she asked.

Ben stopped himself just short of shrugging. "He disappeared before he ever came to trial on that charge. I lost him then."

"He changed his name?"

"Not officially, not that I could find any record of. Doesn't mean anything, though."

"Why?"

"He was a cop. He might have bought some paper on the street. Maybe not even that. Maybe he's just drifted all those years, working in the underground economy, cash and carry. Who knows?"

"Lomax found him."

"Are you impugning my investigative skills?"

She laughed, a real laugh, her voice a little hoarse from the afternoon's excitement, and he felt it strike an answering chord within him. She squeezed his hand, a fleeting impression, there and gone again almost instantaneously, leaving him to close his fingers on the neural echoes of the gesture, a split second too late.

He tilted his head against the sofa back and smiled. "Suffice it to say our host has deeper pockets than I do."

Lara snorted. "Yeah, but he lacks your sensitivity."

"No doubt about that," he said, glancing toward the windows. "What do you know? Maybe our luck's changing. The snow's stopped."

She followed his gaze, her expression pensive. And then she turned back to face him.

"How do you feel, Ben?"

"I don't know." He thought it over for a while, and then he looked up, seeking her eyes. "There's more," he said.

7

You have to tell him, Keel's father said in the darkness.

Keel, still sitting stiffly in the living room of his suite, his guts roiling, shook his head. "I can't," he whispered. "I can't."

You have to. It's the right thing to do. It's the honorable thing.

Keel cradled his face in his open hands. Honor. How it sickened him, that word. How it had weighed upon him all these years. He could see his father in his mind, already an old man when he fathered his son, his body puckered with scar tissue and worse, the empty sleeve and ragged stump that had horrified Keel as a boy—all this for a handful of metal and ribbons. For a handful of trinkets.

And more: Keel suddenly found himself recalling how it had all come rushing back to him that day in Charles Maitland's store, the day he'd finally chosen to absolve himself of this burden, this legacy he could not live up to—this legacy no man could live up to. He had walked into that store to surrender it all, only to find himself confronted with another neatly pinned sleeve, a ghostly vision of the very man from whom he was fleeing. Even now, in memory more than two decades lost, the moment sickened Keel, shocked him.

And now, to have it flung up in his face like this, that word.

He stood, pacing, and snatched a crumpled wad of paper off the desk: the splotched barroom napkin Klavan had given him. Pausing by the window—the snow had stopped at last, and a faint luminescent moon, three-quarters full, peered down between wispy fingers of cloud—he unfolded it, thinking now of Susan Avery. He had given it up, the life he might have made with her, and for what? Nothing. An ink-smeared napkin, a Rorschach blotch, unreadable. He let it drop from abruptly nerveless fingers.

But Susan Avery, once summoned, would not be so easily dismissed. She seemed to hover in the air around him, her scent of coffee and soap, the touch of her chapped lips against his own, her voice in his head, echoing that tired AA platitude about owning up to the exact nature of your wrongs, echoing that and more, saying, *We've got the rest of our lives. It's not too late.*

The phrase echoed inside his head.

And why not? Who said it was too late?

Why not step into the hall and bang on Benjamin Prather's door?

Keel hesitated a moment longer, and then he turned from the window. The doorknob gave beneath his hand. The hallway beyond was desolate. He did not give himself time to reconsider. He lifted his fist and rapped sharply on the neighboring door, once, and then, after a moment's hesitation, again.

No answer came.

He sagged, weariness washing through him in a hazy reverie of nightmarish plunges and distortions, last night's uneasy dreams. He almost turned away, but Susan Avery's voice—

—we've got the rest of our lives—

—turned him down the hall instead. He swung through the lounge doorway unseen—and pulled to an abrupt stop. Prather and the doctor were hunched over a pile of papers like a couple of high school kids on a study date. Even a blind man could have read their easy intimacy.

His guts heaved.

Abel's voice cut through his thoughts—

—ask the nigger, he'll tell you, you don't mind a nigger's sloppy seconds, do you—

—unleashing a tidal swell of jealousy and resentment, and he lurched away instead, not toward his suite, toward the south stairwell.

8

In the same moment, in the infirmary, the sedatives in Abel Williams' bloodstream dropped past some critical threshold and he came suddenly awake, stretched taut on a rack of agony—his thigh burning, his face throbbing—as the events of the past hours poured back to him in a stream of nightmare images. Panic clawed at him—

—*what had happened to him*—

—and then the malevolent presence lying dormant inside him uncoiled itself, banished him to that deep internal pit, and once again assumed its cold dominion.

9

The first drink tasted great.

Deep in the bowels of Dreamland, seated comfortably at Dennis Eakin's desk in the gentle radiance of the gooseneck lamp, almost without memory of the dark sojourn just past, the unlit stairwell and the cavernous antechamber of the central basement, Keel held it in his mouth, that drink, savoring the subtle flavors of charcoal and smoked wood, the sweet evanescence of prime Tennessee sipping whiskey on his tongue. At last, he swallowed. The liquor warmed him all the way down. Igniting a comfortable glow in his belly, it set about the serious business of dispatching calming emissaries to every frontier of jangled nerve ends.

The voices in his head were silent.

Keel leaned back, the chair squeaking underneath him. It might have been made for him, that chair, its arms tooled to fit his arms, the dimpled surface of its seat designed especially to receive him. The whole place felt that way to him—comfortably shabby, lived-in, homey. The sleep that had evaded him upstairs in the impersonal luxury of his suite hung waiting here, high in the crepuscular corners, like a silken net suspended in the shadows to enmesh him.

He hardly needed the drink, the place itself so soothed him. He let this fantasy spin itself out for a minute or two— he'd have one drink, that's all, hardly a major offense, more like a gentle step off the wagon than a genuine fall, and what was to prevent him from stepping right back on, none the worse for wear? Then—hardly aware that he was doing it—Keel lifted the pint of Jack once again to his lips, tilted another slug of whiskey into his mouth, and swallowed it.

A boundless sense of well-being suffused him.

He reached out and dragged one of the magazines closer: *Gallery*, "Home of the Girl Next Door." He studied the cover—a bubble-breasted blonde, her tongue extended in teasing invitation to the giant, rainbow-swirled lollipop she held in one hand—and then he flipped it open, idly thumbing pages as he followed out the line of his thoughts.

The thing was—and when you got right down to it, he really *did* believe this, he believed it to the very bottom of his soul—everything *was* going to be okay. He was comfortable here, that's all. In fact, it was probably better this way—better for all of them. He could sleep undisturbed, stretched out on the sofa as he had slept the other night. He'd have another drink or two—not too much, just enough to dull the edge of anxiety that the whole encounter with Abel, fucking Abel Williams, had honed to razor sharpness—and then he'd sleep. He'd sleep like a baby— remember how well he'd slept here the other night?—and in the morning he'd be fine. He'd be in better shape than if he had slept upstairs, and that would be good for everybody. It would only increase his odds of success in doing just what he'd agreed to do: wading through all the damn snow to fetch back help for fucking Abel Williams.

Right?

Keel eyed the level of whiskey in the pint carefully, comforted by the presence of the two bottles of Crow, like attendants in waiting.

He had another sip, turned a page.

He was well launched into the "Girls Next Door" section by this point, and he felt pleasantly aroused. He'd always been partial to the whole girl-next-door concept: their imperfect bodies, immortalized in cheap snapshots, held an erotic appeal, an accessibility, that the airbrushed models who deigned to spread their empyrean perfection elsewhere in the magazine could not match.

He licked a finger and turned the page.

Take this one here, for example, the dishwater blonde at the bottom of the page, the skinny one with the snub nose and the high tits. Sarah, from Lubbock, Texas. Not bad, not by any stretch of the imagination. She wasn't a surgically enhanced goddess, true, but what she lacked in the looks department you can bet she more than made up for in enthusiasm, else she never would have let—Keel squinted at the text under the photo—she never would have let her boyfriend Jess take the damn picture in the first place, much less submit it for publication. Right? In fact, come to think of it . . .

Keel leaned closer, studying the picture.

. . . she looked a little like Lara, didn't she?

More than a little, actually—and Keel's whiskey-flushed imagination, unbidden, treated him to a private little blue movie of the doctor in action, of Benjamin Prather mounting up in the saddle of her narrow hips, black on white, right there in the goddamn lounge.

You don't mind a nigger's sloppy seconds do you, John?

Keel's lazy sense of well-being dissipated in the cool subterranean air. He separated the page from the stapled binding of the magazine with a single angry jerk, quartered it and quartered it again, and let the scraps flutter down to the untidy mass of paper already on the floor.

It didn't prove so easy to erase the image from his mind, however. Grimacing, Keel reached for the pint—it was almost empty now—and took another drink.

10

"Here," Lara said, pointing to the page.

"What?"

Ben stopped pacing to look over her shoulder. She'd been reading a printout of his notes on Abel's reading—the one session at the keyboard he'd managed without the staccato sequence of interruptions. He'd told her about his nagging sense that there was something of importance there, something he couldn't quite put his finger on.

"I had forgotten this," she said. "The reading in the lobby—it was Lomax's idea."

"No, it was Abel's, remember? We were playing gin."

She looked up at him. "The *reading* was Abel's idea. The *lobby* was Lomax's."

"You sure?"

"You wrote it."

He reread the passage in question. "Huh. Well, so what?"

"This afternoon at the table," she said. "Just before everything went to hell—Lomax suggested we move to the lobby again. Remember? He was kind of insistent about it."

"So what's the connection?" He turned to look at her. "Or here's a better question: Why did he get interested in Dreamland in the first place?"

He resumed pacing, running through the events in his mind. In both cases, Lomax had insisted on a reading in the lobby, where Theresa Matheson had been killed. That had happened two years ago—two and a half now, actually, not long before Lomax had sold off his interest in Eyecom Industries and gone into seclusion—

He looked up, met Lara's eyes.

"Theresa Matheson," they said at the same time.

"What about her?" Ben said.

"She was my daughter," Lomax said from the doorway.

11

Fletcher Keel was drunk.

The booze, after three months off, had hit him harder than he expected. What had started as a swelling sense of well-being had mutated, following that little mind movie of Lara and Benjamin Prather, into sullen resentment. With each subsequent sip of whiskey, the resentment had deepened into something else—self-loathing and a looming sense of depression, finally a formless and foreboding apprehension.

Dennis Eakin's office abruptly seemed neither cozy nor comfortable. It seemed . . . threatening. He suddenly longed for the comfort of his fifth-floor suite.

A long walk, that. A long climb up hundreds of damp concrete stairs. In the dark. With some misguided notion of self-protection, Keel yanked open the drawer containing the tools and fished out the hammer. He heaved himself to his feet and glanced at the desktop, a little surprised to discover that he'd finished off the entire pint and made a respectable dent in one of the liters of Crow.

He reached for it instinctively, checking the gesture just before his fingers closed around the bottle neck. A complex storm of emotions swirled through him—defiance and rancor both, and wrapped up inside of that, like the eye of a tornado, a deep and unyielding pocket of shame. He wondered what Susan Avery would think of him now—and the fact that he *knew* what she would think of him, that she would pity him without judging him, that she would seek to lend him even in this moment of reeling weakness a fragment of her own strength and dignity, somehow made it all worse.

And it wasn't his fault.

He'd been led astray, hadn't he? He'd been coaxed and lured, he'd been manipulated, and now, drunk in Dennis

Eakin's office, drunk on Dennis Eakin's whiskey, he felt dark wings once again beating invisibly around his shoulders.

He lashed at the bottle, slapping it unbroken to the floor, where it leaked aromatic bourbon into the stew of spilled paper and shredded magazines. He hated himself for wanting to snatch it up before it emptied. He hated himself even more for not doing it. If he'd had a match in that instant, he might have snapped it burning into the whole mess, and been glad to do it—maybe he'd get lucky, burn this fucking place to the earth and burn himself up inside it, yielding himself to the bright and purifying flame. Lacking one, he turned toward the door instead, staggering a little. He reached for the lamp to steady himself, and sent it crashing to the floor. Its bulb popped with a soft *whump* of displaced vacuum, plunging the office into darkness.

"Shit," Keel muttered.

He fumbled at the doorknob and let himself out into the central basement, still clutching the hammer in his left hand. Alas, that preternatural knowledge of the building's layout, of every stick of discarded furniture and shattered bottle, seemed to have evaporated. He tried to summon up the blueprint inside his head. Nothing came.

So turn on the lights.

The thought, logical as it was, seemed to come from nowhere, and for a moment Keel wasn't sure whose voice it was—his or someone—

—something—

—else's—but in the end he didn't bother trying to hash it out. The darkness weighed upon him, impenetrable. If he tried to make it across the basement in this condition, he'd probably break his neck. So he reached out with blind, grasping fingers, located the switch, and did just what the voice had told him to do:

He turned on the lights.

12

"I fear that I have been a very poor father indeed," Lomax said, sitting heavily across from them.

"I thought— I thought you didn't have any children," Ben said. "There's no record of them."

"No, there wouldn't be, would there?" he said.

He hesitated, looking at the ceiling, the light gilding his shaven skull. He looked suddenly like an old man, his flesh sagging, his mouth tremulous—as if he had sustained his vitality all this time through sheer force of will, and that failing, he was left with nothing. He sighed. "How to tell it? Lord, how to tell it?"

His hands shaking, he reached into his sport coat for an envelope. He struggled with it momentarily, his fingers prying ineffectually at the flap, and then he gave it up and handed it across to Ben.

Inside it, made out to a woman named Maya Underwood, Ben found a check for a hundred fifty thousand dollars.

13

The lights suspended high in the ceiling came on in staggered clusters, like stadium lights, a line of bright explosions marching down the arched aisle from the super's office to the distant stairwell, and with each fresh burst of radiance, Fletcher Keel cried aloud in horror and dismay.

Bones.

The basement was full of bones, human bones, skeletons limned in interleaving arcs of shadow and of light, still wreathed in the decaying rags they'd worn in life, or in their leathery envelopes of mummified flesh—there must have been twenty of them, thirty, more, who could count, who would want to? Bones, scattered more or less at random the length of the colonnade before him, and the breadth of the basement, too, as wide and long as the nightmare height that towered far above it. Bones, in every conceivable attitude of death, bones supine with arms outflung to the frowning canopy above them and bones facedown in puddles or marooned piecemeal on islands of cracked and drying stone. Bones curled fetal or sprawled in wanton eagerness, ravished now by death. Bones slumped against walls and columns, still cradling the half-full bottles of whiskey and gin and Wild Irish Rose they had died with. It was an abattoir of bones, of curving ribs like the spars of sunken galleons, of shattered femurs and scoliated spines, of fleshless fingers clutching and blank skulls with empty eye sockets staring, jaws agape, and tangled shreds of disintegrating hair still clinging to their yellow-ivory domes.

Keel sank moaning to his knees, struck down by memory, the kindling snap of something fragile underfoot and the sound of Ramsey Lomax's voice inside his head, reminding him how Theresa Matheson's grim assailants had come to that abandoned lobby.

It summoned them, he'd said. *I think it summoned them.*

14

She had shown up at his office three years ago, and he had turned her away—a stranger, what was she to him? His assistant had demurred, and finally, to appease her, he had surrendered. "Very well," he'd said, "send her in," and in she came, eighteen years old, a tiny thing, but possessed of a fierce directness that was somehow tantalizingly familiar.

"So whatever do you want?" he'd asked her, and her reply had shocked him as nothing else had shocked him in forty long years behind that desk.

"I want to know if you're my father," she'd said.

15

Summoned them, Keel thought.

And surely it could do such a thing.

It had summoned him here, had it not, to this dank well? And when, once before, he had lifted his hand to turn on these very lights, it had forbidden him. Everything in its own time, and in this place, in this hellish place, Dreamland set the time: teasing and cajoling and luring them along, trading on their dreams and fears until at last it had them, weakened now, and ripe for plucking, and the moment came to spring its trap upon them.

Dreamland.

It was conscious. It was aware.

He thought of the cold intelligence that had assailed him in the south stairwell all those years ago. He thought of that reed-thin voice—

—it could be any voice—

—and those dark wings beating at his shoulders.

He thought of the photo in the lounge, Dreamland, her eight towers like standing stones, erected all inadvertently, to the service of some dark and hungry god. Who could say what awful intelligence it might have summoned from the void, to batten on the weakness, on the misery and resentment, on the hatred and despair of the uncounted thousands imprisoned in these walls? And when they fled at last, unwilling to countenance such horror any longer, what did it do, what else *could* it do?

It had turned its power outward, extending questing fingers into the city, seeking in its seething masses the helpless and adrift, the forgotten and unnumbered, rendered vulnerable by drink or drug or madness. And when such a one chanced to stray into its purview, it lured him home, it summoned him to its bosom with the siren song of his own unacknowledged dreams.

But why? he wondered. *Why?*

And the answer, when it came, struck him numb and cold:

It had to feed, that's why. Everything had to eat.

16

He had very badly wanted to win her, this girl, this child, with her mother's fierce courage. He was old already then. His wife was dead, he had tired of work, and now there was no one left, maybe there never had been anyone, but a time comes when a man longs for the touch of a hand he hasn't bought and paid for. So he took her to dinner—everyone had to eat, right? He thought it would be a way to win her—tuxedoed waiters, a hundred-dollar bottle of wine.

He had miscalculated, and badly. Bound for Harvard in the fall (it had made him proud when she told him, though what had he contributed beyond a teaspoonful of seed?), she had come to the city for the summer to do mission work for her church. Why stay at home, she said, when there was nothing for her there, her father (stepfather, he silently amended) dead, and her mother lately joined him?

"You can stay with me," he had said, and a funny look had come into her face, as though he had suggested she take up residence in a cave. She didn't want a relationship, she explained. She had just wanted to see his face, to confirm what the check implied.

"You're my daughter," he had said.

"That's biology," she told him. "My father—my real father—died in a car wreck two years ago. You can't buy me any more than you could buy my mother."

Ten minutes later, she walked out.

17

Fletcher Keel whimpered, that phrase—

   —everything had to eat—

   —resonating inside his head.

Terror seized him, paralyzing, and he slumped all the way to the floor, facedown, sobbing. He lay there for a long time—he didn't know how long he lay there, plumbing his own black depths of hysteria—and then an image took shape inside his heaving mind, a nightmare picture of his own bones hunched fetal on the cold stone floor before Dennis Eakin's office, a desiccated husk still draped in the clothes he'd died in, his eyes hollowed into empty sockets, his mouth slackly ajar, his teeth dropping one by one from his decaying jaw as the long years wore on.

"No," he whispered, "No—"

Still clutching the hammer, he lunged to his feet, the basement spinning vertiginously around him, spilling him once again to the floor, face-to-face with a broken skull. Keel stared into those empty eyes for a single nightmarish moment, and then he scuttled away, crablike, fingers clawing at the stone floor until at last he clambered drunkenly erect, unbalanced, all resolve forgotten, thinking now only of the world outside these walls, the velvety night and the snow spinning down upon his shoulders, crystalline and pure. The basement reeled about him. Stone archways lurched toward him. The floor heaved. Skeletal fingers scrabbled at his feet. Keel screamed, kicking at them like a frightened child, and spun, staggering back toward the stairwell.

He didn't see what tripped him, whether it was some upturned spur of bone or merely his own panicked frenzy, but suddenly he was unbalanced, his fingers raking the air as the floor hove up to meet him. He hit the stone with a gasp, his arms outstretched, and plowed face-first into the moldering ribcage of a dead man. He gagged, his throat clogged with the fetor of decay, and then he was still, all the machinery inside him grinding to a halt. He took a breath, willing his heart to slow within him.

Finally, he opened his eyes.

Inside the shattered ribs, couched on yellow bone, glimmered a handful of filthy ribbons and tarnished service decorations. Keel swallowed and pushed out one trembling hand, sooty with the dank muck of the basement. He was bleeding, too, he saw, from the fall maybe, a single bright trickle running the length of his index finger. He lay there, watching this hand that looked nothing like his own hand close around the fistful of medals, and drag them from their cage of bones. He held them on his splayed palm, staring at them in disbelief, reading the name—

—*his father's name*—

—inscribed on each tarnished badge.

No, it couldn't—

Dear God, it couldn't be—

But even as this crazed prayer unreeled inside his mind, there loomed up in the eye of his imagination the seamed and grimy visage of the vagrant to whom he'd surrendered them, his father's medals, oh God, the vagrant, and it all came back to him, the putrid blast of his breath and his yellow food-flecked teeth, his eyes rheumy and wild over the matted lather of his beard, and most of all his raving, he'd been raving about microwaves—

—*goddamn Russian microwaves*—

—and maybe even then he'd been hearing it, not microwaves, but Dreamland's summons ringing deep down in the shuttered chambers of his soul.

Keel's mouth tasted coppery.

His guts cramped, and he vomited, spewing up a bilious flood of churning acid and half-metabolized whiskey, the stench of it overwhelming even the clinging miasma of decay. He heaved again, and then again, fetching up another cupful of liquor, and then nothing at all, just the clutching spasms in his guts, his mind reeling with tangled images, his own finger pulling home the trigger and La-Keesha Turner convulsing as the bullet tore out her throat in a spray of cartilage and arterial blood, and Lisa's face and Susan Avery's and Lara, Ben laboring between her legs, and it was all too much, too much fear and too much horror, too much resentment and too much shame, God, the shame—

And this was the doorway, he understood that now. Fear and shame, the black rivers flowing in the deepest channels of his soul, both of them doorways. Open them up, anything might walk in, anything at all—

Black wings were beating at his shoulders. Keel cried aloud and clutched his father's medals in his hand. He had a final incoherent thought—

—*forgive me God forgive me*—

—and then he surrendered at last.

18

"When I read about the murder," Ramsey Lomax said, "I could barely function. It was all I could do to go on. I kept thinking about that girl across the table from me, a child really, and she was so—" He sighed. "She was so much like her mother." He clutched his thighs with gnarled old man's hands, straightening his back, and took a deep breath. "Six hours," he said hoarsely. "Can you imagine what that must have been like for her?"

He shook his head in baffled disbelief.

"And that's when you quit working?"

Lara's voice was smooth, sympathetic. Ben marveled at it, that voice. He tried to choke down his own rising emotion, to cling to some ideal of journalistic objectivity, but he was past that. For God's sake, look at the man, wallowing there in self-pity, and look at *them*, look at what he'd done to *them*, look at what he'd done to Abel, and why, for God's sake *why*?

He stood jerkily, too fast, the pain in his side straightening him abruptly, cutting through the fog of rage.

"No," Lomax said. "That was later. I was using my

sources to collect everything I could on the case by then, and I got word of Abel's *Hard Copy* reading in the lobby. It had never aired, but I managed to get my hands on a production tape. It was remarkable, that tape—''

He shook his head.

"Abel is a fraud, Doctor. I knew that, I knew the techniques he used to elicit his audience reactions, and yet, when I watched that tape, I saw something else. There's a moment when, when—something happened, I didn't know what it was, but Abel's polished facade seemed to crack. He seemed disoriented, afraid; there's a look of real uneasiness in his eyes—it's remarkable.''

Ben propped himself by the window, his arms crossed.

"That's when I decided,'' Lomax said. "I'd heard the rumors about this place, of course, and the tape seemed to confirm them, at least somewhat. And I was tired, tired of working, tired of everything.'' He shrugged. "So I sold out my shares and dedicated myself to this, this . . . project. It took two years to negotiate the contracts, to track you all down. And there were others, some who wouldn't come back, and some who couldn't, because they were dead or because they were in prison.''

"But it had to be more than curiosity,'' Lara said.

"Oh, yes, definitely more than curiosity.'' He laughed ruefully. "At dinner that night, my daughter, Theresa, said she was glad we'd met. She'd learned a lot. 'What did you learn?' I asked. 'How I don't want to live my life,' she said.''

Lomax hesitated, staring up into the lights. Finally, he shrugged. "I wanted her forgiveness, I suppose. I wanted to tell her that I was sorry for a selfish life. I wanted another chance.''

At this Ben felt his anger tip over into something deeper, something he could no longer contain. "Well, I guess you screwed that up, didn't you?'' he said.

Lomax was unperturbed. "You sound angry, Mr. Prather.''

"I *am* angry. You lied to us, you lied to all of us—''

"Did I, Mr. Prather?''

"Lies of omission,'' Ben said, waving a hand. "The point is, you did it again, exactly what your own daughter despised about you. You *used* us. You manipulated all of us to serve your own ends, and you never spared a thought for the consequences. You, you—''

He bit the words off. He pushed himself away from the wall. Back at the sofa, he knelt and began to scrape up the documents spread out across the coffee table, the clippings and the trial transcript and the smudged photocopies with their imperfectly reproduced faces, the mother and sisters he had no memory of, the cops and lawyers, even a photo of a four-year-old version of himself, a solemn-faced child in an ill-fitting suit, hand in hand with some expressionless court-appointed guardian, the headline announcing in a line of sober black type, SHOOTING SURVIVOR TO FACE ADOPTION, RECORDS SEALED—

Ben felt something break inside him; it was the story of his life, his whole goddamn life, the records sealed, the secrets hidden even from himself, and no one willing to accept responsibility, not even to tell him the truth. He snatched up the documents by handfuls, shoving them at random into the accordion file, and when Ramsey Lomax leaned over to help him, he could not countenance, could not countenance this gesture of—was it pity?—from the old man who had dragged him back here. He shoved the hand away—

"Leave me alone."

—sending a spray of papers high into the air, swirling as the heat caught them up, and drifting slowly back to the floor around him. He slumped against the sofa, exhaustion sweeping over him like a woolen tide, his side aching; he was tired, he was so tired—

"Mr. Prather—"

"No," he said. "Look around you, why don't you, look at how it's ended. You disgust me."

He shut his eyes, trying to block it all out, but Lara's hand closed over his shoulder, summoning him back.

"What?" he said. "What is it?"

She didn't answer, not aloud anyway. Her hand clutched tighter and, wearily, Ben pried open his eyes. Fletcher Keel stood in the doorway, staring back at him from eyes like extinguished cinders. His hair was tangled and matted, his face smeared with dirt and maybe blood. He stank of whiskey and vomit even from across the room. But none of

that, disturbing as it was, really alarmed Ben. What did—
what shook Ben to the core, what sent bright electric currents of adrenaline jolting through his veins to wake him
up—was the object Fletcher Keel clutched in one grime-
streaked hand.

A hammer.

19

In the infirmary, the thing that had been Abel Williams
paused for a moment in its efforts to wriggle free of the
leather straps binding it to the table. The sounds of voices
came to it from down the hall—voices raised in anger, or
in fear. A smile spread across its face in the darkness, and
then it turned once again to the straps, redoubling its
efforts.

20

"You thought you could get away, but you couldn't get
away," Keel said, only it wasn't Keel's voice that came to
Ben, it was the same dead voice that had lately issued from
the lungs of Abel Williams, stroking now the deeper tim-
bres of Fletcher Keel's vocal cords but unmistakable all the
same, like the voice of stones or serpents had they tongues
to speak with.

It was thin and hateful, that voice. It was cold, and utterly
empty of pity. It was Dreamland's voice. Ben had no doubt
of that now, no temporizing, no rationalization, nothing,
just a stark certainty that momentarily froze him there,
slumped against the sofa.

Lara pulled her feet onto the sofa and clambered backward across the arm, putting it between her and the figure in the doorway. Lomax, too, scrambled to his feet, backing away until he passed beyond the limits of Ben's peripheral vision.

And still Ben only sat there, fixed and fascinated.

Keel stepped into the room, his fingers white-knuckled on the shaft of the hammer, a battered, grime-encrusted tool, the black iron head balanced with a curving double-pronged claw, two inches long and maybe longer.

"Fletcher—" Lara's voice, coming from somewhere over Ben's left shoulder.

"Shut up, Doc," the thing said, and its dead eyes didn't deviate from Ben. "Shut up," it said. "Your turn's coming."

"No," Ben said.

"You got away once."

"I didn't, I never got away," Ben said, and sitting there on the floor of Dreamland with the fat accordion folder on his lap, adrift in all that history, it struck him suddenly how true this was: he was thirty years old, and he had never gotten away. "Not here," he said, touching his chest. "Not in my heart."

The thing paused at the other end of the coffee table. "Here?" it said, and it tapped the hammer to its breast in mockery. "Here?" it said calmly. And then a third time, its voice petulant and shrill, like the voice of a child in a fit of angry pique: *"Here? We're here forever!"* it screamed. *"Forever!"*

Still shrieking, the word hanging in the air like some hideous accusation, it lunged at him, bringing the hammer down before it.

21

In the infirmary, the thing that had been Abel had managed to wriggle a hand free at last. As the voices down the hall escalated past anger and into downright hysteria, it started to work on the remaining straps.

22

Ben heard the hammer smash into the table behind him as he scrambled away, and then he was on his feet. He turned, backing now, to see the Keel-thing looming up behind him, its face twisted in fury, its voice echoing in his ears—

"Forever. We hate you. We hate you."

It tangled its feet momentarily in the wreckage of the table, and then it shook free, kicking jagged shards of wood aside. It advanced toward him, raging, the hammer cutting the air. Ben dodged backward, and the blow whistled by an inch short, overbalancing the creature. It stumbled, and Ben took the opportunity to put more distance between them, scanning the room in panic, looking for Lara, looking for something he could use to defend himself—

There was a blur of movement at his shoulder. He cringed, half-expecting an attack from another quarter, but it was only Lomax, his hawkish face combative, his fingers clutching a pool cue. He brought it whistling through the air as the thing straightened. The blow caught Keel just under the jaw, staggering him backward, arms flailing. Lomax pressed the advantage. He whipped the cue around like a slugger swinging for the fences, and this time there was the hollow pop of breaking cartilage. Keel's head snapped back in a spray of mucus and blood.

"Go," Lomax hissed. "Get the doctor, get out of here!"

Instead Ben wheeled around desperately, looking for something—anything—he could use as a weapon. He heard another whistling impact at his back, this time accompanied by the crack of shattered wood. Then Lomax was shoving him toward the door. "Go," he screamed. "Go! I'm right behind you!"

In the same moment, Ben caught a glimpse of Lara moving toward the door from the sofa opposite.

"Go—" Lomax screamed.

He went.

23

When Ramsey Lomax felt the fist close around his ankle, he spun, lashing at Keel's face with his other foot, hoping to drive him back. Instead Keel managed to trip him up completely, bringing him crashing to the carpeted floor with a jolt that nearly took his breath. Still kicking, Lomax flipped onto his stomach, and hurled himself after Ben, trying to reclaim his feet. For a single exhilarating moment, he was free, his legs unencumbered. He pulled himself to his knees, hope blossoming in his breast, and then a stunning blow drove him to the carpet.

24

Lara, not ten feet away, saw it happen—saw Keel rear up over the fallen man, his arm flung back in rage, saw the hammer descend in a twisting blow that buried the claw two inches deep in Ramsey Lomax's back. Lomax toppled forward, arms outstretched, dragging Keel down on top of him.

Keel scrambled to his knees, yanking at the hammer, struggling to free it, and in a moment of nauseating comprehension she understood that the claw had lodged like a hook under the bony ridge of a rib. Then, with a bone-rending crack that set Ramsey Lomax screaming, Keel wrenched the gore-stained claw loose. A terrible wheezing filled the air. Lara moaned and cupped one hand before her mouth, her gaze fixed on the hole in Ramsey Lomax's back, a ragged gouge of blood and gristle from which a jagged shard of rib extended like a broken tree branch. The ravaged fabric of his shirt fluttered with every whooping respiration, and though Lara had seen such things and worse a hundred times in the ER, it was different somehow, seeing a man you had known savaged right before your eyes—

She stood frozen and she might have died there had Ramsey Lomax not lunged up, locking both hands around Fletcher Keel's leg, slowing him down, and even so, for a single terrifying moment, she found herself staring right into Fletcher Keel's eyes, bright and empty and mad all the way to the bottom—

Lomax screamed, his face a writhing mask of agony, his mouth a bloody hole. She couldn't hear anything but the hoarse agony in the voice, the bubbling wheeze as his lungs filled up, drowning him in his own blood. He screamed again, his imperative cutting through the fog of horror, her mind plucking at the sound for meaning—

Go! Go!

And then Ben was at her shoulders, forcibly wrenching her toward the corridor. He gave her a hard shove to get her moving and still she hesitated, her mind filling up with some crazy impulse to go back, to help, to somehow help, and then it was too late, her feet tangled up with Ben's in the doorway, spilling them both into the hall, and a screaming incoherent thought loomed up inside her, filling her brain: she'd doomed them, she'd doomed them both—

They were still unsnarling themselves when Fletcher Keel, dragging Lomax behind him, stumbled into the corridor and cut off their escape route to the stairwell.

· 25

Lomax saved them.

Somehow, despite the burning agony in his back and the blood that filled his mouth with every throb of his racing heart, he managed to hang on for the few steps it took

Keel to reach the corridor—managed even, in the end, to drag himself closer still and sink his teeth deep into the thick-bunched muscle of the other man's calf.

In the heaving instant that it took Keel to stop and lift the hammer to batter him to the floor, Ben managed to get Lara to her feet. Lomax saw it: they were already moving toward the distant beacon of the north stairwell when the first blow fell, like a bomb going off against the side of his skull. And still he clung. He clung with every ounce of strength he had as the hammer came down again, a bright sheet like lightning flaring up before his eyes, and then another blow and then another, the whole world erupting with an incandescence so bright it was almost painful. He felt as from a distance his fingers losing purchase, felt Keel kick him contemptuously away as a man might kick a dog that had been nipping at his ankles.

And then he came to rest.

Through a flickering haze, he saw Keel kneel over him, his arm uplifted for yet another blow.

Ramsey Lomax closed his eyes, and down it came.

It didn't hurt at all.

He felt like he was floating.

26

They might have made it, too—might have made it the length of the hallway and into the stairwell at the other end, might have made it all the way down to the lobby and into the freezing night without—but even as they ran past the elevator bay, the thing that had been Abel Williams shrugged off the final strap and rolled off the gurney. Its legs buckled, but it locked its knees, forced itself erect, and staggered into the hallway to meet them.

27

"Shit," Ben said when he saw Abel Williams looming in the hallway before them. He hung there for a heartbeat, despairing and indecisive, trapped between the Scylla at one end of the corridor and the Charybdis at the other. Then Lara shook him, her fingers tight around his forearm.

"The elevator," she said at his ear.

The elevator. Ben pivoted to follow her, the corridor revolving around him, granting him a final fleeting glimpse of Abel staggering toward them like a human pinball, banging from one side of the hallway to the other on unsteady legs. A blurred swath of innocuous wall flashed past, pierced through with the double-hung door into the kitchen, where all this horror had begun, and then—oh, God, then, then the corridor down which they had lately fled rose up before him. Framed in the milky cone of a wall-mounted sconce, Fletcher Keel hunched like a Neanderthal wielding a club of bone, smashing and smashing and smashing the convulsing figure at his feet, three heavy blows and the arm flung back for yet another one in the single flying second before Ben finished pivoting back toward the elevator. Three blows, like a man pulping a half-rotten melon with a crowbar, each one launching into the crimson air a garish spray of blood and brains and bone.

Then—though he seemed to see it yet, though he thought he would see it the rest of his life, burned like the ghostly image of the afternoon sun not into his retinas but into the gelatinous medium of his brain—then, it was gone. Then he was in the elevator bay. Colored sketches of hydrangeas on the wall and the velvet-padded bench beneath. A decorative urn in the corner with a spray of pastel flowers. He was in the elevator bay, his gorge rising in his throat, the horror behind him for the moment, but coming. Oh, coming.

Lara punched the call button.

Ben wheeled back to face their pursuers, still searching for something—anything—he could use to fend them off. He was reaching for the urn when he heard a circumspect *ding* and the polite clatter of the doors retracting.

"Let's go," Lara hissed, tugging him empty-handed into the car behind her. His heel caught on the metal lip, and he might have gone down but for the brushed-steel railing that ran waist-high around the interior of the car.

Lara stabbed at the control panel.

A light flickered dimly, illuminating the "L."

"L" is for lobby, he thought incoherently, the phrase rolling around inside his head like a child's ABC mnemonic, and then the doors shuddered once again into motion. Through the slowly narrowing aperture, Ben saw Keel turn the corner into the elevator bay. He looked like a vision of death itself; he looked like Thor fresh from the fields of Armageddon, swinging the gore-streaked hammer at the end of one thick arm, his enormous frame splashed in the blood and grime of battle, his face bruised and swelling behind a veil of greasy hair.

"Come on, come on," Ben urged the doors, uttering the words in an earnest whisper, and he realized that Lara, too, was speaking, the same words, almost sobbing them, "Come on, come on," their voices rising up in unison, a chant, a prayer, a propitiation offered up to whatever gods were listening.

Keel—the thing that had been Keel—hurled the hammer after them. Spinning like a thrown hatchet, it rang harmlessly off the metal wall at Ben's back, spattering him with bits of blood and matter—spattering them both, he could see the crimson flecks in Lara's hair. The doors kissed in rubber-bumpered silence, and then they were alone, the hammer on the floor like a token of the horror past, or a calling card, a promise, of others yet to come.

I'm coming, it said. *I'm coming.*

A moment later, as if in confirmation, they heard the impact of Keel's weight upon the door. A wordless scream of anguish and rage followed, echoing inside the car.

A gear clunked overhead. The elevator lurched into motion, and Ben felt a terrible joy well up within him and die away in the realization that followed:

The elevator was going up.

28

Ben launched himself across the car. He punched the buttons methodically, their lights flaring one by one. When the elevator kept rising, ticking without stopping by each illuminated floor, he began hammering the unresponsive control panel, first with one fist and then, his frustration rising, with both fists in tandem. At last, the pressure mounting inside him toward some terrible crisis point, he wheeled on Lara.

"What the fuck?" he screamed. "I saw you, I saw you push the button for the lobby, *so what the fuck is going on here?*"

He gasped, swallowing, his jaw rigid

In the silence, the elevator slammed suddenly to a halt.

They hung suspended, just short of the eighteenth floor. The numbers glowed down upon him, the eight steady, the one flickering and half-extinguished.

Lara clutched the rail with both hands. She returned his gaze in silence, her face pale as fine bone china, her eyes wide, deep-sunken in their orbits, and smudged with bruised-looking shadows of exhaustion.

"What's going on?" he whispered.

She laughed, a grim despairing sound like the rattle of knives inside a drawer.

"Don't you see?" she said, her voice tremulous and small. "It's like the phone. It's not going to let us get away."

29

The moment the elevator doors slid shut, Abel Williams felt the dark presence inside him weaken. He was, for a time anyway, himself; not that that was necessarily a good thing. His nose felt as thick and fibrous as a cauliflower, making every breath screaming agony, his teeth ached, and his thigh throbbed like—well, like someone had driven a knife into it. He took rueful stock of himself: he was barefoot and shivering, probably feverish, and he wore only a tee shirt and what was left of a pair of blue jeans, Lara apparently having decided to split the seam of his jeans in order to stitch him up rather than bothering to undress him. In short, he was a mess.

On the other hand, considering the options . . .

Abel surveyed the elevator bay, apparently unmarred by the violence just past, his gaze settling at last on Fletcher Keel. The other man stood preternaturally still before the elevator, his bruised, bloodstained face tilted to track the numbers over the door. Abel found himself watching them as well, flashing in numerical sequence, until finally, somewhere far above him, something must have gone awry. The seventeen flickered and dimmed, and the eighteen flared momentarily to life; then it, too, died back into a strange shivery half-life, as though the elevator had gotten jammed—or had *been* jammed—somewhere in between floors.

And it had been.

He *knew* it had been. It wasn't conjecture, it wasn't guesswork, and it wasn't logic: it was knowledge, and there was only one way he could have come by it. What the thing inside him knew, he too knew—and so Abel concluded that the cold intelligence *hadn't* departed, not entirely, anyway. It had turned its attention elsewhere, but it had left something of itself behind, like an explorer planting a flag in virgin territory. Or, better, like a vacationer who'd left a lamp burning to light the house for his return.

And where did he fit into this little metaphor? Abel wondered. He wasn't the homeowner, not anymore—that had become abundantly evident. No, he was more like . . . he was more like a mouse, probing with quivering whiskers into a pantry or nosing for crumbs atop a counter, every sense alert for the master who might any moment return, driving him back to the safety of the tunneled wainscoting, the hidden ways inside the walls of—

Abel Williams swallowed.

Inside the walls of his own body. That pretty much summed it up, this nightmarish little analogy: when the owner was in residence, his movements were sharply restricted. When the owner was . . . otherwise engaged—running the elevator say, or running the elevator *and* running Fletcher Keel— then he had more latitude.

Which had its encouraging side. It meant, for one thing, that the owner, whoever it was, *whatever* it was, was not all-powerful. No, Abel sensed that it was more like a newly awakened child, prone to fits of temper and caprice, still testing its limits and powers. He even had an idea—and this was conjecture, though somehow it *felt* right—of how such a thing might have happened: how all the hatred and resentment in this place might have grown over long years, like a charging battery, until at last it had achieved some critical mass, spilled over into a kind of dull half-waking consciousness, stirred now and again to mischief, to sustain itself, then lapsing back into torpor. And in the moments of torpor, or inattention, he was free.

The word rang in Abel's head like a summons: free.

He'd better make the most of it.

Stealing one last glance at Fletcher Keel—he still hadn't moved, he was like an automaton in standby mode—Abel turned away. The corridor outside the elevator bay was a shambles. Gore streaked the walls and it smelled like an abattoir, a nauseating reek of blood and raw meat. Halfway up the corridor, just by the door into the lounge, Lomax sprawled on the sodden carpet, his arms outflung. Abel checked the impulse to go to him: you didn't have to be a doctor—or even a psychic, for that matter—to tell that Ramsey Lomax was clearly beyond help.

He, on the other hand, wasn't—and, as his mother used to say, the Lord helps those who help themselves. So Abel turned in the other direction instead, hobbling off toward the infirmary. His first order of business was locating some painkillers. His second was finding his shoes. As for what came next—well, he'd figure that out when he came to it. He thought he had enough to start with.

30

A few moments later the thing that had been Fletcher Keel roused itself. Ignoring the occasional sounds coming from the infirmary, it headed toward the kitchen. It could deal with Abel Williams at its leisure. For now, it wanted to replace the hammer.

This time, it wanted something sharp.

31

"Who's Katie Wright?" Ben asked.

Lara didn't answer. She was aware only in the most cursory way that the question had even been addressed to her. She felt numb, exhausted, and her brain seemed to have slipped into some lower gear, processing information at glacial speeds. From a clinical perspective, she knew, this could suggest shock, but this insight, too, seemed to have little immediate significance. Right now she was mainly focused on the question of what Ben was doing to the elevator's control panel.

Actually, *what* he was doing wasn't much of a mystery. He had used the hammer, cautiously at first, and with evident reluctance, to pry off the cover. Now he was moving methodically down the rows of buttons, ripping out the wiring. The more interesting question—and it seemed to fill her up at the moment, that question—was *why* he was doing it. Even so, it took her a few seconds to actually formulate the query into words.

"Why are you doing that?"

He didn't look at her. "Say you're right. Say the building can control the elevator, the phone."

"Yeah?"

"So it's got us trapped here. It's only a matter of time before it decides to move us somewhere more convenient, right? Someplace where Keel's waiting outside the damn doors with a machete."

She hadn't thought of that. "You think that'll stop it?"

He looked at his handiwork, bemused. "Shit," he said. "I don't know. We'll see, I guess."

He gave her a tight little smile, and then he turned, examining the ceiling. After a moment, he clambered up on the waist-high metal railing that encircled the elevator—or tried to anyway. The railing—it was segmented and loose in places—stood out maybe three inches from the wall, making balance difficult; after a few seconds Ben half-leapt and half-fell back to the floor, rocking the entire car.

Something groaned far above them.

Ben winced when he straightened, and she saw that blood had started to seep through his shirt on the left side. The wound hadn't been deep—she'd used butterfly bandages to close it; it hadn't even needed stitches. But even in her—altered? was that the right word?—even in her altered state, she recognized that it had to hurt.

Actual words came to her on a ten-second delay, working their way up through the frozen corridors of her brain: "You okay?"

"What?"

She nodded at his side.

He touched the stain gingerly and lifted his fingers to examine them. "At this point," he said, "I figure I'll be lucky to bleed to death."

Wiping the blood on his jeans, he turned his attention back to the ceiling. "So, listen, Lara," he said. "I'm going to have to ask you to help support me on the railing. Can you do that? Hold my legs or something?"

"I guess. Why?"

He pointed at the ceiling, and she saw a trapdoor set high in the back corner, to the right of the flickering fluorescent bulbs mounted over the center of the car.

"I think it's time to get us out of here," he said. "What do you think?"

Lara, still drifting in that numbed and dreamy state, didn't have a strong opinion on the issue. The truth was, she didn't want to think about it just now; the truth was, she didn't want to think about much of anything. But she was willing to help.

"Okay," she said.

He smiled again. "Good," he said, and this time when he clambered up on the railing—it creaked ominously under his weight—she moved in behind him, bracing him with her hands set high on his legs, midway above his knees. He fumbled around up there. Her angle of vision, close against the wall and just under him, gave him a looming foreshortened appearance that made it hard to see anything else.

"So seriously," he said. "Who's Katie Wright?"

This time the question penetrated the frozen tundra of her thoughts. Lara blinked, surprised to find tears sliding down her face.

"Katie died," she said.

32

She hadn't died, though. She'd been killed.

Here was the cold truth of the matter, the cold truth that came back to Lara McGovern in that moment, stranded high in the narrow elevator shaft that cored Dreamland like a spine; the cold truth that came back to her every day, silent companion to every waking thought, and every night as well, an unwelcome visitor in her dreams:

Katie Wright had not died. She'd been killed.

And Lara had killed her.

It had been a simple case, too, a simple case that came into the ER during the thirty-second hour of a thirty-six-hour shift during which Lara had been able to snatch little more than a couple of hours of restless sleep, and even that spread out across a span of hours in tossing increments of ten and fifteen minutes, until finally her eyes felt like someone had worked them over with a fine-grit grade of sandpaper and the hospital assumed a hallucinatory, overlit reality, like an overexposed snippet of film or a place seen in a dream: her third such shift in five days, her body humming like a plucked string with caffeine and adrenaline and vending-machine doughnuts.

And then this child, this girl, this delicate blond nine-year-old who could have been her sister, this Katie Wright: not a complex case at all—she presented with nausea, vomiting, and lethargy. It could have been the flu—but everything is complicated when you have slept maybe twelve hours in the last one hundred twenty, you've been working for more than twenty-four hours straight, and you're juggling a ten-patient backup in chairs, a stabbing, two might-be-acid reflux-might-be-heart-attacks, and a multiple-injury car crash in transit. She'd ordered an IV for hydration and the standard blood work, and when the blood work came back with low magnesium, she'd scrawled an order for an IV push of magnesium sulfate, a holding action while she dealt with the car crash victims even then pouring through the doors.

The rest was all confusion: two belligerent drunks with their faces full of windshield glass and a twelve-year-old with cerebral swelling already convulsing on the table and Lara in transit between with a nurse, a new nurse, this one, fresh out of school, tugging on her sleeve, saying, hey, you mind double-checking this order, and she snatched it away, glancing at it as she pushed through the doors into Trauma 2, calling over her shoulder, "Yes, that's right, just do it," and the nurse, as ordered, just did it. Lara had no clue that anything had gone wrong until low-blood-oxygen alarms started screaming down the hall and by the time she got there, by the time she had tried and failed to intubate the little girl who looked eerily like her own sister lo! these many years ago, by the time she had finished performing a nasty little procedure called a cricothyrostomy—that's a tracheotomy to you—and had gotten Katie Wright breathing again, well, by then it was too late.

"Seven minutes without oxygen," she told Ben, as he worked above her. "Best-case scenario, seven minutes without oxygen means irreversible hypoxic brain injury."

"And worst case?"

Katie Wright's fate: "Brain death."

The Wrights, hoping for a miracle, as parents will, had opted to put their daughter on a ventilator, but Katie's case was hopeless. All the ventilator did was maintain a rosy simulacrum of life. Katie's *real* life, though, was over—Lara had known that even then.

"So what caused it?" Ben asked, and that brought her, as always, to the crux of the matter.

Lara herself hadn't known for sure what had happened, not until later, after Katie's parents had been dispatched to the cafeteria to drink coffee and ponder their futures and the car accident victims had been cleared and the ER had settled back into its routine state of mild chaos. That was when she'd finally found the time to steal a few minutes at Katie Wright's bedside. That was when she finally found the time to examine the chart; it was a simple error, a brain fart Lana would have called it, easy enough to make at the best of times, all but impossible to avoid when you're fatigued and stressed and a thousand things are happening at once. No excuses, though: in her haste, Lara had miswritten the drug order; she'd substituted MSO_4, the chemical symbol for morphine sulfate, for $MgSO_4$, the symbol for magnesium sulfate. The morphine had stopped Katie's breathing. By the time Lara got her back—

Well, she never really *had* gotten her back, had she? Not unless you were going to accept a vegetable on a ventilator as a reasonable substitute for a human being.

Lara didn't know how long she stood there looking down at the child on the bed below her. But for the ventilator, she looked perfectly normal. She might have been sleeping. She would never wake up, though. She would never wake up again, and even now Lara remembered reaching out to trace the line of Katie Wright's jaw, the arc of her skull so visible in repose. Even now she remembered thinking how fleeting everything was, how close to the flesh the studs and beams, the joists and girders on which a life was draped, how big a wind was death, and always blowing, and each human life that turned its shoulders to the gale nothing more and nothing less than a fragile house of bones.

33

Abel was in the north stairwell, heading for the lobby, when the homeowner returned.

Freshly shod, with six hundred milligrams of Extra-Strength Tylenol flowing in his veins, he felt considerably better—so much better, in fact, that he had briefly considered climbing higher into the building in hopes of finding Ben and Lara. Given his own recent history, however, he ultimately decided that it might be wiser to get the hell out of Dreamland altogether, contact the authorities, and send them help rather than trying to render it himself. He'd just begun to nurse hopes that he might actually succeed in this plan—he'd already reached the second floor, four flights from the lobby—when he felt that black presence slipping once again inside his mind, and all his scheming went out the window.

Abel struggled to repel it, but something essential had changed inside him during that final reading. He might not choose to collaborate with his invader—as he suspected (and, given the dark omniscience inside him, more than suspected) Keel had—but having thrown open the doors to admit it, however inadvertently, he could not close them again. So he retreated before it, seeking refuge in the tunneled wainscoting of his own mind.

His husk, outwardly unchanged, paused on the steps, considering. A moment later it resumed the descent.

34

Lara saw a moment too late that the railing Ben was balanced on had passed from loose to outright unsteady to dangerous. She was just getting ready to warn him, her thoughts still fogged with Katie Wright, when a bolt sheared off with a screech and the handrail, unhinged on one side, swung out from under him.

"Shit," Ben cried, and then he was on the floor beside her, the car rocking underneath them once again, as though somewhere in the dark shaft above them, a braided steel cable had started to unwind.

"You okay?" he asked.

"Yeah, I'm fine," she said, climbing to her feet. "Are you?"

He stood, wincing, one hand pressed to his side. "Yeah. Yeah. I'm fine." He stared up at the hole in the ceiling—he'd managed to dislodge the cover, revealing a square of darkness—and then turned back to the broken railing.

"Trouble?" she said.

"No. I don't think so. In fact—" He crouched to examine the railing, now dangling vertically from the remaining post. He twisted it with one hand, the bolt rattling where it entered the wall. "In fact, I think this might come in handy. Here." He glanced over his shoulder at her. "Give me that hammer, will you?"

She stared at it, reluctant to touch it. Ben had wiped it more or less clean before he went to work on the control panel, but just looking at it reminded her of Keel, and what he'd done to Ramsey Lomax. And with that everything else came sweeping back: Abel Williams and the phone that had stopped working and the elevator that had countermanded its own electronic instructions. She felt the fear return, her own panicky observation—

—it's not going to let us get away—

—closing around her throat like a noose. For the second time that day, she put the question of their escape odds to the magic eight ball in her mind, and this time the answer that came swimming up through the green murk lacked even the wiggle room of *Signs say no*. This time the answer came up cold and definitive: *No*.

"Hey, you okay?"

Lara forced a smile. "I'm doing better," she said, and that much, anyway, was at least marginally true. If nothing else, unloading the story about Katie Wright had defrosted her brain a degree or two—her synapses now seemed to be firing only a second or two slower than their normal rate. And if Ben could continue to function, well then, so could she. She picked up the hammer and handed it to him.

"Watch your ears," he said.

Three sharp blows, each one echoing inside the car like a gunshot in a steel drum, finished the job age had started and the burden of Ben's weight hurried along. Ben picked up the severed railing and inspected it critically. Angling the rail against the floor, he struck it twice more, delivering each blow with a purse lipped expression of concentration. One of the two welded anchor posts shot off across the floor and rattled to a halt against the far wall. Ben grunted in satisfaction and displayed his handiwork for her—no longer a handrail but a flat brushed-steel post, three feet long and three inches wide. The tapering wall anchor at the top looked like a spike.

"What do you think?"

"What's it for?"

"Dual use," he said, smiling. "Pry bar. Club." He hefted it experimentally, then looked over at her. "You ready to do some climbing?"

She shrugged. "I guess."

"All right. We're going out through the trapdoor. You go first. I'll come up after you."

"Okay."

She clambered up on the remaining handrail, this one none too steady in its own right, and let him boost her toward the access hatch. She scrabbled for purchase, her fingers sinking into a thin layer of greasy muck, and then, using all the strength in her forearms and triceps, she levered her weight up and onto the elevator car.

She stood, brushing at her blue jeans.

It was dark here, with a sense of heavy mechanical components crowding the gloom. A thick cable of woven steel disappeared into the shadows overhead, and the air smelled of iron, black grease, and corrosion. They had evidently come to a halt—or had *been* halted, she thought uneasily—just short of the eighteenth floor. A narrow vertical line of lesser gloom, starting at about knee level, marked the crack where the doors met. Lara shivered, suddenly stricken with an image of the elevator lurching into motion, smashing her like an insect against the ceiling somewhere up there in the dark.

"Everything cool?" he asked, handing her the pry bar.

"Hurry," she said.

"I'm hurrying," he said.

A moment later, he had scrambled up beside her, gasping with pain. He was nearly invisible in the darkness, but she didn't need to see him to imagine the gradually expanding patch of blood-black seepage under his left arm. When he had caught his breath, he took the length of railing from her. She watched him, a shadow among shadows, bending to slide the flat end into the crevice between the doors.

"So they finally took her off life support?" he asked.

After a moment of confusion, Lara realized that he had taken up the thread of conversation where they had dropped it a few minutes ago: with Katie Wright.

"Yeah," she said. "After a week or so. She didn't last long after that."

"Yeah? So what happened next?"

Ah, she thought. Next.

That was the complicated part.

35

On the tenth floor, a thing that was and was not Fletcher Keel stopped to catch its breath. He felt an aching resentment at having to do so: if everything had gone as planned, he would have finished the matter on the fifth floor; failing that, the elevator should have delivered Prather and the woman both right to him.

The strength beating inside him—that thin, hating voice—had promised him as much. Instead, Prather and the doctor seemed to have disabled the elevator somehow. Smart—he would give them that. He was going to make them pay for the inconvenience though.

And it wouldn't be long now, either, he thought, testing the edge of the blade he had taken from the kitchen. It was a good knife, ten inches long, perfectly weighted, and sharp. Very sharp, indeed. Say what you want about Ramsey Lomax, the man didn't skimp when it came to cutlery.

Keel took another breath, and looked up the stairwell.

The darkness—and it was pitch black in here—did not bother him. Keel was at one with the building now, joined in a kind of joyful symbiosis: he gave it the mobility, the physical presence, it would not otherwise possess; in return it gave him strength, the fearless stone-cold certainty he'd always longed for. He did not need his eyes to see: he had instead an absolute and unerring knowledge of Dreamland itself, an instinctive awareness that infinitely transcended the paltry blueprint it had shown him that first night in the south stairwell. He could feel the fifth-floor furnace warming in his bones, the joists and archways creaking in its subterranean depths were like his own creaking tendons, the wind sculpting the cap of snow on the roof might as well have lifted his own hair. And the footfalls of his adversaries came to him like the sound of mice scurrying through the labyrinth of his own body.

Close now. They were close.

And he had a sudden image of Lara McGovern writhing underneath him. Rewards awaited.

Keel smiled and resumed climbing.

36

"The worst part isn't being suspended," Lara said. "The worst part is knowing that even after I'm reinstated—*if* I'm reinstated—she'll still be dead. I'll still have killed her."

Listening, Ben pried at the elevator doors with the length of steel. Despite the cold—and it was cold here, a blistering blue-black cold—Ben was sweating, a slick feverish perspiration that had less to do with exertion than with the spokes of pain that clutched at his rib cage with every movement, however minor.

Gasping, he released the pressure and stood upright. He lifted his glasses and wiped sweat from his eyes, two fingers at a time.

"How many lives you figure you've saved—or will save— over the course of your career?" he asked.

"Yeah. I've thought of that. It doesn't help."

"Hmm." He wedged the flat edge of the post between the doors, spike pointing in the opposite direction, and pushed. Something groaned deep inside the wall. The door shuddered half an inch, met resistance, and ground to a halt.

"She was nine years old," Lara said.

"It would have been better if she was twenty-nine?" he said without rancor.

"No, it's not that, exactly." In the smoky radiance leaking through the crack, her face looked thoughtful, like a child's face, frowning in concentration over some especially difficult algebra problem. "It's that somehow she got mixed up in my head with my sister," she said finally.

"Lana?"

"Yeah."

"You were twins?"

"How'd you—"

He laughed—a *real* laugh, though a somewhat subdued

one, and how much it surprised him, that laugh. As a reporter, he'd occasionally been struck by the resilience of human beings in the face of even the most horrific adversity. But to see the principle at work in his own life—that was something else.

"Lana, Lara?" he said. "You don't even have to be a psychic to figure that one out. She's dead?"

"Leukemia. She was nine, too. . . ." Lara looked at him again, her face divided along the terminator line cast by the bluish light between the doors. "Sometimes I hear her voice inside my head," she said. She shook her head. " 'It should have been you, Lars.' "

Ben didn't answer, at a loss for words.

He wiped his forehead with the back of his hand and turned back to the doors, the phrase echoing inside his head. He slipped the lip of the bar between the doors and leaned his weight into it. The motion pulled at his side, peeling the bandage free from the slowly drying blood in a lacerating line. Something groaned inside the door. "Help me," he gasped, and she closed her hands over his, adding her weight to the bar. His shoulders shook with the effort. Something snapped far back in the wall, and suddenly the resistance was gone. The door sprang back abruptly, nearly spilling them.

The stench of mold and wood rot rolled in from the elevator bay beyond—the heap of abandoned carpet remnants, he remembered, and that reminded him of something he'd been trying not to think about. Apartment 1824. It brought with it no clutching sense of panic this time, just a numb imperative, a summons.

He straightened.

Both of them stood absolutely still, half expecting some kind of attack from the gloom of the elevator bay. Nothing came. Panting from exertion, Ben turned back to Lara, his head suddenly filling up with the answer that had eluded him a few minutes ago. It arrived full-blown, already formulated in Paul Cook's familiar tones; all he did was repeat it. "Maybe that's not Lana's voice," he said. "Maybe it's *your* voice. You ever think of that?"

Then an impulse seized him, and he did something totally unexpected—something he didn't even know he'd been planning. He pressed his lips gently to her forehead. She did not pull away. She just stood there, watching him out of wide gray eyes.

"It wasn't your fault, Lara," he said. "You don't have to punish yourself anymore."

Embarrassed, he tossed the length of railing into the elevator bay, and clambered out after it. Turning, he reached down for Lara. Their hands clasped, and he was struck for the second time that day by the sense that somehow they'd been made for one another, those hands, perfectly machined to match.

"Now what?" Lara asked after he'd pulled her up.

"The stairwell," he said, feeling the lie inside him and willing it not to be a lie. Bending to retrieve the rail, he repeated the words, "The stairwell," unsure whom he was trying to convince, her or himself.

37

The lie caught up with him at the intersection of the central corridor and the south wing. Lara saw it happen.

In the bleak yellow pall cast by a distant lightbulb, the last bulb yet burning, by the door into the south stairwell, she saw it happen: saw his fingers close around the door handle, saw them blanch with indecision, saw them pull away. As if summoned, he turned, looking down the long dark corridor toward the apartment where his family had died. Another exit sign glimmered down there, a distant beacon, shining over the same door that Lara had hustled him through on their way to the roof the other night.

"Ben—" she whispered.

He looked at her, unspeaking, and she thought of Abel Williams, she thought of Fletcher Keel, both of them out there somewhere, hunting them in the midnight dark. She thought of Ramsey Lomax, slumped against the wall, his body already going cold, and she said, "No, Ben—"

"Lara." The voice was thick with entreaty; it was hardly his voice at all.

She touched his hand, willing some of her strength to pass through into him, as his strength had buoyed her during those dark moments in the elevator. *"No!"* she said.

His voice broke as he responded. "I have to, don't you see that, *I have to*—"

She looked in his eyes and thought of his words back at the elevator—*you don't have to punish yourself anymore*—and another voice cried out within her—not Lana's voice, *her* voice. *Hers.*

And how are you supposed to stop? it asked.

Lara knew the answer to that one. There was only one way. You faced it. You faced it, and you breathed it in, you soaked it up like a sponge. You made it part of yourself. You said, This is the worst thing I have done, and for this I bear responsibility. And you surrendered the rest of it, the part you were powerless to change. You honored it, but you did not own it. And then it could not own you, never again.

Lana had died.

She had not caused it, she had not wished it, she could not change it. If she could, she would. But she would not let it own her.

Katie Wright had died as well.

And that was hers to bear, and there would be others, and maybe worse ones. But she would bear them.

You figured out what was yours and what was not.

And you did it by facing it: it was the only way.

She saw that *this* was the true strength she had to give him: the strength to risk it, the strength *not* to run away, when there were always reasons to run, and good ones. Good enough that if she insisted, he would defer, and maybe that was what he'd been hoping she'd do all along.

If she let him start down that stairwell without facing it—whatever the risks—she would have failed him. She would have failed them both.

"Okay," she breathed, the words turning to vapor in the space between them. "Okay."

38

The clouds were breaking, and a swollen moon hung low in the sky, firing the flawless mantle of snow eighteen stories below with an eerie blue glow that suffused everything.

They stood in the window of a back bedroom—who knows, it might have been his bedroom once—and gazed down at the shattered plaza, and the long curve of the city beyond it.

"What was your name?" she said. "The one you were born with?"

"Jamal." He turned to look at her. "Jamal Turner. My parents heard the story on the news. They arranged to adopt me. It was like—" He snorted. "I don't know, their idea of public service or something."

"You sound angry."

"I was. For a long time I was. They never told me who I really was. I had to learn it all on my own. You bet I was angry."

"And now?"

"Now?"

He examined himself for any hint of the anxiety that had triggered the panic attack. It was gone: the events of the last few hours had burned it out of him, leaving . . . leaving what?

He didn't know.

But whatever it was—and it would be something, he didn't doubt that anymore—he would not find it here. Not here, in this stark, cold bedroom, empty but for the corpse of a pigeon that must have strayed in through the window. He prodded it with the length of broken railing and watched it collapse, a house of delicate bone, tented in dry feathers and leathery flesh.

A hollow thing, devoured from within.

The idea sent shivers up his spine. Paltry sustenance indeed for a place that had feasted on such banquets of misery for so long, he thought. And he could almost feel the hunger in the air.

No, he would not find it here.

There was nothing here but hunger and death and hate. He turned to Lara.

"Now?" he said. "Now, my name is Benjamin Prather."

They were silent then, there in the moonlit apartment with nothing but their breath to warm them.

"Let's go," he said at last. "There's nothing here. There's nothing here but hate."

39

Ben's first hints that something was wrong were the clutching fingers at his wrist, and Lara's shocked hiss of intaken breath. She drew him around, choking dread in his throat, the room airless and cold.

He stood frozen by the figure before him, gloom-shrouded, the long goateed face hanging disembodied in the darkness. An apparition, a hollow thing, not a man.

"Keel," he said, and they regarded one another in silence.

Then the figure shifted slightly. A moonlit blade coalesced in the shadows, a blue edge gleaming. The figure slid toward him smoothly and without sound, the blade grinning, everything so dreamlike and strange that Ben could almost let himself believe that it *was* all some crazy nightmare from which he might wake at any moment. And then he too was moving, pushing Lara back with one hand, bringing the broken length of railing around with the other. It shed a glimmering silver wake, whipping past too fast for his eye to fix and hold, and for an instant he almost dared to hope.

And then Keel, moving with the certainty and grace Ben had first seen at the pool table all those nights ago, reached out and snapped the length of railing from his hand. He hardly seemed to look at it. It clanked away into the darkness, lost, and then Keel was on him, that blue blade snapping down.

"No," Ben said. He darted forward to meet the blow, to sneak under it, snatching at Keel's wrist, but the other man's momentum carried through him. Ben's legs went out from underneath him. He was momentarily airborne. Then he was down, flat on his back, a bright line of agony stitching itself along his wounded side.

Keel came down on him a moment later with his full weight. Breath burst out of him, a glittering fog of condensation. Ben brought his other arm up, clutching the other man's wrist with both hands. The blade hung above him in the moonlight, foreshortened: two feet from his heart, then one, Keel bearing down with every bit of his strength. Ben's forearms trembled with tension. The blade leaped forward an inch, then another.

"No, please," Lara said from the darkness, a thousand miles away.

Another inch. And another.

"Why?" Ben gasped, but he knew why, he understood that now, and when Keel, or the thing that was in Keel, responded, he understood that, too.

"We hate you," Keel hissed, his voice venomous. "We hate you."

And it became a mantra—

". . . *we hate you, we hate you, we hate you* . . ."

—and Ben understood it. It was the hatred of the cold for what was warm, that hatred. It was the hatred the bone bears toward the flesh, the hatred of the hollow for that which is sustained, the hatred of the void for the full and breathing world. And it did not matter where it came from, that malice. It did not matter whether it had been born here, born in the hearts of men, born from long years of misery and despair that at last turned inward, self-hating and self-destructive, or whether it had descended upon this place through the thin margins of the world from spheres of outer dark, or whether it had been summoned, hunger to hunger, hatred to hate. It did not matter. It mattered only that you combated it, at every turn and every crossing. It mattered only that you stood your ground and did not let the darkness own you.

And so Ben whispered, seeking that which yet respired in the hollow places, seeking the warm and living flesh cleaving yet to bone. "Keel," Ben whispered. "Fletcher, please."

Still the knife inched closer, closer. He could feel the bright tip bearing down upon his breast, his shirt parting with a whisper to admit it.

Lara sobbed.

Ben's mind reeled with terror, the first distant memorandum of pain firing along his nerves as the tip first indented his skin, and then bit through, a bare millimeter into the flesh beneath.

"Please," Ben whispered, and then inspiration struck him, something Lara had said to him just moments ago—

—*your name, the one you were born with*—

"John," he gasped, the memory of Abel's words in the kitchen—

—*what would your daddy think of that*—

—slamming through his brain. And he repeated it, seeking the child that lived inside the hollow man, saying, "John, John, please, you don't want to do this, John, this is your father, *John, this is your father, John, you make me proud*—"

Keel's voice faltered, dying, and something flickered deep inside those cold eyes. The pressure of the blade eased.

"You make me proud," Ben said. *"You make me proud."*

In Fletcher Keel's moonstruck face confusion reigned. "Dad?" he said. "Dad?"

He cocked his head, listening, and Ben heard it, too: a distant whistling sound in the air. Ben glimpsed a blur of silver, Keel's eyes widening in surprise, and then, abruptly, the weight upon his chest was gone.

40

Lara, clutching the length of handrail like a bat, had thought the blow would be enough to kill it.

But no, it was not. The impact of the stroke had dislodged it, had sent it rolling across the barren room, the blue blade flashing in the air. But it was on its feet again almost in the same motion, on its feet and coming for her. The impact seemed hardly to have slowed it down.

She saw it, then, she saw its eyes, and whatever tiny fragment of Fletcher Keel had glimmered there before, whatever vestigial humanity had lingered in the moment before she struck it down, it was gone now. Suddenly it was there inside him, entirely *there,* Dreamland, the force of it unbelievable, inhuman, vibrating in the air. It came at her in wordless fury, intent. She screamed and she struck at it again and again, smashing at it with the post, with the jagged spike.

Still it came, swinging the blade at her. Lara swung the metal post, smashing it in the face, the arms—everywhere, everything whirling around her, everything crazy. It lurched toward her, staggering now, and she swung, snapping its head around in a spray of blood and snot. And again. And again. And still it came, unstoppable, backing her and backing her until it had jammed her hard into a corner.

Her shoulder blades rammed the wall. She had nowhere else to go. "Please," she whispered. "Please."

And still it came, brandishing the knife before it, its eyes glittering and inhuman. She swung the length of rail again, swung it with everything she had, driving all three inches of the sharpened spike right through one of those eyes, into its brain. The spike lodged there, hooked inside its eye socket. The thing straightened abruptly. Its hand opened, and she saw the knife hit the floor. It pawed ineffectually at the post, its fingers crooked into claws

Lara moaned. Her mouth gaped in wordless horror, one hand cupped before it.

And then, still spasming, the thing pitched forward, its weight sagging against her, its face empty and inhuman. The last thing she remembered was its fingers raking her face, catching in the fine chain around her neck, and dragging her down atop it.

41

Dreamland shrieked, a soundless, rending cry, splitting the air.

42

In the moment just after Lara struck the thing atop Benjamin Prather's chest, in the moment when it came screaming to its feet before her, its eyes utterly bereft of humanity, Abel Williams, deep inside his wainscot labyrinth of self, felt the black presence in his breast flare like a filament, its attention elsewhere, and slowly die away.

Suddenly, he was himself again, wholly himself.

He staggered to his feet, his thigh aching, to find himself in the lobby, clutching a length of castaway pipe like a club before him. Memory flickered inside his mind, and he knew—knew with that same black certainty—his murderous function here: should Fletcher Keel fail in the warren of empty apartments above, then they would fall to him, Dreamland's blood deeds.

He retched, heaving a vile spew of acid.

"God," he whispered. "God."

He hurled the pipe clanking to the floor. Then, fury rising inside him—fury at himself, fury at the hellish place that had entrapped him—he kicked the pipe, kicked it and kicked it again, launching it at last into the darkness of the gaping elevator shaft. It fell for a long time, and then it hit concrete far below. Echoes rolled up to him through that stone throat, the noise reminding him of his first visit to Dreamland, the empty liquor bottle the cameraman had kicked into the abyss, the sound of shattering glass like hysterical laughter.

He turned away, trembling. He thought of the others, of Ben and Lara, trapped somewhere high above him, wanting to help them, wanting somehow to redeem himself, knowing what he had to do instead.

If he stayed here, it would seize him yet again.

It would use him.

His wounded thigh throbbing, Abel limped toward the plywood-paneled doors.

"I'm sorry," he sobbed to himself, "I'm sorry."

But it was the only way. It was all that he could do. Still sobbing, he shoved open the door and staggered into the moonlit night beyond.

43

Lara came to herself, sobbing, rocking in the warmth of someone's arms. "It's okay now," he was saying. "It's over."

44

That dark presence made one last run at Abel. It found him in the snow, slumped against the distant fence, his face turned to the sky. The cold had already gotten to him by then. His fingers had curled into blue talons. Frost rimed his eyebrows. His legs were like brittle toothpicks carved of ice.

Still, it came for him, a black fluttering like wings about his shoulders.

Dreamland.

All unwilling, Abel stumbled to his feet at its behest, but his legs could no longer hold him by then. He collapsed facedown in the snow, blood congealing in his veins, and Dreamland, seeing he was useless, abandoned him.

Abel laughed aloud in something like joy. Too late, he thought, too late. I beat you. And then, because he wanted to die with his face to the stars, he used the last of his strength to wrench himself over on his back. The moon cast its cold eye down upon him. The chill deepened.

Abel took a breath and closed his eyes.

A long time later, he didn't know how long, he managed to heave them open again. He stared into the cage of shadows on his ceiling, listening to a watch tick in the darkness, time moving on again, the crack down the face of the world healing over at last. It was warm here, with the sheets tucked close around his chin. The snow was gone, or maybe there had been no snow. Maybe he had dreamed it. Maybe he had dreamed it all. He was drifting off to sleep, and still more dreams, when he heard a door somewhere open and felt a shadow fall across his bed.

"Dad?" he whispered drowsily. "Dad?"

The mattress gave beneath the shadow's weight, and rough hands caressed his face. A whisper stirred in the darkness. "I'm here, son," it said, "I'm right here."

Abel tried to open his eyes, to look into his father's face, but he was tired, he was so tired. So he settled for a final drowsy murmur. "I'm glad you're home, Dad," he said. "I'm awful glad."

And then he slept.

45

They huddled together all night, high above a world struck dumb with winter, sleeping and waking and talking quietly in dreamlike intervals where time itself seemed to drag to a halt.

Lara remembered dreaming that the body across the room twitched and lurched up, the broken length of rail still embedded in its eye, and she remembered waking from the dream to stumble to her feet. "What are you doing?" Ben asked. "I want to know he's dead," she said. "I have to be sure." And kneeling down by him, she made herself sure.

Later, she remembered wondering if Dreamland would come for them, as well. Ben didn't think so. "It takes the weak," he said. "It takes the vulnerable. People who are broken inside."

"Aren't we weak?" she said, knowing the answer already, but wanting to hear it on his lips. "Aren't we broken?" she asked. He smoothed the hair back from her forehead. "Not when we're together," he said, and she knew that it was true, knew that hand in hand they could stand against whatever came—even if Abel came, or Dreamland in Abel's guise. But Abel did not come.

And then, sometime in the far reaches of the night, when even the moon had fallen and the lights of the city were distant in the windows, she remembered his fingers in her hair, his lips against her lips.

And then the long night ended.

Just before dawn they stood once again in a window, looking out at a world where the black sky came down to meet the snow, and there was no line between them.

46

In the first blue light, Lara knelt to retrieve her necklace. It was still knotted in Fletcher Keel's fist, the locket cupped securely in his cold, cold palm. She could not bring herself to break the silver chain again, and she would not touch his dead, gray fingers.

In the end, she left it.

47

In the ruined lobby, Ben found himself thinking of Paul Cook. There was brain knowledge, Paul had told him, and there was heart knowledge and they were not the same. The brain categorizes and classifies. The brain divides.

The heart—the heart connects.

"You ready?" Lara asked.

"I'm ready."

And then, like newborn children, hand in hand they stole out across the virgin snow.

Acknowledgments

Many people had a hand in bringing this book to fruition. The experts who granted me cheerful assistance and specialized knowledge include John Dodge, who provided information on caskets and embalming practices, and shaped my depiction of Lana's funeral; Sherrie Bohrman, Sally Deskins, and Karen Singley, all of whom contributed to my understanding of various medical issues; and Steve Sanderson, MD, who developed the scenario of Katie Wright's death and didn't even charge me for an office visit. I hope all of these generous people will forgive me to the extent that I've inevitably misunderstood, misconstrued, or misrepresented the information they were generous enough to share.

I'd also like to thank my agent, Matt Bialer, and my editor, Laura Anne Gilman, for their apparently endless reservoirs of patience, their kindness, and their good advice; Barry Malzberg, Batya Yasgur, and Wayne Singley, for encouraging words during some of the darker moments; and Jack Slay, Jr., both for listening and for commenting on various chapters in progress. My parents, Frederick and Lavonne Bailey, also read the manuscript and made countless other contributions, large and small. Finally, I am especially indebted to those who had to live with me during the process: my wife Jean and my daughter Carson. No mere acknowledgment could convey the magnitude of their support, generosity, and love. I hope a simple thanks will do.

About the Author

Dale Bailey is also the author of *The Fallen*, a finalist for the International Horror Guild Award for First Novel; *American Nightmares: The Haunted House Formula in American Popular Fiction*, a study of contemporary gothic fiction; and a collection of short stories, *The Resurrection Man's Legacy and Other Stories*. His short fiction has been nominated for a Nebula, and his novelette "Death and Suffrage" won an International Horror Guild Award. He lives in North Carolina with his wife and daughter.